REGENESIS

a novel by

Robert Granat

SIMON AND SCHUSTER · NEW YORK

C.1

FIRST PRINTING
SBN 671–21362–8
LIBRARY OF CONGRESS CATALOG CARD NUMBER: 72–83899
DESIGNED BY EVE METZ
MANUFACTURED IN THE UNITED STATES OF AMERICA

Years ago, in the benevolence of youthful conceit, Bob began to keep a journal, in order that the world might someday be able to lick nourishment from his every word. Reality soon moved into clearer focus, of course. But still he has gone on writing things into these notebooks, which have become tools for personal survival. Occasionally now he will pick up one of them and browse through it, and there he finds again his constants and his variables, how little he has changed and how much.

In an early volume recently he happened across an aborted entry —this:

Hotel de la Salud, Pátzcuaro
October 25, 1958

Since the last

This. Nothing more. The rest of the page a total blank. And for a moment his mind too was a blank. He couldn't place it or place the him that went with it. The next entry, written over a month afterward, provided no clues. But as he peeled back the page he was struck by a feeling of déjà vu; and when he saw what had been scrawled there on the Sunday before, October 18th, then he remembered. The blankness recorded the most dramatic week in his life.

1

Hotel de la Salud, Pátzcuaro
October 25, 1958

Since the last

HE SAT STARING into the blankness of paper. An hour, it must be an hour already since he wrote those words. After the mass he'd come running back here to the hotel directly from the Basilica, still resonant, still luminous with his joy, grabbed his notebook from the room and leaped up the stairs to the roof, to this deserted porch. In order to write it all down, to write the whole week down, to compose a love letter, to sing a mass of his own, a psalm of exultation to what he had passed through, to What had passed through him. For the thing we all thought was gone, gone from the earth, gone from our lives, was not gone. Was not!

"Since the last entry everything has changed," he'd begun to write. But then, after three words, an unexpected impulse made him turn back the page. And there it was, sprawled across the paper, that last entry. It had tripped him up like a corpse—his own.

He had laid down the pen and begun to cry.

7

But now he had finished with that, that had finished with him—strange, the need he felt to use the passive voice—and he was left quieted and slowed and altered in mood, conscious of his location on the globe. His body was seated in a tub chair made of orange leather and pink cedar staves and black pitch joints before a small round table of the same materials, resting atop the glassed-in roof of a hollow pile of rocks and lime and baked and unbaked clay, slapped together with tropical haphazard into an organism labeled *Hotel de la Salud—all modern comforts.* The ongoing of his life attracted his attention, the periodic blinking of his eyelids, the steady pumping of his blood, the eddying of air in and out along the membranes of his breathing passages, an occasional swallowing in his throat, an occasional gurgling in his abdomen. Each process proceeding at its proper pace without consulting him. From the streets and patios the ongoing of other lives rose as a bee-like murmuring, accompanied by a soft fluty cadenza from the broken toilet on the floor below. The porch itself was nestled in a spongy white mist that enveloped the town and the lake like a placenta, humid and lukewarm, nurturing a lush profusion of green lives, from the algae that grew in the open gutters and stained the stones and the clay roof tiles to the tall dark slender trees that canopied the plazas, nurturing too the decompositions of death. The air was soaking with smells, the pervading mildews, the flower perfumes, the cooking, the decaying lake vegetation, the leather and resin of the porch furniture. How finely tuned his senses were right now, especially the sense of smell—why, he could even distinguish the faint animal odor of the hide glue in the binding of the notebook in his lap, the cheap business account book—Record No. 1276 —in which he'd intended to record an account of this week's business when he came running back here from the church . . .

This acuity of smell—it was exactly like after shock . . . after electroshock.

"My God, I'm alive!"

He felt a shudder pass through him. He had forgotten. He'd thought he remembered, but he had forgotten.

He slowly turned back the page once more and gazed down at the heap of pen-scratches that lay beneath his eyes. Those words, *he* had written them there. In Albuquerque, New Mexico, last Sunday night, seven days and fifteen hundred miles from now and here. Robert Edward—his mark. An undeniable fact, as facts undeniably went. The writing was degenerate and out of control, now trembling and feeble and barely discernible, now lurching and black with the boldness of insanity—still it was his. It looked like a medical electrogram of a seizure. It was. His.

Yes, he'd forgotten that. Forgotten it probably as his fingers were scrawling it onto paper. And he'd essentially forgotten last Sunday itself. Only pain, it seemed, could really remember pain. Like pleasure. Pain remembering pain, pleasure remembering pleasure—this somehow was a step beyond ordinary memory, beyond time. A step toward the real thing. But the real thing, that—as he had discovered an hour ago in the church called La Colegiata (as had discovered itself to him)— that was still other steps beyond.

Slowly, purposefully, he began to read last Sunday night's entry again, listening intently, as to the gasps of a dying man. Some of the words were completely illegible. He read them anyway.

down—the bottom—again—

the body—I feel it—it's taking me over—the meat sick, the chemicals off, the electricity shorted—to write this, to think, exhausting me—not the pills—too soon yet for them—no, just It—like

9

before, It—a parasite attached to each cell, sucking, sucking, sucking—

heap of pulp, stinking goo, jellyfish on the beach lying drying dying—rotting stinking seagarbage—me, a rot in the rots, a stink in the stinks—

why? WHY? what should I, could I—the Questions—just can't hold onto them anymore—and even if—what for, what good?—too late, too down, the body—tomorrow, tomorrow if, Dr. Hoerchner again—what for, what good?—drug me, shock me, bullshit me, bill me—poor guy, he tries—but he can't—too much for him too, too much, TOO MUCH.

what am I writing this for?—more words, more goddamn words —wordglut, we glut on words, we turn into words—the flesh made word

hope? is it still hope?

hope—h o p e—and what?—wiseguy echoes nope—and now it's Hope Something or other from back in the fourth grade, paste-faced, plaid-jumpered, stick-legged, whiney-sinused, time she farted in geography and began to weep—what else? nothing—hope's another stinking wordshell, more garbage—

one thing clear, one thing only—down, I am down, like last time, down, the bottom—It's got me, It's coming and I can't and Hoerchner can't and nobody can and nothing can—helpless hopeless, hopeless helpless—

Help of the helpless, Hope of the hopeless—where's that from? fourth grade too?

referring, as usual, to you—to You—YOU!

Y O U—you who?—yoo hoo!—who you?—one more wordshell on this stinking beach?—

I AM THAT I AM—all right, but who are you really?—last Mama fantasy whose skirts we grab for as we—what? just go out? is that the way it is?—Pffftt! like a light bulb?—

light bulbs?—why not?—so easy to replace us with your technology!—what's it to you if your light bulbs agonize!

I'm here, in this bed, waiting for the pills—am I alone or are you?—

You—always, back it goes to you—because, simply, what else? what Else!—if only you, You—but why? why should You give a damn? why me? garbage, little heap of rot, minor stink among stinks? You've got fresh ones—billions, BILLIONS!—the species— is that what You care about, the species?—the species is burgeoning!

but—but still, I am here now—aren't I here now?—I feel, don't I feel? I think, don't I think?—of you, You, right now, here, of You! —who arranged all that? did I? am I responsible for all that?—

no! You are! You thought me up! You put me inside this machine! You made me think! You made me feel!—here, now, inside the machinery, the meat, the chemicals, the electricity, FEEL!— You did that! YOU!—so don't you have some obligation, some ethical, rational, reasonable obligation to

oh save me please please save me—

2

"MY GOD, I'M ALIVE!"

And he could, as easily, be dead. If not dead Sunday—he could, as easily, have swallowed the whole bottle of Nembutal instead of just three—then dead Monday, driving insane along the highway, stumbling about on that deserted mountainside. The facts, those magical entrails people kept laying bare, studying, and prophesying from, insurance company truth, the truth that has made them rich, the facts wouldn't have it for his body to be sitting here now, in mental and physical health, down in Pátzcuaro, Michoacán. By statistical rights it should be back in Albuquerque, dead, the bacteria and embalming chemicals tussling together beneath the emerald sod of Sandia Memory Gardens. Or if not dead all, then dead half, slouching slack-jawed and glazed in the locked basement of Bethlehem, vaguely salivating to the bell of feedtime, plugged into imbecile peace by Dr. Frank Hoerchner's little black box . . .

And no sooner was he thought of than he precipitated. There he was again, the good psychiatrist, looking-listening at him again, emitting quiet curls of cigar smoke, a welcoming cottage for lost Hansels and Gretels.

"Frank! . . . Well, how are you? Fine?"

Of course he was fine. To his patients the doctor always was fine, he had to be fine. But now he looked as exhausted as ever, the dark caves of fatigue behind his glasses, his skin gray as rock, the fifty-cent cigar jutting from his mouth like—no, really now, like what? Not a cottage chimney, not a nursing bottle, not a penis—more like one of those nylon swivel-bits acrobatic artists sometimes clench between their teeth as they perform their stunts. Without relaxing his bite, the doctor relaxed his lips and smiled his smile.

"Yes, I thought you might be kind of curious about what happened to me, Frank."

The silence, it must have surprised him, the phone call that never came, from the police, the county hospital, the morgue. The doctor certainly couldn't have expected his crazed patient to get very far when he fled from his office on Monday morning. And yet, for some reason, Hoerchner had made no attempt to stop him, to send after him. What reason? Surely not because he was so anxious to tend to the senile Mrs. Sauerwine. Had Frank finally given up on him too? Or did something or Something . . . ?

"Well, thanks anyhow, Frank, thanks for letting me go, thanks for whatever made you do it. I'll drop by and tell you about it when we get back."

Tell him, not consult him. Never would he be a mental patient again.

How could he say that? How could he say for sure that it—that It—wouldn't come back? It had come back once. It might again.

Well then, if It did, then he knew what to pray for. The strength to live through It or die of It, and offer It to him.

To Him. But he felt certain It wouldn't, it couldn't, come for him a third time, not like that. He felt sane—*saned*, driven into his mind—in a way that was permanent, to the extent you could use such terms in such a world.

A postcard, he'd send Dr. Hoerchner a postcard. He must have heard of this place. It was a well-known tourist attraction with its lake, its butterfly nets, its Indians, its native crafts. Maybe he could find him a view of La Colegiata or the corn-paste image of Nuestra Señora de la Salud inside. Or better yet, a photograph of an Indian, a "typical Tarascan peasant," with coarse brown wool poncho, white manta pajamas, and a dark Asiatic face—a *face*. But what would that mean to Frank? Hoerchner wouldn't see what he himself had seen, even if, by some freak of chance, the man on the postcard happened to be exactly the same man who had knelt beside him an hour ago in the Basilica.

He felt a sudden outflowing of affection for Dr. Hoerchner, a yearning to tell him what he had learned this week, and instantly a sad shadow of intimation that to tell him might be impossible.

"*You shall indeed hear but never understand, you shall indeed see but never perceive . . .*"

Perhaps. And yet, with what he recognized as the eagerness of a convert, he longed to tell him.

Chen-Yu—was that his name, Chen-Yu?—*pointed to Confucius and remarked: "There goes a fellow who spends his life trying to do something he knows quite well cannot be done."*

Couldn't it be done? Couldn't Frank be told, the multi-million Franks who ran this country, this world? To hear they would have to regain the kind of ears they had had as children. That would take a miracle, and could miracles happen to people who refused to recognize miracles? . . .

"Bob, seems to me what you're holding out for is a miracle." Dr. Hoerchner had been half-kidding when he'd said that,

14

he'd had his smile on. But in a way the psychiatrist was right. He *was* hoping for a miracle, what they would call a miracle, and simply because he knew he *had* to, because he knew in his bones that in their cabinet of answers, analytical, chemical, electrical, there was none that would solve the riddle of his suffering, no matter how much they exhumed of Mommy and Daddy, of Baby Bobby's anality and genitality, his fantasies and traumas—and they did dig up plenty—no matter how they tinkered with his brain waves and his body chemistry. None of it and no combination of it would begin to resolve that enigmatic syndrome called human life, not merely the case of it afflicting this particular specimen tagged Robert Edward, but that universal sense of halfness, of halfassedness, of un-homogenized mixture native to human consciousness in every time and place. Hoerchner had nothing in his cabinets to deal with *that* one, and he personally treated his own case of it the way most successful men did these days—by keeping busy, busier, for the longest possible moment, than Hell. When at rare times he could be cornered into voicing a personal word about the meaning of life, he sounded infantile—light-year-old David had a better grasp on the mystery . . .

"Growth," the doctor interrupted, repeating now in apparition what he had more than once remarked in the flesh, "I believe in growth."

Which now, as then, evoked images of cancers and gross national products.

And yet, last Monday morning—God, was it only six mornings behind this one?—back he'd gone to Hoerchner, to Bethlehem, and running. But out of terror alone, out of sheer animal terror for his life. He knew and had known for a long time that Frank could do nothing more than keep him physically alive by means of his medical violence, that no cure would be forthcoming from doctors—no, not even if Dr. Freud had been his personal physician.

"Frank, that miracle you kept teasing me about—it happened."

It happened. But hadn't it always been happening? He'd merely consented to it, that was all. Consented? That wasn't the word. The ego needed for consent had been crushed out of him. He'd had about as much autonomy as a foetus being squeezed into the world or a dying man being sucked out of it. In such a state he had "consented" to fall into nothing.

And that nothing—that Nothing—had caught him up like a mother's arms.

"How's that again, Bob?" A sudden animation broke on Dr. Hoerchner's face. The eyebrows bobbed up over the rims of the eyeglasses, the smile spread sideways again from the cigar. "A mother's arms? . . . 'Ah, the breast that flows sweet 'neath the eyes that love.'" And the real Frank, the next-to-real Frank, came out like a weary sun. Weary, tolerating, disillusioned of all illusions except the hard-edged illusions proper to his time and place, the Frank that smiled indulgently on the Sisters of Charity at Bethlehem Sanatorium, who, as if not fully trusting to his orders for the patients, insisted on praying for their souls as well, kneeling before the saccharine plaster images of their mother-surrogate from the religious supply-houses—those enlarged little girls, fixated in prepuberty by the black medieval arts of that wily old fossil, the church.

Yes, this had always been the worst trouble—that he could read his doctor as well as his doctor could read him. He could read him now, reading him.

"Transient euphoric reaction. Having made his payment to his Shylock with a thick dripping slice of misery, he allows himself a brief time-out, a moment of manic well-being, before he takes the knife to himself again. Near classic manic-depressive syndrome, with typically grandiose religious-type delusional content."

And, as far as it went, he had to admit Dr. Hoerchner's diagnosis did have a certain crude accuracy. But how far, really, did it go? How strange, to be so constantly concerned with the depths, and to remain so constantly on the surface.

"Oh Frank, let's diagnose the earth. What a manic-depressive old ball she is! With what euphoric reaction she bursts loose each spring after that long sado-masochistic winter! At last, after months of self-flagellation, catatonia, and raging, she has assuaged her guilt over last summer's wild libido-spree. Really, in the temperate zones at least, isn't mother earth our archetypal case of cyclical emotional pathology?

"Oh, but there's more to it, Frank, there's more to it than is dreamt of in your philosophy. You don't drill deep enough to strike the living water. That unconscious of yours lies in little dry wells cupped in the soil of consciousness!"

In the silence that followed this outburst, he felt his own lips stretching. His turn to smile. Because there was the doctor looking at him, impassive, unspeaking, with nothing by way of expression on his features except for a small lump that the point of his tongue raised on the surface of his right cheek.

No, Dr. Hoerchner had never gone much for his spiritual rummaging. He listened, of course, as the sick derelict mind went feeling through piles of threadbare words—God, Faith, Meaning, Love—a bum at a church bazaar, desperate to find something to clothe himself with. The doctor listened, as he always listened, to everything and anything. But his patient had seen the little lump rise on his right cheek, had heard the pencil set to doodling in the margins of the note pad, caught the nostril-flare of the sublimated yawn—how keen to such touches the wounded psyche is! The ears that had pricked like a hound's to the whiffs of sex and feces and hatred and dreams fell flat and listless now.

The communication of non-communications. In his fear, his desperation, he tried to unnotice what he had noticed, while up on the surface all proceeded according to procedural standards, the therapist playing his part with that on-stage professionalism his society esteemed so highly (didn't it refer to bombing women and children as "doing a job"?) and rewarded so richly, that antiseptic make-up which sterilized the actor inside it.

"The letter was always perfect, Frank—the letter that kills."

"Come now, Bob, I think you're being a little harsh on me, aren't you? What did I ever say to make you think I'm down on religion? On the contrary, in some cases I've seen it work wonders."

Work wonders—the day-before-washday miracle . . .

"I'll go farther. In some cases, religious faith's the only thing that's been able to pull them in out of left field. I remember one patient, father made a fortune in men's toiletries, typical millionaire playboy . . ." And Frank told him again about Case Smith, the profligate alcoholic who got religion, as previously he'd told him about Case Jones, the Catholic monseigneur who got women and liquor.

"And me, Frank? Is my case a 'some case'?"

"Possible . . ."

Impossible. And what made it impossible was the who in the what, the spirit that tinctured the words. To allow that a man's search for what is real in life could be, in some cases, a useful therapeutic tool—this was enough. The sophisticated spirit that throws off the old prejudices, but won't bother to put on new virtues.

"He who is not with me is against me, and he who does not gather with me scatters."

He'd never understood that remark before, Christ's remark, not until this instant. On some questions there is no such thing as a neutral stance.

For the simple reason that such neutrality is never neutral, no more than that of a news photographer rushing to photograph a victim of violence. Dr. Hoerchner's wasn't.

"Frank, remember the time, the single time I ever really got your goat, the only time I remember your losing your professional decorum? When I brought up Jung, something he wrote to the effect that most of the psychological problems in patients over thirty were actually spiritual problems? And what was it you said again . . . ?"

"Bob, look here. Don't you think we'd get a helluva lot farther if we cut down on all the mystical crap and stuck closer to real things?"

Mystical crap and real things. Real things being, of course, those things our own monitors had been adjusted to register, the "facts." Didn't matter in the slightest how fantastic, how wild, those "facts" turned out to be. All the long buried traumas, all the murders and bestialities, all the loathings and lustings and fearings the id was heir to—always it was the sniff of these that made us paw for pay dirt together. All these "real things" which, when added to the "real facts" of urine and blood and endocrine juices—those multifarious truths that made us prisoners—all this equaled the sum of a man.

A man . . . but even in geometry, isn't the whole more than the sum of its parts?

"Bob, I've told you again and again: my business is to get you well. And to do that we've got to expose the roots of your sickness."

"Tell me, then, would you try to cure a sick tree by digging it up by the roots and exposing them to fresh air and sunlight? Wouldn't it be wiser to feed these roots?"

"With what? Each case I see is different. To be able to help all his patients the therapist must keep himself value-free."

"Value-free! But that's what we're mad with, Frank—our freedom from values! What does 'well' mean anyhow? Social adjustment? Being able to keep a job? No, even in its perverted forms it means having and holding to a set of values. The values that come when a man has recognized authority, has chosen it freely and followed it lovingly. The well man is the man strung fast onto his own nature, from inside, like a hollow bead on the unseen thread. We aren't strung onto anything inside, Frank. We're a chaos of possibilities. I've seen well men, Frank. They are what they are—like water."

"Without the rhetoric, where and when?"

"Here, in Mexico, this past week."

He was thinking, he realized, of the Indian, the man who had knelt beside him an hour ago in the Basilica—his gaze had vaporized toward the image of the Virgin like water toward the sun. And later, when he and his little child had been reabsorbed into the quiet throng of pajamas and sarapes, it was like human drops falling back into a human lake.

The lake. He felt himself precipitate back into his body once more, reinhabit time and place. The joints of the chair creaked under him as he straightened his legs and half-stood on his feet, half-leaned forward on his hands across the small leather-topped table in front of him, gripping the round skin edges. Looking up, he saw that Dr. Hoerchner had vanished, faded away like the Cheshire Cat, down to his smile. He felt alone and refreshed to the here and now, to the invisible presence of the lake, the dank mildness of the mist, rich with the oxygen breath of countless billions of plants. He could smell flowers again, and corn masa frying in lard, the spice of cedar and leather and pine sap from the porch furniture, the damp moldering earth. He looked about him. On all sides the porch windows framed an exhibit of collages: geometric cutouts of terra-cotta rooftop scumbled over with algae and moss, rounded patterns of tree foliage in stippled greens, a foaming magenta mass of bougainvillaea vine, all pasted in varying arrangements on the linen-white ground of the mist.

He listened to the murmuring from below and around him and, tuning his hearing finer, made out individual sounds—a heavy diesel motor starting up in the plaza, children playing in some hidden patio beneath him, chortling and fussing together like parakeets, broom-straws sweeping stone, faucet water plashing into a metal pail, roosters and church bells crowing and ringing intermittently and far off.

He looked out in the direction of the mist-veiled lake. Howell must be out there somewhere. Harry Howell—friend and traveling companion, lay therapist and agent of salvation —out in the fog, taking the local grand tour of Butterfly Nets, Janitzio Island, Paracutín Volcano, and Tarascan Lake Villages, along with his Japanese camera, his French watercolors, his Yankee energy, and his Mexican diarrhea. He wouldn't be back here at the hotel before evening.

Half-standing, half-crouching, on feet and hands both, he waited out this moment of transition and indecision, looking down into the blue-ruled emptiness of the notebook, listening to the endless melodic warbling that came drifting up from the leaky toilet on the floor below.

And now what?

As if needing the evidence of still another sense to decide, he began to slide his palms caressingly over the orange leather circle of the tabletop. They reported more than anticipated: not merely the pored smoothness of skin, but also a sharp little prickling. Looking down, he saw that the animal's hair had not altogether been scraped from its hide. Here and there little tufts of stubble remained and teased at his fingers.

Closing his eyes, he moved his fingertips lightly back and forth over the stiff bristles, like a blind man reading by touch, like a thief feeling out the combination of a safe . . .

Suddenly, not from his fingers but from the very end of his tongue, came a tiny sting of pain, pulsating in weakly, a signal light from a great distance. It was minute, it barely crossed the threshold of feeling at all, and no sooner did he notice it than it went out altogether, as if extinguished by the turning of his attention. He could no longer feel anything.

Yet he *had* felt something. Something, something there. Something? Instantly he'd recognized it, knew what it was. A thorn, a sticker, the last of those dozens of hair-like darts left impaled in the flesh of his hands and mouth by his orgy on cactus fruit Monday evening. A tiny spine of the *Opuntia*, the prickly pear cactus—American, not Mexican—the *tunas* the old man had given them Friday on the way to Lagos were peeled. No, this was from the stunted northern cactus that clung to the slopes of Sandia Mountain east of Albuquerque, the cactus that had put the thought of Mexico into his head, which had put the thought of Harry Howell, who had transported him through the days of this wonderful week. Links in the chain of ordinary events that made up his miracle, the miracle of his . . . regenesis.

Regenesis? Was there such a word? There was now—for him.

With careful concentration now he began to tweeze for the thorn with his front teeth. He grasped nothing. Then he tried rubbing the tip of his tongue lightly over the sensitive inner lining of his cheek. Nothing. He felt nothing.

Nothing? He smiled. Well, he'd learned a little something about Nothing. And besides, hadn't he actually *felt* it? Pain, an infinitesimal touch of pain, which alone can remember pain.

3

SATURDAY NIGHT he had no dreams. But even before he was awake to Sunday, he felt infusions of chill spurt into his sleep, as if the spirit of the day to come stood crouched over his inert body with a hypodermic, injecting it with small intravenous jets of itself. Before mind could think it, body knew it: Sunday would be the worst day.

Sunday had always been the worst day. As a fever rises in late afternoon, the anxiety and desolation tended to intensify at the end of the week. This Sunday depression had been the earliest pattern to appear during his sessions with Dr. Hoerchner last spring. Not such an uncommon phenomenon, either, the doctor reassured him. "Ol' Sunday Syndrome," he'd said with a smile, his smile.

They'd discussed it exhaustively. No, not exactly discussed, since he himself, utterly disassembled like a watch in for repairs, could contribute no ideas at all. But Frank Hoerchner, it soon became clear to him, regarded this Sunday Syndrome as one more symptom of that Dark Age Plague, Puritanism, whose spirochetes could be found at the core of every emotional ill.

"You realize, Bob, we're only now *beginning* to emerge from the Puritan Era?"

Whether by Puritan Era the psychiatrist had meant Christian Era, he hadn't asked. He couldn't have. He was too destroyed in those days to engage anybody in rational dialogue. And Hoerchner probably would have dodged the question anyhow—he'd early noticed his doctor's habit of avoiding clear declarations about anything—even, he suspected, to himself. And yet, without saying it, he'd said it plainly enough. Religion was—or, thank the Lord, had been up until very recently—a scourge on humanity, an insidious disease of the psyche that had severely crippled the development of man.

"Let's, for fun, have a little glance at the Sermon on the Mount. Now if that isn't the classic Puritan document for you, loaded down with repressive threats and impossible demands, sick with anti-life, anti-erotic moralisms. 'If your right hand causes you to sin, cut it off'—guess we know where that right hand's located, don't we?—offering instead the masochism of the cross, the elaborate fantasy-system of rewards and punishments to be meted out postmortem by Big Daddy in the Sky—I just don't see how anybody could come up with anything more pathogenic than that if he tried . . . and to think of the lives that have been ruined by such perverse demagoguery . . . hundreds of millions!"

Not that the psychiatrist had ever come baldly out with anything like this. It was merely said without saying. All he was striving for, he maintained, was an objective view. As a man of science, a clinician, he could not afford the luxury of personal prejudice one way or the other in such things as religion and politics or ethical rights and wrongs. (He did admit to being a partisan of Lincoln automobiles, however, and bought himself a new one every other spring, in preference to Cadil-

24

lacs and Imperials.) No, there was but one article of faith to which he was openly, deeply and unequivocably committed: that people should be getting a hell of a lot more fun out of life than they were in fact getting.

On Sunday too. On Sunday especially. For hadn't old Jehovah himself set the precedent when he took the day off after that first hard week's work of his? Even today you could catch the vestigial Sabbath imperative (Sunday having long ago replaced Saturday) reverberating through the land: "Let there be FUN!" Ah, but the captive Puritan ego, clamped in its iron-maiden of repression, festering with generation upon generation of impacted and abscessed desires, couldn't any longer just let loose and enjoy itself. By now it craved more than the Sunday papers and TV sports, and Mom's pie and a family drive—it lusted to ravish and ravage. Any wonder then that such semi-emancipated psyches as Bob's felt feverish come Sunday and shivered to those seismic Sabbath tremors? . . .

And—another thing—the Sunday Syndrome was often an outlet for neurotic hostility directed against society (i.e. Mommy and Daddy). Like the little child who keeps falling down and hurting himself (and Mommy and Daddy) who grows up into the big child who keeps failing (Mommy and Daddy) by making a big mess of his life. So, if Bobby's folks had—or if he thought they had—obeyed the Sunday commandment to take it easy and have a good time, well, what better way to get back at them than by taking it hard and having a thoroughly miserable time? Actually this was probably the biggest factor in Bobby's case, since it was obvious to them both by now that here was a fellow with a strong neurotic need to rebel against authority, which was, needless to keep repeating, Mommy and Daddy.

All of which Hoerchner said without saying during those first hours of therapy, even before the sessions with electricity, lysergic acid and sodium amytal had been completed. And asked, "So maybe it would be a good idea now to try and work back towards some of the reasons behind this hostility of yours, don't you agree?"

Yes, yes, he agreed. He agreed to anything. He wanted one thing only, peace, an end to suffering, and whatever peace-terms the doctor offered he was ready and eager to accept; and besides, these terms did seem reasonable to him, they did make sense to him.

But strangest thing! Even in his annihilation, in spite of his mind and his will, he felt something inside him still fighting back. Even as he, the general, was signing the armistice documents, one lone diehard sniper held out deep in his ruins.

Pinged now and then by a stray shot, Hoerchner had leaned back in his chair and remarked, "And while we're at it, maybe we ought to talk a little about the reasons behind your resistance to therapy."

Which they did. And the reasons behind turned out to be Mommy and Daddy, just as surely as with a Marxist they would have turned out to be recalcitrant bourgeois tendencies, or, with a priest, spiritual pride.

And, in those days, this pocket of resistance in him pained him more than it did the doctor. With whatever shreds of will were left in him, he tried to snuff it out, tried to believe in the doctor's interpretations, as he might, under different circumstances, have tried to believe that he must dedicate himself to the historical struggle against the enemy class or the enemy nation or the enemy tribe, or believe that the wafer dissolving on his tongue was truly the body and substance of God.

The effort was a dismal failure. The Sunday Syndrome didn't give a damn. No sooner had the effects of shock and drugs worn thin than back it came, as strong as before, utterly contemptuous of theories, explanations and insights into its causes . . .

And now one more Sunday was about to begin, this Sunday, October 18, 1958. Even before he woke up into it, he knew in his veins it was going to be the worst day, knew it before he knew its name or his own . . .

Seven A.M., and already it was wide-awake and waiting for him. He hadn't yet even fluttered his eyes, and he did not now. He did not stir at all, but lay motionless in the bed, trying with his first consciousness to locate it, isolate it, identify it, without attracting its attention, before it realized he too was awake. Like waking at night to a sound in the house and trying to pin it down before deciding what to do or not to do. Like watching a wild animal from a blind.

He heard it and felt it—It—scratching about; as with a fingernail across a chalkboard, both heard and felt the palpable premonition that this day about to begin would be a terrible day, the worst day yet. If only he could wind himself backwards into sleep, and let Sunday pass by without him in it, not show up for October 18th at all. But he'd tried that technique all week, and now he was nauseated with sleeping. The day stood waiting, imposed like a criminal sentence, inescapable. He could see it looming before him now, a long narrow gauntlet to be run, spiked with hundreds of hostile moments.

Well, what is it? Quick, what *is* it? Guilt? No, not guilt, I don't feel guilty. Not panic, either. Nor terror, actually. It's more . . . I feel—well, *what?* Quick now, what exactly *is* this feeling? I feel . . . hopeless. I feel I'm starving to death, have been starving all my life. I need a certain kind of food soon or I'll die. But . . . but there's none of that food anywhere in the world . . .

This thought came clearly, very clearly, as, eyes still shut

27

tight, he hurried to take advantage of this last unnoticed moment to have a look at the Thing that sat waiting for him to stir like some great hideous pet. He'd done the same thing before at moments like this one, and learned that anxiety wasn't a simple feeling at all, but a kind of brew compounded of different essences whose proportions and flavors could vary a great deal. There was the chill minty taste of fear-anxiety for one, with its expectation of impending catastrophe from God knows where, in which every element cringes beneath immanent horror, or rushes madly about trying to scratch out a hiding place in a floodlit cement landscape. Completely unlike sex-anxiety with its fermentation, corked-down fretfulness and itching. Different too from impatience-anxiety, forward straining limblessly, forward peering eyelessly, anticipating fundamental changes (what changes?). Or the bleeding enervation of can't-cope anxiety, in which the mutilated mind runs from battle station to battle station to rally defenders that have all been killed off or deserted. Or the whirling centrifuge of madness itself when the brain is being accelerated back into its component atoms.

But now, this instant, he saw that the anxiety waiting for him was none of these. No, it was the starvation-anxiety, the lack-loss anxiety. The dominant sensation was of hunger, of some vital nourishment missing. Something lost, something stolen from him, something never possessed at all. It didn't matter which. If he didn't get that something he would die.

What? God! How should he know what!

Yet this definitely was It, the It that was waiting to embrace him, surround him with Itself, ingest him like some Gargantuan amoeba the moment It saw him stir.

He lay there thinking, scarcely breathing, trying to avoid the unavoidable motion that would bring down the attention of the day, that stretch of time in which the living had to act—refusing to act was also an act—in which history occurred. He lay thinking that he could still think, for a moment or two more, maybe, about the feelings he felt, the thinking looking down on the feeling, as if perched on some little promontory, without having to contact it at all. From here the reasoning mind could make its observations, spell out its labels and distinctions, call It bad names—and have not the slightest effect on anything. A much more primitive form of consciousness this anxiety might be. But like the day, all the power, all the vitality and reality, were on Its side, and like the day, this It would inevitably rise up and drown whatever part of him was thinking now.

His mind had classified the pain for him. Like all anxieties, this It was essentially pain, pain anticipating pain, the way the molecules in a piece of iron polarize to a magnet that does not actually touch it. A label had now been pasted neatly on it: loss-lack anxiety, starvation pain, not the crushing together of terror or the pulling apart of inadequacy.

But how, just exactly how, does it feel? Right now, this instant, what's it feel like?

As if playing a grim game in front of its executioners, his mind responded. Except for his reason, the anxiety had already drenched his inner works completely. All of them, the organs inside his chest and belly, the networks of arteries and veins, nerves and ducts, muscles and skin, all but the rational center of his brain itself, were tugging at their tethers, roaming as far as they could inside the tight confines assigned them in his flesh, every one of them engaged in a mindless search for something. Something utterly required, utterly missing. The search had long ago become chaotic, anarchic, hysterical. The something, whatever it was, no longer mattered. It was like what happens when a harried man realizes, as he is about to leave for a crucial appointment, that he has misplaced something vitally important and has looked for it again and again in the same places he knows it is not, missing his appointment, until the thing he is looking for and the reason he needed it so badly are both lost in the frenzied tangibility of the mad search-operations themselves.

His thinking looked down now and saw his entire subrational being become a maniacal search party, frantic to find something which, of course, it lacked the faculties to comprehend or go after in any organized or orderly manner. From the little promontory of its detachment (already he could feel the ground beneath disappearing as the It dissolved the edges away) his reason could still attempt to grasp what it was that everything was looking for, could try to name it even. Of course it could do so in nothing but words, and in such sterile, impotent, devitalized words that nothing was standing under its understanding. But in spite of all this, in this ultimate first moment of the morning, even as the maw of the day to come was sealing over it and swallowing it down into corrosive guts, his intellect did a remarkable, even valiant, thing. It tried to make one final valedictory summation as it drowned, to say what, in its own pitiful rhetoric, it was still capable of saying . . .

"Now, Bob, what you are looking for is, quite obviously, God. I am, however, painfully aware that to say this is to say nothing, even on a purely semantic level. The phrase has been run into the ground, become a platitude for lazy minds. And in any event, you have no expectation of finding God. I am sure you wouldn't recognize Him if you bumped into Him. Even this flood of idiot emotion which is overwhelming us now with all the despicable 'triumph' of a spawn of staphylococci doesn't think—beg pardon, wouldn't think if it could think— that it's going to find anything with all this agitation. No, let's face it, God is not about to materialize, crash down through that ceiling up there, yank back the covers and say, 'Arise, Bob, take up thy pallet and walk.' Hardly. But, you see, it isn't

God you want anyhow. Just a sense of Him, a scent of Him, His whereabouts. You have neither expectation nor desire to go to the North Pole or the North Star. But you need to know in which direction North is, simply in order to navigate correctly down here where you are. Because life's taught you this much by now (you are thirty-three, after all, and not exactly new to this terrain)—that if you don't know where your North is, you'll never get your inner bearings, will you? And if you don't know where you are, who you are, what you are doing here, why it is that you find yourself waking up in this bed in this house in Albuquerque, with Sunday, October 18, 1958, here to be coped with, how can you steer a course through this day, through this sidereal river through which you in this spaceship body of yours are so clearly designed to navigate? The happy man—I may already have told you this, but it will stand repeating—the happy man, Bob, is *not* the fellow who's learned to squeeze the last drop of pleasure from the teats of life. He's the man who's sure of his North, who is free from choice in exactly the same way that a tree is free from choice. To do this he's got to find and keep remembering the thing a tree doesn't have the power to forget. For you, Bob, that means nothing less than centering on the core—the sense, the scent of God. This, beyond any discussion, is the heart of your problem. Don't get sidetracked, my boy. However, most regrettably . . . much as I'd like . . . I, as you know . . . am personally . . . unfortunately . . . incapable of . . ."

And down it went, his Professor Reason, beneath closing jaws, floodwaters, barbarian hordes, and that was that. Though he continued to lie as before, still trying not to move, there was no voice left inside him but that of pain, of It. Existence was composed of a headache pressing on the back of his eyeballs like a pair of relentless thumbs, a tightness of the skin of his forehead. His mouth was arid and sulphurous. The teeth in it grated against each other irritably. They had turned into for-

31

eign objects pressed into his flesh, too hard, too big for the tenderness of his mouth, pieces of gravel. His tongue twitched and wandered like some horrid little absurdity, some slug-like animal that had stupidly got itself rooted in the entrance to his throat. His body itself felt like some dilettante's botched, ill-fitting, meaningless junk-construction, whose parts cohered to one another for no better reason than the difficulty involved in separating them. Bone gouged flesh here, then there, muscle groups pulled peevishly against each other. Tiny bubbles of itching rose to his surfaces in undecipherable patterns. Skin felt stale and sticky where it touched the blanket or other parts of itself. Cheek on pillow felt sweaty and dirty. None of these annoyances, though, was in itself acute enough to attract steady attention. Just a physical orchestration for the theme being played out, that was all. He began to shift and turn, and the swarm of petty discomforts shifted and turned along with him. Soon it resolved into a balance and counterbalance between lying miserably in bed or getting miserably up, the frying pan or the fire.

His legs swung heavily off the bed, and he sat up, bent over, rolling his thumbs over his eyeballs to apply a reciprocal pain. At that instant, Sunday, October 18th, spoke, broke in with its keynote remarks of the morning. Two tremendous concussions that rocked the air in the room and rattled the window-panes fiercely. Lack-loss flipped momentarily to terror-from-without. Before the blasts had ceased reverberating, they were punctured by a shrill distant screaming, as if from murder victims or maniacs, and he relaxed in the understanding that this was no more than a couple of sonic booms from a brace of jet fighter-bombers out of Sandia Base, sounds that went on every day in Albuquerque, until one wasn't really conscious of them any more—he thought.

He lifted his body leadenly erect, and covered his lower half with the pants that lay in a heap on the floor. Then he yanked his shirt out of the tangle of bedding, and as he pushed his arms into that, he heard his upper half emit a pitiful sigh while simultaneously his lower half emitted a repulsive fart.

Dressed more or less, he wandered into the kitchen, where all the smells and disorder and dirt left over from the past two weeks greeted him, a desolation of unwashed dishes, unwashed clothes, unemptied garbage, unclosed drawers and doors. From force of habit alone he drifted first to the stove and squinted down into the coffee pot; at the bottom was a fraction of an inch of opaque umber liquid. He turned the burner on and without removing his hand turned it off again. Better not take coffee. What then? Everybody drank something in the morning. There wasn't any milk left in the house, or tea, or juice. He filled a greasy plastic tumbler with hot water from the tap and sat down at the round kitchen table to sip it. It tasted strongly of chemicals, chlorine, fluorine, both.

What should I take? A Dexedrine Spansule to tune me up, or a Triavil to tune me down?

The decision was too much. The problem slipped away.

On the table in front of him lay a letter, Anne's letter. It had come last Thursday, and since then he'd held onto it like a fetish-object, reading and rereading, analyzing the writing, comparing the nibs on all the r's, the loops on the g's, the tiny blot on page two, the crossed-out mistakes, like some insane archeologist trying to piece together an entire civilization by obsessive study of a single potsherd.

. . . we're doing O.K., I guess. Actually it's not as bad as I thought it was going to be—think we can last it out as long as necessary (if that's not *tooooo* long!) My parents say they're "overjoyed" to have us (sometimes they have to clench pretty grimly to that overjoy). But there's a nice park six blocks away, and whenever it gets too rough, I take the children out . . . they try . . . And one thing, the food is good. We're all getting fat. I've put on seven pounds in a week! . . . David's cold is just about gone . . . Cassie's been riding my old tricycle—they've saved it, can you imagine! . . . —seems to like her grandfather best . . .

And you? . . . Not a word in almost a week, and I'm beginning to worry. God, I hope we did the right thing—it was the *only* thing left, wasn't it? I know I was no help at all, almost cracking up myself. Just that much more weight on you. Aren't you a little better, now that you've got some quiet and peace to think? . . . and, if you don't feel like writing, call me, collect, soon . . . and please, if it gets too bad, please, please, go see Hoerchner. In spite of everything, he did help pull you out of it last spring . . . and don't worry about money, we'll get it somehow. You're worth more than money . . . where she got the idea I don't know, but Cassie thinks you're coming here to get us. Every morning she asks me "Is Daddy coming *today?*" . . . and please, take care of yourself, please eat right and take your time and I know you'll get back on your feet sooner than you think . . . and never ever forget, we all miss you and love you and I love you and aren't you beginning to miss us a *little* bit by now? . . .

In his mouth the fluorine and the chlorine of the tap water were reacting badly with the sulphur of his depression. As he laid the letter down and tried to swallow, he found his throat passages had grown stiff and tight, and his breathing had become shallow syncopated sighs. He spit the water slowly back into the glass and felt himself sliding inside, like a collapsing mudbank, giving way to that contemptible self-pity that is the one common factor in all mental illness, mourning himself miserably.

Two weeks . . . was it that long already since she'd left? The first time in the whole ten years. Except for his hospitalization in Bethlehem last spring, Anne and he had never

34

spent more than a night or two apart at a time. They had cleaved together like—like two halves of a wheel that were useless alone . . . or maybe more like two people trapped underground breathing from a single shaft of air. Yet for years, during the worst times, the idea of separating had come up again and again.

"You know, maybe you ought to be by yourself for a while," she said.

"You know, I think maybe I need to be by myself for a while," he said.

"Maybe we both should get a little vacation from each other for a while," they both said, "to get a little perspective, to think things out. I can't tell my thoughts from yours any more."

But it was only this time that the crisis grew to sufficient size and power to force talk into act, to pry them apart.

Pry us apart . . .

He raised his head and looked back into the living room, at the bed he had just left. In that bed, that same bed—oh, God, not again! He shook his head, to shake away the memory.

But it was already again. Two naked bodies, grappling at each other, a pair of hysterical swimmers drowning in the sea of that same bed, trying frantically to take, to give, to find rescue in the solace of love. Impotent, both of them, feeling, both of them, only the thickening wall of anesthesia numbing away the other's flesh, voice, reality, their own flesh, voice, reality—everything growing more remote, alien, fantastic.

The angers, the torrents of cruel trance-spoken words, the silences, the tears, the shames, hers, his. Meaningless, dishonest, exaggerated explanations, accusations, torture-confessions, messages unauthorized, undelivered—and the awful inexorable coagulation of estrangement, the slow, progressive withdrawal of being, of response, from both, the stiffening and chilling of death.

They lay side by side in exhausted, staring silence and isolation, their bodies nowhere in contact. Suddenly she sat up and looked at him, her hair wild, her beautiful pale green eyes red and terrified and ugly. Her voice was trembly and high-pitched, like a child's.

"Honey . . . you know . . . I think . . . I think we're going crazy . . . both of us . . ."

A bolt of terror, cold as outer space. They were!

And then the baby cried. The baby cried and saved them. When she came back to bed, they squeezed hands in a pathetic desensitized clasp and fell into unconsciousness.

If it hadn't been for the children, their incessant demands on her, Anne too might have frozen. Her inner temperature was low enough. But the constant physical and emotional distractions necessary to keeping them going kept her going as well; that agitation alone prevented the ice from freezing over. Even so she was reaching her limits. In her case, though, breakdown would take a physical form. Already she complained of palpitations, shortness of breath, trouble with seeing and hearing, a constant fatigue, and strange unaccountable fevers that came and just as quickly left.

Last spring she had managed to stick it out with him. But when it descended again this time, it was even stronger. Too strong. The nighttime terrors of madness and collapse had metastasized into daytime reality. The simplest things—a flat tire, a haircut for David, fixing meals—were becoming menacingly complex. And like a huge hourglass set in the center of their lives, the money was running steadily out. Last spring there had at least been his teacher's salary and the insurance to pay Bethlehem and Hoerchner. Now . . .

Thank God she at least had got away from it.

For a moment his consciousness wandered down a narrow tributary of fantasy. He was finally out of the way. She was free at last, rid of him—what did she ever ask anyway but a

36

simple, natural life with a decent, stable man (no little to ask these days)? Left now with two kids by her former marriage— *former marriage*—thirty-one, a little worn, but still pretty, more than pretty. Maybe there was some high-school boyfriend still around. Maybe they'd already run into each other, in that park six blocks away . . .

The tributary had become unnavigable.

He pulled out his wallet and opened it to her picture. She was holding an infant—David, seven years ago—smiling with a fresh Kodak American smile. Thick brown hair, pale green eyes, the kind of young woman sentimental painters like—and who was this, anyhow? Had he been married for ten years to this pretty girl with the perpetual Kodacolor smile, this wallet-sized rectangle of glossy chemical-coated paper? He shut his eyes and tried to conjure up the real woman. He couldn't do it. He thought of all the times they had been intimate, all the words, the looks, the gestures, the thousand proofs of their love— everything seemed false, irrelevant, vague—flimsy extraneous evidence that would be thrown out by any court. He snapped the wallet shut and looked again at the disheveled bed in the other room.

The revelations of that night—and there were other similar nights—had been growing steadily more distinct for several years, moving behind screens on long vacant gray days, running naked through desperate nights, until there it stood in un- moving irrefutable reality: the truth. Bob and Anne, who loved each other, who never thought, even in dreams, of es- caping each other or turning each other in for new people, were, when caught, really fouled in the nets of modern life, helpless, helpless to help. This love they believed in—be- lieved in as a baby believes in milk, with a belief all the more vital because it had to support them against their instinctive disbelief in the shoddy pantheon of contemporary gods, in car and country and money-power success and war and institutions and technological bulldozing into the shining glut of the future —this love of theirs had limits, and they had reached those limits.

Nights like that had treated them to a glimpse beyond those limits: they had never spoken to each other about what they saw. But they knew, both of them now, that the aloneness was not, as they had thought, forever behind them. The aloneness had been waiting to be noticed, taken up and carried, each one his own.

It was then that the talk of separation became more than mere talk of separation.

Two weeks ago, the week after he had given up his job with Howell's construction crew, they had, at her insistence, tried to break the spell with a Sunday picnic. They had driven through Placitas, winding up into the ponderosa forests, through the golden groves of turning aspens, to Sandia Crest, a mile above the city, and then home by way of Tijeras Canyon. A marvelously brilliant fall day, the best the Southwest has to offer.

It had eaten up a few hours, but done nothing to lift their desolation. When they got home, Anne went mechanically into the kitchen to heat up some beans, and he lay down on the bed while Cassie climbed over his inert form, trying vainly to tug it into a bouncing horsey. Suddenly Anne appeared from the kitchen and sat down on the edge of the bed.

"You know, why don't I just take the children and go visit my folks for a while? They've been begging us to for years. I mean, I simply can't think of anything else to do at this point. What do you think?"

Think? He had been thinking, "You two little people are going to have to go through a fire." The woman at the honeymoon hotel had said that, that highly rouged divorcée who read their palms with eyes almost as colorless as water. And the two little people, triggered to laugh, laughed and wandered back upstairs to make love again.

"Remember our honeymoon, that woman?" he said.

"Woman?" she said.

"It doesn't matter." He said nothing more, being now unable to say anything more. He turned and looked at her levelly, as if they were on a seesaw. Steadily the balance shifted, and his pity for himself shifted over to pity for her. He drew Cassie to him and looked away.

She got up. "I'm going to go next door and phone them. Right now. Is it all right with you?"

"Remember what she told us . . . about the fire?"

"What did you say?"

"Nothing. Go call."

And instantly now the kitchen itself seemed to fill with the whistling shriek of the jet, and there he saw them, sealed hermetically behind one of those many strung-out little portholes, a pair of arms fragilely waving, like wisps of grass, and her miniaturized face looking seriously, sadly, down at him. Just as it turned animate, as she tried to convey something to him, the fretful motors accelerated into a raging howl, and, its metal hide flashing swords of sunlight, the great mechanical whale pivoted away, and they were gone into the sea of space. He sat here, exquisitely, acutely, sentient to the distance stretched between them, as if some attenuated filament fifteen hundred miles long had been grafted onto his own nervous system.

His body, as if in horror at that, gave a convulsive shudder, got up from the table and took him to the bathroom. As he walked in, he saw his face loom up at him from the medicine cabinet, bearded and grim as a skid-row bum. Something in the woebegone expression released a drop of irony into him, and he saw the corner of the mouth in front of him crook upward a little on one side. How pitiful, how inaccurate the human face was when it attempted to force its simple musculature into ideograms of the complexities unseeable and shifting behind it—but how very hard within its limited means it did try.

The water turned on in the tap and he watched the face being treated to the morning routine of washing, shaving, brushing, as if the hands that worked over it belonged to some Salvation Army missionary who was even now attempting to boost his broken morale and start his day right. But even as he watched he knew that no efforts of any kind could prevent today from being today, the culmination somehow of what had been building up and tearing down in him for weeks, maybe years. Today, he knew already, would be the day in which he would sink or swim. Today would make him or break him. And what could that mean really except that today he would sink, today he would break? And there was nothing and nobody that could . . .

"Muss es sein? . . . Es muss sein!"

A strange sensation of inevitability, of unavoidability, yes, even of necessity. He could practically hear it, it was so intense, a high-pitched buzzing, like a radio beam guiding him in to God knew what unknown landing.

Again his body, by means of another little convulsive shudder, broke him loose from this fixation and took him from the bathroom to the main room, pulled open the front door and delivered him outside—into the public reality, Albuquerque, October 18th, 1958.

4

A SULLEN OCTOBER DAY, tamped down with gray wads of cloud. Mean-looking but toothless, fall was playing at winter, panicking the yellow leaves of the poplars and cottonwoods with gusts that were incapable yet of making them release their hold. Still, a light scattering of leaves lay on the drive-way, and across the fence the neighbor's wife was already going at them with a systematic vengeance, as if punishing her patch of lawn for messing itself. The sight of her scratching away made him retreat back into the house again.

To see, heaped over a chair, his corduroy jacket. Upon which cue, the cheery Salvation Army remnant (which he knew was just pretending to be fighting It, while really playing out its comic bit-part in the whole absurdity) took advantage of the weakness of transition. "A little walk will do you good."

He pushed into his jacket and reemerged. Eyes carefully averted, he began to move quietly over the gravel toward the open street.

"Mornin' there, mister." Her Texas drawl fell onto him like a rope.

He turned and gave her a half-glance. Vigorous, mindless old age. Weathered waspy church-and-business lifetime, spick-and-span conscience tuned to Sunday neighboring. What was her name?

God, he couldn't summon up the woman's name. He'd known it for months. He knew it a few days ago. He nodded and turned to go.

"How you gettin' on with the batchin' life?"

The second nod aborted into a jerk and the accompanying smile into a twitch.

"Okay."

"And what you hear from Annie? Enjoyin' her stay back East?" A reedy quack, a badly played oboe.

"She's okay."

Now, he saw, the message was finally getting through to her. Her next words got away from her before she could rein them back.

". . . Was fixin' to bring you over some biscuits." The *biscuits* barely made it across the fence.

"Thanks." The *thanks* barely made it beyond his lips. He turned and walked on. Mrs.—what the hell *was* the woman's name? Some Freudian thing there?—no, she wouldn't be bringing him over any biscuits. She'd always been suspicious of him anyway—something off there. It was "Annie" she liked, felt sympathy for. Probably the most unitive force among women, that, cornerstone of all the female clubs that proliferated across America—the common misfortune they were saddled with: men.

At the public sidewalk, he turned to the right and looked slowly about him, at the real world, the one they all readily acknowledged was there.

Bleating a warning, the blunt blue nose of a car pulled across his path into the driveway in front of him. He could see nothing else, it seemed, but cars. They dominated all the views.

Everywhere his eyes looked, there they were, these large gleaming blobs of color and sound and motion, purring, blinking, gliding, farting contentedly . . . such powerful and healthy imitations of life that the smaller species that went along with them, working their controls or grooming their glossy flanks with sponges or their padded interiors with vacuum hoses, seemed faded-looking and unimpressive, misshapen even, imperfect, like factory rejects. Not only did the streets belong uncontestably to them, but as they squatted beside their houses and lawns, they turned their variform nates and chromium smirks onto the world as if these too were theirs.

All of which set off inside him the first peculiar undulating sensations of the confusion of paradox. Of power that was flabbiness, of reality that was illusion, of meaning that had no meaning, of order that was utter chaos. As if everything bore officially approved mislabels. Other Sundays, taking similar walks for similar reasons, he had felt these same unnerving feelings of inversion . . .

Suddenly, from the rear, an undulating scream like a police siren, a high sustained squeal like a fighter plane—two pursuers at six o'clock, rapidly closing. He wheeled, adrenalized, to the sight of a pair of crew-cut ten-year-olds on skateboards plummeting down the cement at him.

"Outta the way, outta the way!"

He obeyed, but his reaction time was half a second slow, and they came close to collision. Through the brief roaring intensity they threw him the look of Hitlerjugend to whom all grownups, were Jews. "Creep!" They ground off down the sidewalk ahead, and he felt his heart slowing gradually to normal.

Is this all me? Is it all just my subjective state?

"*Ils sont dans le vrai.*" Flaubert, watching the Sunday crowds along the Seine.

Again he looked about, picking out people from among the cars. Besides the car attendants, there was a young wife squat-

43

ting on the lawn, her flowered yellow shorts drum-tight across her hefty haunches. Here, a young man was tossing a ball to another young man who tossed it immediately back to him, there, a fellow his age was doggedly casting and recasting a fly rod up his cement driveway; several more were trailing sputtering mowers around their patches of grass; an older man was erecting a cinderblock wall between himself and his neighbor, another screwing a chromium Scotty dog onto his mailbox. Down a front walk a toddler was pulling a robot that shot colored sparks out of its eyes. And tearing through the shrubbery was a small pack of children in camouflage suits and battle helmets, chasing each other with futuristic death-ray guns.

Flaubert, come here a minute, will you. Say that again. "*Ils sont . . . quoi?*"

He quickened his pace, head lowered, eyes beamed to the inrolling band of cement a few feet in front of him. He watched his feet come kicking one after another up into his field of vision. He didn't look up for another block or two, and then did, as if to find out where those feet were taking him.

Beside his right shoulder now, a high cyclone fence, stout steel poles set fast in concrete and lashed with tempered steel mesh. He felt eyes on him, and sought them out. They belonged to a huge black German shepherd that crouched like a lion on the grass behind the fence, eyes that tracked his every movement with the merciless silence of an artillery rangefinder. Two loud flat reports next, gunfire, and there stood a gray-haired man beside his younger, taller double, father-son obviously. Both held identical blue-steel rifles, and both were sighting at a life-sized paper man fastened to a backstop of sandbags piled against a cement wall. The paper man serving as target was of a radically different physical and psychological type from father and son, clearly a legitimate kill—swarthy, unshaven, a cowering coward, a sneak, a gangster, a comic-

44

strip undesirable, indefinitely Jap, Chink, Red, Mex, Nig, Yid, Hip, whatever the times called for. About to twist and run, he stood transfixed, not merely in an extremely vulnerable pose, but over his left chest glowed the outline of his X-rayed heart, the same red symmetry that floods the nation yearly on February 14.

The boy's rifle cracked, and the paper man gave a slight shudder. "Nice one, Wayne." An acrid whiff of gunpowder. Behind, in a driveway, a big red car with a flasher on the roof sat awaiting orders. "Sheriff's Posse," said the tag over the license plate. On the windshield there was a numbered decal of Sandia Base, perfection center for nuclear weaponry.

How much of Albuquerque's income did Howell say came from the military? Sixty-seven percent, was it?

He realized he had stopped at the same instant that father-and-son realized he had stopped and was looking in at them. Their eyes joined those of the dog to form a battery of six eyes that had him fixed in a suspicious once-over. He felt his skin pigment darkening, his beard grow visible, his features thicken into undesirability, his body cringe and twist to escape. He felt the six X-ray eyes picking out his heart, and it seemed not merely possible but reasonable and certain that the rifles were being raised behind him, and that after the annihilating explosions, there would be yet one split instant more in which to hear one final human voice: "Nice shot, Wayne."

But it was only the dog that broke discipline, suddenly leaping up to rage savagely after him, rattling the steel netting as it tracked him to its master's property line, and then, with a similar abruptness, desisting.

Piggy-Wiggy next. Piggy-Wiggy Shopping Plaza. Ten or twelve flattened acres of asphalt, a great solidified tar pit for cars to wait on while their occupants shopped at the complex of steel and glass structures that lined the shore. Dominating

45

the scene was the great P-W Supermarket. Out front, welded immovably aloft on a steel mast, the chain's famous trademark, the twenty-foot-tall humanoid Disneyoid pink porker in a butcher's cap, welcomed in the crowds with the professional smile of a convention host. Solid steel, pastel-enameled.

Everything was striking him as if he'd never been here before, as if all the callouses of habit had been pared off.

OPEN SUNDAY—huge fat spend-money letters in day-glo plastic.

Open . . . Sunday . . . food . . . I'm hungry . . .

As if the entire place tilted, he stepped forward, highly aware of how legitimate, how primordial, this motion, this reaction, was, conditioned into flesh over hundreds of millions of years. By cell-squiggling, skin-rippling, torso-writhing, tail-lashing, jet-squirting they moved forward. By tentacle, fin, feather, paw, foot, wheel, they propelled themselves to food. The food-getting urge, Urge Number One, the very same sensation of need that gave the first protoplasmic jelly-dots a *Weltanschauung*, a *raison d'être*, and led them, eon by aching eon, out of the Cambrian slime, towards Albuquerque, towards Bob the Hungry Homosapiens, moving across this hard black residue of primeval lives at this utterly latest instant of all evolutionary time, now.

Obsequious as a courtier, the glass door swished itself open before him and ushered him into the city of food. The bustle and hustle of communal life. Up front the wire carts banged and the checkout machinery plinked and whirred. Up above show-tunes seeped out of invisible ceiling jets like a sweet narcotic gas onto the slow traffic circulating below. He took hold of a wheeled basket and began to steer it through the blocks of cans and bottles and packages and signs and prices, gripping the handle against the dizzying waves of the sensation of paradox that now were suddenly stepping up their assault.

46

At the frozen-food zone he loaded in a can of orange juice and moved on in the direction of the bean, bread and banana neighborhoods, trying to keep from bumping into the strolling pastel buttocks of housewives, yet forced by their very numbers to consider them closely. In shape they struck him as rather naively streamlined, like the rear ends of models designed in an earlier, less sophisticated period. Nevertheless the constant parade of these soft bilobate forms, these animalized nectarines, tensing and relaxing symmetrically down the aisles, had its cumulative effect, scattering spores of lust, abstract and depersonalized, which budded fungi and rotted immediately, adding their weight to the bolus of despair that was dragging him down inside like a dead foetus.

This too he'd discovered already. Dr. Freud, Dr. Hoerchner, to the contrary, sex and death were not necessarily opposites. Eros could form a marriage of convenience with Thanatos.

Suddenly he was afraid. For the length of an aisle, all the way from the instant teas to the cake mixes, he wondered whether he would be able to complete this process, to make it out through the checkstand without crumpling to the floor. He reached out and grabbed hold of a chocolate cake and tried to keep himself afloat by studying carefully every word written on the package. But as he read through the long list of chemicals that comprised the Devil's Food, he knew this wasn't going to help. He was sinking fast.

As he went down, he desperately jettisoned his load of provisions and with the moment of added buoyancy, just managed to squeeze out through the checkpoint, holding his empty palms out to the girl as proof he wasn't stealing anything. If she had uttered a word to delay him—but she didn't.

In the parking lot it had turned warm and sunny, courtesy of a gap of sky between the slow clots of cloud. He made it to the first row of cars and propped himself against a round black

47

fender, panting like a rabbit that has momentarily evaded its pursuers. He looked in fear around the cosmos of Piggy-Wiggy Plaza.

Where am I? What am I doing in this place? What world is this? What species is this? Mine? Am I, from outside, just like them? Are they, from inside, just like me?

Shave-and-a-haircut—two bits! A horn beneath him blasted out the rhythm. The fender he was resting on was sliding away. His body jerked straight and jumped free. Without his noticing it, the car had swallowed an entire family. The driver was grinning at him through the windshield.

I've got to get out of here, got to get home.

Clenching his teeth and fists for strength, he began to walk down a lane between the ranks of parked automobiles. Then, behind him, he heard the rattling and palpitating of an old car, as if someone were tailing him. The paranoia hardly surpri—

"Hey Bob, you fucker!"

Wheeling, he recognized the dark vibrant smile instantly. Griego, pick-and-shovel operator number one on Harry Howell's construction crew. Until three weeks ago they had shared a side-by-side intimacy of hard labor together. Griego had taught him a thing or two about balancing a load of cement and puddling a slab floor and sharpening a spade. He'd also given him a complete course in Chicano profanity as he sweated all week in order to drink, fornicate, fight and go broke each Saturday night.

"¿Qué 'stás haciendo, chingado?"

"Nothing, I . . ." He could take his psychological measure by his fluency in Spanish. Now he could barely dredge out a word of English.

"Trabajando muncho?" The smell of Tokay reached him now.

He nodded. It was not a question of truth or lie. It was a

48

question of disengaging from Griego as quickly and inoffensively as possible. From the dingy recesses of the car he saw half a dozen small black-eyed faces staring silently out at him. All scrubbed and combed for Mass. The lavender and pink and yellow dresses of the girls looked like parasitic orchids that had bloomed from the substance of the used, prematurely old woman who was giving him a gapped smile from the back seat. He nodded to the wife, tried to force a smile for the children.

"No quieres un traguito?" Griego's arm was holding a half-drained flask of dark yellow liquid out the car window to him.

"No . . . gracias."

"Waiting on the old lady?" Griego tried one last time, in heavily accented English, but his voice had lost its warmth, as if this were suddenly just another gringo, not his compadre Bob, who'd talked with him in mexicano as they hammered in studs together.

Again Bob nodded, trying like a prisoner to slip a message out to him through the surrounding walls: Griego, forgive me. I'm the same. But today, today, Griego, I'm very sick . . .

"Bueno, Bob, take it easy."

"Bueno."

As the car pulled away, it tore open a new pang of desolation. Why had he come out into the open? Just to pile up witnesses to his condition? He didn't have the dignity of a dog. A sick dog curled up in a far corner and stayed there until it recovered or until it died.

He was still very weak and trembly. Unless he rested a few minutes he'd never make it back to the house. In the center of the waves of car tops he spied a small concrete atoll with a phone booth erected on it like a lighthouse. He made his way toward its glass isolation. If he could sit down a little while, then perhaps he could gather enough of himself together to set out for home.

49

He closed the folding door and looked out for a moment or two through the smudged panes. Family convoys were crossing the asphalt expanse, flagship mothers with fathers and children in tow. Out on the perimeter small organisms sifted steadily through the great cetaceous maws of the stores like plankton through baleen.

Gratefully he felt the welcome touch of anger that stiffened and centered him a little.

"No, it's not. It's not all just me, just my morbid condition. It's out there too. Something out there that's wrong, that deserves to be resisted. Something I'm right to fight against. All right. I won't eat today. I'll fast. That's what Gandhi"—a sudden bilious distaste to hear himself linked with Gandhi in the same thought. "But still, low as I am, I can do that much. Fast. Maybe it . . . anyhow, it's something. A fast—against cars, shopping centers, autonomous buttocks, chemical cakes . . ."

Something was heaving in on the island now. A teen-aged boy in a black plastic jacket; he wanted to phone. Without thinking to, Bob reached out and picked up the receiver. If he wanted to occupy this sanctuary any longer he'd have to start phoning.

Who? Whom did he know in Albuquerque? He knew Howell. He shuddered as he pictured Howell's once-born good nature slopping heartily out of the earpiece. "Well, Bob, what d'you know? Where the hell you been keeping yourself?"

What about the other people he knew in Albuquerque? Was there no one he wanted to talk to? No, no one.

Hoerchner? Maybe he—no. At least, not yet, not unless—

The boy's face was looking in at him, puffing on a cigarette.

Anne. She was worried. He hadn't written. It was Sunday. Cheap rates. He put in a call to Ohio, person-to-person, collect.

"Collect, you say? The flat small-town voice of his mother-in-law, confident, unified in single-visioned sleep. "From Albuquerque, New Mexico?"

The connection was faded and poor. But, he knew, she'd heard perfectly well the first time and was only making the operator repeat everything for the benefit of his ears.

"Will you accept the charges?"

Would she? A hesitant silence with which she spoke eloquently to her daughter's husband again. "Well . . . all right."

"Honey!" Anne's excited voice. "Is that really you?"

Was that really her? He realized, with disconcerting remoteness, that he was now actually hooked electronically to her. The Bell system would verify that. Another reeling swell of the sense of paradox. The non-Anne of this Anne. This non-connection of a connection. The abysmal separation of this closeness. Her voice was distorted by the poor circuit, but still he was struck by a new regional intonation in it, a family resemblance to her mother's. As if she'd regressed there, rejoined her past. The accent unnerved him—after all, she hadn't really wanted to go there, and if it weren't for him, she—

"How are you? Get my letter?"

"Yes." How could he talk to that accent? His own voice sounded regional too, as if it were being transmitted from some other phone in some other part of the country.

"So tell me . . . wait a second. I'll take it on the other phone."

A pause, faint electric cackling, a cluck. "All right, Mother, thanks. You can hang up now." Another cluck, slow, reluctant.

"Now tell me the truth. How is it?"

"Okay."

"You're lying. It's worse, isn't it? I can tell."

He struggled to sustain it, this connection that was disconnection, this voice that wasn't his, that voice that wasn't hers.

He could almost see the interminably long and leaking copper cable.

"I guess. A little worse."

Through fifteen hundred miles of wire he heard her draw a mobilizing breath, and when she spoke again her voice had put on a brave and touching front of authority and decisiveness that was altogether foreign to it.

"Where are you phoning from? Mrs. Morton's?"

Oh, it was Morton. Mrs. Morton.

"Where?"

"No, Piggy-Wiggy." Through everything he felt a sudden pressure to laugh. If he didn't yield to it, it was out of fear he wouldn't be able to stop.

"Listen—can you hear me all right? Your voice sounds funny —there must be something wrong with this connection."

"I can hear you. How are the—"

"They're all fine. Now listen: I want you to get in touch with Dr. Hoerchner right away, you understand?"

"What can—"

"I don't care. Just do what I say. He's an M.D., too, don't forget. It might very well be something physical. A vitamin deficiency, glands or something. You yourself said it always has a physical side mixed up with it. I'll bet you're not eating right. What did you eat today?"

Like many women, Anne did her best to find a nice physical explanation for all the mysteries. Though she rarely attacked his spiritual interpretations directly, he knew she regarded them very skeptically, hardly more impressed with them than was Dr. Hoerchner. In May, during their last, lighthearted session together, the doctor had put an affectionate arm around him and laughed. "Bob, you're an atavism." And when he'd told Anne, she'd said, "Well, aren't you?" It wasn't merely that her husband's words were always so vague, so general, and seemed to do nothing at all to alleviate the misery that almost invariably accompanied them. (Even Socrates, whose mystical life was concrete, satisfying and joyful, had failed to impress his wife.) No, at base she suspected her man's desire to enter into relations with God as adulterous.

"You haven't been fasting, I hope." A note of sardonic electronic clairvoyance. He could hardly blame her.

"Don't be silly . . ."

"You eat, hear me. How much money have you got?"

"Enough, maybe a hundred. Why, you need some?"

"No, Dad lent me some money. Now tell me, are you going to see him today? I mean it."

"Today's Sunday."

"I don't care. You call him up—right now. You promise?"

He felt something like a sea-swell rise beneath him and float him away a little distance. It was not altogether unpleasant.

"Honey? Honey, are you still there? What's the matter?"

"Nothing, I'm listening."

"I want you to promise to call Dr. Hoerchner."

"But—"

"No buts. Will you call him?"

"All right. I'll call him."

"Really?"

"Yes . . ."

He heard her sigh as she took off the mask of authority. "You miss me?"

"Yes . . ." The boy in the plastic jacket was leaning on the glass, his face not ten inches away. He had lit another cigarette and was signaling to his pals in the car with bravado jerks of his head.

He closed his eyes. "You know I . . ."

"What? . . . I can't hear."

"I do . . . you don't have to ask."

"Well, that's something, anyway. Now I guess I better hang

up. You call Hoerchner right away and write me tomorrow. Was there anything else?"

"No, I guess not." There was, of course, a lot else. But not through this paradox, these plastic ears and mouths, these proxy strangers discussing their affairs with such familiarity.

"Well, then look at me."

"What?"

"Look at me."

Closing his eyes he could conjure her face, but eroded and blotched, like a wirephoto sent over this same faulty connection.

"Kiss me."

He opened his eyes. Inches away, the boy's face was laughing voraciously, probably at some inanity yelled at him from the car. Thin lips, sharp young teeth, red tongue glistening with saliva, a panting, lupine laugh. The fresh, beardless complexion was mottled red, and the tendons of cheek and jaw stood out in lean tight topography.

Shielding his face behind his hand like some criminal suspect being hauled past news cameras, he made and heard the sound of a kiss. The phone gave one ultimate squawk and fell dead.

He replaced the receiver and vacated the booth, unsure whether the call had been for better or for worse. He felt his emotions churning, unsettled inside him, rather than just dragging him down like dead weight. And he did feel steadier on his feet now, his legs felt stronger beneath him. As he threaded his way among the cars, he gave one last glance up at the enameled steel icon of plenty. Beside it, a marquee announced glad tidings in heroic letters: "Tendertouch Tissue —10 rolls $1." And at the end of the cluster of stores, he noticed the sign of a new one, spawned since last he was here. A sexy blond sow in a décolleté gown. *"THE PAMPERED PIGLET—Fashions 'n' Things."*

He set out for home by a different route . . .

Moaning. Low, muted, harmonic—an organ. Before him now a neatly bluestoned parking lot with well-groomed cars lined up in silent order. Behind, a great new A-frame church, set on a carpet of lawn, striking, simple, tasteful. He stopped, looking, listening.

What was that hymn? Wasn't it—yes, it was. He knew that one, had learned it once because it was Gandhi's favorite.

Lead, kindly Light, amid the encircling gloom,
Lead Thou me on! . . .

The dwarf pines seemed to be taking well. The privet ushers lining the walk were prim and trim, the grass practically as green as artificial. The rosebushes had a few last blooms still, though most of the leaves had been blackened and the petal edges whitened by the first touches of frost.

Sunday, October 18, 11 A.M. *Crisis in Christendom—Christendom in Crisis* . . .

The fish in the sea, the sea in the fish—small white plastic letters in black slots, like a lunch counter menu, removable.

. . . Dr. Bill Crawford, D.D., Minister . . .

Another professional. Add an S and he'd be a dentist.

The night is dark, and I am far from home—
Lead Thou me on! . . .

Suddenly he felt something tremble inside him, like a stringed instrument in sympathetic vibration. He felt almost like crying.

I do not ask to see
The distant scene—one step enough for me! . . .

He took a step between the hedges, pulled forward by a force almost as ancient as the need that had drawn him into the food market. Only after he was actually inside, under the sudden scrutiny of well-polished faces and glittering eyeglasses, did he remember the public reality and how he must look. Quickly he slid into the closest empty pew and sat down on the orange velvet cushion, casting his eyes immediately downward, to check his fly. It was, thank God, properly zipped. The foam rubber seemed to accept his bottom as readily as anyone else's, and one by one the faces pivoted away from him and back toward the altar.

Unobserved now, he began to observe. Up front a great peaked isoceles triangle, aglow with stained glass—the rich ultramarines, emeralds, rubies and amethysts of medieval cathedrals, yet thoroughly contemporary in treatment, being a pleasing arrangement of shapes and hues that represented nothing at all—a "religious-mood" window. Before it, a stark walnut lectern in Danish modern, and bisecting the window, like two fast strokes of a draftsman's pencil, a thirty-foot-high cross in four-inch stainless steel tubing. No one was hanging from it.

The building, obviously, was brand new. The smells of varnish and synthetic finishes and wood mingled with the smells of perfume and cosmetics and dry-cleaning and mimeograph ink, forming an incense of fresh energetic beginnings. It was redolent too with the spirits of recently departed architect firms and design associates, color schemers and subcontractors, fund-raisers and bank officers, contract lawyers and building inspectors, all those whose coordinated effort had raised here this splendid motel for God to relax in during his Sunday stopover in Albuquerque. Electric kitchens and pastel bathrooms assuredly stood at the ready in the wings. The word made flesh.

A young man was standing before the cross. Dr. Bill Crawford had risen to speak. Tall, slim, thirty, soberly suited and tied, he might have been a junior sales executive or a vice-consul in Caracas. His head was narrow, and his rather protruding ears glowed in low translucency like tiny panes of the great window behind him. His appearance beneath the stainless steel cross—his pattern as he raised his arms for silence seemed artfully to repeat the dominant theme somehow—stirred a rustle of bulletins and bodies settling into attentiveness. A decent number of decently handkerchiefed church-coughs rose and shrank to silence in the steep wooden perspectives above. The young man spoke:

> I looked on the earth, and lo, it was a waste and a void;
>   and to the heavens and they had no light.
> I looked on the mountains and lo, they were quaking,
>   and all the hills moved to and fro.
> I looked and lo, there was no man,
>   and all the birds of the air had fled.
> I looked and lo, the fruitful land was a desert,
>   and all its cities lay in ruins . . .

He stared around in awe . . . the words, those words! There was the speaker up front, standing impassively like a junior executive making his report to the board, but the words, richly bassed and trebled, were coming not from him, but downwards, thundering down from everywhere above, just like Jehovah of the Wide Screen. He threw his head backward to the Alpine heights above, searching among the massive fir beams for the strategically hidden woofers and tweeters of this amplifying system.

He couldn't locate them and after a while dropped his head again and began to gaze emptily at the velvet padded kneeling bench, feeling increasingly trapped beneath this rain of words

—of platitudes, clichés. For the Crisis in Christendom, it was already evident, was due to a flagging respect for law and order, to communists, anarchists, atheists, extremists, drug fiends and sex fiends, and these had to be met with the only thing they respected: force. Onward-Christian-Soldier power.

Head bowed, he waited out the deluge, miserable as a horse caught in a downpour. Why weren't ears equipped with closable lids like eyes?

A stereophonic stereotype—but such a stereotype he could hardly believe his ears. No ranter and raver, Dr. Bill Crawford. A status quo buttresser, a statistic compiler, an authority quoter . . .

"As Paul told us in 2 Thessalonians 2:7 . . . as the President told us in his news conference last week . . . of the college students called up for military service, more than half . . . of the college girls interviewed, less than 14 percent had never experienced intimate . . . the shocking reluctance among our youth to enter the world of science and business . . . the steady drop in church attendance . . . the steady rise in crime rates . . . in the fifth chapter of Matthew, Jesus . . . in this month's *Digest*, J. Edgar . . ."

Ah, there it was. The *Digest's* sermon-of-the-month club, the pre-digested Word, processed for your listening pleasure . . . the *Digest*, the newer than new Testament, featuring our beloved secret police chief as spiritual father, J.(esus) Edgar—hey!

Hey! what are you doing! Adolescent wisecracking! College-boy cynicism—aren't you beyond that yet? That *is* neurosis, you know, that Hoerchner *could* explain—going at that poor guy as if you expected he had something to offer you, when he's empty himself. He didn't invite you in here. What are you sitting here for anyhow? Don't tell me you still think you're going to find spiritual things in a *church!*

" . . . not merely our Christian heritage, my friends, but

the very fabric of our democratic free enterprise system itself.
Why, in the past twelve years alone . . ."

A little click as another tumbler fell in the lock of this day.
He yearned to get up and walk out, but he didn't dare. Without the protective shell of irony he felt himself naked again to
the waves of paradox. He leaned forward, resting his head in
his palms as if in grave meditation upon the Crisis in Christendom, and wormed the tips of his forefingers into his ears. That
helped. The sermon moved off to a decent distance. Trying
to shift his attention from hearing to seeing, he began to
stare fixedly at the wooden back of the pew three inches in
front of him, as if to lose himself wandering in the intricate
grain. A year ago, probably, that wood had been alive . . .

Alive a year ago. October. A raw fall afternoon at Taos
Pueblo. The great golden trunk of the ponderosa pine, limbed,
peeled and coated with grease, and then erected in the packed
earth plaza between the mud halves of the ancient communal
dwellings. High up at the top swung the slaughtered ewe, sacks
filled with food tied beside it, streams of yellow and red tie-
cloths whipping in the cold mountain wind. The *koshares*,
six or eight of them, their naked bodies smeared white with ash
and black with soot, prancing and clowning around the base of
the tree, grabbing women from the circle of onlookers and pretending to mount them, downing a small boy and pretending
to slice off his genitals (no, he'll never need you, Doctor),
shooting impotently up at the sheep and the sack with their
toy bows and tiny arrows—all their humor grounded in wisdom
and proportion, the pettiness of man's pretensions before nature, all of the acts deriving their vitality, their authenticity,
from their perfect anonymity, not competing, not mugging to
upstage, just roughhousing together like bearcubs, frustrating
one another's efforts to climb the slippery trunk. Until, finally
and at the proper moment, the ritual one did slither to the
top amid the laughter and applause of the crowd, exactly as

59

he had done on this day for unremembered ages. And peering up at the naked, ash-covered human body untying the prize, agile and small as an insect against the harsh gray expanse of sky and the great blue-black hulk of the Sacred Mountain, he felt something so strongly that he turned suddenly to his wife and said, "There it is." More than that he couldn't have said. Yet, at that instant, he understood, and understood precisely, just what had been removed from our lives, just how our way was a crippled and a lonely way—and was meant to be—and that what these Indians had somehow managed to preserve against the ruthless pressures of the materialistic society about them, we, in our lifetimes, would never regain. And yet, he understood too, for that instant, that this lonely way was the way as it was meant to be for us, the way appointed for us, and that therefore, somehow, it was right . . .

A moment, the most peaceful and confident moment in years. Even remembering it now made that peace echo momentarily, so that he might easily have stood up and left under the guidance of it. But he was too absorbed in the board in front of him, drifting along the maze of eddying lines the life tides had left in that anonymous tree.

By the time he was back in the here and now, it was once more too late to act.

". . . the assurance of things hoped for, the conviction of things unseen . . . truly, my friends, this Christian faith of ours is walking through the valley of the shadow of death. But if we cling steadfast to the way, the truth, and the life of the Good Shepherd, our Lord, Jesus Christ, we need fear no evil. Let us pray."

The service shifted down into a silent neutral, as if double-clutching into the final hymn, and in the sudden quiet his It ambushed him again. First the thought, then the dread, then the certainty, that his mouth was about to spring wide and bay forth in terrible groaning howls. The hidden private scandal erupting into public scandal. The shouts, the rough arms, the vilifications, the police, being shoved down a long line that led to Hoerchner and his little electric box . . .

Please!

A pair of hands seemed to be prying irresistibly at his clenched jaws. But then, at the terminal instant, they relented, as if under orders. A new voice entered his head and the sound of it calmed him instantly. Gratefully he recognized his friend and teacher, Søren. On and off for weeks he had been reading, struggling to read, his *Concluding Scientific Postscript*, and now the gentle, lucid intelligence, the proportion, the sanity, and the authority of Søren Kierkegaard had come to rescue him. "See now," he whispered, "we have here an excellent example of what I was telling you, just what I meant when I said that what is true of itself may, in the mouth of such-and-such a person, become untrue. In the old days, only an individual here and there knew the truth; now everybody knows it, but the inwardness of its appropriation stands in inverse relationship to the extent of its dissemination."

"Let us rise."

The congregation rose amid a clearing of throats, a creaking of bone and wood joints. He and Søren rose with the others, turned, both of them, and walked out the aisle together, leaving a wake-like hiatus in the service. It was just beginning to fill with rustlings and whispers when the great tidal moan of the organ came down and engulfed them.

He brought home a sense of purpose—to recommune with Kierkegaard. Before drinking any water, he troubled to rinse out the glass. He even thought of doing a few dishes, tidying up a bit. Later. He went and searched for Kierkegaard and found him under the bed among shriveled brown apple cores, crushed wrappers, and bolls of dust. Back in the kitchen, he settled himself at the round table and split open the anthology.

"*The crowd is untruth . . .*"

Right. You knew, God how you knew. Even a hundred years ago, more, you knew, you saw it coming. Here, listen to this:

As if to demonstrate something, as if Søren were standing there listening, he reached out and clicked on the transistor radio that stood, scarcely ever played, at the center of the table. Slowly he rotated the dial.

". . . so when nervous tension strikes, reach for a bottle of Tranquin tablets and start to swing again . . ."

". . . twenty-three FLN terrorists were killed today in what government sources described as the most successful and encouraging . . ."

". . . doowit, doowit, doowit, doowit, doowit tuhme, baby, come back an doowit again . . ."

". . . black and white, red and yellow, Jew and Gentile, rich and poor, we're all Amer . . ."

He sliced it off. Any hour, day or night, the same, rarely a thing that wasn't an offense. You were right when you said the mob had mounted the throne, the crowd had replaced the kings as tyrant with its retinues of sycophants and lapdogs. You were right, like Christ and Buddha and Socrates and Gandhi and thousands of other individual souls who, like you, loved the truth and refused to kiss the crowd's ass—even if they were murdered for it.

You are right, all of you are right, and I—I'm partly right too. My sickness *isn't* all inside me, it isn't! I'm not just sick, I'm sick of—and it isn't all due to my morbid imagination, my infantile history, my economic class, my conceit, my misanthropy, my masochism, my obstinate refusal to adjust to "reality." All around is this huge collective insanity that dwarfs mine, like an artificial atmosphere imposed under a monstrous plastic dome. And into it the crowd manipulators pipe their "breathing mix" concocted by their hired technicians, a gas which asphyxiates every impulse towards spontaneous life . . .

every contact with it makes me shrink, from its sales pitch to buy whatever its factories are turning out at the moment to its expectation you'll hate whomever the government is making war on at the moment. What trivia, what sham divinities it sets up for my devotion! What awful vapid faces it engraves on its old people—faces without a wrinkle of wisdom, just youth broken down, rusted out, ready for the junk heap like old appliances! Every breath leaves me dying for air, every touch makes me want to pull away.

But where? Into myself? I am insane too with isolation and inadequacy. Can I create a world, a civilization, inside this rented house? I was born for community, for reciprocity, and here I am stinking, rotting away like an unvisited flower!

Oh God!

And he saw the hands that held the book trembling. With anger. Anger—there is no madness without anger, none. To be mad is to be angry, as the language observed long ago. Beneath all despair, beneath his despair now, there was a glowering red coal of rage, and it was burning, he knew, not against society really, or against other men—who were they, after all? what real authority had they? No, it was directed through them and against God Himself, against God for creating a creature capable of creating such a nightmare. And it wasn't merely personal, either, for His cat-and-mouse way with him personally, the way He let him taste Him, like that afternoon at the Pueblo, leading him on, whetting his hope and desire, then dropping him flat like an infuriating girl. He was angry at His everyday way with men, His unconcern, His impotence, His indifference, His injustice, His silence as the liars expropriated His Truth and smeared it over the earth like excrement, forcing brave and honest spirits to deny His existence entirely and try tragically to assume His responsibilities alone. These were the heroes, the doomed heroes, of our times . . .

And here am I, sitting on my ass, sniveling over myself!

Yearning again for support and companionship, he turned back to Søren. But Kierkegaard didn't want him now. He was in a dense, verbose, dialectical mood, having a grand time heaping ridicule upon Hegel. Too much, too much . . . he could not follow him there.

He slowly closed the book. The anger, the madness, he had launched outward at infinity, he felt it bending in obedience to a time-space mathematics beyond his comprehension, circling back to sear through his own heart, leaving a charred hollow for his lostness to reverberate dismally inside. He pushed himself miserably to his feet, dragged himself into the other room and lay face down on the bed . . .

Neither then nor a week later on the porch did he know what happened during those two or three hours at the middle of Sunday. Continuity did not take up again until he was roused by the bell.

5

HE WAS ROUSED BY THE BELL.

Not one bell, many bells . . . the church bells that had started ringing again. The first, drifting in from somewhere far off, was overlapped by a second, and then by a third, a fourth, a fifth, as if out of sympathetic vibration, until it seemed every last church tower in Pátzcuaro was sounding off. He sat listening to their music, slowly sinking into the rising deluge of sound that swamped his mind and unmoored and floated away his thoughts. All lesser noises were engulfed like tidal pools—the warbling of the toilet downstairs, the bee-buzz of street life below, the cryptographic murmuring of his own flowing consciousness. Geysering up from who knew how many church tops, the resonations poured down over the town. The village, the misty air above it, seemed to dissolve into banging and bonging. Bells of every size, rung by every method. Some—he could distinguish them—must be stationary. Boys were beating on them with hammers. "Bong . . . bong . . . bong . . ." steady, forthright, sober. Others,

65

their clappers jerked by ropes, cried out with an excited, stammering clangor. The Basilica, La Colegiata, he thought he could pick out above the others. Several very heavy bells, it seemed, fixed to great wooden yokes and iron axles, were slowly rolling over and over on themselves like amorous whales; their loose tongues, tossing and lolling wantonly, boomed out in gargantuan delight, in good-tempered thunder. While they were at it, the church bells, there was nothing for him to do but sit back in the leather chair and let himself be bobbed about like a duck in the waves.

He of course was vulnerable to them—he was not accustomed to hearing church bells on a Sunday morning—last Sunday, certainly, there had been none. With time probably, Sunday after Sunday, you'd get used to hearing them, the way in Albuquerque you were hardly aware of the Sunday screaming of jets and sirens and the blaring of car horns. After a while church bells too would soak down below consciousness.

Not that he hadn't known bells in his life—that was the first thing he'd heard under Hoerchner's LSD—a bell. But that bell, like the others, was mechanized, made by a neurotic metal pellet pulled between ever-shifting attractions and repulsions. Alarm clocks, front doors, back doors, telephones, school fire-drills, class-period bells—sudden blasts, Pavlovian stimuli, all of them.

Now they were dying down again. One by one they dropped away until just two were left, the first from someplace nearby, the other shimmery with distance, from down by the lake somewhere. They took turns—definitely, they were having a bit of dialogue. "Bang! Bang! Bang!—¿Qué hay pa' 'llà? What's new over there?" "Bong-bong, bong-bong, nada-nada, nada-nada . . . not much, not much." And now they too called it quits, and the agitated molecules gradually slowed and drifted back to their normal speeds and positions. Air became air again, the town reemerged. Into the new quiet the

66

broken toilet was the first sound to insinuate itself, with humble endurance, like sparrows after a thunderstorm.

He wondered what was wrong with it this time. In every place they'd stopped, except the outhouse in Nombre de Dios and that fancy motel in Lagos de Moreno, the toilet had been broken. Not that the chirping annoyed him. Actually it was like sitting beside a brook. Funny. In Albuquerque, the trickling of a leaky toilet was always a source of irritation.

Plinngg! And there, suddenly, came another bell, a high-pitched little tinkling from inside the hotel. He got up and walked to the top of the stairwell, and looked down the axis of the spiral of pink tiles, and flimsy iron railings and potted plants that fell the flights to the musty dimness of the entry hallway. Again the little bell chimed from down there, some sort of contraption on a spring, bounced by a tug of a string outside the door.

"*Ya voy, ya voy* . . ." A female voice, husky with aging sensuality. And down the terra-cotta canal of the hallway came a large soft bundle of flowered chintz, boudoir pink and blue, as if a set of bedclothes had gathered itself into a bulky ball and were rolling to the front door. The *patrona*, the manager, the manageress. From above, it looked like a huge tropical water-lily floating down a muddy channel. A fumbling with locks, and a bright rush of sunlight washed into the shadowy interior. A straw peasant hat, a woolen sarape, two brown chunks of flesh and leather—feet. "*Buenos días, Señora, fresas traigo* . . ." A luminous scarlet disc hovered between them, a basket of fruit, of strawberries.

"*Muy frescas, muy dulces* . . ." The phrases drifted up the stairwell like curls of thin smoke. The dressing gown shifted, bulged toward the fruit.

"*Un poco verdes* . . . *cuánto pides?*" The woman's voice was stronger, deeper than the man's. She sampled, bargained, sampled some more, and did not buy.

"Es que no tengo nadie ahora . . ."

Nobody, nobody here, she'd said. The two gringos, her only guests, were both off for the day . . .

He walked quietly back up into the porch and stood for a few moments looking out in the general direction of the lake. Dark undulating treetops, geometric sections of clay *teja* roofs. The lake itself was still unseeable, perhaps permanently hidden by intervening objects, or perhaps only temporarily shrouded in the mist, which seemed to be thinning, absorbing sunlight. But he could smell the lake, its dank watery exhalations that entered his lungs with each breath. It was there, all right. It was there.

Details began to fall into the range of his attention: single tiles, the cracked, the crooked, the odd-shaped ones; a luxuriant miniature marsh of algae in a gutter pool; the window edge, the way the frame had been mortared into the wall; variations in the greens and the cuts of the leaves, the salmon-pink dots of hibiscus—while through some center of his mind the leaky toilet gurgled away. So that, as the mental patterns began to reform, they seemed of their own accord to dip themselves into that bubbling stream, to let him see which, if any, had a glint about it . . .

And of course it presently came again, that Sunday, that room, that household chaos, that bed with that body—his—sprawled across it, motionless and stiff as a waxwork figure in an historical museum. Revulsion rose in him at the sight of it, revulsion against returning, even in memory, to reinhabit that body and that consciousness again. And why did he have to, anyway? It was a figure out of the past, gone, dead. Why couldn't he just let it lie there and molder into time? He'd made it to here, hadn't he, and now. A healthier man in a healthier place. Why not leave this porch, go down to the plaza and have a plate of enchiladas and bottle or two of cold, dark Dos Equis?

Not a single argument rose up to oppose this suggestion. Still he made no move to leave. Rather he turned around and sat down in the leather chair again, took the notebook from the leather table and opened it to the same pages again. Again he sat studying the blue-ruled emptiness beyond the trail of words, "Since the last . . ." and even turned back the paper and read again the terrible testimony to the reality of last Sunday. And without hearing any reasons for it, without hearing the voice of thought at all, he understood that, for reason beyond reason, the only way out for him was through that inert and unhappy form lying on that bed. It was a kind of window to be leapt through. Who would jump out of a window? Nobody in his right mind—not unless the room behind were in flames . . .

6

HE WAS ROUSED BY THE BELL. A series of shrill assault waves upon the beaches of awareness. He came alert instantly and lay there listening in terror, like one caught thieving or in an illicit sexual act.

"Brrrn . . . brrrn . . . brrrrrrrnnnnnn!" Like a dentist's drill, a jackhammer, its sharply concentrated violence chewed down beneath the hard top, the enamel of his stupor toward the nerve. When it hit, his body writhed spastically and twisted up, his stare fixed like a rifle at the back of the door. Hard with fear, he made no move to speak or to rise; the idea of answering the doorbell never even germinated.

Finally the bell gave up. He heard feet shifting on the cement stoop, a tiny scratching as a paper mouse slid itself under the sill. Receding steps, cardoor opening and slamming, carengine waking with a roaring snort, cartires rolling away in a fading crunch of gravel.

Propped on an elbow, he continued to stare at the door. Then he got up quickly and walked back to the bathroom. As he sucked water from the tap, he checked his wristwatch. It had stopped. Outside the light said mid-afternoon. Automatically his fingers went to rewind the watch, but they barely made contact. Only then did he walk back to the front room, to stare down at the edge of white paper under the door. Finally he bent and picked it up.

Bob—
Sorry I missed you—just checking. Got two weeks free between jobs. Thought maybe you'd like to take a spin someplace—Coast or somewhere. Drop over—
Harry Howell

The words, as he read them, did not come through in Howell's easy Southwestern voice. They sounded with an acrid sarcastic bite, as if Howell were merely the dummy of some worldly and depraved ventriloquist, wise only in absurdity and relishing this "wisdom." He could almost hear the low mocking laugh of the sadist that had thought to dispatch Howell to his door at such a moment with such a proposal.

The crushed bit of paper fell to the floor, and he, feeling depleted again, sat back down on the edge of the bed and delivered his face to his hands, which immediately began to knead the flesh of it roughly over the bone of his skull . . .

Harry Howell was the closest thing to a friend he could claim here in Albuquerque. It was Howell who had given him a job with his construction crew last spring when he was released from Bethlehem, disjointed with electricity and dizzy with chemicals, hardly capable of doing the pick-and-shoveling the work required. Howell was a contractor—of whom there were many in this mushrooming city—but one who by choice remained small and independent—one house at a time, built by himself and his crew of six or eight. He specialized in ranch houses on 150 by 75 foot ranches, ranches whose owners raised not cattle but incomes, and he made a real effort to keep these

71

houses as esthetically valid as the mass designs and his patrons' calloused sensibilities allowed. He'd been trained as an artist and still had much of the open, easygoing and enthusiastic nature found so often among mediocre painters, the kind that paint out of sensuous enjoyment of colors and shapes, out of a childlike attraction toward things that are good to look at or feel or taste or smell. After the war he'd gone to Paris to study painting at government expense, put a couple of years into Latin Quarter studios, cafe philosophizing, and making Parisian love, and then married a middle-class French girl and brought her home to America when his money ran out.

He'd first met Howell last May when he'd gone to ask about a job, too shaky and fearful still to face the school authorities again, not sure even that he could handle construction labor, afraid to look Howell in the eye.

"Sure," Howell had said, "be here Monday morning." And then he'd taken him straight out to his studio to show him his work. " 'Course, this is all old stuff," he'd said, pulling the canvases out one after another, blowing the dust off and cocking his head at them appraisingly. "Wouldn't paint like this now."

The would-be day laborer had nodded in confused silence, trying to adjust to the unexpected shift in relationship. The painting itself was not bad, nor was it good. Utrillo-style cityscapes, Cezanne-style still lifes, Matisse-style nudes, led to abstractions in the manner of the late forties and early fifties. "Was just getting into abstract expressionism when I quit," Howell had said.

"What made you give up painting?" he'd managed to ask.

"What do you think? Wife and two kids? Had to get out there and hustle." He picked out a paintbrush from a coffee-can of fifty of them and worked the soft tuft back and forth in his palm, clearly enjoying the feel. "Yeah, the abstract started going out when the concrete started pouring in—Georgette was turning them out faster than me." He gave a small smiling sigh and then suddenly raised his arm and painted a vigorous flourish on the air with the flair of an épéeist. "But don't count old Harry out yet . . ."

No, it was obvious that Howell hadn't altogether hardened into solid citizenship. He still sought out the friendship of artists and oddballs, helping them out with small loans and hiring them for his crew if they could manage to do the work. He loved talking to any sympathetic ear about the good old days at the Grande Chaumière and the Deux Magots, as if half-convinced that this middle age and economic harness were just temporary impediments, that the future would see a return of the past, that as soon as he got the youngest kid through school and paid off this and bought that . . .

"You wait," he'd promise over a can of beer after a hot exhausting day, "one of these days now I'm going to get back to painting. I'm beginning to feel the old urge. You know, I was thinking if I just got up at five every morning, I could get in two good hours . . ."

Why Howell so often assumed this apologetic tone with him, he wasn't exactly sure. He was no artist, just an ex-high school teacher trying to come back from a breakdown. But it was apparent that Howell did feel drawn to him especially, that like a director in pressing need of an actor to fill a certain part, he had assigned this role to him. Perhaps it was his very convalescent condition that attracted Howell, the fact he had so little personal ego left himself that he could listen without distraction and with something that approximated interest. In a way Howell was using him as—what a joke!—almost as a therapist.

But as the summer closed, the depression began to grow again through his spirit like some temporarily arrested malignancy, and the days came more and more often when he didn't have the strength to lug its weight to work, or if he managed to show up, he felt so leaden, so removed, that he knew he couldn't possibly be earning his pay. Still Howell kept him on the payroll, whether out of compassion or out of need for his ear he was never sure.

Finally, a month ago, he told Howell he had to quit, fabricating the excuse that he was expecting to be called back to teaching—this in September, after the school term had already begun. Since then he had avoided Howell, as he had avoided everyone else, more so, fearing the scalding splash of that exuberance on his raw consciousness, the painful touch of that once-born nature.

And now Howell had come to seek him out, had stood right there on the other side of that piece of half-inch plywood, the dupe and dummy of whatever sneering force or impotence was in charge of arranging the absurdities of his existence.

His hands, through all of this, had been bullying his face. Now they had taken thick pinches of cheekflesh on both sides between thumbs and forefingers and were pulling on them, outwards and backwards, as if to peel his face back off his skull like a thick-skinned fruit. It resisted painfully at the mouth and where the tendons were attached to bone. Giving up on this, they began to push his face upwards and inwards, until both eyes were buried in flesh and his breath snuffled out through the misshapen nostrils in noisy pig-snorts. But the hands quickly wearied of this game, too, and they fell aside as he stood up once more and walked back into the kitchen, where again he stopped and looked despairingly about.

The round wooden table; on it, the letter from Anne, the open book by Kierkegaard, the transistor radio, grouped like actors; all around it, the encircling disorder, attending in silence, like a theater audience. He sighed and sat down and

74

reached out and absently picked the letter up again, not to read it, just to stare at it.

Hoerchner, he'd promised her he'd call him . . . if it got worse he—well, had it? Had it got worse?

Is it worse?

A problem. He sat trying to concentrate on it. Then, the problem still unsolved, he noticed that the letter was trembling in his hands, quivering like a singed and fallen moth.

Automatically, orders went out to his hands: stop that! They did not arrive.

He watched as it got worse. The paper began to rattle. His hands, his arms, his whole upper body was trembling. Hunger? No, he felt no hunger, none localized in his stomach. Drugs? Couldn't be drugs, he hadn't taken any all day. Maybe it was no drugs. Or maybe, more likely, it was just It, the chemicals, the electricity, the meat, slowly taking things out from under him.

The letter he had been gazing at was gone. Instead there was a whiteness, flickering and variegated, like swirling snow. He blinked into it. Shadows, dim emerging forms. He strained, peered. Dark shapes. Human figures, yes, a small mound of people, huddled together as if lost in a snowstorm. A woman, two small children clinging to her legs. Swathed in windblown rags, all of them, dark, filthy rags. Eyes sunken, black-circled, all of them, huge with fatigue and fear, fixed on his, all of them, as on something monstrous—no, not on him, *through* him, he wasn't there—as if they were trapped in the path of some great pitiless mechanism that was bearing inexorably down on them all.

The image set as he stared, growing gradually clearer and firmer, all in blacks and whites like a stark Kaethe Kollwitz tableau of famine and war, her lithographs of mothers welcoming death. What? . . . Who?—but suddenly he recognized them. They were his! There they were—and where was he, who should be interposing himself? Gone! They were looking through him!

He opened his mouth with a desperate shout, to warn them, to attract their attention, to assert his existence. What he heard in his ears was a small, murine squeak.

It was the sound that made him understand he was hallucinating. He wrenched his head and his body violently, to break out of it, feeling through his fear how feeble the movement was, how sapped he had become. Of himself he might not have gathered the necessary force, if the chair beneath him had not tipped backwards and his body not crashed against the floor with the jolting power of gravity.

He lay there gathering his breath. Then he scrambled to his feet, and ran to the front door, and stood on the stoop gulping in draughts of the cooling afternoon like some health fanatic. When he regained enough stability, he began to walk, to run, to the nearest phone, a drug store three blocks away, and dialed Frank Hoerchner's home number.

"Hello . . ." A woman. His wife. He half-pictured her. He had met her once, last summer, when he'd visited Hoerchner at home. A dyed blonde, forty-fifties, sophisticated, bitter, with hysterical edges.

". . . please speak to Dr. Hoerchner."

"I'm sorry, the Doctor's not in right now."

Her voice fell strongly onto him, as if it, like light, were being fractured into all its components, as if the phone, his state, something, were acting on it like a prism; all at the same time he heard poise, anxiety, resentment, irritation, weariness and a sort of neurotic self-pity exactly like his own. All this in those first few words.

". . . someplace I can reach him?"

"I'm afraid not. He's off on a hunting trip this weekend, and I don't expect him back till late tonight."

76

"He left you all alone?"

Like a red dye a new element flooded into her voice: suspicion. "No, I'm not alone. I have two large German shepherds—who is this calling?"

"Hunting?" He felt distracted, almost forgetting his purpose, like a small child. "He went hunting?"

"Ye-es, that's what I said. Who is this? If you don't tell me your name, I'll have to hang up."

He told her his name. "Hunting what?"

A short silence, as if she were slipping into uniform. "Is this a patient calling?" Her voice narrowed to cool blues, a professional man's professional wife.

"Yes—no . . . I mean I was . . ."

"Oh . . . oh, I see. Well, you can reach the Doctor in the morning, at the San."

"Deer?"

"What was it you said?"

"I said deer. Is he hunting deer?"

"Oh Look, why don't you get in touch with Dr. Jacobsen? He's on call. I mean, if it's something urgent . . ." The voice was mauve-gray, parental, yet wary, as if dealing with some other woman's child. "I've got his number right here."

". . . maybe I'll go see him tomorrow."

"But why don't you let me give you Dr. Jacobsen's number anyway? Have you got a pencil?"

"He never told me he liked to hunt."

"Oh, it's just an excuse to get away from—now listen, I really think you ought to get in touch with Dr. Jacobsen."

"Away from what?" He was listening to himself too, almost as surprised as she was.

"Yes . . . well, that's all right. He'll be in his office at nine tomorrow morning at the San. And now I'm afraid I have to hang up. But I still think you'd better call up Dr. . . ."

"Maybe I'll go to the sanatorium tomorrow."

"Good. Why don't you plan on that, definitely? And if I were you, you know what I'd do? I'd try and get myself a good night's sleep and then get up bright and early in the morning and go straight over to Bethlehem. I think that's the smartest idea of all, don't you?"

"Yes, I do. Thank you, Mrs. Hoerchner. I'm sorry he left you all alone." It wasn't exactly that he felt sorry for her; he felt sorry he hadn't a drop of sorrow left over to spare for her. "You, too, get a good night's sleep."

The line was dead before he finished.

Good advice, though. A good night's sleep. A nice time-out on it, a nice stretch of nothing. But sleep, he knew, wasn't going to come to him of its own accord tonight. It would have to be captured and dragged in. How?

He looked up into the white fluorescence about him, realized he was in a drug store, and remembered the prescription in his wallet. He went over to the drug section, a high embankment of small bottles and boxes and packaged medical gadgets, from a rectangular slot in which the well-scoured face of the pharmacist smiled down on him. "Yes?" He handed up the prescription Hoerchner had written out the last time he saw him, to use "in case." It looked dogeared and grubby gray from the months in his wallet.

As the druggist read over the dirty slip of paper, his bright eyeglassed face dimmed visibly, as if the current supplying it had momentarily slackened.

"Nembutal, hmm—this stuff for you?"

He nodded. His mind was lagging behind the pace of actuality, the flow of events. It was still dwelling over the spectral voice on the telephone, picturing the psychiatrist stalking through the underbrush, rifle at the ready, in a phosphorescent pink jacket and cap.

"Happen to have any identification with you?"

He handed up his driver's license, and the druggist's expression brightened again as power was restored to it. "O.K., sir, fine . . . just verifying, you know . . . the way things are these days with narcotics . . ."

He nodded again. The way things were these days. Like a child he watched as, up at chin level, the scrubbed pink fingers spilled a little puddle of shiny green and yellow capsules out onto a special glass tray, counted out twenty-four of them by twos with a stainless steel spatula, and funneled them into a small cylinder of sparkling clear plastic. The operation was very impressive. So neat, so sure, so beyond ifs and buts, and the little pills looked somehow so happy about it all, so snug and comfy under the sterile cotton bolster of their little bed, such bright cheery little siblings they were, so perfectly formed, so brand new, such a twinkling lemon-lime, drops of innocence, drops of purity.

How many would kill you? Less than two dozen, that's for sure.

"All righty, sir, here you are." The druggist smiled on him with the friendliness of business and the confidence of science, and passed down to him a small crisp white paper bag—down, since he was standing on an elevated platform behind the drug display, and his head—the living bust of him, rather—was a foot above his own. As he accepted the medicine into his hands, he felt a small surge of optimism inside, of hope, as if he himself had just been accepted into the skilled hands of medicine. It wasn't only that the infallible means of restful sleep, temporal or eternal, had now been vouchsafed unto him, but that the whole ceremony was so legal, so condoned, so open and over-the-counter. These lemon-lime fruits of research, produced by a free economy, purchased on the free market . . . they were, in fact, precisely what the doctor ordered!

And then, all at once, all the great array of bottles and boxes and plastic gadgetry and sundries seemed to glitter on their tiers with a heightened intensity, like votive lights, as if he were standing before a great altar, from the heart of which this immaculate priest in his immaculate white vestments had given him the guaranteed makings of an up-to-the-minute, do-it-yourself communion. An altar of glad tidings, of comfort and joy, banked high with new miracles to ease all the ancient human woes—as completely stocked with responses to every possible human question as old Mother Church herself.

No, there was no comparison. This temple had no need of obscure corners, no flickering murk of mystery. This purity, this knowledge, could stand the whitest light.

> . . . the Papal blessings, broadcast to Lourdes by radio. The paltry miracles of the Gospels side by side with the radio!

Where had he read that? Somebody's diary—oh, Leon Trotsky's.

"And what else for you, sir?" the pharmacist was saying in the tone of someone repeating a question. He realized he'd been standing there a few seconds too long.

"No . . . nothing, that's all." As he turned toward the cash register, he took one long last breath of the drug store, as if to renew his blood with the air of order and asepsis. And almost gagged.

Into his nostrils, his bloodstream, came the unmistakable stench of human filth. Above him he saw the druggist's smile capsize into a deep frown; his inner light had suffered another, more serious power failure. Behind him he saw a shadowy new tableau. Into the store, as stealthily as germs, a small family of Indians—man, woman and child—had come, and now stood silent and dark amid the gleaming cleanliness. They were Navajos, three out of those hundreds who, for one reason or another, had become separated from tribe and land

and now wandered dispersed and disoriented through the wilds of the white man's city. He'd seen them often, mostly along the outlying roads, more conspicuous for being almost the only people left who still went about on foot—clusters of slow dark figures garbed like gypsies, joyless, music-less gypsies, working at dirty jobs for exploitative wages, sleeping in sheds and fields and grubby rented rooms, living in order to buy the sweet wine that took living away.

Three of these, a young couple and their infant, had just stepped into his here and now. The father, still in his twenties, stood wavering slowly in his torn black boots, his body a thin forked stick wrapped in begrimed denim Levi's and jacket. Beneath his big and battered black felt hat, his face bore swellings and scabs and shiny purple bruises from brawls and falls, and his unblinking black eyes looked fishlike and glazed. His mouth, half the teeth already gone, hung open on its hinges, as if he'd been clubbed; from it bled the reek of digesting alcohol. A little behind him stood his wife in her filthy many-layered skirts, clasping a black-haired baby to her green velvet blouse. The baby's face was crusty with mucus, which bubbled slowly from small openings in its nostrils like volcanic mud-pots. It stared around at this lighted white world, blinking dully and breathing through its open mouth, as if trying to avoid its own smell. The woman wore no jewelry except a string of dime-store plastic beads—the last of her turquoise and silver had no doubt been pawned. Her pretty face was wasted and wizened, and her skin a sick yellow. Her eyes, in contrast to her husband's, were glittery and black. For a few moments, husband and wife stood before the tabernacle of medicine in speechless awe, like pilgrims who have walked hundreds of miles to a holy shrine, staring up at the immaculate white figure of the druggist, who in turn stared back upon them with an expression of unconcealed horror, as if a great chance of some loathsome dark-age pestilence had suddenly broken out anew on the flawless complexion of his pharmacy.

His mouth was just moving to form his standard professional "Yes?" when the woman began to cough. Not a polite, well-kerchiefed church-cough. No, a prolonged fit of desperate gagging which tossed her frail body about so violently that the baby, in an obviously conditioned response, instantly dug its tiny brown fists deep into the velvet folds of her blouse, like a sailor in a squall. The woman, as if she had already learned that all resistance was futile, abandoned herself utterly to her paroxysms, making no effort to cover her mouth, coughing wherever this terrible ecstasy happened to throw her head— up toward the druggist, around at the others, out onto the neat displays of bottles and packages, the perfumes and cosmetics and underarm preparations, the toothbrushes, the gift chocolates, the toasters and hair-dryers and radio clocks. The druggist had plunged his nose and mouth beneath the starched white wing of his jacket, leaving only his round-glassed eyes staring out like a horrified owl. The baby clung tight to its rigging, and the young man waited with the patience of a tree for his wife to subside. Which, at last, she did, and stood doubled forward like a broken plant, panting in wide-eyed exhaustion. Only then did the husband act; he raised his right arm, pointed it first back at his wife and then slowly swung it about and up until it was aiming directly at the druggist's face. It was another few seconds and out of another deep silence that he finally spoke, pronouncing each foreign syllable with a slow, drunken deliberation. And somehow it became suddenly like a courtroom, with the defendant accusing the judge.

"You! Wha you ga fo ha?"

And he, standing there watching, felt each of them, the weight of each of these terrible syllables that seemed to attach

82

themselves, one by one, to the weight of the misery inside him. So that again, as this morning in the supermarket, the same dread of impending bodily collapse made him turn and flee, not waiting to watch this little drama played out, never learning what, if anything, this white medicine man had for "ha."

Outside the sun had given up, for this day anyhow, all efforts to break through to Albuquerque, abandoning it to a turbid gloom in which the colored electricity had begun to wink and shimmy and imitate life like the incandescent lures of deep-ocean predators. Very slowly he began to walk back up along the same path down which he had recently come running, back to what he didn't know, didn't think about. The brief bubble of faith in pharmacy had, of course, popped, and he felt, if anything, lower than before.

But in a different way. Colder, in a chill pit of desolation. No longer heated by panic, or hallucination, or hectic searching.

He knew why, what had altered it. The human contact, such as it was. The refracted voice on the telephone had struck a theme, and the Navajo family had developed it, raw and unadorned—he, Bob, wasn't the only one suffering; others were suffering too. He had felt the touch of pain that was not his own, undeniable proof that he wasn't the only one who'd been hit on this battlefield, that if he happened to find himself wounded now—where? the head? the heart? the electricity? the chemistry?—if he were staggering about down here, bleeding and hurting, he wasn't unique. Far from it. On every side the casualties lay strewn—all you had to do was notice them. Some just nicked a bit, others crippled and disfigured, still others already in terminal agonies. He had recognized them, heard them, and he knew that if one single thing remained right and certain in this confusion of ifs and buts and maybes, it was to respond to such cries. But here he was, horribly wounded himself—how could he, who was himself in desperate need of being helped, help anyone else? Yes, to help might mean to be helped, but . . .

But God, I can't, I can't even—"Eeuuaaghh!"

Disgust, rising in a thick, nauseating wad up his gullet, forced open his mouth and came out as a vomiting sound. Again he felt, almost smelled, the gangrene of his own condition. What a repulsive wound, his, with its unseen inward hemorrhaging and rotting. Yet God knew it was real, real as hunger and tuberculosis, real as love and dream gone dead, real as a leg torn off. Already it was reaching the stage of visibility, of becoming a public event.

"We've all got troubles." What he'd just understood had long ago ossified into platitude, and some people, the least troubled, the least sensitive to pain, tried to buck you up with that. Yes, how true, how undeniably true—and what a lie. Pain was never "we." By its very nature it was alway singular, striking individuals only, individuals isolated behind thick walls. The singleness of pain. Even where many were struck together, they were instantly torn from each other and hurled into separate prisons, and there dealt with singly, each to get what was coming to him, hardened criminal, tender infant no matter, each walled off. That Navajo baby, born into cold, malnutrition, sickness, neglect—why? Or even lucky babies—his own —wailing all night with teething, shrieking from a touch of the stove or a fall, whimpering and sobbing and hot with fever—the hours they'd spent hovering about those locked little dungeons, he and Anne, always outside, unable for all their willingness to absorb the torment from those little bodies into their own . . .

He'd been to this brink before, more than once. The torture of children. In a single sentence of Matthew ten thousand babies were butchered in the fruitless effort to murder the infant Christ. And Ivan Karamazov: "If the sufferings of children . . . I protest that the truth is not worth such a price . . . I hasten to give back my entrance ticket."

Every delivery room was a courtroom in which an invisible judge pronounced sentence: "You are guilty of being born, and for this you are hereby condemned to suffer in the flesh and in the spirit and to be subsequently put to death in an unknown manner and at an unknown time . . ."

It wasn't merely a fact. It was *the* fact. The Fact of facts. All human arguments and explanations withered and rotted before it, all the word-logged theologies and philosophies went down—what eternal music could drown out a single groan from a victim of this life? The cardinal truth of life was death, was pain, the sadistic, the *cowardly* infliction of pain, on helpless and isolated individuals. At any moment anything alive could be seized and dragged off to the torture chamber, always singly, always alone. To pay for what crime?

"*Original Sin.*" He could practically hear it, the transistorized sing-song of the A-frame preacher: "*In Ad-am's Fall we Sin-ned all.*" Oh, for Christ's sake, wasn't it time to come off that one at least! No wonder the church's body was collapsing, stuck in the paunch by a few pointed truths. Men didn't invent murder. Men didn't invent atrocity, injustice. It wasn't the Marquis who thought up sadism. Parasitic mites sucked the life out of the trilobites in the Cambrian slime, the weaker lizard writhed on the fangs of the stronger lizard, and the sudden lava immolated them both. Eons before Jesus the moth hung crucified on the spider's web. No, don't credit man. The rule for this creative set-up had been fixed from the beginning: Life shall live on death.

"*Eeeeeeee!*"

He heard it again, the rabbit, the cottontail he had shot as a boy, the voiceless rabbit which in its anguish was granted a voice. He'd stood gazing down at what that small curling of his forefinger had wrought, while the rabbit screamed up at

85

him, screamed like a child! What was that bunny's Original Sin? In what did its soft-muzzled Adam disobey its Creator? When will its flop-eared Redeemer come?

"*Selfish craving* . . ." Ah, now it was the Buddha speaking, in the firm black voice of Janson typescript, from out of the mildewed pages of the book he'd found three years ago in a secondhand book-store in Denver. "*Suffering is caused by selfish craving.*"

And this was true, very true. True as far as spiritual suffering went, at least. (It does hurt, does it not, Exalted One, to be burned by fire, or to be torn by rocks and metal, even if you have conquered all selfish craving? Those poison mushrooms you ate at your last supper—didn't they cause you suffering, the way the nails, we know, hurt Jesus?) And still you were right. Selfish craving brings suffering.

But what, then, is life? To want to eat, to love, to breathe, to learn, yes, to yearn, O Gautama, for the Norm, the Way—what is this if not selfish craving? And so if to live is to crave, then our suffering is caused by being alive—and to diminish the suffering, as our civilization does, with drugs and material abundance, is also, as we are learning, to diminish the life.

To live is to suffer. This was the law before Manu and Hammurabi and Moses, before Adam, before the first enterprising fish flopped up onto land. The Original Sin, if there was one, belonged to God . . . men's evil was to follow the evil built into them, the evil they saw all around them. The management of the universe fueled it with victims, the way politicians run societies with violence and threats of violence. Like a coral atoll, life was built of the bones of the dead—the very word "to die" was a euphemism—who *died?* what *died?* All things were *killed!* Any expedition to understanding that didn't set out from that spot was irrelevant.

And what journey could start with that? The base camp a

vat of lye! Any other was a vat of lies—yes, the punning, the schizophrenic punning—and so, so what?

So Nothing! Nothing then, if Nothing was the truth! "You shall know Nothing, and Nothing shall set you free . . ."

What set him free this time was his nostrils. The smell of broiling meat released him from the crushing constrictions of his incoiling thoughts and turned him out onto Fourth Street. Glancing quickly about, he saw he had wandered too far, almost half a mile beyond his corner, and stood now within the atmosphere of the circular drive-in called "Royal Burger." Above him hung the great nationally known plastic hamburger, illumined by internal light, wearing on its bun a small golden crown and resting on a throne of white vinyl words that said "OVER 3 BILLION SOLD!—39¢" Beneath and around, encapsulated in metal, satellite hungers consumed the soft food and soft drinks brought to them from the bright central planet by girls in white military caps and blood-colored stretch pants. Before, the place had been nothing to him, just another of the long string of commercial encrustations along Fourth Street. But now, as had happened before in strong subjective states, good ones as well as bad ones, every trivial detail seemed electrified with significance, charged with personal message . . .

Over three billion? Why? The population of the globe, a Royal Burger for every man, woman and . . .

"Oh, brother, big deal . . ."

The cymbal-crash of laughter, like falling glassware, drew his attention down to where a blond girl, her hips cocked like a rifle, her butt sleek and smooth and round as a hamburger bun, stood leaning against the shining curves of a sedan-load of young men, flirting and taking orders, combining business and pleasure. "Let's see if I got it now—that was three emperors, a king, and two princes . . ."

87

Instantly he noticed that the boys were capped in exactly the same way she was, only in airforce blue.

"How about the princesses?"

"Sorry, dear, we don't sell princesses . . ."

Another tinkling explosion of laughter. The sound communicated itself as unfeigned joy at being alive, with an intensity equal and opposite to the vibrations of misery from that little family in the drug store. Why? Wasn't it obvious? Because they were happy, happily rocking in the embrace of selfish craving, that was why, craving they knew would be satisfied, for hamburgers and Cokes at the moment, but the real intoxication came from easy, uncomplicated sex. That hamburger girl, had she ever once, at some off moment, received a picture of bulging bovine eyes, of slavering bawling bovine terror, of the sudden hot flush of blood and gush of feces, of the terminal nerve-spasms, the last wild pumping of the outraged bovine heart? Did those clean-cut laughing boys recall for an instant that their purpose in life was the infliction of pain and death? As they munched their Royal Burgers, did they think once of the broiled meat of fire-bombed children?

Of course they didn't. The laughter told him that. And why should they? They were happy, in happy harmony with the universal law of men and society, the law of pain. Happy because, for the moment, the pain was turned in other directions.

As he stood looking and listening, heavy clouds of alienation moved into the intervening space like evening fog, distorting and isolating. He turned away and back, and with his body went his thoughts, his anger, his madness, into himself.

All right! All right, and who are you, who the hell are you! From what personal superiority do you rebel against man and nature? How much sick envy lies hidden by your righteousness? How much would you give if you could laugh like that, if you could relax under the reign of this Royal Family and flirt with those well-done human hamburgers who offer soft food to still your cravings? How much to unlearn all you think you understand? How much?

His head was shaking. I don't know.

Oh, you don't. Well, try this one then. What was it really that sent you soaring up in the clouds of abstraction a minute ago? The touch of other people's pain, you say? Hoerchner's wife, that Navajo couple? Because you were too down yourself to do anything for them?

I don't know. I don't—

Yes, you know! You were afraid, afraid of where those battlefield analogies of yours were taking you, so up you went, so high you could look down on God.

All right, I was afraid.

But now he was not afraid. He was too exhausted, too emotionally spent, to be afraid. How much he envied the happy people he didn't know. But he did know it wasn't just because he was incapable of helping that he ran from the unhappy ones. No, the truth was that he—that part of him that was doing its best to take full control of him now—*resented* them. Their misery competed with his, made the chances of attention—from whom? from where?—mathematically that much slimmer. He, that part of him, hated suffering people for suffering, and probably hated happy people for being happy. And to feel this loathsome part of him mouthing him, consuming him more and more, as if his lower bowels were sucking down his head, as if he were being gradually swallowed by an enormous infant with unhingeable jaws, made what was still left of him, of *him*, despise and despair of himself even more profoundly. For he knew he was utterly powerless to pull free of It, this It that was now intent on assuming his entire identity. And what's more, this It was so stupid, composed of such insensate flab, that the process was beneath both tragedy and guilt . . .

The front door, half-open, was before him. Behind him the

lighted swish of car after car, above the artificial blue moonlight from the streetlamp. Through the metal venetian blinds of Mrs. What's-her-name's, the sliced blue glow of the television flickered and twitched, accompanied by the muffled conversation, not of herself and her husband, but of some concocted couple who were now having the same concocted family quarrel in tens of millions of American living rooms.

He reached out and pushed the door wide. He could see through the darkness to the kitchen windows, and he remembered again the hallucination, the panic, which had driven him from the house an hour ago. Now, in contrast, his mind seemed wearily, coldly, rational. Again, as early this morning, it seemed to be "understanding things," as if the little rhetorician, indigestible, were emerging whole, if somewhat befouled, from the anus of the day. He seemed to see him now, out spading among the garbage, ready to provide analysis.

Anal ysis . . . psycho-anal—the sight of him brought no pleasure.

Because what difference did it make? Nothing changed, nothing. A garbage heap is a heap of garbage, analyzed or unanalyzed, understood or misunderstood. The day was living up to his expectations all right. No matter what fell into its hopper—infantile terror, numbed torpor, highflown philosophizing, drama, poetry, rational and irrational analysis—it crushed it all down into garbage, the same stinking, dripping mash.

Half-aware, he thrust his hand into his jacket pocket, and there his fingertips met something he could not at once identify, a hard stubby cylinder wrapped in crisp paper. Oh . . . and all at once he seemed to see the gross enigmatic features of Hermann Goering, listening impassively to the judgment from the docket at Nuremberg, his pudgy fingers resting lightly over his belly, over the tiny lumps of cyanide embedded in the ample fat of his navel.

He took the package from his pocket, unwrapped the bottle and held it close against his eye in the direction of the street-light. The pills twinkled green and golden in the crystal clarity of the plastic. A neon springtime wonderland. Then he began to shake the tube, and it rattled gently like an infant's toy.

7

HE STOOD ON THE CONCRETE STOOP, hesitating, peering in
through the door left half-open when he fled the house. The
day hadn't finished with him yet. There was a concluding act
to be played out, and it would begin the instant he passed over
the threshold. And now he would, simply because he could
think of nothing else to do. For no better reason than that—
this was the only thing that was presenting itself as possible.
Not that it reassured him any to have this sense of direction.
A man falling to his death must also have a fine sense of
direction.

Through the dimness of the living room and the kitchen, the
gray rectangle of the sink-window came into focus, and against
it a small black silhouette of flowers in a drinking-glass. It was
the spray of asters the children had gathered three Sundays
ago today, on that pathetic last drive into the woods, dead now
in a dry glass. The sight of them released a feeling he had felt
before—long, long ago.

Long, long ago his father had taken him out to a huge
metropolitan cemetery to visit his grandfather's grave. And as

his father stood looking solemnly at the headstone, he himself had strayed, first by eye, then by foot, over to a square Greek temple nearby. He looked up at the rich family's name blasted in the granite above the entry—some very ordinary, even funny, name—Crump, or Funk, or McGee. In the heavy bronze door was a small glass pane, and he could, on tiptoe, just peek inside. Dim, milk-gray silence, veined white stone, smooth, oily, cold, like bloodless flesh. On either side, a great chest of stone drawers from floor to ceiling. Neat bronze labels on each. A person's name, the person who stored his stuff, his bones and hair and things, inside. On the far wall, a small window of tinted glass with a bunch of flowers that had died and dried, unlike the plastic blooms of today, which never wilt, but which have never lived, either.

Then and there, here and now, he felt the feeling, the touch of stone draining his body warmth.

He took one last quick glance back at the world he was leaving, the neon-pink city sky, the passing headlights, the twitching electric life of the neighbor's TV. If he was looking for last-minute possibilities, he got none. He stepped through the doorway, knowing without formally thinking it that he might never step out of it again. He felt himself lured, but not by that, not by death. He was lured by the sense of this-is-it, only this, no choice existed. Not for him, here, now. This and nothing else was presenting itself for his doing.

He closed the door behind him and turned the latch, walked through the main room and stood in the kitchen darkness, just stood and waited. It didn't take long. He began to hear a soft humming that rose, inside him or out, a harmonic anarchy, like that of a pit orchestra tuning up for an impending performance. And when he reached out and snapped on the light, it was the round kitchen table that came suddenly to theatrical life. It was a stage, and on it three actors already stood in dramatic juxtaposition: the little chrome and plastic transistor radio, the letter from Anne, the open anthology of Søren Kierkegaard. Beside them he now set the thing he had been holding in his hand, and it instantly filled out the company as a fourth, the plastic pill bottle, as shimmeringly at home beneath the lights as a leading lady. And then, simply because no other action was possible, he sat down in the chair, and began to gaze carefully at these four objects, examining them one after another, in various combinations, as a group. He wasn't unaware of the peril in this—this pastime. Yet stronger than his fear was that strange sense of necessity, or rather inevitability. That whatever was coming would come, and that to try to run from it, or even to want to avoid it, was, in some way much too complex to understand, to want to escape himself. As futile. And what's more, he felt sapped, profoundly exhausted, incapable any longer of *doing* anything. All he was fit for was to follow passively, to slide in whatever direction the ground was sloping, to wait for whatever was coming to come.

And, eventually, it did. As happens in the theater, the distance, the distinction, between stage and watcher gradually narrowed and vanished. Whether the players on the round table came to him or he to them he couldn't tell, whether they turned human or he subhuman. It came to the same thing. He and those objects leveled together. They began to speak and he began to understand.

The radio first. The goddamn big-mouth radio! Slick, brash, nervy smoothy he was, smiling smugly with his instant potential to sound off. Not one original idea in his transistor brain—all he could do was parrot the party line, the real of the realists, the facts of the factualists, a squawker with a lackey's insolence.

He squinted down into that chrome-plastic smirk with a growing hatred, fear and distrust . . .

For without his touching the switch, a low static, a crackling, rattling, spattering sound, had begun to seep from the radio's mouth like venomous spittle. As it grew louder, he could make out the millions of minuscule noises that composed it. Scratching penpoints, clacking typewriters, clicking machinery, rotating gears, snapping circuitry, droning wires, shifting mechanisms, monotone voices quoting figures . . .

A spy, that's what the son-of-a-bitch was, a household spy and a mouthpiece for Them, for the Forces of Occupation. The People of The Bookkeeping, the Doers of The Number. A spy for their General Accounting Staff, whose legions of men and machines and hybrids of the two were relentlessly consolidating their positions over the earth. These accountant armies swarmed everywhere, these Super Ants, stacked up in echelons, spread out in phalanxes, ceaselessly busy perfecting methods and equipment, endlessly, indefatigably, rendering account, turning to account, everything accountable. Accounting, recounting, miscounting, discounting . . .

From the precision circle of the radio's mouth, the roaring spittle oozed through the precision grid of its teeth, as from a planetful of artificial insects rustling in the endless artificial summers of offices, laboratories and factories, filling the kitchen with their tintinnabulating tabulating. Word counts, head counts, body counts, blood counts. Counting off, counting on, counting up, counting down, counting in, counting out. Counting with and over countless counters, tolerances, valences, variances. Salaries and calories. Split-seconds and light-years. Batting averages, hits, runs, errors; battle casualties, deads, woundeds, missings. Distribution systems and delivery systems. Production units, radiation units, profit ratios, kill ratios, box-office ratings, academic credits, median incomes, bust measurements, pollution levels, Gross and ever Grosser National Products. Heights and depths and widths and lengths, tonnages and megatonnages, computer data, computer dating, carbon dating. Age groups, pressure groups, subversive groups, fighter groups. Physical, physio-, psychological types. Socio-, anthropo-, bio-, zoo-, onto-, morpho-, geo-, teleo-, pathological types. Cell blocks, building blocks, voting blocs, mental blocks. Mental cases, attaché cases, criminal cases, terminal cases, shell cases. Statistics and ballistics, logistics and fishsticks. IQs, IDs, VDs, VIPs. BMs and IBMs and ICBMs. A and AAs, B and BBs, C and CCs. 1-2-3-4-5-6-7-8-9-10 and 10-9-8-7-6-5-4-3-2-1—BOOM!

The General Accounting Staff—it seemed to him he could hear every last member of it, hordes of men at machines, machines at men, men at men, machines at machines—every last one of them an accountant, and not a single one of them accountable. Counting incessantly and yet not really counting at all, not counting at all what really counted . . .

Now, he realized, he was hearing more than the popping spittle roar of the mechano-human world. Above it, ever louder, came a tight whining chanting, the mad hymns of insanity.

But he did not turn away. He couldn't. The spotlight seemed to shift to the pill bottle and he turned to confront it. No, not it, her.

She stood there in her see-through dress, glittering with jewels. She was from Them too. But she had been personalized, her body bore his name, she was his private prescription. She knew him, the statement of his personal account, the fingerprints and mug shots and urinalysis of his identity, the case record, the criminal dossier with the evidence of his guilt, his self-separation from the sanity and order of his fellowmen. "Because you have turned your back on reality, because you are infected and infectious, because you love death better than life, yourself more than your fellowmen, I have been sent to you, the gift of the generous, life-affirming united free citizens of this society. Come to bed with me. A kiss or two will gently ease your sick brain. A few more will tenderly close your poor bankrupt account for good . . . for good . . ."

"Socrates . . ."

It wasn't he that thought of Socrates, though with more nurture, that is what the embryo might have developed into. It was she who pronounced the name, having delivered it *in foeto*. A temptress trained in medicine, and in history too.

"Oh, so now you're Socrates, and I'm your hemlock. The pathetic arrogance of you people—how boring, it's always the same. Socrates—if it's not Christ or Napoleon, or Joan at the stake, or Mozart or Isaiah, it's Socrates! Come on now, deary, come off it. Let's us go to bed, you and me. Just a little loving'll bring you blessed nightlong relief from all the nagging discomforts of insanity. Or, if you're really serious, we can make it all the way to eternity—I'll stick with you till death do us part. How about it, lover-boy . . . ?"

He slammed his hand down over the bottle to shut it up, and sat quivering in the silence. Was it the real truth, all that? Was all this just the imaginary ego of the egoless, the pains of an amputated limb? Did he really—Socrates?

No, hardly Socrates. Once maybe. At twenty you could dream yourself into anything. Not now. Besides the other things, all the other things, Socrates loved himself tremendously. He was pleased to publicize his ignorance, knowing it was wiser than all the knowledge of the others. I don't love my—myself? What is that? which self? I couldn't even recognize it. I don't love my ignorance. My ignorance splinters me, makes me just what they—he focused an instant back on the radio, the hand cupped over the pill bottle—just what they say I am, sick, a mental case among mental cases. Just because I half-believe everything, them, myself—myself? what self?— half-believe my worst, half-believe my best, half-believe the outside, half-believe the inside. Half-believe—that's what

97

breaks a mind, that's what all us neurotics have in common. We half-believe. We're all spread-eagled over a widening pit, trying to keep hold to all sides . . . to all possible truths, all possible selves, not knowing which might be real . . .

Know thyself—was that Socrates? No, it was carved over the temple at Delphi.

He seemed to see a brief fade-in—Dr. Hoerchner's office door at Bethlehem. On the frosted glass, in neat business capitals: *Know all thy selves.*

He withdrew his hand cautiously from the pill bottle, ready to clap down again if it should attempt to pipe up. But it had said its lines and stood there alongside the radio, both of them complete in their undivided beings, happy slaves, as surely themselves as he was unsurely himself. All that was necessary was a simple mechanical motion of the fingers, and either one of them would do their programmed stuff . . .

He left them and turned to the letter. Two frail translucent leaves, two tissues of fragile existence, adrift among the crushing gears and lethal voltages of the accounting machinery. Private life, the subworld of unaccountable affections and unnewsworthy events.

He waited for the letter to speak, but it remained mute, even though it was a thing of words. ". . . better, now that you've got quiet and peace to think?" The thin trail of the pen looked imprecise, inarticulate, feeble and perishable . . . obsolete.

And wasn't it? Wasn't it as perverse to love one woman and remain loyal to one woman as to claim and be loyal to a single self? Didn't everything single, everything personal and private, look outmoded and irrational, even perverse? It was like holding on to some worn-out and antiquated piece of equipment when everyone else had gotten improved models. And just in terms of survival, wasn't a family a liability? You presented a bigger target by spreading your emotional identity over other people. How many families were left intact anyhow? Among his friends, his contemporaries, he could hardly think of one. The cowed, the dull, the conventional—these were the ones that stuck it out, often chained together by mutual hostility.

And was it even love? Could you call that love, exposing them to his disease year after year? Wasn't it really a frightened dependence, wanting somebody near in the darkness? Wouldn't real love mean leaving them, while Anne could still find herself a happier, healthier man, while the children were still supple enough to bend to a better shape of things? What had he done? Locked them in his sickroom.

"What I do, see, every time I fly, I take out $300,000 in the wife's name—you know, you never know." Somebody, probably Howell, had said that to him. He had no insurance, no money for premiums. He had nothing to leave her but the old car—and liberation from him.

Beneath the glare of this stagelight, his love for his family looked dirty and selfish and cowardly. It looked like a fraud. Compared to the glittering substantiality of the pills, the letter seemed hardly there at all.

What was the truth? What was the truthful act? Oh God, what was the point going on with all this futile thinking? Every movement of his mind just entangled him more hopelessly in the net. Why had he been issued into this world as a man, with this awful capacity to think? Why had be been born with a brain, a brain like this!

A thoroughly modern brain, a brain that was a miniature office, a production line, a bureaucratic agency. A brain with all the fragmented selves in their various cubicles, at their various stations, attempting to process the ceaseless inflow of raw thoughts and feelings and information, while somewhere up front some harried managerial section, some switchboard analyzer, was supposed to evaluate each item as it came in, shunt it down to the proper department, assign it to the proper self to deal with. Selves who hadn't the faintest idea of what the whole operation was all about, what kind of business they were working for. Who weren't even acquainted with one another, who mingled only during breaks, always in a state of nervous exhaustion.

The modern brain went mad when this data-processing equipment broke down, when the management couldn't keep up, when the wrong thoughts and feelings started landing on the desks of the wrong selves.

No sooner did he discover this than it began to happen. A sudden rising turbulence inside, a sudden circular whirring and whirling, as if an unseen typhoon had come slamming into him. Everything speeded up violently, broken bits of thought and feeling came roaring in from all directions at once, every one of them seeming right, true, every one contradicting and negating the others. Where was the front office? Who was supposed to be sorting, discarding, categorizing, ranking, deciding? He was. He?—who, what, which was he? Where was he?

"Where am I!"

He heard the shout, and he gripped the table beneath a drenching swell of terror. No saliva in mouth—the report slipped in parenthetically, a battle message, an office memo, and something in the chaos noted it down as being a perfectly normal fear reaction. More insistent was the pulsating signal shooting up from inside his chest. He felt it strike brain-flesh with an electric flash of pain. It was his heart, coming in louder and clearer, drumming out a syncopated throb, hollow as a jungle tom-tom. Through the racket and the chaos, it kept beating in its one rhythmic phrase, one primitive communication, till he could pay attention to nothing else. "Wit's End," it was saying, "Wit's End, Wit's End." Again, again, again. "Wit's End, Wit's End, Wit's End, Wit's End . . ." As the heartbeat took words, the words now took substance. A narrow-gauge railroad track, a loudspeaker announcing the upcoming stop: "Wit's End, Wit's End next." Ahead, a cliff, the raw rock-edge of nothing. And along came he, reeling and rocking, a runaway handcar . . .

"Wit's End!"

He gave a hoarse sucking gasp, and his flying mind, flailing out wildly for something to grasp, seized on the last object on the table, the open book, which lay beside the letter. Both hands grabbed it at once, and his fingers dug hard into the crevice of the binding.

It worked. Instantly he felt himself stopped with a violent inertial jolt, shake furiously for a moment, and then begin to move slowly back in the opposite direction.

No, not this time. Not yet.

His eyes closed in relief and gratitude, while his hands began to slide like a blind man's over the surface of the book. The smooth cool curvatures of the paper beneath his palms reassured him. The book was there. It was an object. It was real, real as the radio, the bottle of pills. Kierkegaard's book was real. It was here, on the table.

He opened his eyes. There it was, right there, lacking none of the credentials of reality, volume, weight, color, mass. Yet where was the book? The *book*—where was *that?* It lay invisible, impalpable, unmeasurable, a kind of psychic incense clinging to the little black stains that filled the paper. Even less substantial, actually, than the letter. Behind the letter was a real live woman. He'd seen her, touched her; he'd spoken to her a few hours ago. Even the radio would confirm her reality. She had her mechanical, electrical, chemical basis too, her circuits, her ducts, her structural components. As many as the radio had, more, and more complex.

But the book—beyond these tiny tattooed marks that fingers couldn't even detect, who, what existed? What creature had passed this way and left these tracks? An eccentric bachelor, it was reported, a slight, rather twisted human male, who for an interval of a very few years, had been observed upon the streets of Copenhagen, who had, in the year 1855, collapsed onto one of them and vanished from earth forever, aged 42. And behind that brief historical apparition which, presumably, functioned by means of a legitimate set of respiratory, digestive, nervous, vascular and endocrine systems, what? The man, the *man*, had existed not even then and there really, but, even more dubiously, in the inward journeys of his head and heart, from which he sent back a series of long involved letters to the world. No, not to the world. The world couldn't have cared less. To someone he called "the individual," a being he created out of imagination and faith. And what did he say to this "individual" of his, this strange little man? "Truth is subjectivity," he proclaimed with a defiant objectivity, and the news was received with a total indifference punctuated perhaps by a snicker or two. And yet, somehow, all these little mindprints, every scrap of paper, had been devoutly gathered together and preserved. And now, a century later, though the world itself still could hardly care less, more and more individuals were turning up to recognize themselves, and were paying more and more attention. At this instant, in this room, Søren Kierkegaard seemed more alive, more present, than the 200,000 living souls who actually surrounded him here in Albuquerque.

He looked down at the book, at the letters peeping out between his thumb and forefinger. "one in dia." He slid his hand aside:

> . . . alone in dialectical tensions which (without God) would drive any man with my imagination to madness; alone in anguish unto death; alone in the face of meaninglessness of existence, without being able, even if I would, to make myself intelligible to a single soul . . . make myself intelligible to myself . . .

Again, as this morning in church, he felt the rescuing embrace of a friend, a sense of parallel suffering that blended into the happiness of mutuality, like two lonelinesses coalescing and vanishing. With Kierkegaard beside him, he knew for sure it was real, the nonaccountable world, real as "theirs," more real. Their ant-armies hadn't wiped it out, nor could they or would they. Because to their dials and sensors and tabulators, it did not exist, being neither here nor there, now nor then, big nor small, heavy nor light, acid nor alkaline. It couldn't be produced, priced or marketed. It eluded the most sensitive of their artificial noses, eyes, ears, tongues, brains. It was proof against formulation, reagents, beneath infra-red, beyond ultra-violet, too deep in for X-rays, too far out for radio-scopes. And just as the professors were explaining it away, and the social engineers were about to relax to the smooth purring of the human machinery, there it was again, sprung up in the hollows of starving hearts, shooting up through the moldering centers of power and system.

Why should he feel cursed to believe, even to half-believe, in the reality of the world within? Wasn't it the same thing as Christ's Kingdom of God? No, he ought to feel proud, feel graced that . . .

He glanced back down quickly, feeling the need for another bit of contact, of reassurance, incapable of going any farther alone. He got no help from the page. Kierkegaard had wandered off again. The marks refused to cooperate. They turned into letters all right, and the letters into words, but the words themselves balked, refusing to take the final step into meaning. Sounds that said nothing, as if they had lapsed back into Danish . . .

And what if it was all madness? A confident, immovable madness in such towering misfits as Kierkegaard or Christ, a weak, wavering madness in the likes of himself. What if it all, as Frank Hoerchner implied, was just a homespun web of defense mechanisms, rationalizing fantasy, designed to veil from his own eyes the sight of some overwhelming truth, screen away his terror, impotent anger and inadequacy before the facts of reality? Suppose he had been able to, could even now, come to some sort of terms with society, even at this stage, would he lose all this need to feel about for imaginary "Kingdoms of God"? Would he, fitted into some snug and sheltering social niche, performing some useful social function, join the others, accept and enjoy the facts of this life as it really was? Just that passing instant of unity with Kierkegaard a minute ago, that feeling of solidarity with one single, long-dead man, had been an instant of strength and happiness. What could it be like to feel that way with thousands and thousands of ordinary people, with the living society around you?

Impossible to know. His mind was a shambles, what could it know? If it knew anything, would it let itself lie here helplessly, lacerated by random, uncontrolled thoughts and feelings?

"Yet from an objective point of view, the subjective point of view . . ." He recognized the pedantic accents: his own personal rhetorician. Kierkegaard might have gone, but this little academic was still around. Like a bored student facing a boring lecturer, he settled down, hoping to doze. The poor fellow—he meant well enough by him and might even come out with some wise or truthful things. But he couldn't help it—every word, every insight, that passed through him emerged anesthetized, drugged with the abstraction that was his element.

"Proposition: The subjective is objectively real; an invisible kingdom does actually exist in more than the unhappy imaginations of maladjusted psyches like yours. Proof: its universality. You're not an isolated case, nor Kierkegaard either. Millions have been dreaming this same thing for millennia. Everywhere and always, men have been stirred by this same dream of perfection beyond all possibilities of this material world. And in general they've always cherished it as the greatest gift they've had—with the exception of certain decadent periods when it's been fashionable to dismiss it (such as, regrettably, the one you happen to be living in). The dream is evidently standard, built-in equipment in Homo Sapiens. Now then, where could it have come from, the dream of perfection? From only one place—Perfection Itself . . . you've read that, too. French philosopher, can't think offhand which one. And besides philosophers, wave after wave of poets and artists and prophets and saints and mystics—and droves of many more everyday people than you can possibly imagine in your present distortion—they've all hankered after an inner reality that offered more life than the one we commonly live. Are they all mad, then? And what's more, men haven't only wanted it, they've experienced it, felt its presence. Everywhere, always, people have tried to put this experience into words and shapes and colors and sounds, into symbols other people could grasp. And sometimes they must have caught a little something too, because the race has preserved and cherished these symbols long after empires and great men have been forgotten. So the problem for you, my boy, shouldn't be whether such an inner reality exists or doesn't exist. It exists all right. What you should be concentrating on is this: 'Where is it, here, now, for me?' "

"Thanks," he heard his voice murmur, only half-sarcastically, "thanks, I'll do that." And his mind, some part of it, began to do just that . . .

Where is it now? For me? Why can't I hear a thing above the noise of the radio? Now when I need it, where is it? In this book here? Am I supposed to squeeze this book like an orange and drink the truth? It exists, it exists somewhere, but somewhere is somewhere else. How does that keep a man from starving, to know there's really such a thing as food and that it exists—somewhere? Where is the scrap for me? This kitchen's empty. Where do I have to go? Out of my mind? (Once he'd seen the Buddha-smile on the face of a deep psychotic at Bethlehem.) Out of my body? (He'd seen the smile of peace on the shriveled gray lips of a dead child during the war.) Am I just too scared to read the signs? Is this the wonderful keystone of insight Hoerchner worked so hard to pry loose? That I am meant to go mad, to die? If not, why, while I'm still alive and sane—partly alive, partly sane—isn't there a drop, a crumb, for me, nothing?

In the pressure of the answerless silence, he felt himself suddenly giving way. He sank forward onto the table and laid his cheek on it, choked under a thick bitter flow of sobs, caught up, sucked down in it totally, except for a tiny sliver of being which hovered above it all like a hummingbird, fully observant of the mudslide of self-pity going on beneath it, disgusted, appalled, but powerless to affect it in the slightest.

Gradually it subsided by itself, and consciousness pulled free again, too weak to think. Instead it attached itself to something outside, a shimmering droplet of clear liquid quivering precariously on the ridge of his nose. His entire awareness became absorbed in this huge, tiny thing, this momentary existence balanced out there, a blurry half-inch from his eye, anticipating that in a second it would have to relinquish its drophood, its life apart, collapse and rush down the ravine of his nostril. Which, in a second, it did, bequeathing him a series of light, drifting images of sun and earth and rain, that turned the table top presently into a landscape, the varnished grainy wood into a plowed field in a sunshower, the rises of his hands and wrists and forearms into a horizon of protective hills, the radio and pill bottle into a small city with its silo or standpipe. For however long it lasted, he was disburdened, and when he finally pushed himself back upright in the chair and wiped his eyes and nose with his shirt-tail, he felt both calmed and strengthened . . .

For another fifteen or twenty minutes he was left relatively unafflicted by thoughts and emotions except those that floated by like high clouds, far above him personally. He sat motionless, listening for his next breath, watching for his next eyeblink, exhausted out of selfness, as if by a stretch of physical labor. Then, just as he felt his mind being brushed with intimations that the process was about to start up again, he heard a strange and startling whisper, transparently clear, enter his head:

"I am God."

Not a booming resonance like some movie Jehovah. Just a voice making a quiet statement. And where had *that* come from? Had it been cranked out by some mental machinery of his, did some underground workshop of his brain just invent it? No, that was still another thing he'd read somewhere and stored—it had merely been released to the surface like a marsh bubble. Somebody else had said that, somebody you wouldn't ordinarily connect with such—Nijinsky, that's who said it, Nijinsky the dancer. He said it, kept saying it—after he had lost his mind.

"Lost his mind . . ." what a funny expression that was. "*He* lost *his* mind." And after *he* had lost *his* mind, what and where was the *he* that remained? Who, what, in people was capable of losing a mind and still remaining? Or a life? That also sounded perfectly natural, didn't it—"*He* lost *his* life?" Just as natural as "*He* lost *his* umbrella." What became of the *he* that had lost its life?

When had he read it, Nijinsky's strange remark? Five or six years ago, it must have been. He didn't think he'd paid much attention to it, then. It sounded like insane raving. But now, here, it sounded like exquisite sanity. I am God, no matter what the I was labeled, Nijinsky or anything else. The *real* I, if you could find it—that would be God. Maybe not God Almighty, no. But yes, too, in a way. A drop of water was water, as much water as the ocean was water—even if it wasn't as *much* water. If you only find yourself, your *Self*, then you find God.

He remembered people had said that about him for a while, relatives and other well-wishing elders, to mask their dismay. "He's trying to find himself," they told each other, meaning he was looking around for just the right part to play in the social comedy, a prominent and well-paying part, of course. Finding oneself might easily be defined as losing oneself. Most of his contemporaries "found themselves" early, by simply ceasing to look.

It seemed to him that this was all new, that he'd never seen it in quite this way before, that it was *himself* he had to find and there he'd find God too. Yes, it was exactly the same as that Greek thing, that "Know thyself." He'd never wasted much attention on that, either. It too sounded like romantic raving, an illusion. Because how could anybody possibly find out all there was to know about himself? All the fluctuating, evanescent and multi-layered elements every person was composed of? You could spend your whole life collecting facts and observations and scraps of knowledge, and you'd never be able to piece it all together into a whole, *yourself*. There were elements you couldn't see or even think. A self couldn't take its own measure. It couldn't know itself.

But here and now this phrase was suddenly making limpid sense to him. He'd had it wrong; it didn't mean you had to study and understand everything. It meant you had to *locate* yourself, your Real self. It would have been less confusing in some other language which, unlike English, had two words for *know*. Like *savoir* and *connaître* in French. One meant comprehending, swallowing with your brain. The other meant recognizing. It was *that* know. It wasn't something restricted to people with clever brains, it was for everybody. It meant: recognize which of all those shifting selves is your real self and identify with that. That self is God. Know that Self and you know God!

Like all discoveries, big or little, actual or illusory, this one released a sudden burst of fresh energy in its discoverer. No longer able to sit, he rose from the chair, thrust upward into indeterminate action by the burning determination not to waste a second in setting off on the obvious next step of exploration, to locate and know himself once and for all. His trajectory took him into the black of the living room, along the walls of his spatial confines, and into the bathroom. There he switched on the shaving light and found himself under that brilliant globe, looking out at himself from the mirror.

No, it was just his face. Familiar as it was, it gave him a shock to see it there suddenly confronting him again, the kind of shock it had given him often before. Is that me? His fingers began to feel of it, prodding, pinching and pulling at it curiously. It was his face, all right. But still it looked strange. How come it had this look about it and no other? Why hair that color and texture? Why that mole there and not here instead? Why greenish-brown eyes? Why not blue eyes or black eyes, or yellow or purple eyes? Why not three or four eyes? Why skin and features from this race and not some other race? Why a man's face, why not a woman's? Why a face reflecting this particular age, just beginning to sag out of youth? Why should it register thirty-three when inside he didn't feel thirty-three, no more thirty-three than any other arbitrary number? It was his face, yes, but it didn't necessarily have to be. It would look just as right on somebody else's skull. And it could look completely different—it had thirty years ago, it would thirty years from now—and the he inside was always the same he. It was simply a face, the one he'd been issued. A gift, or a loan, for a while, to him.

Him . . .

But maybe he felt strange with his face because he didn't actually see it very often. Maybe with some more familiar part of his body, his hands—he didn't even have to look for them. His hands rose instantly into his sight and set to wiggling and twisting about in front of him, in a demonstration of agility. What wonderful things! You didn't even have to think "wiggle," and already there they were wiggling for you. Marvelous when you stopped to think about it. He held them out at arm's length in order to get a better perspective, and they turned slowly and assumed poses like fashion models. Rather graceful, winglike objects they were, beautiful from certain angles. Still, it made him feel strange to think he had the pair of them just growing out of him arbitrarily. But these certainly were *his* hands, he recognized them thoroughly as his. Without them he would be in sad shape, why deny that? Yet, nevertheless, these things, like his face, were tools loaned for his use, not really a part of himself.

Oh no? In a sudden pique of disobedience, his hands flew up on their own and embraced the hot lightbulb. Not part of you, eh?

He pulled them off with a small howl of pain. But still, no. Even though they were capable of obliterating his self altogether through agony, the facts remained. "My hands hurt me. They're killing me." Subject verb object. Where was the object, that's what he had to find, where was the *me*?

His gaze turned downward, his chin pressed to his chest bone. The hands, loyal servants again, anticipated his wish and pulled open his shirt, pushed up his undershirt, unbelted his pants and hurried them and his underpants to the floor, where his obedient legs stepped clear of them. Each obedient foot in turn helped slip the moccasin and sock off its mate. Then he began to concentrate on what lay below, what was holding him aloft here, like a man in a tree.

A pair of low symmetrical mounds lay closest, on which a scant crop of hair was growing. To what purpose? Such a measly fur could neither warm nor protect. And that pair of wizened pink buds that could never blossom, what were they doing there, anyhow? Were they some sort of reference points, or mere decorations? If so, why just two of them? Why not a dozen, a daisy chain of them strung in a graceful loop across his breast?

No, it was obvious. These male nipples and this human fur were leftovers from an earlier age. The body he inhabited was clearly a transitional form, up from the animal, the bisexual creature, in the process of evolving toward—toward what?

Yes, and if the human body was a temporary in-between thing, then why couldn't the human mind inside it also be in a stage of evolution, containing elements out of its more primitive past together with others from its future? Couldn't that explain the civil war that always seemed to be going on in the human consciousness, its inborn sense of disharmony?

Yes—yes, it could. And so what?

He turned down again to the terrain beneath him. That chest, it housed heart and lungs, utterly vital things, both of them. Without them he wouldn't survive ten seconds. Yet no, still no, this body of his was no more him than his face. It just wasn't. It was his, but it was not him.

Oh, but what about that, those?

The tree seemed to have inverted. Now he was down at its base looking up, not in the branches looking down. The thick barky central trunk and from it the two sets of sturdy limbs branching off, each of them terminating in a single thick and primitive leaf. And there, sprouting from the main crotch, a somewhat dark, figlike mass that must certainly be its fruit. What about that?

His genitalia did nothing, made not the slightest effort to cooperate in his investigation, and so his servant hands cupped them and lifted them up, pulled them down, so that he could observe more carefully. What a peculiar-looking ensemble. Was it really part of him or a separate creature altogether? The color, the consistency of warm earthworms, it seemed more like some foreign organism of the genus found in moist earth, in caves and wells or fathoms deep in oceans, that had managed somehow to fix itself here with the suction of a leech or squid, amid these smooth sturdy shafts of bone and muscle and skin. Or—another possibility—it might be some organ of the viscera, designed to remain inside and unseen, that had accidentally slipped outside, where it clung to an unnatural and highly vulnerable existence, its sensitive lumps and pulps protected inadequately by membrane. Lying in the lean, alert fingers that held it on display now, it looked almost as if it *hadn't* survived. Torpid, flaccid, formless, a still-warm corpse.

It looked. It *looked!* He sat down on the toilet lid, his energy dissipating under the sudden awareness of the complexity that confronted him now, the demands thinking about *this* would make, not at all sure he could find the strength to go on with his quest. This thing, all this thing symbolized, wasn't to be dismissed like a face, a set of hands, a chest, with a glance of intuitive non-recognition. Sex—what was sex to him, to *him*, or he to it? Did they interpenetrate, sexual reality and *his* reality? How and how much? Sighing at the questions, he looked down again. Left to their own, the organs had fallen away, practically out of sight, indifferent that he was thinking about them. Inert, passive to gravity as a hanged corpse.

A corpse—this should have released a smile. But no smile came. Too late, too far down, for a smile to surface from the thought that here was a corpse capable of ten thousand resurrections, that could spring prodigiously to life, that was in itself a spring of life. Hadn't his very existence—half his genetic being, wasn't it—come gulping forth in life-teeming spasms from a corpse just like that one? Compared with hands —how could you compare *this* with hands! This was no ideal servant, clairvoyant to its master's whims, leaping to his orders. This had a master's nature itself. *It* felt the whims, *it* issued the orders. Tyrannical, a spoiled child, it could drive you crazy with its nagging and whining for attention. Yet it was magical too, an Aladdin's lamp with a powerful genie that could sweep you up out of mind and body into a kingdom of delight, which, if it wasn't actually *that* kingdom, must surely be similar in its thoughtfree thingfree reality. Reality— again, he knew that at another time he would have smiled at the irony. Because at this instant nothing on earth or off it could have had *less* reality for him. The feel, the memory, the efflux of erotic desire or feasting was just as remote and lifeless to him as its instrument, the sodden fleshsack sagging sullenly between his thighs. He had to think about it—but how could he think about it, this unthinkable force, which, totally absent now, had so often returned and might again return like a tidal wave, not merely to batter thought but to undermine it and sink it beneath itself?

He felt something like that now, a sort of tidal pull on his thinking, as he sat naked on the toilet lid like a man at the edge of the sea, staring absently at the hairy gooseflesh of his knees. Not the warm tropical lapping of desire, but the icy brine from the arctic coasts of that same ocean, the frigid undertow of despair. And instinctively he did as such a man would, stood up quickly, backed away and looked about for his clothes.

He had to go on with it, had to find what was really him. It was the only chance of keeping—of keeping It off. Having gotten to sex, he had to think about sex, no matter how unreal, how blasted his mind. But first, get dressed. You could think better dressed than naked. Why else did civilized men make so much of clothes and costumes and uniforms?

Dressing quickly, he left the bathroom and went back into the kitchen, shocked a little to see everything waiting there exactly as it had been—the lighted table, the radio, the pill bottle, the letter, the book. The past become the present, ready now to become the future. The chair was pulled out from the table, inviting him to reseat himself and take up where he'd left off. He touched it, about to sit down again, and hesitated. Oh, a pen and paper—he'd need these, these further artifacts of civilized man, before he entered the jungle of sex.

He went to look for his notebook and found it, together with a ball-point pen, on the floor by the bed where he'd dropped it a few nights ago. All right, then, clothes, writing equipment—anything else? A bit of refreshment. A hot cup of tea would be nice. There was no tea. He drank another glass of tepid tapwater, feeling his nerve beginning to erode under this procrastination. Decisively he sat down in the chair, sat up in the chair, pulled the cap off the pen, split the notebook open to a fresh page, parodying an efficient clerk with the bravado of his inadequacy. The white expanse of paper confronted him with the virginity of outer space . . .

8

THE SQUARE WHITE LANDING PAD came settling up beneath him . . . the sensation of touching down again, returning from a flight. He glanced around at the familiar landmarks. To the northeast, the place, "Hotel de la Salud, Pátzcuaro"; the time, "October 25, 1958"; the substance, the entry to the entry, "Since the last" that opened onto the field of vacant white, faintly ruled in blue.

His mouth felt dry. He touched the tip of his forefinger to his tongue and borrowed a bit of the scant moisture to pull back the left-hand page, as if expecting to find—but he didn't; it wasn't there, what he was looking for. Again, still, that outburst of scrawls from last Sunday night. He turned back another page. Not there, either. Instead, three or four short entries, the last written a full week earlier, October 11th.

Six days since she left. No better. Being alone hasn't changed anything. It's getting steadily worse, as if It knew where It was dragging me. Last spring all over again. And I can't think of a thing to do about it but what I'm doing, or not doing. Been trying to read Kierkegaard, fits and starts. I sense that he knows about It and how to make It serve him. But still he's somebody else. I envy him, not so much his tremendous intelligence, but his tremendous faith. God, if I could pray . . .

He took a slow deep breath which, in this solitude, became an event. As if the moist tropical air itself were charged with it, he felt a mild current of rapture pass through him, the same kind he'd known this morning at the mass. It seemed to arc across some electrode gap inside him to radiate a sort of silent brilliance through his body, a tremulous sense of pity and marvel, of sadness and exaltation. He stirred, the leather chair creaked beneath him, and the spark of feeling went out. Then he began to riffle through the blank pages of the notebook from the back cover, looking still but no longer expecting to find, while his body was gradually taken over by a new feeling, a double imbalance of fluids—too little in the mouth, too much in the bladder. He stood up, supporting himself on the round leather table, stiff and achy from sitting so long. How long? His faithful arm presented its wrist for inspection. It was naked, just a pale band on the skin where his watch used to be. Oh, that's right, he'd lost it, in Juarez the first night, when he'd taken it off to reach into the toilet tank and forgotten to put it back on. But, as he stepped out onto the tile roof, blinking in the sun-laden mist, he realized that it wasn't as late as he might have expected. Two-thirty, maybe, or three. Time was tricky. He passed the white cement water tank, the pair of small twig-burning *calentones* for heating water, and down beneath a low arch to the next level, the bathroom.

The toilet was chirping away like a canary, and for a few seconds he accompanied it with a small trill of his own. When he reached out to flush it, the metal knob came off in his hands, its function purely esthetic. He carefully rebalanced it into position. Whatever was the matter with the toilet had been the matter with it for a long time. The bowl was streaked with minerals and rimed with green algae, like a forest spring. He felt a slight curiosity to lift the lid of the tank and have a look into its mechanics, a curiosity too slight for his hands to even stir. Instead he went into their room, drank two glasses of lukewarm *agua purificada* from the glass decanter by Howell's bed, and began to retrace his steps back upward to the porch. On the roof, he looked around a few minutes before climbing back up into the glassed-in lookout that perched on the main body of the hotel like the bridge on a ship. The mist was thinning rapidly. Probably it would be clear very soon. This was the last of the rainy season.

His eyes moved without friction over the view. The dark-furrowed rooftops of baked earth seemed to mimic the small geometric fields of plowed earth, with the church steeples puncturing up through them like great pinkish bamboo shoots. On the highest hill, dominating the town, he saw part of the Basilica, one bell tower unfinished, the other not even begun. A pair of small amorous yellow butterflies, each half as large as the cathedral, chased each other across its façade in a twirling *pas de deux*. Around and beneath him the rosy inner flesh of the hotel patio. A small rainforest of slender potted palms lifted their fronds to the roof and higher; a maze of orchids, geraniums, begonias, and tropical succulents grew from all kinds of containers, including trenches scooped into the cement railings. Right beside him here was a huge bougainvillaea vine in blossom, a great glowing puff of vibrant purple. He gazed into it. What cries of undiluted delight it was pouring out into the world, what hosannas of singing silence. It, like all the other plants in the patio, seemed to have its voice pitched just beyond the range of human hearing.

And thank God for that. The choir of this little patio alone might be too much to bear. He had never seen a bougainvillaea up close like this, and when he reached a hand out to it, he half-expected it would drift through it like cloud or ectoplasm, feeling nothing. Instead his flesh was met instantly by the sharp thicket of prickly twigs that lay just beneath the surface of petals and leaves. Parting it, he looked into the under-structure. A complicated network of ugly gray, tough wooden ganglions and tendons that led back and down to a gnarled and varicosed trunk as thick as his arm, which in turn made its way down over the edge of the roof and disappeared into a small black plot of raw earth left open in the pink-tiled patio floor.

He picked one of the purple blossoms, which, he saw, were actually terminal leaves suffused with a sudden blush of glowing color. He split the notebook he was still carrying, and placed the flower carefully inside, spreading the petals gently to reveal the fragile loveliness of its sexual parts, the tiny sticky pistil, the encircling anthers yellow with pollen. It was then that he noticed the rough-edged stub from the page that had been ripped out here.

Could this be the . . . ? He tilted the book slowly against the light and caught the imprint of letters, embossed by the pressure of a ball-point pen. Not very many, a few scribbled words here and there that could not be read. But at the top, in large block letters, underlined and obviously worked over again and again, he deciphered a phrase: *SEX AND SELF*.

9

SEX, ʜᴇ ᴡʀᴏᴛᴇ, SEX AND SELF. In slow, heavy block
letters.

He did not go on. Instead he began rolling the ball-point
back over the words he had printed, making them heavier
and blockier.

Blocks. Granite blocks. Tombstones. "Here lies Sex." . . .
"Here lies Self" . . .

Oh God, I can't. How can I if I can't think? I can't, and
I've got to. If I don't—

Start! Start where? At the start. Start at the start. When
was that? In early infancy, they say—did I or did I not babble
all that to Hoerchner under drugs, about my mother caressing
my little—bullshit, pure bullshit! Feeding the dog his dogma.
How could a baby—brainwashed, I let myself be brainwashed.
I was so down, so desperate, so destroyed, that anything—
nice lukewarm babybath. Soft attention felt good, from
Hoerchner, from Mama, to a baby, to anybody. That's what
they mean by sex, whatever feels good. Sucking in through
your lips, pushing out through your anus—for an adult the

genitals *feel* better than anything. No, that's a lie. They don't, not always. Not if you're thirsty—a glass of water feels better. Not if you're exhausted—sleep. Not when you've got a stomach ache, not when you've burned your finger—no-feeling feels best. No, sex only feels best when you feel like it, when you happen to have a charge of that kind of current. What good is it if you feel like me—what good is it to me now? Supposing some golden goddess out of an adolescent fantasy came sidling in here this second, took things over as perfectly as only dreams can—would that change anything? No. Not now, not any more.

But once, yes, once sex would have distracted him, for a little while at least. Sex could, sex had done that—and up to not so very long ago. Admit it, for God's sake, admit the truth. You believed in sex, you worshipped it. Exactly the way almost everybody believes in it these days—or pretends to—the Hoerchners, the admen, the philosophers, the artists, the writers, the teachers, the preachers even. Sexual joy—man's highest good, the healthy sap of well-being that flows from a vigorous and rich sex life, cradle to grave. You too, you believed that lie too, admit it. No matter what you claimed or wished you believed. Big talk, big illusions about higher things, spiritual joys, "purpose." But when you got down to bedrock it was *that*, always *that*—pleasure, feeling good. And the biggest pleasure was sex, both in actuality and in anticipation. Off flew your mind, your mouth, while made you clung to it, to *feeling good*, as the *real* salvation, the only one you could *feel*. Clung? Yes, clung, clutched, like a baby monkey, and you know why? Because the instant you stopped feeling good or anticipating feeling good, you felt bad, so unbearably bad. Suffocatingly bad and sad—which fish is it? The shark. It's got to keep swimming. If it stops, it sinks, asphyxiates and drowns. Same thing. Keep feeling good, or rather keep swimming around the hope of feeling good soon. Stop and you choke, you drown in the futility of living, your living. Futility you *feel*, that's *real*. If you failed to keep yourself distracted—and sex was the realest, most powerful distraction—down you'd go, down to . . .

. . . to here, to where I am now. That's it, that's what's happened—I've run out of distractions!

What do they do, the others? There must be others, I couldn't be the only human being in the world this happens to. Do they buy new distractions? This society produces enough of them, God knows—the Great Distraction Industry. Drinks, drugs, TV, books, fashion, sports, travel. I guess that's what they do, most of them, get themselves "involved," keep themselves terrifically busy, seeing, talking, doing, coming, going—what they label "living." Never let a blank open up in the appointment calendar. Like gyroscopes—go round in circles fast enough, and you don't fall down. Seems to work. Why don't I then? I don't know. Just never could, never wanted to. Always felt so fake. Sex, at least, isn't fake. It's real. And besides, it came to me naturally. I didn't have to go out and buy it.

Tell the truth: sex *saved* you. It kept you alive, alive inside. And it arrived just in time, didn't it? Just when you were about to die inside, when you were about to be convinced that there was nothing real *in* you, that everything real had to be out there, someplace else. Tell the truth, tell the truth!

He heard his breathing coming heavier, each breath stirring his vocal chords to a low embryonic moan. He had to try, he had to try. Even if it was too much for him, he had to try.

Was it the truth to say that, then, to say sex had "saved" him? Well, looking back from here, it seemed like it, it came at such a crucial moment. Before, as a child, there'd never been a moment's doubt about where reality was located. Inside you. Everything outside had to prove itself, convince you, the skeptical judge, that it did indeed exist. Dreams and feelings, they were real, of course, and good stories (the ones you felt inside), your mommy, your daddy. But the fire had to burn you, the electric cord shock you, the ground come up and cut you. Two and two had to repeat themselves endlessly before you'd concede they were four, and it took endless mornings of pledging allegiance to make you finally grant there was a nation indivisible (and invisible) somewhere. But such things were in a minor and unimportant way, never the way Kenny was your friend and Miss Snyder was your enemy, the way getting a scooter was nice and getting a stopped-up nose was awful.

But education kept piling up on the other side of the balance. By the time you were about twelve or so, you knew for real that the window you broke wasn't going to fix itself by even the most fervent wish, that an F in Arithmetic was a much more serious matter than God's wrath, that Teddy's nice, sweet-smelling mother had really died of cancer and was in a box rotting just like that poor Easter chickie you'd buried and then dug up, just to see, no more up in heaven with the angels than it was—because there was neither heaven nor angels (they were things you told little kids). And that you yourself hadn't been bought in some baby store or been delivered by a stork, but had come out of your mother's stomach in some nasty way, most likely when she went to the bathroom on your birthday. And that you weren't strong and bold and fine like Robin Hood or Sir Gawain, but just another skinny kid with a nose that was growing bigger every day. It was then, exactly then, when you might, who knows, have been peacefully weaned over to radio reality, that what should start in but this, sprouting up out of the dead tree of childhood like a powerful green shoot, inside again, invisible but real, ferociously feelable, upsetting the balance all over again . . .

That's when it began, unhappiness, right then. He'd never been unhappy before, not that way, this way. This double way, *inside* versus *outside*, *was* versus *could be*. Never before had he seriously wished things were different, more, better than they were. He could place the very day. The day—he was thirteen—the day they went on that trip to the city, the Museum of Natural History, the ninth grade class. Hours of old bones and dead stuffed mammals, birds, fish, reptiles, bugs. Acres of rocks in glass cases. Stifling boredom and aching feet. And then the noisy, shaking bus ride home. Mary Wiggins and Ellen Martin across the aisle. Great breast-buds live and bouncing, sturdy rippling thighs, everybody singing *Vive la, vive la, vive l'Amour* and fooling around. And that night they came back, Mary Wiggins and Ellen Martin, or maybe they'd fused together into a single Maryellen Wigginsmartin, and he was fooling around with them or her in ways that might be very unclear but which made him feel delicious. More delicious and more, till he felt too delicious for his body to contain it and down came a typhoon and syphooned him up, up, into the clouds. And when he woke up, shivering and panting, awed and sticky wet, he almost followed the old trail of habit into his parents' bedroom to relate to them the strange and marvelous thing that had happened.

But he did not. The double life had begun . . .

Oh God, what use to go wallowing into all this again? Like one of those sickeningly "sensitive novels about adolescence"— a self-cannibalism, adult feeding on child. And hadn't he and Hoerchner spent hour after hour spooning through it already— and gotten where? To regurgitate your past and then try to read it like a soothsayer reading entrails—that, for him, was an exercise in futility. Where am *I*? That was the question. *Am.* Now. Was sex him? Suppose there were no sex, what would be left without it? There'd be no love, no Anne—my God, was that all there was at the foundation of his love for Anne? And no children? Sex? Chemicals? Love was organic chemistry? If he'd been born a eunuch, then what? Would he then be incapable of knowing love, would he have no self? If sex had never come awake in him, would he now be contentedly believing in the world? Would he not then see with his eyes, hear with his ears, know with his heart? (Was the heart a sexual organ, too?) Sexless, would he believe lies, not feel pain? Was a eunuch ignorant of death, of cruelty and injustice and mercy? Would the radio satisfy a man without balls?

Ridiculous. Obvious. He—anybody—was alive more profoundly than *that*. Yet where had he put his hope, really? There, in that. No matter how much he denied it—no, no, he wasn't denying it, he was through with denying—what had he counted on to save him? That. The values of the materialism he'd marinated in all his life had soaked to his core. Like the rest he'd used his best energies in the pursuit of his own happiness—it was in the Declaration of Independence, wasn't it— the red-hot chase after pleasure, ever faster after a forever faster shadow. For happiness had come to be a synonym of pleasure, little more, feeding your egotism, feeding your flesh. The ego delighted in its superiority over other egos, the flesh in having its senses titillated. The ego and the flesh were the real things, always with you; all the rest was mere poetry and daydreams. And so he, like others, had tried to exact from the ego and the flesh more than they were meant to give, to make up for all the lost joys, the lost joy of genuine community, the lost joy of real work, the lost joy of seeing oneself and one's brothers as noble and immortal spirits, at one with the Spirit that made them and loved them as Its children.

And now both his ego and his flesh had broken down beneath the overload. Whatever else, it hadn't surprised him. He'd seen through their limitations for years, seen through them, and at moments even felt through them. He'd caught intimations of the silence and the stillness beyond. Life dead and gone, his life, Anne's, the children's, the lives of every person here now or to be born. He'd seen this whole mighty human order consume away like last year's passions, the whole teeming earth freeze to ice, burn to ash. And yet he'd kept on clinging to this God of Atheists, this ego, this flesh, this world. Clinging to what he saw crumbling to dust before his eyes. And yet he'd placed his reliance on what he knew perfectly well could not be relied on, and kept trying impossibly to keep the absurdity hidden from himself . . .

Oh Frank, oh Dr. Hoerchner, this, this once and for all, is it. This is our neurosis, the neurosis that is killing me and us. Neurosis, we agreed, involves clinging to worn-out, regressive and inadequate forms and meanings. And I and we have kept clinging to the childishness of our sophistication too long—too frightened to let go, to leap out for better, even though the truth of our situation has become transparent to us. And once transparent, nothing, not all the rationalizing, narcotics, and know-how in this world can make it opaque again. On all the walls we erect around it the afterimage imprints itself . . .

An afterimage imprinted itself on his thoughts, a war photograph from Russia, a small child wailing and tugging at the ice-hard body of its frozen mother. A phrase imprinted itself, from Russia too, from Gorki: "an orphan upon the earth . . ."

Mothers, Dr. Hoerchner, fathers? We have no mother, we have no father. We're orphans, all of us, mothers and fathers too, orphans upon the earth . . .

"And what about that famous Father in Heaven of yours, the one you were always trying to talk me—I mean, talk yourself into? . . ." It seemed Hoerchner himself had spoken it. His inflection, his gentle all-tolerating cynicism . . .

Yes, there was that. The one thing that still remained a possibility. The thing they called God. The one conception his mind could conceive and not encompass. Because as soon as you understood God, had him pinned-down and stuffed and labeled and set out for display in your museum of natural history, this ultimate idea burst free, like Christ from the tomb, like the dimensions of the universe, into vaster definition. Idea—what did he know of God besides ideas? Had he ever actually—yes, it seemed to him he had; he had experienced a moment here and there when he'd sensed Something. The reality of something unspeakably wonderful, totally satisfying. And merely to sense that had charged him with a kind of freedom, a fearlessness, a lucidity, that was no mere sublimation of sex either. He'd known them both. The ecstasy of sex was a release from human awareness into a state of pure sensating energy. Lovers fused only to dissolve apart in a flow of bliss. An exquisite disintegration. But this was not that. This was the bliss of integration, of consciousness heightened to crystalline clarity, of the panorama of perfection, of obscurity illuminated, contradiction resolved, multiplicity made one. This bliss was the bliss of belonging, of feeling at one. There'd been moments—there *had* been, there *had*— when the heavy blanket of pollution that enveloped his life had thinned, been pierced by a flicker of unearthly light; and instantly some sleeping unearthliness in himself had stirred awake and turned to face it like a sunflower, like a baby turning to its mother's footstep. Instantly all the undisciplined atoms of his existence had ionized into glorious alignment.

He'd never convince Hoerchner of it, nor perhaps Anne either. But such a thing *had* happened, perhaps two or three times in his life. He couldn't remember the circumstances now, and he could no more recall that sensation to himself than he could the sensation of sex. Still these moments were as much facts of his life as any others.

But what good did that do him now? Now when he needed a return of that vision, now that neither sex nor psychiatry nor thinking nor anything less than God could save him, God did not choose to take notice. The feel of a glance, the slightest rustle or stir from the only authority left that his mind and intuition could still recognize as legitimate, and all this agony would turn to peace, all this chaos to order. But God did not choose to notice. God did not choose . . .

"Lord, turn not Thy face away . . ." David—hadn't other men been here before, from the beginning? Yes . . . but maybe not. Those men believed in a society that believed, a world of mutual myth. But here he was, a misfit, an atavism, in a world that had tossed religion on the junk heap of the obsolete and done with, trying to jerry-build his own Divinity out of scraps, cemented together with the sap of his own desolation, his own isolation. An orphan on the earth . . .

He looked around with a vision like an X-ray. He could see through everything. God was a darkness where his mind could not penetrate. If there was no God in that darkness there was nothing at all.

And nothing-at-all was the disease the spirit died of . . .

Suddenly he ceased to breathe. He would not breathe again until—

"Lord come, Lord come, Lord come Lord come Lord come Lord . . ."

The stale dioxides exploded through his lips, a dismal flatus of defeat.

"Shit, shit, shit . . ."

After a moment, several moments, when he looked down at the notebook in front of him he saw that, scribbled across the page: Shit. Apart from this there was nothing, no written evidence to mark his investigations. Just the heading, SEX AND SELF, and this had been traced over so many times it was barely legible.

With a grunting moan he ripped the sheet of paper from the book, crushed it small and threw it fiercely across the room in a paradigm of futility.

Futile, it was all futile. No God was going to save him, neither by swooping down, Deus ex Machina, nor by rising up in power and glory in his breast. He looked about at the chaos of the kitchen. God hadn't saved him from the madhouse last spring, he wouldn't save him now. What would come instead was *It*, like last time. Only worse.

It had already happened. Nightmare had become inexpungeable public record. The schoolteacher from Llano, New Mexico, had had a nervous breakdown, much to the dismay of the students, the school board, his family and the Providential Insurance Company. The wreck had been towed to the garage at Bethlehem, where the medical mechanics had put it back into running condition with a skilled application of electricity, chemistry and mental reconditioning. The repair had lasted three months.

What could he do now with his life? What if Jesus had broken in Gethsemane, vomited up his cup? What if Socrates had confessed to the citizen court? What if Buddha had cracked up under the strain of that night beneath the Bo-tree? They wouldn't have *been*, that's all. What of the millions of smaller spirits who had simply not come to earth endowed with the strength to endure? They just *weren't*. How many flawed poets and artists, saints and heroes and thinkers, had gone mad or died before, not after, they'd done their work? Who had ever been discharged from a mental hospital to regain his manhood?

"I believe in growth," Hoerchner used to say. Well, here he sat, with those months of therapy, those volumes of talk, those milligrams and millivolts, that treasure of psychiatric insight, those days and hours of thinking, added to his life like so much cancerous growth. Feeling the unmistakable feelings of last spring, that the skin of his life, torn once and healed over, was rending again at the scar, about to spill him out like a flayed body . . .

He looked about miserably, feeling the seconds come biting at him one after another like piranhas, voracious little mouths that could be filled with nothing but further torment. What to do next, what to feed time next? A flash of silver caught his eye: the radio grid. It was laughing, laughing at him. He reached out and grabbed it and would have sent it smashing against the wall if a sudden terror hadn't stopped his arm. The blow, instead of destroying it, might set off an alarm, a powerful electronic howl that could never again be switched off. His trembling fingers opened and the radio tumbled back onto the table, onto its face. This, came the thought, this is exactly the way the hounded mind slips across the frontier.

The next moment shifted to his lips. They were in restless movement, pressing themselves against one another, pouting, grimacing, grinning, frowning, kissing air, drawing themselves coyly back inside his mouth, dragging themselves along the hard edges of his teeth. Behind them his tongue was roaming and fidgeting and pulling like a chained animal, unable to find a position of comfort. The walls of his throat were contracting again and again, too dry to complete a swallow, and air was trying to force itself through constricted passages that didn't seem to want it . . .

Time moved up and inward next, to his brain. He could *feel* it, a locus of irritation, inflamed and congested, a stomach in the head, swollen with partially digested, no longer identifiable lumps of information, observation, realization, connection, distinction—a swill that had exhausted the power of the mental enzymes to assimilate. Nausea, pain of engorgement, need to vomit. But this stomach had no plumbing for evacuation—the ears, the nostrils, the eyes, the mouth, were all fitted with one-way check-valves, none outgoing. Inside, the fermenting stew was pressing harder and harder against the thin brittle bonebottle that enclosed it—he could already hear the preliminary creaking and cracking. His skull was about to EXPLODE!

The desperate, faithful-servant hands were fluttering about

below him, pounding the table for attention, claiming the next moment. And finally they succeeded. He was divided. He looked down. He saw them fumbling frantically through the pages of Kierkegaard, shaking, patting, palpating the book, as if trying to rouse the inert body of a physician from a century of death to rush to their master's aid. Suddenly they laid bare a passage heavily underlined in red pencil, marked in the margin by a date, 8/22/58, and a comment: *"The truth, God knows."*

The hands, solicitous, willing, but illiterate, stopped there, as if sensing. They wiped over his face hard, like a pair of squeegees, to help him see better.

"Nowadays not even the suicide . . ."

It was as if he'd been paged by name: The Suicide.

". . . not even the suicide kills himself in desperation. Before taking the step he deliberates so long and so carefully that he literally chokes with thought. He does not die with deliberation but from deliberation."

Stop thinking!

He jerked to his feet, sending the chair clattering to the floor behind him. His chest was heaving, his breath rushed in and out as if he'd been fleeing pursuers or making love.

The Kingdom of Hell is within you.

Get out! Get out of my head! Stop thinking!

How? Where—

Stop! Stop thinking! Stop!

Take something. He shot a glance down on the pill bottle and it locked his eyes instantly like a street whore. It had been watching him all along, glittering with its saliva-washed predator's grin.

No! He broke free into action and began searching through the kitchen drawers and cupboards one after another, looking for the bottle of brandy. It was the only liquor in the house. Apart from an occasional gallon of red wine when they had the money, they didn't drink much. There was only the half-pint of brandy, kept mainly for massaging the baby's gums when she was teething.

He couldn't find the bottle. Go out and—he'd never make it, beyond him now. Anyhow it was Sunday, they didn't sell—what about this? He picked the two-ounce bottle of vanilla extract off the spice shelf: "Alcohol content 35%." He gulped it down, put his mouth to the sink faucet and sucked in a few swallows. Then he let the cold water stream over his head and face . . .

It was like that night of the toothache. The nerve had abscessed under the filled cap of a molar, the pus and gas of putrefaction trying to burst out through the hermetic seal of enamel and amalgam. Rinsing with ice water, with hot water, picking with a pocket knife, burning the gums with creosote drops, and finally drinking a whole bottle of Cointreau. Same thing now, except that now it was his entire skull.

His head and hair dripping wet, he began to move again, to walk, to march, steadily on a course along the walls of the four rooms like a toy train on its set of tracks. When he arrived back at the sink again on the second circuit, he began to count steps.

". . . sixty-five, sixty-six, sixty-seven. Sixty-seven steps around. Exactly sixty-seven steps—hmmm!"

He began his third tour. "One two three four five six seven eight . . . twenty-nine   thirty   thirty-one . . . forty-three forty-four . . . sixty-five sixty-six sixty-seven sixty-eight sixty-nine. Sixty-nine. Sixty-nine steps that time—hmm!"

The fourth time around it was sixty-four, the next sixty-eight, the next sixty-six, the next sixty-seven again.

Sixty-seven. Take sixty-seven as an average. Say it's sixty-seven steps. All right, then how far exactly is that? One step equals three feet. No, not that much. His step was thirty-one inches, he'd measured it once. So, thirty-one inches equals one step. Then thirty-one multiplied by sixty-seven—that's too complicated. Say thirty, thirty inches even. And make it sixty-eight steps, to compensate. Thirty times sixty-eight is more or less the same as thirty-one times sixty-seven. No, it's not, but close enough. So, thirty times sixty-eight, O.K.? Let's see, a zero at the end first, then three times eight is twenty-four. Put down four, makes it four zero and two to carry, right? Three times six is eighteen plus two is twenty. Total of two thousand and forty. Inches. Two thousand and forty inches—that's how many feet? Twelve into twenty goes one with eight remainder. Twelve into—wait a minute, let's see: eight, bring down the four, eighty-four. Twelve into eighty-four goes how many times . . . ?

So, still fighting, wasn't he, and to stave it off, to stay alive. The balance might be tilting, but he was leaning back on it with whatever weight he had left. Why? Because he wanted to keep on living, even on these terms? The inertial thrust of life toward further life? Or the reverse? Scared of death, scared to death of death? Flinching before pain? Pain? What pain? Death was no pain. All right then, the idea? Yes, that— the idea—horrified at the idea. The idea, mainly, of its prematurity, of cutting himself off before he was cut off, of not enduring to the end.

Enduring why? Out of hope, still out of hope.

Hope? On what grounds hope? Because I'm me and death can't happen to me, even if it can to everybody else, because they aren't me? That's what we all hang on, everybody, greatest among the wonders of the world: all the rest except me. Yes, for years, that was what he'd held onto too, but not any more. That suit of soap-bubble armor had popped last spring. It could happen to him.

So then, what basis for hope?

Well . . . justice.

Justice?

Justice. It simply wouldn't be just that he should die this way. He was, at least relatively, innocent. So it was only justice that he should live. Whatever his crimes, they were venial, petty. They didn't deserve the death penalty.

Deserve? . . . *Deserve!*

Yes, he'd done disgusting things, cowardly things. He'd hurt people. But it was out of weakness, not malevolence, ordinary human weakness. He'd done nothing most people don't do, done nothing any human judge would sentence him to die for. And how could human justice be more just than . . . ?

Than . . . ?

The words that fit were obvious: Divine justice. But they sounded strange, archaic. They sounded mad.

March!

He felt himself being trapped again. And why not, what was supposed to fend it off, two ounces of vanilla extract? There were a dozen Triavils in the bathroom. Simple tranquilizers—they couldn't kill you like Nembutal. Yes, they could, they could kill you—

Move!

He was moving, he hadn't stopped, just slowed down a little, wandered off the rails, lost track. Now he began to concentrate on the pacing legs below him, the pacing computation inside him. O.K. now, where was it he left off? Figuring the distance around the course, converting inches to feet. Dividing by twelve. Correct. How many inches was it again? Two thousand and something. Something? No somethings allowed here, two thousand and what? Well, let's see, it was sixty-eight steps multiplied by thirty inches for each step. All right. Zero first, put down the zero first. Then three times eight is . . .

Was this why they loved to count and move and calculate?

133

Was this what kept them sane and contented even without knowing who they were or why? Count, march, left-right, left-right, hup-two-three-four, hup-two-three-four . . .

Multiply! Multiply upon the earth!

Three times eight. Three times eight is thirty—no, twenty-

The numerals decayed in his grasp. He couldn't get away mathematically, either. Others might, but for him there was no—

His faithful, self-sacrificing hand had thrust itself between his teeth. He bit down on it and continued to walk his round. For a few moments this too seemed to be working. All the pain and complexity was drawn into a small circle of hand-flesh, localized and simplified.

In relief he completed another three circuits, at the controls of the situation like a machine operator, easing up or clamping down with his jaw as needed. But halfway through the fourth orbit, his will suddenly drained out like an emptied gas tank, and he gave up trying. He slumped down into the single broken armchair in the living room and dropped his head and his resistance.

All right . . . come . . .

And nothing came. Instead Sunday itself seemed to come to a stop, like time at a sports event. Just long enough to let him wonder exhaustedly what guise It was going to assume next. Then, through his drooping gaze, he saw. A florid technicolor face looking determinedly up at him from the floor. It was the President.

He returned the look. It had arrived last Wednesday or Thursday, the magazine, along with a fistful of junk mail. He had picked up one envelope. "Pray for Peace," it had stamped on its postmark. Official hypocrisy, they wouldn't dare print "Act for Peace." When he'd torn it open, it was like prying the lid off a pop bottle; up fizzed a carbonated sugared voice,

person-to-person, telling him, in the latest, most highly per-
fected phraseology of mass intimacy, how much his life would
be enriched by subscribing to a news weekly designed for just
such "thinking doers" as himself. It was the same magazine
he'd taken for years, the same one he had dropped then and
there to the floor, where it had lain since, unopened, President up.

His right arm, hanging limply over the chair-arm, stretched
its fingers, tweaked the President by the ear and brought him
up close. "Man at the Top" read the cover caption. Since the
President was scrutinizing him so relentlessly, he began scrutinizing the President back. The Face of Decision. Strong, set
chin, tight mouth, tight eyes, tight nostrils. Not a line betrayed
a wandering thought, a thought irrelevant to purpose. And
these eyes, which could surely recognize his, Bob's, irrelevance
instantly, which wouldn't normally have wasted two seconds
on him, were nevertheless fixed on him now, so exclusively,
and with such unwavering force that they seemed to be trans-
planting their own healthy vigorous corneas onto his blurred
and distorted vision. The miasma cleared, life shone forth in
clean well-lit geometry. Power, he could see now, at the heart
of everything was power. Nothing could be done if you didn't
have power. Power was the thing to be studied, understood and
loved. But power was meaningless without people to use it on.
Therefore people too must be studied, understood and loved,
used creatively, the way an artisan understands, loves and uses
his tools and materials. Two molten elements—personal destiny and human destiny—must be fused to make the only alloy
tough enough to forge history. The final goal of man, of course,
was to produce history, since history was the ultimate arbiter of
greatness. Yesterday lay to the rear, tomorrow lay ahead. You
learned from yesterday to use today, the raw stuff for tomorrow's history. Great history could only be created by great

135

managers of men, by leaders who had mastered the complex technology, the formulas and processes of power, and who did not flinch from exercising it—the great men. And if you were by chance looking for an example of such a man you need look—

The President vanished, faced about suddenly by a capricious flip of the wrist. And instead of the back of his silvering head, there was a young couple sitting on a rock by a mountain stream, inhaling cigarette smoke together and experiencing what was described as "deep-down satisfaction."

But still, how else could one govern? The human problem as a human problem was simply insoluble. To work with it at all you had to lop away all the uneven, ill-defined edges and square off what was left into usable blocks. To figure it out you had to crush it into symbols that fit into political calculus. Only then could you work toward the final solution of the human problem.

Emerson, who never studied power hadn't he written something into his journal about this, during the administration of who remembers which president? "The great public problems all have private solutions . . ." "Every wall is a door," Emerson said that, too. "Every wall is a door . . ."

He sighed and looked down at the happy couple on the rock. Unlike the President, they had eyes only for each other. He passed quietly around them, opened the magazine, and entered it backwards like a Hebrew book. The bright lithography of a liquor ad attracted him immediately. A chic penthouse party was in progress, handsome young people gathered gaily about a giant whisky bottle. A sleek blonde in silver lamé was holding a sparkling highball out to him. "You've tried the rest—now try the best." He accepted gratefully. As he sipped in the luxurious decor of his new surroundings, admired the fashionable modern abstractions on the wall, he felt himself being relieved, almost undressed of his dreary self and his dreary condition. He turned and became engrossed in a clever review of a movie on hot-rod racing, turned from that to listen to some expert predictions on the upcoming national elections. Slowly he made his way forward through the magazine, absorbing everything, enjoying everything, accepting everything. Every word, every bit of information and commentary, every scrap of advertising art, every photograph of everything, every caption and credit line, even the page numbers were objects for contemplation. He became the Ideal Reader, the Publisher's Delight. He bit at every lure that dangled. Every hook hooked him. Each item in backward succession, no matter what, gaffed his attention like an assembly line grapple, performed its intended operation on him and swung him back to the previous one. News events of any kind, great and trivial, features, editorials, blurbs for chewing gum, industrial chemicals, giant corporations, columnists, letters, the very masthead with its harem of research assistants—he bought them all. All were selling and he was buying, buying, buying. Everything they offered he snapped up. No need to pay cash. Infinite credit, minuscule installments, eternity to pay. A glorious spending spree. Race murder in Chicago—great, wrap it up. Gun manufacturer's rocketing profits—wonderful, I'll take it. Latest greatest pop musician—send it. Sorry plight of U.S. Protestantism, saintly old doctor in Africa, simpler cheaper detonator for H-bombs, worst famine in fifty years in Asia, peek-a-boo bras, record mile, extra-strength pain reliever, bodies of war victims and sex queens, daring new brain surgery, zany new Broadway hit, disappointing new novel from Nobel author, laser-beam can opener, new attitudes among Negroes, rundown on aphrodisiacs, growing sense of social responsibility in big business, embezzlement scandal in Congress, Coke bottles bedded in ice cubes, rammed up the rectums of Algerian rebels. Latest in cars: tail fins. Latest in philosophers: Søren Kierkegaard.

He looked at the portrait of Kierkegaard, the boyish curls, the large serious eyes, but did not dwell overlong on it. It did not surprise him to find Søren here too. He was, after all, one more item in this stupendous variety-store called life, with as much right to be offered for sale as whisky or famine or crimes or starlets or medicine or war or politics or cigarettes or ball bearings or anything else. And he bought him, bought Kierkegaard, as he was buying everything in the house, all sterilized and refined and buffed and repainted, all wrapped in such neat attractive packages and merchandized with such skill. He stowed him between the Mideast crisis and a star dancer's million-dollar legs.

For an hour at least, perhaps two, he fed on all the nourishment the week of October 12–19 contained. He knew it backwards. He could have conducted a seminar.

With a shudder, he realized he had reached the last page, the first page. He dallied as long as he could on the final ad, caressing the luxurious white car on the luxurious estate driveway, its proud owners so obviously members of the democratic aristocracy, and then stepped apprehensively through the front door and was outside again. The President as before. And now (he tried to ignore the oscillating streaks of fear) and now what? Was It about to take up again where it had left off? Or had the long time-out altered things? Even as he wondered he knew. Something had changed, fundamentally. Now It would be different. It would be worse. He couldn't pinpoint it yet. But he noticed the new tremor, the tic, in the President's face. He could not confront it now, and let the magazine slip away, back down to the floor.

He felt It pouring itself back into him as a new and ominous sensation. Desperately he tried the old trick of mastering it by definition—where was his rhetorician anyway? Gone.

The bottom. He'd thought he'd reached the bottom already.

138

And he had. But the bottom was now giving way beneath him. The bottom was hope, and he'd taken hope apart on that disassembly line, he'd killed hope. Guilty—he was guilty. No longer could he plead for his life on the basis of his innocence. Willingly, happily, he'd allowed himself to be stripped of the last of his integrity. Willingly, happily, he'd allowed himself to be pandered to, taken whoring after cheap lust and bored violence and vacant novelty. He had feasted on food that was not his to eat, that to him was poison. He had lost his case. His hope of justice had been turned into a dread of justice. Justice—any sentence meted out to him now would be just.

Now it was not just his condition, his fate, that he loathed. It was his very life. It seemed to him that his *I*, that ultimate Self he'd been searching for so desperately, the I that was God, lay limp before him now like the small corpse of a raped and ravaged child. His head fell forward at a sharp angle, like that of a murderer awaiting his blade or bullet. He fully expected and believed in the blow that would rid the world of him for good.

Inside, his consciousness was already dying, devolving swiftly downward, below human awareness, melting into a kind of dream fluid, image and feeling dissolved in one another. The collagens of human form had broken down. Down, down, ape, mammal, reptile, fish, marine jelly. A beach, ebb tide, dead bloated fish, rotting seaweed, stinking mollusks. A small glutinous heap, himself, his remains, drying-dying, more stench already than substance. A healthy place, a scene of ecological well-being, natural selection, the perishing of the unfittest. The tide would come back, not miraculously to revive, but at its own mathematical time, to wash away the stains—

"OOWEEOOWEEOOWEE!"

A police siren, screaming hysterically down Fourth Street, slashed through to him. He jerked up in terrible reawareness of himself, in this room, in Albuquerque, in the world. He stared at the front door as if it were about to splinter beneath a policeman's shoulder.

It did not. Silence sealed back in, and he listened to the silence, the pulsations in his temple and throat. A dull iambic beating, like a knocking at someone else's door.

"duh *duh* duh *duh* duh *duh* duh *duh* . . ."

After a minute or two the duhs turned to words. ". . . to *him* who *knocks* it *will* be *opened* . . ."

He didn't think them or hear them. He saw them, a bouncing lyric to accompany the low pumping of his body's hydraulics. Projected on a sort of screen like a dim lantern slide, boldface roman type on the lower right-hand half of a page. It came from last spring, Bethlehem, when he'd memorized the entire Sermon on the Mount, along with verses from the Bhagavad Gita and the Tao Teh Ching. He'd forgotten them all. But now it was coming back, faint but legible, in a long-delayed afterimage.

". . . to *him* who *knocks* it *will* be *opened* to *him* who *knocks* it *will* be *opened* to *him* who *knocks* it *will* . . ."

A little at a time the rest began to rise into view. A tiny figure 9 and then: "Or what man of you, if his son asks him for a loaf, will give him a stone?" A tiny figure 10 and: "Or if he asks for a fish will give him a serpent?" And 11: "If you then, who are evil . . ."

Who are evil—that phrase had upset him profoundly. Evil? How could we be called evil, who were just creations, who'd been given no say about the kind of natures we came equipped with? Could you reprehend a fly with "If you then, who are filthy . . ."?

Nothing of this now. "Who are evil" slipped smoothly upwards to make room for what followed. "If you then, who are evil, know how to give good gifts to your children, how much more will your Father, who is in Heaven, give good things to those who ask Him . . ."

Ask him *ask* him *ask* him *ask* him . . .

He saw that his hands, his devoted hands, had risen on their own and come together, as if they'd begun praying without him.

"And in praying do not heap up empty phrases . . . for your Father knows what you need before you *ask* him *ask* him *ask* him . . . Pray then like this: . . ."

He squeezed his eyes, his entire face, shut and began to mutter.

"Now I lay me down to sleep, I pray the Lord my soul to keep, If I should die before I wake, I pray the Lord . . ."

Bars, he seemed to see vertical bars. A crib, a prison, a locked ward; he seemed to smell urine, pine disinfectant, ironed starch, floral soap, cigar smoke.

Time hung in suspension. His praying stopped, his senses died out. Then he felt, he heard, a tiny click inside him, like an automatic machine switching into cycle. His eyes opened like louvers. In some little-used corner of his central nervous system an amber signal bulb blinked on. A faint electric humming from the timing mechanism. He sat motionless. Then there was another click.

Now

His hands lowered, his body rose from the chair, walked to the kitchen, picked up the bottle of pills from the round table and continued walking into the bathroom, smoothly, without hesitation or waste movement. His right thumb and forefinger twisted off the white plastic cap, pulled out the cotton plug and spilled the pills into the positioned palm of his left hand. They lifted one from the little green and yellow heap, laid it on his waiting tongue, and his mouth, salivating well now, swallowed it down easily, without water. When it reopened and the tongue resumed its position, the second pill was just arriving. The operation repeated itself, and then a third time, without the slightest deviation from pattern and with no more in the way of inner consciousness than the "on" of the little amber signal light.

The fourth pill was being laid on his tongue when the machine blew up. His whole body lurched madly under the sledge hammer that had struck it, not from outside but from inside. As he fell, his faithful hands flew out and clutched at the towel rack, tearing it instantly from the wall. On the way to the floor he felt his head hit the edge of the iron sink. When he saw again, he saw the round white underside of the toilet bowl—for a moment or more in between he might have passed out. He continued to stare upwards into the porcelain blankness until he felt a small warm trickle slip out of his hair and into his ear.

Slowly he began to pull himself up from the floor, climbing on the toilet and the washstand, and stood, back to the wall. The mirror was there but he did not look into it. He stared down at the pills that were broadcast over the tiles like the beads of a broken necklace. He snapped out the bathroom light, walked through the kitchen, snapped out the kitchen light, and lay down on the bed. He did not know how long it would take the pills to act. He did not know how many he had swallowed or what their effect would be. He neither considered taking more nor throwing up the ones already dissolving in his stomach. He thought about the empty space beside him on the bed. He thought about Anne putting the children to sleep in those strange beds in Ohio, living that strange routine, waiting, waiting for him to do something. He felt his eyes tearing, not just for their sadness, his and Anne's, but for the sadness of everyone who loves. Life would be simpler if we couldn't love. He wanted to speak to them. What could he say? What words were left to say? What was left of him that could say anything? But he—he couldn't just—

He got up in the dark, felt his way to the notebook on the kitchen table, and brought it back to write them a letter under the bedlamp. But what he wrote instead was that entry. He must have, though he never could remember writing it, not even a week later on the porch in Pátzcuaro when he seemed to remember everything else.

10

MONDAY CAME DIGGING DOWN FOR HIM, but it had to work hard. The pills had buried him deep, and the exhumation was slow and in stages. Minute agitations at first, almost imperceptible ripples through the oblivion, brief intermittent scintillas of something showering down on the surface of nothing. The sprinkling came and went and came again a little stronger—not as dream but as dabs of dream, snips of sequence, flecks of color and sound, random molecules that took a long time to build toward a kind of pointillist form, but a form of no objects, only sensation. A sensation that gradually accumulated definition and focus—it was the sensation of being sealed away, filmed over, muffled, gagged, walled, boxed. Next, and also little by little, in accord with Newton's third law, something equal and opposite began to react, reactivate, from within the darkness. Not consciousness, not even dream-consciousness, but a kind of low-grade counterthrusting, a primitive mindless will. A will-against which began to stir and push itself in opposition to the waking process, as certain embryos are known to resist the process of birth. With its own amorphous substance it set to plugging the chinks through which October 19th was attempting to seep in, nuzzling for its own darkness, nursing at nothingness. For a critical moment, on the threshold of wakefulness, the suckling grunts of annoyance and exertion penetrated faintly in through his ears. They ceased as Monday was finally beaten back again, and the effort not to wake was rewarded. Perversely. Because no sooner was he securely encauled away once more than the darkness suddenly bloomed into full-blown dreamlight, vivid with mental and sensual orchestration, all of it sealed tight and buried. He was wide awake now, but to a subterranean day.

He recognized the place, the situation, instantly. He'd been here before. He even remembered the date—April 6th, the day he broke down. This insight, for all its interest, was irrelevant. He was no less totally here now, no less deeply in it.

In the cement, the ocean of cold wet grit he was sinking into, going down vertically, slowly, like a stricken ship, into the gray and viscous sea. He looked out over the shiny leaden waves of its surface—out, not down on, since it had already taken his entire body and was sucking its slow way up his throat.

"It's a dream, the same as the last time. It's a dream, a dream!"

As if to prove how unreal it was, he tried with all his strength to move his arms and legs. Impossible; they were sealed in heavy cold wet pressure. His arms were pinned to his sides at military attention—even his fingers would not move. And yet his body was moving, was being moved. Down. The icy slime had reached his chin and was beginning to ingest it in a python's swallow, lethargic, relentless. Reptile-cold it began to push insistently against his frantically tightened mouth. The smell of caustic, of lime and earth. A small, gritty tongue forced its way between his lips—the taste! In a great spasm of panic he succeeded in wrenching his head backwards, away from it. Face up, he sought the sky. There was no sky. Instead, a gray concrete lid hung inches above the surface scum. The smell of alkali. A moment's reprieve. He used it to count fifty gasps against the pressure on his lungs. The moment ended. Already the cement had plugged both his ears. He was deaf; and now the suffocation, the last phase. Again it had climbed to the corners of his mouth, and lubricating their way up his lips with their own slime, two slugs of it were sliding the final inch to his nostrils, flaring and snorting in horselike terror. As the cement oozed into his nose, his mouth opened wide and gave one ultimate screaming blast that seemed to rupture his heart.

The scream liberated him, delivered him from the cement into Monday. He heard it in both worlds, kept on hearing it, as the concrete cover suddenly gave way to the plaster wall behind the bed. His head was arched unnaturally back on his neck, rigid as if in a tetanus seizure. Farther down, his arms and legs, suddenly released, were thrashing hysterically in the thick tangle of bedclothes.

Suddenly they stopped. His spent body lay still for a few seconds and then sat bolt upright on the edge of the bed, mouth open, gasping like an animal.

Today! . . . *Today is today!*

Clawing his clothes together over his body, he ran to the bathroom. Two gaping wounds of Sunday greeted him first, ugly gray gashes where the towel rack had been. Something tiny crushed under his feet and he looked down and saw them, the green and yellow seeds, broadcast over the tiles. He had forgotten. He looked back up, and there that face was, staring at him again, bearded, bloated, blanched, with a streak of red rust across the temple, with swollen red eyes and thickened dry lips that sagged in parody of the mask of tragedy. The face of the clown, the caricature of suffering that always and everywhere has made men laugh. Other mornings, after looking at him intensely for a moment or two, the face would inevitably break down and smile; sometimes a meager and bitter smile, like yesterday, but always that miserable stare gave way. Now it did not. The expression in the mirror intensified, grew tight with horror. The man stared out at him as if he were the devil himself come to take him off to hell. The eyes quivered at the sight of him, the puffy lips began to blubber.

Today wasn't yesterday. Today was today. Hoerchner. Get to Hoerchner, get to Hoerchner now!

From some atavism of habit, he set to sprucing up a bit for the doctor. He managed to connect the electric shaver and apply it here and there to his beard. He dashed cold water onto his head and tried to rub order into his wild hair with his palms. His mouth was putrid with the taste of drugs, and seeing nothing else to rinse it with, he used soap. But there was no time. Yesterday there had been time, a glut of it. That was yesterday. This was today. Today there was no time at all.

Get to Hoerchner, get there or—the fuse was lit and sizzling, how long, how fast a fuse, there was no telling.

He threw on his coat, slammed the front door behind him, and was halted on the stoop by the sudden push of morning brilliance. From a corner of his grimace he saw the woman next door halted too, staring at him through the puritan whites of her washline. He dashed for the car and slammed himself inside. He reached for the key, the key to his fate. Would the car start? For two weeks it had stood here unused, since the day he took them to the airport. The battery was on its last legs. After a weak complaining whine, the motor coughed irritably and caught. Thank God. He shifted, rolled out into the public thoroughfare and began to drive, surprised, as last spring he had been similarly surprised, at the way the ability to operate a car stuck with you to the last. More than that, the act of driving calmed him. He felt he'd been granted a temporary stay of execution. As long as he drove this car It couldn't get at him. As his long-practiced body moved through its motions, and the car responded knowingly with its own, he felt himself meshing into intercourse with his machine, felt the conjugal intimacy being established between them, it the driver, it the driven. It and it, an unbeatable team. Itted together like this, he was safe. Even from that other It.

Effortlessly as sweethearts, man and car glided without a misstep through the ballroom traffic. On all sides of them, the road became packed with car-man couples dancing their way toward nine A.M. and The Job. And how beautifully the two of them fitted in, Bob and Chevy, so similarly intent on beating the clock to the madhouse. What a sense of communion it gave him to look out upon this centaur race of car-men that surrounded them, united to them and one another, not merely in appearance but by a common faith and assurance in destination.

Most of the others reached theirs first. He watched as the major part of the flow divided off and poured away through the double gates of The Base, past the armed guards in their booths, between the big signs, "*Air Force Weapons Laboratories—Directorate of Nuclear Safety.*" He felt a pang to see them leave, the good sane folks who spent their days and their lives in the healthy, normal and rewarding effort to perfect and stockpile the wonderful devices of nuclear safety.

Ah, but he had no need to envy them. He no less than they had his mission to accomplish, his job to do, his place to go. A pre-image of that place appeared in coordinates on a grid in his mind, a complex of tile roofs and foliage, buildings erected in the Spanish Mission style of forty years ago for rich tuberculosis patients from the East, adapting itself later to the changing fashions in disease. It was still four or five miles away, north of town on the Santa Fe highway, atop a small irrigated mound of green, rising from the once desolate but now steadily subdividing desert, maintaining its lawns and elm groves through the relentless pumping of its five-hundred-foot wells. Toward this oasis—no mirage, thank God—he was heading now like a parched Bedouin.

No, hardly like that. More like a ballistic device. The tormented human brain of yesterday seemed to have finally burnt itself out, leaving a kind of radar intelligence. No extraneous or unprogrammed thoughts could intrude on it, no fruitless deliberations about philosophers and psychiatrists, pills or prayers, no isometric wrestling between self, society, eternity, no guilts or innocences, truths or deceptions. Now merely a keen receptivity to flight commands, an unerring sense of target. Inside this hurtling steel jacket, his instrumentation recorded nothing but the parabola from pain to peace, drew bead on nothing but the red tile roofs ahead under which relief awaited him. He hardly noticed the familiar landmarks along his course—the long windowless stretches of the superstores, the big yellow mylar banners out front proclaiming "Goodwill Cash Nite," the ten-foot jets of orange flame spurting from the roof of the Fireside Manor Lodge, the fiery sign that sizzled "Charcoal Grill—Live Girls, Live Lobsters, Man-sized T-bones," the gleaming aluminum and enamel freightyard of the Vista View Trailer Estates, the cyclone-fenced acre of iron tentacles, rails, wheels, cockpits, rods, light bulbs, dynamos—the frivolous mutants of hard-working factory machinery, corralled here together under the huge neon aegis of "Family Funland." Even the great dusty rock of Sandia Mountain that towered on the eastern horizon was scarcely registered.

And suddenly he saw it for real, with his naked human eyes, the yellowed greenery of Bethlehem, a bushy clump set amid the flesh-colored aridity, as startling as a pubic patch. The

149

booster thrust cut out instantly, and as he whistled down the arc of his trajectory on perfect target, he began to rehumanize. The first human thing he felt was a whimpery gladness.

Entering the grove, he passed through the visitors' lot and parked in the gravel area behind the main building reserved for staff and the few in-patients who had delivered themselves personally. He'd be in here for a while. Good. He wanted to stay. With a trembling eagerness he passed through the doorway under the wrought-iron sign "Admissions—Office."

At the desk he saw Sister Mary Consolata going over forms with a man and woman, asking quiet questions, filling in quiet answers. If she noticed him it was only as the shadow of somebody entering. He sat down in an orange pastel chair to wait. The fiber-glass embrace felt good on buttocks and back, a strong plaster cast on shattered limbs. The terrible sense of urgency had eased off. He'd made it, he was in good hands now. The quiet order of this room and of the lives going on in it was a tranquilizer after the shambles of his house and life, and he sat sipping it down with a patient's patience. Behind the desk, on a wooden table, the Virgin stood in three-quarter scale. An exquisite child, a perfectly formed lady midget. She had on a long gold-spangled cape of baby blue over flowing cream robes, drawn apart at the bottom to show her pretty white feet which tread weightlessly on a submissive and happy serpent amid a general scattering of pink roses. The Virgin of what, Fatima? Her head was slightly elongated and compressed from her Gothic forebears, and her canted face with its perfect features, ivory complexion and tiny rosepetal lips, gazed down with somewhat cross-eyed and Italianate compassion upon the room, himself included. It was like one tender poignant note being drawn from a violin with an endless bow. Beneath the Virgin Mary sat the Virgin Consolata, a large figure of shapeless solidity and force, a tight-packed bundle of immaculate laundry, her face white and lumpy as a snowman patted out hurriedly by a child and fitted with a pair of rimless glasses.

His eyes moved up and down, back and forth, between the cold plaster perfection of divinity and the warm animate botchiness of humankind.

"Thank you, Sister, thank you so much . . ." The woman's voice was reedy and broken. She was weeping. ". . . been so kind . . . we're so grateful . . . we never thought . . . appreciate . . . anything you can do for Linda . . ."

The couple turned and walked past him out the door, the woman dabbing eyes from which the mascara had run, reducing them to charred holes, the man's eyebrows warped into uncharacteristic astonishment by something beyond his understanding and control.

The nun was putting the folder into the file cabinet when he got up and approached the desk.

"Yes, sir, can I help you—oh, why, it's—oh, no . . ." His eyes began to burn as he saw her recognize him, recognize It. Her face made an utterly spontaneous, utterly sincere, and utterly impossible attempt to look like the one in the bathroom mirror. "Oh, dear, no . . . oh, don't tell me . . . oh, dear, I'm so sorry . . . and we were so sure . . ."

He closed his eyes, tried unsuccessfully to swallow, and to avoid looking at her opened them on the Virgin. Her loving gaze was now directed a few inches above his right shoulder. He had stepped out of the beam of her compassion.

". . . dear, and I thought everything . . . you were doing so well—does Dr. Hoerchner know?"

He shook his head back and forth. Too fast.

"Oh, and you know he hasn't come in yet. He just now phoned to say he was leaving home. So he should be along soon, ten minutes at the most. Now, wouldn't you like to just wait for him in his office? Are you—I mean, do you feel well enough to—you could just lie quietly on the couch if you wanted. You remember—or would you like me to have someone take you there?"

"No, I'm all right." All right.

"I'll send him in the instant he arrives."

Gluey tongue sticking to gluey palate; a gluey, whispered, "Thanks."

"I'm so sorry . . . you poor dear . . . you'll feel better soon . . ."

He stepped through the inner door into the interior.

The central corridor was dark and varnished, and the rooms were arranged around it, like a hotel. The locked wards, arranged otherwise, were underneath, in the cellar. From behind him came the clatter of crockery, the peculiar unappetizing odor of the dining room. Ahead, at the end of the hallway, lay the large recreation room. Instinctively he looked toward Number Six, his, last time, and saw a stout middle-aged woman sitting on the edge of his bed in a quilted dressing gown of bride pink, staring down through her laxly parted knees at the hooked rug, his rug. Through the open doorway of Number Nine he saw a familiar body sprawled on its stomach across the bed and snoring erotically—those black serge pants, that thick brush of gray hair, could belong to no one but Father Callahan. A few steps onward, a closed door ahead opened a slice, just enough to frame a lifelike illustration of a lovely young girl, a sleeping princess lying in a deep and silent swoon. It closed again soundlessly as Dr. Mayer, the Chief Psychiatrist, emerged, milking his dark Vandyked chin, too preoccupied to take notice of the passing recidivist.

In the recreation room, the magic fishbowl of the TV had still not been switched off. The indefatigably grinning housewife inside was still shoving that box of something forward with unflagging enthusiasm, still trying to push it out through the glass surface of her world into the room. Nobody looked at her. Nobody looked around at him either, and thankfully he realized he knew none of these people. A youth in a white college sweatshirt and white tennis shoes was playing listless ping-pong with a dark-skinned female attendant. Three menopausal women were playing cards with a pink-pated man in a yellow Polynesian-print sport shirt. A scattering of other patients sat in armchairs with reading matter closed in their laps. One of them, an old man, white and frail as ash, was nodding in feeble metronomic rhythm over the dripping-wet body of a beach beauty on a picture-magazine cover, as if ticking off his final heartbeats. Another, an overrouged and overweight young woman, whose globular breasts were sheathed in black jersey, and heavy flattened thighs in nylon, sat crushing a cigarette into the coils of a ceramic ashtray from Occupational Therapy. Suddenly, with no warning, she glared up at him in ferocious hatred, and just as quickly looked away again, furious with him still for daring to be a different man. From the black billows of her bosom, a heaving diamond crucifix flashed out signals of distress.

"But you'd better act now. This offer is limited." He shot an anxious glance about to see which of them had spoken. It was, of course, the housewife in the box.

Hoerchner's office was behind a partitioned section off the rec room. It was empty and unlighted. When he had closed the glass-paneled door behind him, he started for the brown leatherette couch along the wall, but stopped, turned and sat down instead in its similarly upholstered mate, the "patient's chair" which waited with open arms in front of the desk. It received him in soft female conformation like a maternal lap, and from it he looked up, out, on the depressing familiarity of the scene. Nothing in the office had altered. The stained dark woodwork, the chalk-white walls, the fixtures in black "Spanish" iron, the framed diplomas, the framed snapshots of wife and kids and boxer and shepherds, of Lincoln Continental and ranchhouse and kidney swimming pool, these sights his eyes had fixed on through so many therapeutic hours that they had laminated their images to those feelings and those memories. He leaned forward to reexamine the green plastic ball on the desk, the same object he had picked up and rolled about in his hands so often, not a sphere but a dodecahedron, a calendar with a month to each surface, the many-faceted gift of Abbey Labs. Inc., Evanston, Ill. That, yes, had changed. Now it was October on top . . .

11

". . . YES, YES, SISTER, I know she is. When *isn't* she, the old—"

Hoerchner's voice, a strident whisper, like a cop barging in to break up some illegal goings-on. Hoerchner's voice, out of nowhere, at the door.

At the sound of it, his body jerked in reflex and sat him up, disoriented and bewildered, in the leather chair. In the *leather* chair, the real, not the imitation, leather chair, the pigskin chair. And as before, his first movement was to seek his bearings from the wrist that had been naked of time since Juarez. But even without being pinned numerically down, the present began to reassemble its pieces together around him. From down in a courtyard somewhere a small radio with a rattly paper speaker flared up to assist him. ". . . *la voz encantadora de Flor Mendoza* . . ." and the enchanting voice of Flor Mendoza bellowed forth into Pátzcuaro like a cow in heat:

155

Soy el último romántico
De este siglo frántico . . .

The soda pop commercial that followed was even louder, screamed out. But nevertheless the force of the radio died rapidly away, allowing the piccolo piping of the defective toilet downstairs to bubble up into audibility again. Reestablished in Mexico, in October twenty-fifth, he relaxed back into the chair; the cedar staves creaked at their joints of pitch.

Was it true? Had it really happened? Was he remembering something or daydreaming it up?

No answer. No surprise either. Perhaps there was none. But . . . but it had all seemed so real, so sure in all its details. Still, nobody in the condition he was in last week could possibly have been so alert to all that. Nobody, a week afterwards, could possibly recall this much. Obviously not. So where, how . . . ?

No answers. Frowning, puzzled, he began leafing absently backwards through the notebook toward last spring, stopping at a place where two sheets of yellow manila paper had been stapled onto the white of the bound page. Unfolding them, he began to read what was typewritten there.

May 23, 1958—Autobiographical Sketch
I am writing this autobiographical sketch at the suggestion of my physician, Dr. Frank Hoerchner. Because I have recently undergone an extensive series of electroshock therapy, I am unable to recall many details of my life. But I will try. I was born . . .

Still frowning, he refolded the yellow pages and laid the open book back on the round leather tabletop.

One thing at least he felt sure about. He had *heard* it, just now, Hoerchner's voice, Hoerchner's words, just as clearly as he'd heard the enchanting voice and words of Flor Mendoza. More than that, he was as *there* when he heard them, as slumped in that patient's chair, as he was here and seated in this pig leather tub now. Five minutes ago his essential being had been back in Albuquerque, in Bethlehem Sanitorium, in Monday. But if that was true of five minutes ago, was it true also of six days ago, of Monday morning itself? Did it happen that way in reality—in factuality, rather—just like that? Or was he making it up out of nothing, inventing it?

Inventing? But he himself had done nothing! He'd simply sat back and been there, that's all. The there had become here. But was this there the same as that original there, or was it new and changed? Did the past remain fixed in taxidermy like a museum exhibit, or did it evolve to suit the present?

No answers. Except that as he puzzled over this mystery, his glance happened to be resting on the yellow rectangle of manila paper, which did gradually happen to remind him of a similarly yellow rectangle he'd happened to see two or three days ago, a sign they had driven past, in front of a pharmacy along one of the main streets of one of the towns—Fresnillo, Zacatecas, Lagos de Moreno, he couldn't remember which— an ordinary Kodak-yellow sign with what struck him then as an extraordinary black word painted on it: REVELACIÓN.

Howell's pocket dictionary had cleared the matter up. The Spanish word *revelar*, it turned out, had a double meaning— to reveal, and to develop films. An incident quickly forgotten among incidents.

So how come he should be thinking of that sign now? Could it be a *revelación* that all this was *revelación*, that this sequence of life he had been "reliving" for the last hour or three hours or whatever, was something that had impressed itself frame after frame onto some sensitized plate in the obscurity of his mind? Was he viewing rather than reviewing, seeing for the first time material "exposed" but unrevealed? Was this light-filled porch a darkroom? How strange . . .

Warm and invisible, a cloud bearing the sweet odor of onions and peppers frying in lard drifted up from the patio below, along with scraps of dialogue between patrona and maid, the caws of command and tweets of assent, "Sí Señora muy bien, Señora . . ." reminding him again that his single life was going on in the midst of millions of lives, reminding him of a college word that had once intrigued him with its combination of silly sound and hideous meaning—solipsism, a sort of philosophic basis for madness.

But it didn't worry him now. He had no sense now of isolation, or of creating something out of his own will or substance. He felt no feelings of effort expended, no exhaustion. No, he felt the opposite, refreshed, as if all this were being fed to him fresh from—from where? Where was all this coming from?

No answers, but at the sight of the next unanswerable question he felt himself smile: "Where am I coming from?"

Where was it going to, that might be more to the point. An hour ago, or three, whatever it was, when he'd come up here to the porch still resonating with that experience in the Basilica, it had been to write what was essentially a letter to Dr. Hoerchner, to explain, to justify, to vindicate himself before that father, authority, official representative of the spirit of the age. He'd been able to summon up his image easily, picture the psychiatrist sitting—in the patient's chair perhaps—listening, maybe learning a thing or two about the dimensions of existence. But now, when he refocused, he could no longer conjure up Hoerchner's face at all. All he could see, and that only dimly through his nearly shut eyelids, was Hoerchner's back . . .

A rear view of him, a suit he'd never seen him wear before,

brownish wool with a green undertone, a muted autumnal tweed, well-tailored, double slit in the jacket, bending slightly outward through the doorway, getting rid of the importunate nurse.

"Oh, give her a big red sugar pill, tell her a fairy story. Tell her the truth even, that I've got an emergency, and I'll be in to see her in twenty minutes."

"And if she throws another tantrum? She may break more than just my glasses this time."

"Bring up one of the boys from down below. Threaten her with restraints if you have to."

"Well, I'll see what I can do with her, Doctor."

"Good girl. I'll testify at your beatification, Sister."

"Doctor, you are *terr-ible!*"

Hoerchner slowly pulled the door closed, and he peered out at him through the drawn shutters of his eyelids like an attic idiot. He did not stir but remained shriveled and involuted in the chair, knowing he was holding this miserable cringe to impress the doctor with his desperate condition, knowing his condition was that desperate by the very need to impress. The doctor's smell reached him before his eyes — cigars, aftershave lotion, something else. When Hoerchner did turn, his first look, which didn't look, was a smile. "Bet you can guess who that was, Bob. Old Mrs. Sauerwine, our lecherous millionairess. Didn't I tell you how under LSD she tried to tickle my fancy?" Yes, Hoerchner had told him about Mrs. Sauerwine, and about the Reverend Father Callahan and other fascinating cases of his during those last few weeks when they'd talked and argued together like friends, almost like equals. It was as if Frank were still half-hoping he'd just dropped by for another of those pleasant chats.

A rodent from its burrow, he squinted out at the man who stood with his back to the closed door looking down into the hole. Though Hoerchner was in fact an inch or two the shorter, he loomed huge above him now, father above child, health above infirmity, youth above senility, boss above hireling. As he watched the warmth cool from the face, some delicate instrument inside was registering the swift sequence that passed over it.

1. Boy, if that ain't a sight for sore eyes, first thing Monday morning.
2. Here we go again. Exactly like the last time, same sick cat some kind soul threw back on my doorstep.
3. Jesus, what am I supposed to do with him now?
4. Oh for the life of an ophthalmologist, a proctologist even . . .
5. The poor benighted bugger—the knots these contortionists can twist themselves into . . .

And then numbers 4 and 5, the two pities, for self and for other, coalesced to form a weight much too heavy for a single man's resources. So that the personal, staggering under the enormity of the mutual situation, fell back against the surgical steel bars of the professional discipline, the job-to-do-ism of the secularized Calvinist. The burden transferred, then and only then, could the mechanism of cure begin to unwind.

Hoerchner activated. He began to cluck softly, shaking his head from side to side in rhythm. Like a priest beginning a mass, his face took on a ritual set, not of piety, but of maternal concern, and his voice intoned the liturgy of a doting mama whose baby has skinned his knee or been jailed for shooting a cop.

"My goodness gracious, what's all this they tell me, what's this, what's this now . . . ?"

On this cue, he understood, he should at least try to smile, and he tried to smile. But it was much too late for that, and he felt the smile on the left side of his mouth only, as a crooked wince. Hoerchner came over to the patient's chair, sat down lightly on the arm and began to tousle his hair affectionately.

A cloacal sense of repetition, of stale worthless repetition, of life-waste, of starting in again on something already finished. He knew exactly what Hoerchner was doing. They'd discussed this too last June, agreed together that the safest approach to a severely depressed patient was mothering, that certainly if there was one thing a mangled ego could not bear it was fathering.

"Dear-dear-dear . . . my-my-my . . ."

Cluck-cluck-cluck. The all-enveloping mother hen, the louse-picking mother monkey. But now the touch felt oppressive, pain upon pain, and he was relieved when the doctor had gotten up and was looking at him from the other side of the big desk instead, thoughtfully down to business, chin cupped in palm, forefinger on nosetip, conjecturing eyebrows lifted, meditative lips pursed. His skin, usually a sallow gray, was slightly ruddied from his weekend in the woods, and the edge of one sideburn was slightly out of kilter, as if he too had shaved hurriedly this morning. Suddenly the pose shattered. The physician had made his decision. He reached for pen and pad and began to write out his orders for this patient.

"My old buddy's not feeling any too chipper right now, is he?" he said, continuing to write and without looking up.

He managed to give his head a small wrench, jarring loose a warm pocket of tears.

"Well, we'll see if we can't do something about that pretty quick."

He watched the scrubbed white fingers coercing the pen firmly along the pad. The long-held-back tears continued to flow soundlessly, while inside a steady barrage of emotion and thought exploded salvo after silent salvo. He felt a quivery dog-gratitude to this man, a dog-joy to have reached this safe kennel in time, to have his leash taken up by the skilled hands of masters who knew and would bring him what he needed soon, very soon—a doggy desire to repay this man for his goodness by means of a few woofs of normal conversation—to ask him, for instance, about his hunting trip, whether he had shot a deer. But simultaneously he felt the human pain at his dog role growing and spreading, the despair at having come whimpering back through that door, the humiliation that this second breakdown in six months had ceased to be private and hidden, but was being written right now into the public record, into radio reality, that more stones were being lashed onto the life he would have to carry from now on.

He saw the doctor reach up and stifle a yawn, and he realized that Hoerchner was dead tired, remembered that for his fifty thousand dollars a year Hoerchner worked sixty or seventy hours a week, a field surgeon in a battle that never ended, remembered his telling him how, every month or so, he'd escape, drive to Santa Fe or Taos, check in at some motel and sleep for twenty-four hours. He remembered the embittered, unhappy voice of the woman on the phone yesterday. Hoerchner too carried his stones, and he, Bob, was one of them.

As he sat watching the doctor write, his focus began to fix itself on Hoerchner's tie. It was an expensive silk foulard in the same dusty metallic tones and pattern he himself had dearly prized once, in college and for a year or two afterwards, when he had looked on clothes in the same way a crustacean regards its shell. He followed the tight crisp knot as it rode the wave of the Adam's apple beneath the slack overhang of the jawflesh, while the wool and cotton broadcloth of the chest rose and fell at regular intervals and the pen performed beneath the supervision of the eyeglasses. And suddenly it seemed, the tie, to be a ribbon of rank, the slender dark band down the white shirtfront a kind of Fraunhofer line, locating the wearer not merely in the social spectrum but on the evolutionary scale. With this tie went a fixed life-view, a fixed set of values, a fixed hierarchal position. It spoke of assurance, of a sense of power, of performance and reward, a kind of integration that was not individual but collective, not personal but conferred by a social body upon its members in return for their loyalty, through an unspoken pact of mutual assistance. A stockbroker could wear such a tie; a pawnbroker could not . . .

He found this thought obsessing him as he waited for Hoerchner to finish. This man, the physician, was intact. He, the patient, lay in pieces. He envied this man. And yet, at the same time as he envied the wholeness that allowed this man to function, to be of help to others, such as himself now, he didn't envy *that* wholeness. If Hoerchner had somehow been able to graft it onto him, his organism would reject it, even now, even in this condition. An unexpected, unsought, unwanted feeling to have to feel. But it was there whether he liked it or not, the feeling, or the impression, that this man in whose power he lay, into whose mercy and wisdom he had delivered himself, this man writing out orders for him there, aromatic of cigars and aftershave and success, playing his role so competently, so humanely, was somehow ten years, that tie's spectrum location, behind him! Behind this great human larva curled in his examination chair awaiting his disposition! Despite the arrogance, the illogic, the insanity of thinking such a thought, this blighted grub had, in some strange way, already passed beyond that man!

But the mental content of all this was remote and ephemeral. It made itself felt as a sudden surging intensification of pain. The struggle seemed to have broken out of its arena, the benumbed spectators were being attacked. He heard his teeth as they grated together, and the quiet tearing turned into sobbing. Like a singed worm he could only try to coil tighter into his shame and isolation.

Hoerchner had noticed. He saw the eyes look up from the page, and beam down at him through the glinting glass lenses, the pupils adjusting to refraction and distance. He felt not merely naked, but dissected, beneath scientific scopes.

The doctor laid his pen aside, sniffed, and ripped the pages smoothly from the pad.

"How about the family? Made some arrangements?"

He could not speak. He gave his head a shuddering nod, not to answer him, but to stop his asking.

"Good. Because, old timer, I think maybe we'd better figure on your spending a little time here with us, don't you agree?"

His chest gave a sudden noisy heave, and like a caught fish, his mouth gaped open, sucked in a great gulp of air and held it, useless, suffocating, inside inflated cheeks until it escaped with a pop.

". . . no . . . don't . . . don't have . . . no more insurance." It was a shuddering sob. He didn't know how he'd spoken the words, much less how Hoerchner had made them out. But he had.

". . . Well, that may complicate matters a bit, but we'll worry about that later. Right now, let's both just concentrate on breaking up those old gloom-clouds of yours . . ."

"How long?" This came out more distinctly. The sobbing seemed to be easing off.

"I don't know, Bob. If I gave you a date, I'd be lying. I can only promise we won't keep you here a day longer than necessary."

". . . necessary . . ." It was hollow, an echo, but clear.

Hoerchner slapped both hands on the edge of the desk, about to rise.

"So—the sooner we get started, the sooner—"

"What are you going to do to me?" This question was much louder, almost in a normal tone. It was because something new had begun to happen in his interior, a new process had started. Some gland directly beneath his navel seemed to have ruptured and from that center an astringent cold was beginning to radiate outwards through his body, tightening and hardening the flesh as it spread.

"I haven't got any new tricks, Bob. Why do you ask when you already know the answer?" Hoerchner smiled, trying to keep it light, but he couldn't prevent the escape of a sigh.

Inside the process was fanning out, overwhelming pockets of token resistance, taking a rigorous military control. It was the chill of terror again, but terror of a different kind. He felt his body stiffening, his muscles growing taut. Already it had straightened him out of his foetal curl and was sitting him up higher and higher in the chair.

Hoerchner noticed. "What's the matter? What are you looking at me like that for? My goodness, you don't suppose I intend to repeat the LSD, do you?"

He had forgotten the LSD. Hoerchner had a foundation grant to experiment with this newly synthesized Swiss drug, to test its possibilities as a therapeutic tool. He had tried it on him three times. Later they had gone over the transcripts of those hideous sessions together he'd even presented him with one as a "souvenir." Now this reassurance he wouldn't use it again served only to accelerate the process of refrigeration.

"You know I'm on your side, don't you? I'm not going to hurt you. All I want is to stop that pain . . ."

He hardly understood the words. Already Hoerchner was becoming peripheral to his attention, which was enveloped more and more by the tumescence of his body. It was as if the animal in him had sensed with its animal acuity a peril the human understanding was still unaware of and could not pin down. He saw his shoulders rising on either side, hunching up, like those of a cat which has smelled a dog.

"Why did you wait? Why didn't you get in touch with me earlier?"

He stared at the blurry shape behind the desk, hardly able to define its outlines.

"I'm your friend. All I'm interested in is helping you get well."

He started. Thin smoky veils seemed to be dropping one after another over Hoerchner.

"Look, we pulled you out of it last time, didn't we?"

Last time!

He felt the galvanic electricity bolt through his meat like the prod of slaughterhouse prongs.

"Bob, I've always been level with you. I don't do that with many patients. I can't. And maybe I was wrong to make an exception in your case, but I'm not going to try to fool you now. You know the story as well as I do. And at this point I know of nothing else that's going to do the trick . . . but somehow, I've got a feeling it's not going to take as many this time . . ."

THIS TIME!

". . . may not even need a full series to unscramble that old mixed-up noodle of yours. Eight, maybe even six, might be sufficient this time—"

THIS TIME!

Hoerchner never finished.

"No!"

He lurched to his feet, his flesh hard and quivering as that of a man leaping from a poorly strapped electric chair.

"NO! NO-NO-NO-NO!"

* * *

He stood, hands clamped to the round table-edge, blinking down into the orange disk of pored and bristled pigleather, talking to the man he could no longer see . . .

Yes, that did catch you by surprise, didn't it, Frank? I know you've seen just about everything there is to see in the line of human behavior. You've seen old Mrs. Sauerwine lay bare her grizzled thatch to entice you, listened to Father Callahan, O.P., intone his obscene litany to the Virgin Mother and cast his blasphemous maledictions on that Son-of-a-Bitch, her Whelp. You've seen six-figure corporation executives sit in wet pants wailing for Mommy and had a distinguished father and civic father beg to caress your penis. Nuclear bomb experts have been frightened you were about to spank them, and shy young girls have tried to knife you with nailfiles. And as for myself, under drugs you've watched me gasp and choke as I emerged from the obstetrical mucus, perform unpunished bed-wettings, tear pillows apart and toss the feathers into the air like the flower petals of mad Ophelia.

But that, I think that did catch you by surprise.

It did me too. That such violence could explode out of such inertia the instant you touched the trigger.

Trigger? Those two little words: this time. I think if you hadn't happened to use those particular two words, the whole story might have been utterly different. I think I would have allowed myself to be led back to the electric bed again without a murmur. What, finally, did it then? Stark terror, of course, what else? Terror is the only thing that can pierce down into that kind of depression, we know that. Pain was clutching the very edge of bearability, terrified of that extra gram that would send it plunging over that brink.

But why should the prospect of your little black box have frightened me so, that's what I still can't explain, not, at least, in any terms you could possibly accept. Because it wasn't more pain you were offering, it was a speedy release from pain, a round-trip vacation into peace. I wanted death and you had death to give, a marvelous healing death, not merely painless but complete with a built-in resurrection.

I just don't know—that is, yes, I do know, Frank, but not how to tell you. All I can say is that your *this time* was the claw that finally ripped open the scar of *that time*. The feel of pain after it's gone is as hard to summon back as the feel of delight after it's gone. But pain remembers pain, and on Monday morning, there in your office, *this time* remembered *that time*.

12

Ice. Ice and nice. They know. They come, always they come, just on time, and freeze it up again, right where it's thawing. Ice and safe. Just leave me alone, that's all. Just leave me alone.

The ice is clear, a little white and a little green. I can watch. I can hear. I can smell. I can think. Maybe I can talk too. I don't know, I haven't tried.

Green. Green and white. The walls are green. Not grass green, dollar green. Not yellow green, gray green. The cots are white. White paint, white sheets, white blankets. Our gowns are white. The nurse's uniform is white. The orderlies' coats are white. The floor is white and green. Green squares with white foamy lines. The squares are all different. No two are the same. I know. I've been watching them. Some have faces. The one down by the cot leg has a cat's face, whiskers and everything. The one by my left foot has a naked woman burning into smoke. The one on top of that is funny. It keeps changing. First it's a clown. Then it's a devil. Then it's nothing, just lines. Funny.

Three times a day the orderly comes with a white mop and

mops the floor. When he gets to feet, he lifts them if they don't lift themselves. The professor never lifts his feet. The Mexican doesn't lift his feet, either. But I do. I lift my own feet.

My left shoelace is broken. I need a new shoelace. But the orderly won't come till it gets dark in the windows. He just finished and he didn't notice my shoelace. Maybe because I lifted my own feet. Maybe next time I won't lift them. Then he'll have to lift them. Maybe he'll see I need a new shoelace.

This place smells funny. Some stuff they use to cover up the other smell, the sweetish one that comes from people who mess their pants and don't tell anybody, just sit in it until somebody comes to look. The professor messes his pants. The Mexican does, too. But I don't. When I have to go to the bathroom, I go to the bathroom by myself.

The windows are high and low. Low but high, high but low. Low in height but high up on the walls. Way up by the ceiling. That's because this place is the cellar. The windows have blurry glass with chicken wire in it. You can't see out and nobody can see in. Just blurry. Light blurry when it's day and dark blurry when it's night. On my window there's a shadow that goes back and forth, back and forth. I know what it is. It's a branch with wind blowing it. A low shrub but high, way up there by the ceiling. Low but high, high but low. Because up there, that's the ground. Straight through from here, from my bed, is just dirt, six feet down. The roots of that shrub up there, I bet they don't come down this far, to where we are. My bed is lower than the roots. Funny.

The lights are on. Gray pink tubes in the ceiling in our part, yellow over there in the nurse's part. She's in there now, telling the old orderly about her sports car. She's buying a sports car. "Yeah, well, I don't know, I kinda go for the Caribbean blue, but I'd have to wait maybe a month. Maybe I'll just go ahead and take the fire red. I don't know . . ." There's music on her radio. *Boo-boo-beedee-beedee-bap-bap.* Music, talking, music, talking, all day. The nurse is pretty old, but she's trying to stay young. She's not a sister. She's a lay nurse. The young orderly says she's a hot lay. Her hair is yellow, the same as a specimen. She has red greasy lips. The old orderly has thin hair. He combs it a lot. He's combing it now. His mouth is full of brown teeth and has a bad smell. I think he's a big drinker.

The door is jiggling. The knob is wiggling. They keep it locked. The orderlies and the nurses and the doctors have all got a key. But we don't. The door has a little round mirror in the middle. Not exactly in the middle. Higher than the middle. They say people can look in from the outside. Once when I went to the bathroom I looked out, but I could only see in. The same thing I see now.

Oh-oh, here comes the young orderly pushing Gramps ahead of him. Gramps never moves unless somebody pushes him. "O.K., Gramps, let's go now, that's the boy. We're back home now." Gramps has his shiny blue bathrobe on. His face is all red. He doesn't like people to push him. He's really mad. His pink gums are snapping up and down. He's raising his fist at the orderly, shaking all over, hissing like an alligator. But he won't do anything. This is just the way he is. He gets mad at everything. Even when they feed him, he gets mad. He hisses at them between swallows.

I hate the young orderly. The old one and the nurse leave us alone. They stay over in their part and drink coffee and talk and smoke. They don't bother us. This other one is a smarty-pants. He sticks his nose into everything. He talks too much. He uses big medical words and acts as if he's a doctor. He tells people he's a pre-med. I think he's lying, but maybe he is one. How should I know? I just don't like him. If he starts bothering me like he bothers some of the others, I'll—I don't know what I'll do.

He's taking off Gramps' bathrobe and hanging it in the closet. The old man has his mouth open, hissing at him like an alligator. He hates the young orderly too, but he won't do anything. He hasn't got any teeth.

"Guess that's the lot of them—oh, what about Rose?"

"Haaanh!" He woke up Mr. Rose. Mr. Rose sleeps all day in his wheelchair. He looks like he's dead already. He's whiter than anybody. White face, white hair, white gown, white blanket. So white you can almost see right through his face and hands. He's jerking and feeling around for his glasses. There's not much left of Mr. Rose. His legs are both cut off. But what's left hates the young orderly too.

"Don't-wanna-go-for-a-walk! I'm sick. I-had-a-loose-stool!" Mr. Rose is crying and shivering, like a little baby. That's the way he is. Sometimes when you think he's just sleeping, he starts crying, "Waaa-waaa!" In a little tiny voice, just like a baby. I don't cry. I never cry, I don't bother people, and they better not bother me, that's all.

"Hey, what's the deal on Rose?" The young orderly's got his hands on the handles of the wheelchair. Mr. Rose's eyes are blinking fast behind his glasses. The bumps of his stumps are shivering under the white blanket. His mouth is opening and closing, and he's saying "Waaa-waaa" but not out loud.

The old orderly puts his comb back in his pocket. "Nah, no walk for Rose today. Got a little diarrhea."

Mr. Rose makes a funny noise through his nose. "Yee-aaannnh!" and lies back in his wheelchair.

But now he's looking at me. I hope he's not going to bother me, that's all. He better not bother me because if he does I—

"How about the new guy?"

"Him neither. Dr. Hoerchner says no P.T. for him yet."

The young orderly looks around at all the beds and then he goes over to the one where that big man is stretched out, staring up at my window, watching the shadow of the shrub going back and forth, back and forth. The one who was shouting and fighting so much this morning.

"How we doing, Mr. Kinney? Feel better now?" It sounds like he's just asking nicely, but he isn't. He's got a funny look on his face. He just wants to bother him.

"Listen, man, when you guys gonna give me back my thirty-eight?"

"What thirty-eight? I never took your thirty-eight."

"Cut the shit, will you? One of you guys stole it. I had it right here under this pillow. It's my gun and I want it back now, you hear me?"

"What do you want a gun for anyway, Mr. Kinney? You're safe in here. Nobody's going to get you in here."

"Goddamn it, how's a man supposed to defend himself if bastards like you steal his gun?"

"I'll protect you, Mr. Kinney, don't worry. She'll never make it through that door. See that lock? That's the same kind they use at Fort Knox."

"Don't make me laugh, kid. A squirt like you stop that woman? Squirts like you she eats for breakfast. Now give me back my thirty-eight, for Christsake."

"I'd just like to see her try, that's all. Stick her snout through that door, and I'll give her a blast with my EST."

"Jesus, you're thick! Think she's gonna come herself? She'll send an agent, one of her goddamn nigger-jew lovers. Dressed up like a doctor—you stupes'd never spot him."

"I'll spot him, Mr. Kinney. I wasn't a CIA operator all those years for nothing, you know. Who do you think engineered that takeover in Bango-Bango? See this here—looks like an ordinary wristwatch, doesn't it? Well, it's actually an ultra-micro agent-spotter. It can spot an agent a mile off. So just relax."

"Christ, kid, will you cut out the bullshit. I mean it. She's gonna kill me, you hear, kill me. So please, you got to give me back my thirty-eight. I'm not asking for your gun, am I? All I want is what's legally mine, my own goddamn property that you thieving bastards stole from me. Please, you hear me?, I'm saying please . . ."

It's the same thing he was shouting and yelling about this morning. But now his voice is weak. This morning he smashed a bottle on the floor, and they had to tie him to the bed. Now he's not tied, but still he won't do anything. Like Gramps. You can tell, he's on ice too . . .

They know. Those doctors, they really know.

Oh-oh. He's waking up again. The Mexican in the next bed. That means trouble. He's going to start bothering people again, I just bet. Like he did before, bothering me and the professor until the nurse came and gave him a shot. I hope this time he leaves me alone, that's all. I'm sick, and if he starts bothering me, I don't know what I'll do.

Now he's sitting up in bed and looking around at everything and picking at his mouth with his finger. He opens it wide, like a hippo. What an awful mouth. On one side the teeth are all white. On the other side they're all gone. All bloody and awful. His head too. Half of it has the hair shaved off and there's a big awful cut across it that gets white when he opens his mouth wide. Then it gets red again, like the nurse's lips. He looks very dark in the white bed.

Oh-oh, he's starting to think now. I can tell. His face is changing. His mouth is starting to make words. He's looking around for somebody to bother. He's going to bother us again. Just what I said. All I hope is it's not—

It is. Me. Here he comes dragging his bad leg. His bad leg is all wrapped in white bandages. He's talking in Spanish. Maybe if I don't look at him, maybe if I just look down at my shoes— oh-oh, I knew it. There they are, his two feet, one brown and the other big and white. And he's got his big heavy hands on my shoulder, pushing me down.

"¿Están bien, todos?"

Oh no. The same thing he was asking before. I can understand him. I understand Spanish. "Are they all all right?" That's what he's saying. What's he asking me that for? How should I know what he's talking about? What's that got to do with me? I'm sick. I'm here because I'm sick. I can't answer. I don't even know if I can talk. I don't know anything. I don't want to know anything.

"¿Están bien, todos?"

He's trying to lift my head up. He's strong. I have to look at him. He smells like medicine. His face looks funny. The cut on his forehead looks like a zipper, two little rows of brown dots from the sewing. His eyes look wet and wiggly. Why is he bothering me? Why do they let him bother me?

"¿Están bien, todos?"

Why does he keep asking me that, if everybody's all right? Who is he talking about? How should I know? Please, make him leave me alone. Where's somebody to take him away? The old orderly and the nurse are still talking over in their part. The young orderly is sitting on Mr. Rose's bed reading a newspaper. Nobody looks. Nobody helps me. Nobody cares.

"¿Están bien, todos?"

He's pushing at my head. He's crazy. He might hurt me. Maybe, maybe if I give him an answer, he'll go away and stop bothering me. But maybe I can't even talk.

"¡Diga! ¿Están bien, todos?"

He's getting mad. His eyes are wiggling. Black dots in red jelly. He's crazy. He's going to hurt me.

"Sí."

So, I can talk. It sounds funny, my voice, full of mucus or something. But he heard it. He's looking at me. His mouth is hanging open. Half white teeth, half purple hole.

"¿Están bien, todos?"

"Sí . . . sí."

His hands hurt my shoulders. They're shaking me, shaking me. But he's not mad, he's smiling. He's happy. He's hugging me. He's kissing me!

"¿Están bien, todos?"

"Sí . . . sí, sí, sí."

It worked. It really worked. He's going to leave me alone. He's dragging himself over to the professor's bed now. The professor is sitting quietly, shaking and spitting on himself like always. His shirt is all wet from spitting and there's a puddle of pee on the floor. The Mexican's feet step right in it. He's got the professor's face in his hands. His big brown hands are shaking because he can't stop the professor's face. He's shouting at the professor's face.

"¡ESTÁN BIEN, TODOS!"

Now, now they know he's bothering us. The young orderly looks up, puts down the paper and comes over.

"O.K., Pancho, let's not disturb the professor now. He's got to cogitate. Vamos . . . let's go now." He takes the Mexican by the shoulder and pulls him off the professor. The Mexican looks around at the orderly with a big awful smile.

"Oiga, Doctorcito, ¡están bien, todos!" he tells the orderly.

"Yeah, Pancho, you bet. Truer word was never spoke. Now you get back in that bed and stay put a while, O.K.?"

The orderly goes and gets the mop and comes back to the professor's bed. The professor is pointing down at the puddle of pee and his finger is going back and forth, back and forth.

"You know, Professor, I'm damned if you're not the most absent-minded professor I ever did see. How many years were you head of the Chemistry Department? What is this stuff you're working on here now? Looks a lot like that same old $C_5H_4N_4O_3$ again. Have I got the formula right?"

The professor shakes his head and his lips make a funny fizzy noise, like opening a beer bottle. The orderly goes to rinse the mop and then goes inside the nurse's part.

The Mexican is sitting on his bed and feeling at his cut with his fingers. He's starting to look around again. He's looking at me again. But he's not smiling any more. His eyes are wiggling. He's starting to talk to himself again. He's getting up again, he's coming over here again . . .

"Hey! . . . Hey!"

Oh-oh. Now everybody's looking at me, the nurse and both the orderlies. Now everybody's going to bother me . . .

Hospital No. 7251

Name   Robert Edward   Room or   6   Hoerchner
                                        Ward No.   Doctor

        Date   NOTE PROGRESS OF CASE. COMPLICATIONS. CONSULTATIONS. CHANGE
                        IN DIAGNOSIS. CONDITION ON DISCHARGE. INSTRUCTIONS TO PATIENT

4/21/58
9:30   L.S.D.-3 cc I.V.
a.m.

10:00   Pt. says he was confused and de-
         pressed before taking drug. "I can't
         seem to make sense out of anything
         . . ." Every effort overwhelming.
         Visits yesterday from wife and
         school colleague. Disturbed that
         they "should see me like this."
         Dream last night: all the tires on
         his car broken, kept trying to pump
         them up, but they kept going flat
         faster than he could fix them.
         (Wife mentioned she had to take one
         tire to garage.)
         Filled with feeling of "more than I
         can cope with." So much anxiety at
         this point can hardly articulate
         clearly.
         Pt. made final decision as to
         whether to take this med. again.
         "Sometimes you say yes when you
         really mean no." Says episodes un-
         der drugs "haven't been pleasant at
         all. Each treatment leaves me more
         confused than before." Feels hope-
         less, without energy. "Energy comes
         from hope, don't you think?"

10:20   Pt. feels dizzy, buzzing in ears, difficulty getting breath. Can't verbalize. Shivering convulsively, teeth chattering. Says he's sorry but he can't stand it. Begs for something to ease tension. Obviously experiencing intense neuro. stress.

10:35   3¾ Sod. Amytal—20 mg. Meth. I.V.

10:45   "I'm all mixed up. Feel if I let myself drift I will die. Yet at the same time I know this is the effect of these drugs."

11:00   Pt. keeps squinting and rubbing face, as if trying to clear his thoughts. "I don't know why I consent to this. I don't like being under drugs. I hate the idea . . . madness to cure madness. This whole thing is mad. Last few weeks a

resis-   nightmare. How long have I been in
tance   this place anyway?" Admits feeling some hostility towards Dr. "This is more or less just another brain-washing procedure."
"This treatment . . . in effect it's an attempt to get me to accept and fit into a way of life that is it-self sick."
Dr.: "I don't give a darn what way of life you choose, as long as it makes you happy."
"But you yourself have accepted the dominant middle-class, materialist, anti-spiritual way, and you can't

help but communicate that, even when
you tell me to 'take any direction
I like.' You think your own life
doesn't matter? Sure, on a rational
level I can understand it. You've
had to make compromises. But on a
deeper level, I can't completely
forgive you, can't completely trust
you."
Dr.: "I never asked you to trust me,
Bob, just to trust yourself."
Distressed expression: "Oh God, why
do I have to see you as a whole person? Why can't I deal with people
impersonally?"

11:45   All kinds of hallucinations. "It's
hard to distinguish between what's
real and what's imaginary . . . who
couldn't honestly say that? . . . I
hear a bell. It's real, isn't it?"

12:05   Thinking about ther. again. "Yes,
I've seen things under this drug,
seen the roots of things. But it
hasn't changed anything, hasn't
helped." Grants possibility of Dr.'s
suggestion that reluctance to admit
improvement part of resistance to
ther. "But that in itself is an ob-
stacle, that idea . . . (tries to
say something, shakes his head, silent a moment) . . . your—well, your
glibness about what a cure's supposed to be like, that in itself is
a barrier."

Dr.: "Bob, you'd have made a good analyst."
"Sure, that's what they taught me, to analyze everything, tear everything apart. But never to put anything together . . ."

12:15   Lunch tray brought in. Pt. sits up to eat, takes a few bites and falls back in bed, buries face in pillow. Shakes head angrily to suggestion we feed him. Left alone for twenty minutes.

12:40   Pt. lying on back staring at ceiling. "Oh, what's the use of talk-
flight   ing!" Wishes he could go to sleep. "The only thing is to go to sleep."

1:05   Strong urge to urinate. Doesn't know if he can navigate to bathroom. Goes to toilet but could not urinate. Feeling strong sensations. "Impos-
block   sible to put into words . . . emergency situation . . . need to urinate but I can't." Irritated by my remarks. "All right, let's try to break the block. I wouldn't do this for the fun of it."
Dr.: "What would happen if you just let go and pee in bed?"
"I'm wet and cold."
"Anything else?"
"Maybe a certain fondling of that area."
"Does it also bring a fear of father?"

"I can't tell . . . yes, maybe."
Denies anxiety over wife touching
penis. Says recent impotence "just a
part of the whole existential anxiety."

1:35 Crisis past. Hearing aural hallucinations now "quite different from
the ones outside—airplane motors,
sirens." (These are actual sounds
from outside.)
Quiet.

2:05 "I seem to be going back to a period
when I could sleep without—" Suddenly, face brightening: "The whole
world is mother!" Laughs; drug has
made him admit one of Dr.'s postu-
lates. Childlike smile: "I've got a
very beautiful sensation of being
born without any cultural connec-
hallu- tions . . . only spiritual connec-
cina- tions . . . it's really quite an ex-
tion traordinary . . . everything is
right, everything being taken care
of . . . a mystical sense to everything . . . really beautiful . . .
I wish you could . . ."
Dr.: "Associations?"
"No associations . . . nothing different . . . everything mine, I'm
everything's . . . like waking up
for the first time."
Smile fades: "But the world's not
like that. The world's demanding."
Dr.: "In what way demanding?"
"Making sense out of it."

"Any idea why you feel this terrible
compulsion to make sense?"
"I don't know. Maybe because I
can't, I just can't, accept the
sense they make out of it."
"They?"
"People. Most people in this country. People like . . ."

pro-   "Like Mama and Papa perhaps?"
jec-   Nods; "People like them, people like
tion   . . . you." Looks up imploringly.
"Can one person create a whole new
world?"
Dr.: "A lot sure try."
"Oh, you mean psychotics."

2:55   Dr. away 30 min. Pt. says he returned to pre-anxiety level. "I
guess all I want is to go back to
the womb. I need help but the help
doesn't help . . . (mumbling,
barely audible) when you doubt
. . . even the things you look to
for help . . . need them, can't do
without them, but they are inade-

ambiv-   quate." Asked who, replies, "People,
alence   parents, doctors, drugs . . ."
"I know it isn't any real escape,
hiding. But I feel physically tired,
can you go along with that? You can
direct my thoughts if you want to."
Dr.: "If you feel up to it, perhaps
we could tackle that block in urina-
tion again."
Pt. is lying with eyes closed. Cannot or will not communicate.

3:30   Dr.: "Regression again?"
"Yes."
"To?"
"About six months, definite sexual
impressions . . . mother must be
manipulating—father is coming,
father is coming!" Face anguished,
both hands on lower abdomen. "Must
keep dry, must keep dry . . ."
Dr.: "Antagonism?"
"Too young for anger . . . can't understand why . . ." Interrupts Dr.'s
questions with "Leave me alone,
maybe I can make sense out of it."
Breathing heavily, whispers: "I
can't get my breath (repeats 3 x's)
. . . don't know why, I can't get
my breath." Looks at me in bowilder-
ment, as if expecting help. Whispering, only a few words audible.
"Can't . . . got to sleep . . .
can't get my breath" (2 x's). "Don't
keep my breath from me, please don't
keep my breath from me . . ."

hos-   "Who is keeping you from breathing?"
tility   "Too young . . . can't tell . . .
toward you . . . why are you keeping my
mo.   breath from me . . . my mother . . .
keeping my breath from me." Respira-
tions shallow, gasping, acts out
air hunger. Shakes head to question.
"Can't you let the adult you help
the baby?"

4:15   Long period of intense suffering.
Asks for "something to knock me

184

out." Says he wishes he'd never
been told he was toilet trained at
six months. Denies his mother actually cut off his breath. "I don't
hold that against her." Parents just
did what people in their class were
doing. Says he looked up subject in
old medical encyclopedia. Authorities recommended it. It was the
fashion thirty years ago. Accepts
as possibility: to submit to breathing = to release bowel and bladder.
Asks me to leave him alone to "fight
this out by myself."

5:00   Dr. returns to find Pt. has re-
        gressed further. "Real relaxation
        now . . . pleasant, not in sense of
        feeling good, in sense of no pain,
        no demands, everything being taken
        care of. No, I don't want you to
in   deliver me. I would resent your
utero   pulling me out of here, giving me
status an antidote . . . strange, very
        strange: I'm inside here and yet
        I'm there too—didn't you say that
        this stuff was isolated from the
        blood of schizophrenics?" Eyes
        close, grows non-communicative.
        Shakes head negatively to sugges-
        tion he eat his lunch.

5:40   Pt. is sitting up in bed. Reports
        steady buildup in tension. "I'm just
        a little irritated . . . feel some
        hostility toward you, but more to-

ward myself—for being so completely
dependent on you." Kicking at bed
with left foot: "Useless, this is
useless."

6:00   Pt. has become increasingly hostile.
Digging at self, digging at bed,
pulling at pillow. Annoyed with me
for saying things he's heard over
and over. "The point is, I just
can't believe in this, in the drugs,
or in shock either."
Dr.: (slightly annoyed himself). "Is
there nothing you can believe in,
Bob?"
"Nothing. I wish I could believe in
God but . . ."
"But . . . ?"
"But I can't."
"You mean God's inadequate too, like
the rest of us?"
Staring, eyes shining with tears:
"No . . . I am . . ."
Pt. has been quiet for several minutes. Is beginning to trace a large
plus sign onto bed (cross perhaps?).
Movements becoming more violent.
Angry slashes: "I want to rip it
up."
Ripping pillow now, biting, tearing
sheets: "I don't know why . . . just
can't—goddamn, you don't have to
write this down, do you?" Asked what
he is angry at, replies, pain,
everything that causes pain, at life
because it is so full of pain. Sob-

ag-
gres-
sive
re-
lease
bing, hysterical: "Shit on it . . .
just leave me be . . . no, you don't
have to lock me up again." Has begun
to throw food (cake) about bed.
"Don't know . . . what makes me do
this . . . depressed when I started
. . . all just to come back down to
this . . ." Throwing pieces of cake.
"Write down 'Futility, utter futility.' . . . put me back downstairs
if you want to, put me anywhere, I
don't care . . . don't care . . .
don't care . . ."
Violence has gradually subsided. Pt.
growing increasingly depressed.
"Let's just call it quits, O.K.?
. . . yes, I'm hungry, but no I
don't want to eat . . . yes, I want
to pee in bed, but no I don't. Yes,
I want to be well, but I don't . . .
No, you don't have to put me in restraints or force-feed me. Oh shit,
oh God, what a mess!" Pt. shivering,
sobbing, shuddering as if with
chills. Knees drawn to chest,
foetal posture. Voice has become
practically inaudible. ". . . back
downstairs . . . can't take any more
. . . more than I can take . . .
real psychotic state . . . sorry

total
with-
drawal
for myself, that's all . . . anything to comfort me . . ." Pt. has
become totally withdrawn. No focus.
Agitation, hostility, being entirely
repressed. No motor response.

6:35   50 mg. Thorazine, . . . 3 gr. Sod.
Nemb. I.V.

7:00   Pt. able to verbalize once more.
"Need a little ego to survive this
stuff . . . don't think I was up to
this Rx . . ."

8:05   Night nurse in to relieve. Pt. had
sandwich and glass of milk. States
he feels better.

Better. Much, much better. Dr. Hoerchner said this morning he feels very encouraged about the fine progress I've been making. He said I would probably be ready to go home for good in another week or ten days. He just wants to give me two or three more of these treatments first. I am scheduled for one any minute now.

Actually I feel well enough to leave now. But Dr. Hoerchner thinks I should wait and I don't mind. I don't let every little thing upset me like I used to. I feel very calm and detached about everything. Not a bad feeling. Maybe I shouldn't even call it a feeling at all. It's more a freedom from worrying. I couldn't worry if I wanted to. And I don't want to. Worrying is a waste of time. I wouldn't have had to come here in the first place if I hadn't worried so much.

It's the effect of the treatments, Dr. Hoerchner says. I think I've had six of them, but Dr. Hoerchner says nine and I take his word for it. Because I can't remember things like that too well. This is perfectly normal, Dr. Hoerchner says. Another effect of the treatments. It will wear off in a few weeks, he says.

Still, it's sort of funny. I can remember things pretty well up until about Christmas time. I can remember the trip we took to Guaymas over Christmas vacation. But after that it gets fuzzy. I know I began getting very depressed. I must have been pretty bad because they tell me they had to keep me downstairs in the locked ward for almost two weeks. I can't remember anything about that and I'm glad I can't. It must have been a nightmare. I sort of remember the sessions under the new drug Lysergic Acid-D. Dr. Hoerchner says he's going to go over his notes with me when we start intensive psychotherapy. He says I'll be surprised at what I said and did. But I feel no connection with any of that now. Sometimes I try to figure out what I got so depressed about and can't understand it. I had a nice family, a good job, three months off in the summer. Last Sunday Anne and the children came and took me for a ride along the Rio Grande. I kept asking them all kinds of silly questions like "What was the date I stopped teaching? When did I write to so-and-so? Did you come last week or two weeks ago? Is this a new shirt? Did you just buy it or have I had it a long time? What grade is David in now? When's your birthday, Cassie?" The children thought it was a new game. "Oh Daddy, don't act so stu-pid!" They laughed and had fun. What sweet children they are.

I wish I could be home now instead of here. I wish I didn't need any more of these treatments. But Dr. Hoerchner says he wants to complete the series and he knows better. He is a very fine doctor and a good human being too. I am very grateful for all he's doing for me. I was certainly lucky that I got him and not Dr. Mayer, the chief psychiatrist. I dread to think what would have happened. Mayer is a real phony.

Speak of the devil. There he goes now, down the hall, looking in at me, sniffing as if he's disappointed I don't belong to him. He really does look like the devil, like Mephistopheles in that opera. He's got that little trimmed goatee, which I'm sure he grew to make him look like Dr. Freud and which really impresses all these rich provincials. He even talks with a fake accent. But Freud was handsome and honest-looking. Mayer is ugly and dishonest-looking. And the strange thing is, he's got a very good reputation. He cures people. Of course most of his patients are rich women. He works wonders with them, most of them. I watch them and listen to them in the dining room, all the silly talk. "Yes, Doctor. More cornflakes, Doctor?" He eats breakfast with us sometimes and always looks angry. They love him. Because he scares them, I think. Which must be what they are dying for, a strong hand. Their husbands—I've seen a few—must be too easy to manage. Once Dr. Hoerchner and I were discussing Dr. Mayer. I don't think they get along too well—Dr. Hoerchner called him Herr Sigmoid Sphincter. Dr. Hoerchner says lots of patients are big babies who want mothers, married to big babies who want fathers. Mayer provides the dominant male, the stern father, the cruel lover. While he's got them they're not anxious. I thank God he hasn't got me.

But he's got poor Aguero though. That's probably where he's going now, to give Aguero his treatment. Aguero is in room five, through the bathroom from me. I think he was downstairs about the same time I was. I was talking to him this morning for the first time. In Spanish because he doesn't understand English. He was telling me about his big fancy house in Chihuahua, his family and servants. He was in a car wreck but doesn't remember anything about that. He doesn't even seem to wonder about what happened to knock out most of his teeth and break his leg and leave that huge scar on his head. I don't know whether it's because of the shock or the shock treatments.

But I know his story. Sister Josepha was talking about it yesterday. He was a businessman in Chihuahua and he made a lot of money in some way. Maybe he won the national lottery. Anyway, he decided to take his family for a big vacation up to the States. He was on his way home at night when his car missed a curve on La Bajada Hill, between here and Santa Fe. He was going eighty-five. His wife, his mother and three of his four children were killed. He barely pulled through himself. But he got a big insurance payment and that's how he could afford to be sent here after the regular hospital released him. For mental treatment. Because Sister says that in spite of that terrible cut on his head there wasn't any brain damage. It was all psychological, due to shock.

So that's why they've been giving him shock treatments. They must be helping him, or else they would still have him locked up downstairs. Still, I don't think he's got any idea what's going on, where he is, or why. He doesn't know anything about mental illness. I don't think they have so much of it in Mexico.

Yes, I was right, though. There's Mayer in his room now. The doors through the bathroom are half open. And there's that big Sister Thomasina and that orderly from downstairs, the young one. Poor Aguero, he's asking them questions a mile a minute in Spanish and they're talking to him in English. God, is he scared of them. They're setting up the black box on the table by the bed. They must have given him pills to quiet him down, but still he's trying to put up a fight, kicking at them with his good leg and yelling. He sounds like a goat when they hoist it up by its hind leg to cut its throat. I guess he can't remember the other treatments, that EST doesn't hurt. Because he's had a lot of them already. He's just hysterical, I guess. They're wrestling him down, the three of them, leaning on him, slipping the restraints over his wrists, and he's squirming and bellowing with his mouth stretched wide open. What an awful-looking hole with half the teeth white and perfect and the other half gone. Oh, now they see me looking. They're closing the door. I'm glad they did. But still I can hear him loud, loud. "Ay, ay, ay, ay, ay—!" There, it's stopped, like a radio switched off.

The door to the bathroom is open again. Mayer comes in to wash his hands. Behind him I can see a part of Aguero's body on the bed. He's unconscious, but the upper half is heaving and flopping and snorting. It sounds like the only thing his body cares about now is getting air, air, air! It sounds like a leaky bicycle pump.

My turn next.

I feel a little scared. I don't know why, but I'm beginning to be a little afraid of these treatments. Funny, because you don't feel any pain or anything. Just zzzzt! and instant oblivion, that's all, deeper than sleep, deeper than anesthesia. And it's not dangerous either, Dr. Hoerchner says. Some patients have had dozens and dozens with no harmful effects. Oh, you might get a strained back muscle or a bitten cheek, or as happened to me once, a burn on my forehead from the electrodes. And no denying they do help. They have helped me. Still there's something awful about them, the idea. I'm lucky they're only going to give me one or two more. And I'm lucky it's Hoerchner, not Mayer, who gives them to me.

Here they come, through the bathroom. It's always the same team, Sister Thomasina and the young orderly. The "shock troops," the patients call them. They're wheeling the black box on the little white table up to my bed. I lie back down. I want to cooperate. I wish I could smile or say something, but I can't. I guess I'm not as calm and detached as I thought. Besides I just don't like either one of them very much. I can feel it, the fear, like some animal waking up inside me, moving around, disturbing things. I'm trying to relax, but instead I can only tighten up, make my hands into fists so they won't tremble. I'm afraid of them, both of them. The young orderly, he's a smarty-pants and a sadist. He likes to do this. And Sister Thomasina, she just doesn't care, she's stopped being human, somehow. A hard-boiled medical virgin who lost her spiritual reasons long ago and just goes on working here because she's working here already and has to work someplace. I don't think she's ever known any real joy. No surrender, either to a lover or to Jesus. Just to the force of circumstances. She's caught in the ice of resentful and barren service and lost her will or capacity to get loose. I feel sorry for her. But right now I don't feel sorry for her. I feel afraid of her.

Here comes Dr. Hoerchner, through the other door. A quick smile, that's all. No words. When he gives EST he's all business. He's wheeling the black box closer to the bed and checking the dials. It looks like one of those arc-welders, and in a way that's just what it is. He explained the whole thing to me once. He's going to shoot 110 volts at 950 milliamps through my brain now for maybe half a second. I sort of wish I hadn't asked him.

Sister Thomasina and the orderly have put me in the sheet restraint so that my arms are bound to my body. Dr. Hoerchner is rubbing the salve on my temples and clips the electrodes onto my head. I can smell, smell everything, like a dog or something. This is another strange effect of the treatments— you can smell like a bloodhound. I smell the salt in the salve, the wrapped cigars in Dr. Hoerchner's pocket, the aftershave on his face, the sweat from Sister Thomasina's armpits, the detergent on the sheets, the wax and disinfectant on the floor, the lamb roasting in the kitchen, the sour metal and smoky electricity in the black box, the cleaning fluid on the doctor's cuffs, the silver on his watchband, the antiseptic soap on his hands.

Sister Thomasina is standing right against my chest. She's got one hand on my shoulder and the other on my forearm, and she's leaning forward over the bed so that her weight is pressing down on me. And she's a heft. Her bosoms feel like they're filled with sand. On the other side, a little lower down, the orderly is doing the same thing.

Dr. Hoerchner gives that little sigh, the one he always gives at this moment. I feel a little sorry for him. It must be harder to give these treatments than to get them. I would hate to start off each day giving ten or twenty of them. He's stuffing the bandage roll into my mouth now so that when I have my fit I won't swallow my tongue or bite it off. I taste the soapy skin of his fingers and feel the little ridges on my tongue. And now, even before it happens, I feel the electricity streak down through my body and my hands are grabbing the meat of my thighs under the sheet and pinching as hard as they can.

Through his glasses his eyes exchange a glance with mine—an eye conversation which says instantly what there are no words to say. I'm watching the left corner of his mouth because any second now it's going to give that little twitch which means the—

I am writing this autobiographical sketch at the suggestion of my physician, Dr. Frank Hoerchner. Because I have recently undergone an extensive series of electroshock therapy, I am unable to recall many of the details of my life. But I will try. I was born on August 26, 1925, in New York, the second of two children. My father was a successful corporation lawyer and my mother was a successful corporation lawyer's wife. They were fairly well off but not wealthy. One female servant. I was not breast-fed. I was toilet trained, I am told, at six months. My therapy has brought out that this early training plus a strong oedipal conflict was a major factor in my later emotional problems. My older brother and I fought a lot as children. Probably he was jealous, since I was always the favorite child. He was killed in the war. When I was five, my family moved to the suburbs and I attended public schools in Westchester County until the ninth grade, when I was sent to Devonshire Academy in Massachusetts, considered one of the finest prep schools in the country. There I was editor of the paper, at the top of my class in scholarship, and voted one of the most likely to succeed. There also I suffered from a moderate case of acne and masturbated. During my final year my best friend tried to engage me in a homosexual liaison which I rejected at the cost of his friendship. In 1942 I entered Yale University, majoring in physics. But I found myself strangely without interest in my studies and devoted most of my energies to pursuing and being pursued by girls. Although I had a deferment because my studies were considered vital to the national interest, my low marks caused me to be drafted into the Army in 1943. I saw considerable infantry combat in Europe in World War II. The war taught me much more than Yale, mainly to question social values I had previously not thought much about. On my discharge, however, I returned to Yale, mainly because I could think of nothing better to do. As before, my main course of study was girls, together with bull sessions on politics, psychology, and philosophy. But I managed to receive my degree in Social Psychology (whatever that means) in 1948. After graduating, I went to work on the editorial staff of a large New York newspaper. In 1949 I married a girl from Ohio, Anne Clark, whom I met while she was a student at Columbia. For several years we worked and took courses and made love in New York City. During this time also my inner conflicts began to catch up with me. Finally in 1952 we left the city for good and settled in New Mexico, where I had spent a vacation as a child. We have lived here since, with a few intervals in San Francisco. I have worked at a variety of jobs such as social worker, hospital worker, and for the last two years as a high school teacher in the small Spanish-American village of Llano, New Mexico. We have recently moved to Albuquerque in order to be nearer Dr. Hoerchner. Beginning next week I shall be employed as a day laborer for Mr. Harry Howell, a local contractor. My wife and I have two children, David, 8, and Cassandra, 3.

Since adolescence I have been subject to periods of restlessness, dissatisfaction, anxiety and depression, a sense that "something" was not "right." I have never been able to decide on the cause, whether it was personal, due to flaws in my own character, whether I was just "sick" or "weak," whether it grew out of my childhood history and family, whether it was a result of the spiritually empty and shallow nature of the society or social class I was born into, or whether it was in reaction to a fundamental Buddha-like confrontation with the set-up nature has provided for human existence, the "unfinished" quality of human consciousness and the horrors that go along with finding yourself alive in flesh. The pressure of this unhappiness has made me "study" and "experiment" at various times with such things as psychology, sociology, politics, philosophy, and most recently, religion, attempting to find answers, or rather, to find peace. Each of them gave different, often contradictory, views and insights, and in the end only increased my confusion and sense of lostness. Until recently, however, I had always managed to avoid actually breaking down under the stress, usually by a kind of spastic change in my life-situation, moving to another place, quitting or changing or getting a job. But this spring fate finally caught up with me. I cannot now recall the details of my breakdown. I do remember that my energy and interest in teaching seemed to drain out of me and it required more and more effort just to keep level with my classes. For a time I managed to bluff my way through, hoping that the condition would lift and that I could last it out at least until the end of the term. But this proved impossible. On April 7th, 1958, I committed myself to Bethlehem Sanatorium. During my seven weeks there, I received extensive therapy of many kinds under the supervision of Dr. Hoerchner. These included LSD, Sodium Amytal and other drugs, and about a dozen electroshock treatments. Since my release from the hospital, I have continued to see Dr. Hoerchner twice a week as an outpatient. I feel that my psychotherapy has helped me a great deal and that I have gained many valuable insights into the subconscious causes of my illness. I am hopeful that this new understanding will enable me to handle future stress situations and maintain a normal degree of stability and productivity from now on.

"Independence Day," July 4

Haven't written in this notebook, I see, for three full months, since last April. I'm not even going to try to sum up what's happened in the interval. Simply that the bottom fell out of my life. I broke down and spent seven weeks in a mental hospital. They gave me everything in the book. Luckily my psychiatrist turned out to be a good man. Saw him for the last time yesterday. Says I don't need him any more. Hope to God he's right.

For the past three weeks have been working as a laborer. Hot, hard, mindless work, focused relentlessly on the daily five o'clock beer. Feel strong, brown, etc., a body-confidence that carries over (to a certain extent) into the emotional life. Like the army. Haven't really thought about this fall. Haven't even contacted the school superintendent. Don't feel up to it yet. Still living day by day, beer by beer.

A few weeks ago Dr. Hoerchner lent me a book to read: *The Disastrous Death Complex*, by a Dr. Korngold, M.D., Ph.D., etc. A leading authority. Said he was curious to know what I thought of it. At first I was very stimulated and impressed. Very erudite man—432-title bibliography, footnotes, statistics all over the place. Korngold claims we can now pinpoint the "Anxieties" as the real demons that torment mankind, and the "Satan" of them all is Death Anxiety. Everybody lives in continual dread of his own impending mutilation and death, sometimes consciously, always unconsciously. This horror often gets pathological, and the prime agent of this "Disastrous Death Complex" is (but of course) our own mothers. As infants, even as incomplete embryos, we were acutely aware, as she wasn't, of her filicidal impulses, her unconscious desire to mutilate and destroy us . . . and this from the "only other" in our world, the one whom we must depend on utterly for life itself! Hence, naturally, the Disastrous Death Complex—universal, since even the immaculately conceived had mothers. All this Korngold documents impressively with case histories and research statistics, and submits further that all anxieties stem from this original death anxiety, and this anxiety is the real cause behind war, racism, etc.—all man's evil.

Who can deal with it? Psychiatry. Why? Because, says Dr. Korngold, "Psychiatry has discovered that anxiety is of inter-personal origin and can be cured."

Cured. Cured of anxiety. It made me think not only of the Garden before the Fall, but also of the cadre-rooms at Ausch-witz. Still I was fascinated, as I guess Hoerchner knew I'd be, by the subject and by the very intelligent and earnest way Korngold was approaching it. And I wanted to find out where this leading authority was leading us, what he had to say about how we should face mutilation and death, since, as he readily admitted, even the most brilliant program of psychotherapy can't keep any of us from undergoing either one.

Finally, on page 263, he gets to it.

"Let us recognize our human situation for what it is. Science has amassed overwhelming evidence to show that man's life has no intrinsic meaning or purpose. Man has arrived where he is through a fortuitous 'throw of the dice,' and according to mathematical laws of permutation and combination. Further, man must confront the inevitability of personal disaster, and the probability, bordering on certainty, that death means total annihilation."

And to deal with this appalling prospect he recommends . . . that we be brave.

"I may say that I regard courage as the only true positive at-titude. Not the courage to be in spite of non-being, but the courage to master the anxiety of disastrous death. This re-quires courage to face its true meaning (above). Religious faith, incidentally, offers no true courage. It is precisely the lack of courage that creates the need for religion . . ."

Here I dropped out of the course. Professor Korngold didn't need all that learning, all those footnotes and statistics, that 432-title bibliography, to tell me that.

But the book upset me. What can you say to people like this who research so earnestly into everything but their own hearts? Didn't Pilate ask "What is truth?" while looking truth full in the face? Mohammed said somewhere, "There goes a jackass loaded down with books." But who was Mohammed? A paranoid, a nut.

Still, no two ways about it, there seem to be two ways about it: Kierkegaard's "to find the one thing needed," or to pile higher the Tower of Data. The spirit in a child or fruit tree, or the Ultimate Computer. No doubt which way is on top now. But somehow I feel—I don't know why—the pendulum is about to swing. All the latest news about space exploration, for example, is beginning to have a curiously antiquated ring.

But who am I to argue? Feeling the need to find somebody big enough to stand up to this famous doctor and present the case for the other side, I looked up my favorite lawyer and found this:

On life's meaning and meaninglessness. "What I want to achieve, what I have been pining and striving to achieve these thirty years, is self-realization, to see God face-to-face, attain liberation. I live and move and have my being in pursuit of this goal. All I do by way of speaking and writing and all my ventures in the political field are directed to this same end."

On mental illness. "Prayer has been the saving of my life. Without it I should have been a lunatic long ago."

Would Korngold or Hoerchner understand what he meant by "prayer"? Or, for that matter, by "lunatic"?

But now to "disastrous death and mutilation." The lawyer had even more reason, in his life circumstances, to be concerned about these than most of us. The way he looked at it, "God saves me as long as He wants me in this body. The moment His wants are satisfied, no precautions on my part will save me."

And he got a chance to practice what he preached. History records him raising his hands and crying out God's name as the bullets tore the life from his heart. Religious faith, the need for which stems from a lack of courage.

But the scientific mind likes the measurable. So what were the measurable results of the life of this lawyer whose first concern was liberating himself? His most famous by-product was liberating his country—a fifth of the world's population—from colonial domination. His most important was to winch one notch higher—and in times like ours!—what can be meant by the word "man."

I had my rebuttal all nicely prepared for Hoerchner yesterday. But strangely, when I handed him back his book, and he looked at me and asked, "Well, so what did you think of it?" all I could say was: "If I believed this I'd wish I were dead."

13

"SIT DOWN," HOERCHNER SAID, "sit down, sit down . . ."

Saying which, the doctor himself stood up and began to work his way around the desk and closer, talking as he came. "Gracious me, who ever heard of such a fuss about a little EST? My goodness, anybody'd think we were going to hurt you. And you know that's not true at all. You know that in a little while, a very little while, Bobby's going to be feeling better, much, much better. So come on and sit down, sit down, my friend, and let's talk this whole thing over sensibly, you and I."

But he didn't sit down. Instead he backed away, kept backing away, slowly, just as slowly as the doctor advanced on him, maintaining the gap, watching the arms that were speaking to him too, in semaphore, the left one extended at forty-five degrees, pointing to the soft seat of the patient's chair, the right one reaching out toward him, palm lifted and fingers spread in the gentle cup of benediction. It was this right hand he fixed on, this vanguard that wished to soothe, to bless, to canopy him, that he stared at and retreated from.

"No . . . no—"

The door pressed flat and hard against his back. The cool hard ball slipped into the socket of his hand, and as he grasped it Hoerchner came to a stop, let both arms fall to his side, and smiled. Like a mother, just like a mother.

"Now now, come come come . . . what's my boy so darn upset about, hmm? Tell me, tell me all about it." Or was it Mama? Tell Mama all about it?

The doorknob, cool polished metal egg in his palm, dynamic with potential as the dial of a safe, the grip of a pistol.

"Listen, Bob, I want to tell you something. If you feel like running away, I won't chase after you. I'm not a policeman. But I do think that running away now would be a foolish thing to do, a very foolish thing to do. And, in the condition you're in, a dangerous thing to do as well, a very dangerous thing to do . . ."

The voice reached him as the low hypnotic hum of a well-tuned machine. The reason, the health, the peace of a machine. The sanity of a machine which, according to one college definition of sanity, was capable of holding down a job.

He saw the doctor turn, walk back to his desk, sit down and look up at him again, calmly, with his easy, tired smile.

"I mean, really, don't you think so too? You've got intelligence, use your intelligence. Doesn't your intelligence agree that the intelligent thing to do right now is to sit back down and let me help you slip out from under that awful load that's crushing you, shift some of the weight onto me? Two backs are better than one, aren't they? Use your intelligence. Think about it."

Think about it! There was no thinking about it. What there was was an exquisite sense of teetering, of knife-edge balance that couldn't last. Now, whatever he does now, the slightest thing, the most trivial movement, word, will tip it. His breathing stopped as he drew a tighter bead on the man behind the desk.

Hoerchner said nothing more. He merely shifted his head slightly to the left. From the panes of his glasses twin points of light flared like a pair of prison searchlights.

His hand squeezed metal. The door behind him gave instant way, and he fell backwards through it.

"Oh, Doctor, please—oh, dear!" His body knocked the body of the nun aside as it plummeted into the recreation room. He did not see her or the room, merely a cloudy blankness upon which a set of lines immediately superimposed itself, a map, a floor plan of the route from here to there, from where he stood now to where his car stood now, with a heavy line that led through the hallway, through the admissions office, around the hedges, trees and buildings, to the parking lot.

"Bob? . . . oh, Bob? . . ."

He began to pace it, the line that lay in front of him, aware of nothing and no one extraneous, straight forward first, then a sharp left oblique, past Sister Consolata's desk, through the beam of the Virgin's compassion, and out into the sudden sunlight. None of which slowed him. He followed the wide curve, hearing the sound of his footsteps as they altered from wood to concrete to dry leaves to lawn to gravel. Nothing intercepted him, nothing obstructed him. And there, abruptly, was the car. He climbed in, started the motor and continued his moving. Around the looping driveway, down the slope of Bethlehem's hillock, out through the twin stuccoed pillars that supported the iron entry gate. On momentum alone, because the map was gone.

STOP. The looming command, red, octagonal, unequivocal. He stopped. Ahead a graded gravel road. To the left the city, home, where he'd come from, back. To the right the desert, empty, away.

Without hesitation he turned—to the right. As if he knew precisely where he was going. But he did not. No new map, no new route to follow, no new destination had come to replace the other. But no new anxiety either. He was heading somewhere, he felt that. And he was on his way there now. He would get there, wherever it was, without detours or delays.

Relief. He had made his last choice. From here on no further decisions would be required of him. Everything was being decided for him. It almost seemed as if the old car itself had been issued explicit instructions, for whenever a crossroad or other decision-point arrived, the decision came along with it, instantly and automatically. Right, left, straight ahead, slow, stop, brake, clutch—like guiding a train through pre-set switches.

STOP. Again the command, the bright red circle. The car stopped. Out in front an important road, four lanes, east-west. To the west the main arteries of Second and Fourth streets hissed with colored corpuscles being pumped to and from the heart of the city. To the east, and without warning, a gargantuan rock seemed to come crashing in through the safety glass: Sandia Peak. As he recognized it, the fright eased out of his shock and left a kind of awe. In the gray haze of morning, the great granite mountain seemed to be floating with the ponderous buoyancy of a basking whale.

GO. The light glared green. The cross-traffic halted for him and he turned—to the right, the east, the mountain.

The entire windshield filled with mountain. Dry, remote, mummy-brown, a great fractured earthbone that punctured a mile up through the desert's skin, its splintered ridges silhouetted high against the colorless sky. And as he looked at it the mountain seemed suddenly to take note of him, to return his look. He knew now where he was going.

But the road caught him in a loop then, a cloverleaf that spun him around and threw him out onto the new Santa Fe freeway, heading north and no longer toward the mountain. Instinctively he slowed.

SLOW TRAFFIC KEEP RIGHT.

He kept right. A steel fence had interposed itself between the highway and the mountain, and the car prowled along it, searching for weak points. This kind of fence would have none. Beyond, running parallel, he saw the former road, narrow, deteriorated, but still serviceable. How to get through to it? Seemingly he was trapped by this fence that rolled on relentlessly mile after mile, fed by an inexhaustible output of new steel. Still he felt no anxiety. He waited for a sign.

EXIT: ACCESS ROAD.

He exited and began driving back along the narrow bumpy access road. Back across the fence the highway traffic sizzled north and south like an artillery duel. He kept his eyes on the old road, still looking for a sign.

When the sign came, he almost missed noticing it, since it was no more than a small weathered board, sawn into a crude arrow and nailed to a low stake that had been knocked so out of vertical that it pointed over the mountain entirely and into the sky, though still generally eastward. The painted letters were so mud splattered and peeled he had to stop the car in order to make out what it said:

"JUAN TABO."

Juan Tabo? Who and what was that? Somebody's ranch? He looked about and took his bearings, startled by what he saw. To the left a new wall of chain link fencing had sprung up, making the road a passage between fences. Within the steel mesh he saw a lawn as electrically green and wet as an Irish cow pasture, a perfect square of encaged emerald turf, as if a giant block of maritime sod had been dug out and inlaid like a jewel in the discolored wastes of the great American desert. A mirage. But the mirage had a sign.

SANDIA MEMORY GARDENS—Perpetual Care.

Perpetual care?—oh, of course, a cemetery. And evidently a brand new one, because as yet hardly a footstone punctuated that vividly glowing carpet. But in the center, in white marble robes, the Lord was already sitting and waiting for guests with the welcoming smile of a professional host. The Lord of hosts.

This wasn't all. A few feet away from the corner of the cemetery fence, across a narrow dirt alley, another mirroring fence-corner took up. This, he saw, belonged to another block of enterprise set into the wilderness. In size this second square looked like a twin to the first, but clearly it serviced a lesser species. Within it, lying in ragged rows, were hundreds of bodies and chassis, all of them more or less stripped and mutilated, and to the rear a great pyre of them was smoking wanly. For these bodies not merely had no grassy plush been imported, but every scraggly clump of native weed had been scraped away. In the center of this charnel field a wooden shack stood glittering with hubcaps and grills like a cannibal's hut with skulls and thighbones. And onto the steep-sloping roof had been painted its sign:

SANDIA WRECKERS—USED PARTS.

Used parts . . . perpetual care. The signs looked new and vigorous, both of them, the junkyard's a rowdy splash of red and white enamel, all set for the swift wheel-and-deal, the graveyard's cast into the solemnity of immortal bronze, duly licenced to contract from everlasting unto everlasting. And down here, below the right fender, askew, and on its last leg, the crude wooden arrow that pointed between and above, to the sky over Sandia Peak, voicing its feeble and strange "Juan Tabo."

The narrow passageway walled with galvanized steel led eastward between the two compounds and emerged as a faint rutted trail that wandered and wavered and got lost in the desert flats beyond. He turned and entered it. The wrecking yard accompanied him for only a few hundred feet. The car bodies became progressively more battered and broken, and finally there came a great machine that was crunching them, one per bite, into flat portable sheets of rusty steel. The cemetery carried on a little farther, though the green sward terminated halfway back, leaving the dead and naked clay in the rear to await resurrection via projected deaths. But the fences gave out and again the desert was as it had been.

The road was bad. Obviously it was no longer being used, superseded by a new one somewhere else. It heaved the car back and forth inhospitably among the hardened ruts of former muds. To both sides the plain was a dull gray with a mold-like fuzz of atrophied sage, so endlessly brutalized by wind and drought it seemed to have cringed into a limbo between living and dying.

He drove. Feet worked pedals, hands worked steering wheel and gear lever. Beyond this nothing, for nothing was being asked. Again, as under LSD, that state Hoerchner had labeled regression, the conviction that "everything was being taken care of." And within this caul his weary mind rested from what had been and for what, whatever, was about to be.

From the valley the broad semi-arid expanse leading to the mountain had looked level and even, with the great umber rock jutting up perpendicularly through the surface; now it was turning out to be a choppy sea of petrified waves and trenches. The complaining whine of the engine testified to a steady climb, and the rearview mirror backed it up. Already the highway, the populated valley, the cottonwood and willow groves that edged the river, even the small hirsute mound of Bethlehem itself, lay hundreds of feet below him, fading and losing reality in the swirling wake of car dust. And here the sagebrush had begun to stand up for itself, tall—a clear water blue, with dark hulls of juniper and full-rigged chollas floating in it here and there. The road was an all-but-healed scar, studded with rocks, pocked with hollows and sand bars to be negotiated in low gear. The shoreline of foothills advanced. In the distance he could make out the toy yellow machines of the land developers, scratching and tugging at a fold in the mountainside with the tiny industry of dung beetles. The future "Sandia Pines Estates," no doubt. Thousands of feet above, atop the crest, two watch rubies glimmered on the filigree of the television towers. The impressions slid over the glass surface of his vision.

To drive, that was all, to keep driving.

Which itself was becoming close to impossible. The road was barely identifiable (to the right he caught glimpses now and then of the real road, the sleek new ribbon of blacktop). Again and again the arroyo sands all but trapped him, and sudden rocks and holes wrenched the steering wheel from his grasp and bounced his head to the car roof. But the car kept inching ahead somehow, grunting and whining, forward and upward into the main body of the mountain.

It had begun to creep now into a deep and wide canyon between two massive escarpments that came tapering down from above like a pair of enormous parted legs. Their towering mass walled away the sights of civilization, and he could no longer see either the valley behind or the summit ahead for the outcroppings of stone. For these great open thighs enclosed a world of rock. Titanic slabs, shelves, fangs, columns, spheres of it, jutted, hung, leaned, balanced overhead, and on all sides the ground was strewn with huge broken chunks of mountain. In among them grew trees, a few yellow cottonwoods, a kind of low bushy oak with grayish, hollylike leaves and, increasingly, tall straight-trunked pines. Desert had given way to forest.

"CIBOLA NATIONAL FOREST."

The sign was of Forest Service varnished logs, ahead across a steel Forest Service cattleguard. Beyond it the dying road revived suddenly into graveled and graded Forest Service normalcy.

"Juan Tabo Recreation Area →"

The smaller sign's arrow pointed deeper and steeper into the canyon. Several times he read it over, half aloud, his lips slowly forming the syllables, like a semi-literate. "Juan Ta bo Re cre a tion A rc a . . . Re creation Area" before he turned to the right and followed its direction.

The road now snaked adroitly upwards between boulders and pines, wriggling toward the wooded obscurity of the crotch where the great rock thighs joined the body of the mountain. But squirm as it might, the obstacles proved too much for it. It petered out into a narrow foot-trail impassable to cars.

Steel scraped rock with a loud screech. A hard terminal jolt, and all motion ceased. End of the line.

Here . . .

He sat listening as the hot motor caught its breath with the soft companionable panting of a hound. His fingers touched the ignition key and hesitated. His toes even ladled out a few more swallows of fresh gas. Then, as the car lapped in noisy pleasure, he gave the key a leftward twist. The car, with the final incredulous shudder of the murdered, fell silent. His own body took up the same shudder as a swift knife of terror stabbed into it.

He stared through the windshield at the rock that marked the end of fleeing, a lump of granite larger than the car itself. Two lumps actually, since the boulder had been split open by the driving force of a ponderosa pine, whose orange-barked shaft thrust up thick and straight between them, a monster sprout between its cotyledons. His eyes, drifting gradually upward along the trunk a hundred feet into the dark nest of branches and needles, suddenly shut tight. Like some giant inhuffing breath he heard the word: *Now!*

Instantly a great bell jar of silence was set down upon the world, and in that environing silence he sat sightless, motionless, all but breathless, listening, only listening. And when, after a while, he began to hear things in that silence, they came not as sounds but as the negatives of sounds, the hollows that sound displaces, not additions but further subtractions, the decrease that, in vacuum and silence, increases.

A very faint, very high shrilling first, joined at once by a very faint but very low reverberating, the one just above, the other just below the range of normal human hearing. Again a stab of terror. It made him seek protection in labels. The high ringing—that must be insects, millions of tiny legs and wings and antennae; and the other—the other was just the voice of inorganic natural processes, the frictions of air against mountain, of earth and sky rubbing one another, solid against gas, energy in one phase meeting energy in a different phase, energy speaking to energy.

He gave up labeling and sat rigid with attention, eyes shut, ears open wide. The resonating grew steadily louder, but still with that uncanny reverse loudness, so that instead of diminishing the silence it intensified it more and more, endowed it not merely with a voice but with a will, a presence, brought it to a life that was terrible in its power and endlessness. A life that had already lived forever and would live on forevermore.

He still did not stir, could not. But his eyes opened and tried to look around. And here, too, he felt that awesome sense of reversal. He looked out with negative sight. Instead of seeing he felt himself seen, being looked into, through his own eyes and from every direction. Rocks, trees, sky, sun, all seemed to be scrutinizing him. The tables had turned. Subject and object had switched roles. The initiative had been seized by the inanimate and insensate, passive, impassive nature. A life was examining him now, a life which to his human life had always been unlife, a background, but one which had now come alive, or rather revealed itself to him in its measureless and timeless livingness, and his own petty life was laughable by comparison. To one side a set of mighty granite pillars loomed hundreds of feet above him, ruins which had never supported any architraves, but which had served to perfection in the architectonic task assigned them and were serving it still. High on the body of the mountain, dark jagged wounds gouged by ten million seasons of soft scant rains laid bare the heartrock, liquid patiently conquering solid. Energy at play, at work, with energy in an unending unbeginning creative tussling that left all as it was, that destroyed nothing, that added nothing. Not a fraction of an atom, not a fraction of a second, had been gained or lost by this life. A life without an opposite . . .

A life without a death!

And within this life he sat, in his man-life, alone in his man-life, in the frail lukewarm flower whose opposite and enemy and implacable destination was the killing freeze of death. Alone, the sole speck of man-life within this rock world dubbed Juan Tabo Recreation Area, he waited in his vulnerability, while around, beneath, above him, earth and air held murmuring council, as if to decide what to do with him.

But his fear, that was past. Not the slightest apprehension remained. He rested in the spent patience of creatures who know they have been caught once and for all beyond escape. And now, unlike an hour ago, when he sat in that soft leatherette chair, there was no dissenting voice. He felt only awe and respect for the final authority of what held him now. If this was madness, let it come. If this was dying, let it come. It was right, it had to be. His struggle and his wish to struggle both were over. He was at ease. "Thy will be done." He neither thought it as a thought nor felt it as an emotion. With a literality, an actuality, inconceivable before, it took him over.

In the passivity of defeat he waited in a kind of fearless peace he had never before experienced. And no sooner had the old set of feelings finally ceased to flow than a new and very different kind of feeling began to trickle into him. But such feelings—who has the words to describe such feelings? It was life, life that was beginning to redescend, to re-penetrate. But not his man-life renewing itself. Not old life. New life, the one that embraced far more than just his mammalian species or himself. His personal life, that drop-let of liquid sentience, held together by a momentary sur-face tension, of that he had lost awareness. The thirty-three-year trail that led to this instant was effaced, gone. Name, age, sex, race—gone. Knowledge about, language to describe —gone. He wouldn't have understood a question in English. Bob was gone. Yet *he* was not gone. He was conscious, alive, becoming more and more so. But not as himself, and not as a human being. This was life beyond definitions, life without life span. It was rock-life, with a rock's utter assurance of being, of being within being, of faithful conformation to being, beyond all fears, all possibilities, of non-being or cessation or deviation from being. The life that men, himself among them, had always thought of as non-life. And this new consciousness was not what men, himself among them, had always called consciousness, not the instreaming of agitations, not the patternless tickertape of inflowing sensations and images and attractions and repulsions and partial isolated re-lationships and contexts, not—

14

"NOT . . ."

He said it aloud, aloud enough to reawake himself momentarily to Pátzcuaro and present time, to find himself on his feet pacing the glassed-in perimeter, taut and tremblingly alert, like Odysseus steering his way between Scylla and Charybdis. It was as if he had not already passed through that narrow strait between utter madness and a mystical vision so intense it would destroy a man for further life. It was as if, now, he had to negotiate between rock and whirlpool for the first time. He put both hands to his head and held it tightly as a ship's tiller . . .

Not, not . . . no not. Not that—but then again, not this either. Not this and not that. No, words simply wouldn't work. Words were invented to communicate with men. For intercourse with rocks, with trees, with silence, they were worse than useless. And so either you exhausted yourself in nots or else you beat a retreat down to lower octaves, to analogy, and to the only analogy, the same old makeshift that for ages has been coerced into serving as proxy. To desire, to erotic desire.

Lust then—he was consumed by lust; a slow pervading lust for mountain and forest and air, a lust to fuse. To fuse *again*, to fuse *back*, in the way male and female, as if once a single creature, lust to fuse back. To die? No. Life, death, the old categories, men's categories, held no more meaning. Emptied shells of illusion and ignorance. There was no death. Not an electron could die from the universe. Man-flesh enamored of earth-flesh, that was all, energy infatuated with engery.

But flesh felt it as flesh, within its own narrow gamut. His body seemed to electrify with sensual longing, but a longing so cool, so slow, so disengaged from self and species, it was more like a magnetic field, a gravitational pull.

He would now turn back into dust, air, moisture, sunlight, devolve back into that invulnerability, that integrity, that power, and the return passage would be through ecstasy, coolly sensate at first, like the mating of reptile or insect, and then down into the soundless, motionless lovemaking of plants, ever simpler, ever slower, as the pain and perplexity and insecurity of man-life bled away in lowering lengthening waves of bliss.

Transfiguration through orgasm, the way all melting and freezing, oxidizing and burning, volatilizing and synthesizing, fusion and fission, is orgasm . . .

And to oppose it? Nothing. Of "will to life" there wasn't enough left to dredge up the smallest bleat of pro-forma protest. Not even some old-aunty irrelevancy, "Not nice. Nice people never . . ."

Sequence stopped. The film went blank.

It was midafternoon when man-life picked up the traces again and replaced him in Bob.

Sun-drenched boulder and ponderosa trunk, a huge golden *lingam* through the windshield . . . a gouging pressure

216

against his chest—the steering wheel, across which he lay, his arms hanging limp on each side . . . a smell of pine and old car . . . a throbbing, not of silence, but of blood in body and bugs in world. Despite the discomfort, he did not sit up immediately, but raised his eyes to the mirror, effulgent with afternoon sunlight, while thought-feeling began to crank up dully inside. Back again.

Again? . . . why? . . . why am I here again? . . .

Here again—spread across the steering wheel, he lay nursing that, aggrieved by that, betrayed by that, outraged by that, but in a feeble and distant way, without the vitality, the control, to act on it. With more of either he might have devised something: cut his wrists, converted the car into a gas chamber, hanged himself. If he had eaten, if he had taken a Dexedrine Spansule, if—but to end life requires life, a certain amount of it. Suicides, as Hoerchner said, come with convalescence. And he lacked it now, that critical amount. Even his wish to sink back into the sea that had just cast him up was weak and remote.

Coagulated, he looked up at the fiery pillar ahead through the dulled vision of a sacrificial animal, waiting . . .

Suddenly, without warning him in the slightest, his body jerked up, his left hand yanked on the door handle, and he all but fell from the car. His legs, unprepared too, buckled beneath him, and he just avoided crumpling face down into a bed of cactus, prickly pear cactus, that the front wheel had come to rest in. Supporting himself on the fender, he stood unsteadily as needles of pain stitched up the nerves of his legs, gazing down into the silent congregation of green sticker-studded hands extending their fat stubby fingers of purple-red fruit. After a few minutes, he pushed himself free of the car and began to drift across the uneven slope, weaving and stumbling like a drunk among the boulders and trees and clumps of cactus and rabbit-brush, stopping frequently to take on a little strength against the great sun-warm flanks of rock. His awareness had narrowed to a chink, sensitive to temperature mostly, the contrasting feels of the open patches where the sun could pour in and the cold dark shadows where it could not—two basic elements, distinct and different. He was slogging wearily up the sandy bed of a small arroyo when his strength suddenly deserted him entirely. He sank down, sat erect for a moment, and then lay back into the warm sand, while the sunlight spread itself over his body, a weightless yellow blanket.

He lay there the rest of the afternoon—no, to say that wasn't true either, to use time was wrong. Because time had still not returned. He lay in the sand as he had in the car, voided, motionless, unawake, unasleep, in the passivity and patience, if not of a rock or a tree, then of a snake or a lizard, a cold-blooded seeker of sun-warmth. His resentment too was gone or forgotten. He was here, simply here, along with the rocks and plants and insects and rodents who also were here. Comfortably sandwiched in the warm embrace of sun and earth, content. He found he could look directly into the sun without blinking or pain, and for a long period he did so. If he had feeling and thought, it was, again, in no human sense. Nothing happened that could leave its trace on the—

No . . . no, wait. There was something, one thing. One thing that was revealing itself now. Oh yes, the hornet . . .

He is here. He is lying on his stomach. The sand cups his left cheek. His arms are spread to either side and he is looking out along the right one. It leads away, a long tapering escarpment, enclosing a sunlit world of pebble boulders, weed trees and insect roads, a pre-Columbian world that terminates with a sharp abrupt edge beyond which lies impenetrable darkness, a world of stillness and order, satisfying to gaze upon, to gaze upon and gaze upon . . .

Oh, but what's that? Something moving? Yes. Out there,

in the shadow of that great rock, something has begun to disturb the peace, albeit in a very minor way. In that obscurity something is stirring. So that's where it settles, his watching, on that little locus of agitation. From here, down here on ground level, he can't get much of a view. Too many hills, bushes, stones in between. To see well, he'd have to climb higher, lift his head a few inches and improve the angle of sight. But he neither lifts his head nor even considers lifting his head. He lies here where he happens to be lying and watches what he can watch from here, just as the rocks and other things lie where they are and watch from their own heres. But this much is evident: something, some small something, is kicking up a commotion out there, something that isn't very significant or very forceful, but something whose existence lies somewhere within the animate range. This information is sufficient, he does not crave more. The movement is providing a nice little resting place for his open eyes, and he uses it for that, waiting out the intervals when it ceases to stir, without curiosity or anticipation, unaffected when it does start in again.

And so it goes on, like this and like this some more, until now has come to the moment to stir himself—to stir, himself. To shift position, because the sand has gotten critically gritty on his cheek, and his neck and ribs are critically achey. His body is ready to alter its pose. Which it does, turning onto its right side, propping its head on its folded inner arm, and from here, from this elevation, it happens, it has become possible to see what it is that is moving around out there.

A bug. A winged bug. A bee or a hornet or a wasp. Incapacitated in some way. It too is lying on its right side, but unlike him it is struggling, working its six legs sluggishly, in exhausted desperation, the top three clawing futilely at the air, the lower three kicking against the earth, just as futilely, since all they can manage to accomplish is to push its body around in the same small insignificant circle, getting noplace. Its wings look intact, yet it makes no attempt to fly or even to buzz. Evidently it has lost control of them. Then what's the matter with it? Nothing visible. From the outside it looks normal, at least for a bug in human sight. Perhaps it has some internal injury, perhaps it is numb from being in the cold of the shadow. No, more likely it's much less complicated than that. The creature has simply arrived at the end of its little life span and is in the process of dying. Yet, obviously, undeniably, it is resisting that process. Sluggishly, impotently, absurdly, it is nevertheless putting up a passionate resistance to death. Its yellow-banded lower abdomen, the most active part of it, keeps up a continual writhing motion, feeling about among the grains of dirt like a tiny trembling tongue, ejecting and retracting its even tinier stinger, as if searching for a tender spot on the earth's skin to stab it with one last angry sting. It is dying and it is resisting death.

Even it . . .

Now, exhausted by its passion, it has stopped struggling and lain back. Immediately, in the distant millimeters, two new forms stir. A pair of red fire-ants, who have been watching unnoticed, close in quickly and begin to palpate the inert body of the hornet with their quivering antennae, going over it with the nervous expertise of a team of diagnosticians, crossing each other's path and holding many minute consultations, their black pinpoint eyes utterly serious. Has the patient expired? One of them reaches out with its forceps and takes a decisive hold on a leg—instantly the victim begins to writhe again. The ant holds fast for a second or two, tossed aloft and dashed back down by the flailing leg, and then releases its grip and steps back a few paces to rejoin its partner, to observe as the dying hornet once again enters an interval of struggling.

They continue to watch, the ants—and himself too until

the bone in his cheek begins to pinch against the bone in his arm and his body shifts again, back onto its stomach, but looking away now, to the left, onto a scene that is very similar to the other, but devoid of any activity except the occasional swaying of plants in the breaths of wind. He does not think about the hornet, about anything. Yet later, when, in the normal course, his body moves again and his eyes fall on it again, he looks at it again. The hornet is still in motion, but now both ants have clamped themselves on it as if they meant to stay, easily eluding the stinger which makes feeble attempts to twist itself around and get at them. And now the ants have begun to pull, in concert, in the direction of his open hand. And when, after a laborious dragging, they reach it, his hand suddenly acts on its own, grasping the whole mortal struggle between thumb and forefinger. An instant later he feels himself being stung, distantly, insignificantly, but enough to make his fingers open again. The tangle of bodies tumbles soundlessly to the sand in front of his face. One ant has disappeared, the other scurries off in panic. But for the hornet rescue has been the coup de grâce. It lies faintly quivering, and out of the tip of its torn abdomen a tiny droplet of cloudy fluid is oozing.

Again he turns away, and later, when his position once more permits him to see in that direction, he notes, without commentary, that the hornet is no longer there . . .

And here the film did go blank again. Very possibly he fell into an actual sleep.

15

Sɪɢʜᴛ-sᴏᴜɴᴅ-sᴍᴇʟʟ-ᴛᴀsᴛᴇ-ғᴇᴇʟ: with the throw of a master switch all of his senses came humming on together. Smell of resins and rocks, sound of clicking teeth and machine-gunning breath, sight of earth heaving as if the mountain had gone into eruption. Taste of dryness, feel of cold. More than anything that—feel of murderous cold.

The sun had left. The warm bed had chilled into a grave of shadow. He rolled over and sat up. Instantly some giant grabbed him and shook his whole frame ferociously, rattling his jaws, convulsing his arms and legs like those of a marionette.

Cold, he felt nothing but cold. But God, oh God how he felt it!

Felt it . . . felt—

"Jesus, I'm freezing to death!" Even the thought-words came in slivers and fragments, like a shattered icicle.

Thought, he thought—

Cold, he thought cold, he felt cold. Cold that had him in its coils, round and round him, freezing and squeezing, a refrigerated serpent. Everything else gone, nothing left but cold that wanted to kill him and was killing him, cold he must fight.

Nothing? Nothing left? Nothing, just cold, merely cold.

"HA!"

The yell shot out and exploded against the mountain, jubilant and mad.

"HA-HA!" The mountain fielded it, doubled it, and hurled it back at him.

"Ha-ha!" Again he yelled it, deliberately, consciously this time. Again the mountain tossed back twice as much as he had given it. "Ha-ha! . . . ha-ha!"

Oh . . . oh God!

He worked his body around to its hands and knees and rested there a moment, quivering, panting, like a dog.

Oh God, oh dear God!

Slowly and stiffly he clambered the rest of the way to his feet and began to stagger about, like a paralytic at first, and little by little loosening up, massaging his arms and legs, flexing and flinging them about, slapping his cheeks, chest and thighs, clapping his hands, kicking at rocks, and finally sparring and leaping about wildly in a dervish frenzy.

Oh Jesus, oh God . . .

The joyous excruciation of thawing, the ecstatic pain of de-congealing. The welling sap of gratitude, the gratitude of spring, inconceivable to what has not known winter.

Oh God oh God . . . thank God, thank God . . .

The "Gods" came puffing out in small a-rhythmic combustions, like a reviving engine. What he was saying, to whom he was saying it, he had not the least idea. But oh, thank you, thank you, thank you! Whoever, whatever, thank you, thank you! And if you are God, then thank you, God, and if you are Luck, then thank you, Luck, and if you are Nothing, thank you, Nothing, thank you! Thank you, thank you for remembering me, for loving me, thank you and take my mite of love, my poor offering, my gratitude.

Out they poured, the thank yous, poured forth wantonly as perfume from a flower, water from a spring, fluids from a body in passion.

Reeling, dizzy still, he braced himself against a rock with both arms, head arched between them, and stood breathing deeply and loudly until he felt calmer and steadier. Then he began to retrace his way back along the dark trench of the ravine until, suddenly and unwarned, he stepped from shadow into a pool of quietly glowing amber light and a vast unobstructed view of the long narrow river valley and the volcanic hills of the desert beyond. The arsonist sun had ignited the horizon and fled, leaving the long-extinct craters aflame again with the bloody incandescence of old, spewing streams of molten crimson. They were twenty or thirty miles west of here, and between and below lay a tremendous sweep of the Rio Grande basin, from Algodones and Bernalillo to the north down past the southern outskirts of the city itself—

City? He ceased to walk, stood still and gaped down: nothing was there! It was gone—city, river, earth, everything, gone, volatilized. Below him the crags plunged steeply away and vanished, drowned in a sea. A sea of dust, luminous pink dust streaked with the fast cooling reds from the rims of the volcanoes. Not a thing moved in it, not a sound rose from it. A sea of silent phosphorescent dust.

With the awe of a last survivor he stood watching as the alizarine warmth chilled to mauve and indigo, until, at last, the first pinpricks of light punched up through the haze and down from the darkened sky.

He shook his head vigorously, like a stopped watch. And now? . . . and now—what? Was he actually supposed to go back down there again, submerge himself again in that raucous silence, that hurly-burly motionlessness, rejoin his fellow sea-lice in their twitching, their trivial anxieties and preoccupations, their microbic tragedies and triumphs? Back down to that planktonic fearing and hoping, dreaming and scheming, loving and hating, giggling and howling . . .

He wheeled suddenly and looked back up into the dark of the mountain. Instantly, he felt its response—a cold, almost physical pressure. It had had enough of him. It wanted him gone.

Go . . . go down, go back where the likes of you belong.

But what . . . what should I do?

Again the response was instantaneous. A light snapped on in the center of his body. His stomach became a sudden burning presence. Hunger. He felt hunger, in precisely the way a little while ago he had felt cold. He was starving. Hunger was killing him. He had to fight, to eat, and now. Eat. Until he found something to eat, until food entered his body, all other thoughts and acts were absurd. He must eat, and eat now.

What? He began to pace in stooped circles, on all fours practically, sharp famished eyes sweeping the ground, nose all but sniffing . . .

Ow!—his skull butted hard into the trunk of a tree, one of those holly-like oaks with stiff pointed leaves. Rubbing his head, he looked up—acorns! He fumbled through the dry thorny branches. Sure enough, there they were, a few small green nuggets scattered among the leaves. He picked one and bit into it greedily. Aaach! A puff of bitter dust filled his mouth and he spat it out. He tried a second, cracking it between his teeth first and then prying it open with his fingers. The kernel was gone, reduced to a bit of dry black powder. Something had destroyed it, some worm or disease. He tested a dozen more. All of them the same, worthless.

Bugs, how about bugs? Listening, he thought he could hear the nearby shrilling of crickets and grasshoppers. He dropped to his hands and knees. John the Baptist had subsisted on locusts. He rooted about with the urgent efficiency of a bear, turning up rocks, feeling into places too dim to see. In David's *Beginners' Book of Insects* it said Southwestern Indians had eaten crickets, considered them a delicacy.

He found nothing at all. Bad time of day, bad time of year, for an inexperienced human to be hunting bugs.

He stood up again and started walking back toward the car, feeling that if he didn't find food very soon he would collapse here and die. It was like holding your breath, a short and definite life span of crucial possibility. He broke into a stumbling run, urging himself on with fantasies of peanuts, cookie-crumbs, apple cores, raisins, chocolate bits, a veritable hoard of food, spilled over years and waiting in car-seat caches for him to scavenge.

When he saw the front door of the car hanging open to receive him, he made a final dash for it. But just as he reached it, he felt a sudden jaw of pain clamp viciously on his right leg. Horror-struck, he looked down for the snake, and his mind flashed in counterpoint lightning: This, at last, finally, really, is it; rattlesnake meat isn't merely edible, it's another gourmet delicacy. But under these circumstances, when it has already sunk its teeth into your meat first . . . ?

Slowly he realized that it wasn't a snake, not any fauna that had attacked him. He had been bitten by the flora. He had stepped smack in the middle of that forgotten bed of prickly pear. Cactus!

Cactus . . . ? Well, why not? The flat green paws rose in a crowded circle of confirmation around him, close to the ground, directly up out of the ground, as from arms buried to the wrists. They seemed to be applauding his idea, their fat little fingers clapping like the hands of an audience. Carefully, hissing and wincing, he extricated his leg from their midst and yanked out a few of the larger needles. And then, without hesitation, he reached back down impulsively and was immediately stung again, not as fiercely this time, but in what felt like fifty tiny places at once. This food would not be free. Even the fruits themselves were studded with tufts of minute thorns. He nipped at his fingers with his front teeth, trying to tweeze out a few of them, while his other hand set about the operation once more, keeping a cautious balance between price and demand, twisting the soft egg-shaped fruit off with sacrificial thumb and forefinger, bringing it up close to examine it. He'd never tried eating a cactus before, but this was obviously not something you just popped into your mouth like a grape. That leathery thorny skin had to be removed. He tried peeling it off, but this was beyond the capacity of his trembling fingers. Finally he pressed the soft fig-like thing open with both thumbs and turned it inside out. And now it was like a bird's gizzard, stuffed with a mass of small gravelly pits. He sucked them, chewed them and spat them away. This would never—he examined the flayed hide more closely and saw that there remained a thin slimy layer of vivid magenta flesh, a meager underskin. This he scraped off with his teeth. It yielded almost nothing, less than a teaspoonful, but an almost nothing of marvelous and succulent sweetness.

For the next hour or so he worked with the careful concentration of a jeweler, consuming fifty or sixty of the cactus fruits, gorging himself on minuscule portions, paying for each one with another batch of tiny darts which now grew in a thickening stubble from fingers and lips and tongue and palate. At last his hunger felt assuaged. Gathering another dozen or so, he placed them in a little pile on the car seat and then climbed in beside them, to consume one by one as he drove back down. The familiar feel of the seat, the wheel, the familiar old-car smell, added to his well-being, and he felt himself smile. He drank down a deep breath of cool fresh air and on a sudden impulse slapped his hand down hard on the horn, just to see if it worked.

It worked. The blast shattered the crystalline stillness and went ricocheting among the unseen cliffs and crevices like the mating honk of some terrible Mesozoic lizard.

He twisted the ignition key and as the car leapt back to palpitating life around him, it seemed to jar loose a fresh flow of that melting joy. He felt himself deliquescing once more into molten gratitude, so that peering up at the obscurity of towering forms outside, he said, softly but ardently, and aloud, "Thank you. Thank you very much." To the mountain, to his guardian angel, to his lucky stars, he extended his thanks, his heart's thanks. To whomever, whatever, it might concern, to the Something whose reality in the here and now he had felt and still felt, so infinitely more present than himself that —yes, for that very reason—it remained and would continue to remain utterly beyond his power to prehend or comprehend.

And this ignorance did not bother him in the slightest. He felt as much interest or curiosity as a nursing baby does in the chemical composition of its mother's milk.

After a moment, he began to back carefully down the trail, turned at the first widening and started the long easy coast down the slope of the mountain, his left hand guiding the wheel, his right reaching over to the mound of cactus fruits beside him, preparing them one after another, with some method and skill by now, one-handed, like a cowboy rolling cigarettes.

He did not return by the old road. He followed the gravel to the new blacktop, shifted into neutral and glided easily and quietly downward as more and more lights plinked on in the saturating dark ahead. Before his eyes the city emerged again, but in a transmuted form, in the clean and simple dimensions of night. Below him now lay an organism of ten thousand luminous cells, in the living hues of stars and diamonds, shimmering in the black. He could distinguish the greenish constellation of the power plant on the eastern edge, the bright nuclear cluster of downtown with its hovering pink nebulae, the long pearly strings of the mercury streetlamps, the blinking red giants of the radio towers, the streaking twin meteors of the cars, even the dim yellow glow of Bethlehem's hill. There seemed little difference now between heaven and earth. Etherealized by night, Albuquerque lay pulsating beneath him like a fallen galaxy.

It wasn't until several minutes after car and body had descended to the valley and were moving back toward town along the freeway that his mind followed them and sobered to the lower altitude. It came upon him gnawing absently at the skin of the last cactus, reluctant to leave off, even though all of its sweet flesh had been consumed and nothing remained but a tiny rag of membrane.

And now . . . ? And now where? . . . What? . . .

The down-to-earth questions were finally articulating themselves. He listened for the ensuing anxiety more than for answers.

Neither came. There wasn't time. Instead his attention was suddenly taken over by the clamoring of the cactus thorns. Although dozens of them were impaled in his mouth and hands, he had been all but numb to them. But now his fingers, lips and tongue suddenly flamed up with a spread of rash-like little prickles of pain. His brain too seemed stuffed with cactuses. Big and small, of every species, saguaro, ocotillo, opuntia, cholla, desert plants in every fantastic variation, and all of them writhing slowly about inside his head, rustling their infinities of needles together. And out of this soft crackling din somehow, a thought—no, it was more a single word, delivered itself.

Mexico

"Mexico," he repeated under his breath. But he had no

time even to reflect on that word and its implications before a second word came forth.

Howell

"Howell," he repeated.

This was all. The pain in his flesh, the crackling in his brain were superseded by something new. And although there was time now to think, he didn't. He didn't have to. He acted. At the Alameda turnoff he turned off the highway, crossed the Rio Grande to the suburban village of Corrales, and came to a stop in front of the ranchless ranch house of Harry Howell.

16

A LITTLE GIRL OF THREE OR FOUR opened the door to his ring and stood staring wordless and open-mouthed up at him. From behind her a mongrel of stimuli came leaping out onto his senses, aggressively friendly as a puppy. Not an unfamiliar mix either, odors of floor wax and baby powder, roast and pastry, piñon and tobacco smoke and beer. Rumbling blurts of TV, crackling of evening paper, whir of kitchen machinery. Above the child, a lighted slice of living room, a sofa edge, a green swatch of carpeting, a strip of antique-white wall with one of Howell's old Montmartre street scenes staring out, dull as a prisoner, from its heavy French plaster frame.

"Is . . . is your Daddy home?" His voice was dry and wispy.

The child continued to stare at him.

"Well, Debbie, who is it, for God's sake?"

Debbie did not see fit to respond to either of her questioners. Instead, bracing her little arms against the door, she slammed it shut with all her diminutive might.

Ten seconds passed and the door was yanked open again;

there, framed inside the heavy frame, stood Harry Howell himself, short, sturdy and beginning to paunch, shirt open and out of his pants, in his socks, smelling of beer. Like his daughter's, his mouth fell slightly agape at what confronted him, and for a moment he too said nothing.

His former employee smiled a little and nodded his head a little, even reeled back a little under the sudden push of this completely other and separate human entity, finding it nevertheless welcome and not unpleasant.

"Well, son-of-a-bitch, look who's here. I been thinking about—Jesus, man, what in God's name hit you?"

For the first time in a long time he was privileged to glance at himself through another pair of eyes.

"I guess I must really look a sight. The thing is, I've just come down from . . . I mean, I spent the day up on the mountain and—

"Come on in, come on in, have a beer. What in hell you been doing up there, wrestling with the bears? Buddy, I mean, you look like you've really had it."

"I guess maybe I have. Actually I just, you know, wanted to break things up a little. I wanted a change." The splash of Howell's being, so scalding before, felt like a balm.

"A what—hell, I can't hear with this goddamn thing on." He went over to the television set and switched off the volume. In the armchair from which Howell had just risen the plastic cushion was slowly making a comeback after the crushing inflicted by his behind. The ashtray on the end table beside it was filled with half-smoked cigarettes and ringed by three empty beer cans. In another chair a larger child was holed up with a stockpile of comic books. He did not glance out to notice either the visitor or the sudden squelching of the TV. Finally, seated stiffly side by side on the sofa, was an elderly couple dressed in dark formality, an anomalous item of furnishing amid the casual disorder. These two did look up, and with a horror even their good manners were unable to mask.

"*C'est un ami de moi,*" Howell muttered at them. And turning, with an eloquent calligraphic twist of his heavy brown eyebrows: "My in-laws, Georgette's folks, they're visiting with us from Tours for a couple weeks . . . yeah."

The old couple produced their sets of nods and smiles like involuntary tics, while continuing to stare at this "*ami*" with undiminished dread, as if he were actually some thug their American son-in-law had hired to bump them off and deposit them in shallow desert graves.

"Howell," he said, "listen—"

"Let's get you some beer." Cupping a palm around his mouth, Howell beamed a yell toward the kitchen. "Hey, Chérie . . ."

His wife emerged, wiping floury hands on her apron. At the sight of him, she stiffened with shock but managed to conceal it more flexibly than her parents as Howell zipped through the vestiges of a formal introduction.

"Oh yes, 'arry has spoken of you." She smiled with the vestiges of *patisserie politesse.*

She smelled of onions and baby. She looked soft, plump, creamy-skinned and might or might not be pregnant. Except for the narrow, even arcs of her plucked eyebrows and a certain Gallic definition in her heavy shiny eyelids and thin rose-pink lips, she might have passed as just another American suburban housewife. As she took in her guest's appearance, the voluptuous curve of her relaxing throatline drew up in an instinctive rigor of distaste.

"Please excuse me, the way I look. I've been up on the mountain all day . . . roughing it a little, you know, hiking."

"Oh, of course, that is nice. 'arry, why you don't ever take up a nice sport, climbing mountains or roughing it or something? It would be good for you."

"What'll you have, Bob, Coors or Bud?" As he saw Howell turn for the kitchen to fetch the beer, he seized him by the shoulder.

"Thanks . . . no . . . I mean I can't stay. The reason I came by was . . . that note you left at my place yesterday— tell me, you still want to go on that trip?"

Instantly husband and wife looked at each other and froze, as if caught at their intimacy.

"You mean, you really feel like going?"

"Yes."

"Funny. Georgette and me were just having a little discussion on that subject before you got here—I'd more or less decided to forget the whole deal."

But Georgette had come to life. Her eyebrows flattened, her eyelids rolled up like bedroom blinds at morning and her odalisque throat grew purposeful. It was her turn to seize Howell by the shoulder. "Listen to me, 'arry, you go, *tu comprends! Tu as besoin d'un petit* break, *eh* . . . *et moi aussi. Un petit* break *ne me ferait pas de mal* . . . *surtout en ce moment!*" Her eyes were large, brown and sparkling, and her wagging head set her words into italics.

Howell now shot a swift glance at his *beau-père* and *belle-mère*, who, having heard their native tongue, were looking up in discreet and apprehensive curiosity.

Georgette, her feminine distaste at the visitor's wild and dirty condition forgotten, now addressed him with sudden familiarity.

"Friday he was ready to go, you know. Then no, and after that again he was going, and then perhaps yes, perhaps no . . . every moment he changes. Really, it is already too much, you know . . . especially under certain special circumstance —I am sure you understand . . ."

"Where you want to go?" Howell cut in, continuing to ignore her.

"Mexico."

"Mexico? I mean, I was thinking more of the Coast."

"I'd rather go to Mexico."

"Mexico? Whereabouts in Mexico?"

"I don't care."

"Just kind of a little spin around, you mean?"

"Yes."

"Well, jeez—I don't know, I mean, when were you figuring on taking off?"

"Any time."

"You mean like—tomorrow morning?"

"Fine."

"Well . . . I mean, give me a minute, got to think about it." He reached for his beer and took a deep suck, his thick eyebrows seeming to wrap themselves around the rim of the can.

"*Chéri*, I have already thought about it. *Tu vas avec ton ami, mon petit*, and enjoy yourself. How do they say it?—she indicated the old couple with an adroit little wriggle of her large round eyes—it is necessary to get while the getting is good . . ."

"Yeah, guess maybe I could stand a little breather."

"Others also could stand a little breather, *mon amour*. Honestly, this one, when he is between jobs, it is impossible, absolutely." Her little pink mouth flared into a startling and flowerlike smile and he saw what Howell saw in her.

"About how long were you figuring on—I got this remodeling job starting the second week in November . . ."

From the kitchen now came a metallic banging which he easily identified as that of a baby's tin cup on a high chair. The old couple still fixed on the conversation with anxious attention, as if it were their fate, not his own, that was being deliberated here.

"O.K.! O.K., it's a deal!" Instead of shaking hands on it,

Howell gave him a short vigorous whack to seal the agreement. His face played with emotion like a musical instrument. "Won't take me an hour to get packed. Even went and had the wagon greased and tuned. How about me picking you up at your place at six in the morning, O.K.?" He went and got a beer for Bob and another for himself, and as they drank on it, Georgette murmured the few magic words to her parents that relaxed them instantly into shyly blinking smiles before she went off to relax the impatient baby. The older child in the chair glanced up dully at the life-and-death gunfight that was blazing soundlessly away in the lighted rectangle, and after a killing or two, returned to the mayhem in the little printed rectangles of an older medium. Howell was stuffing his shirttails back into his pants, and as he watched him bend over to retie his shoes, he couldn't help feeling the little resurrection play going on in front of him as a kind of parody of his own.

"Hey, I know. I'll bring my paints. O.K. with you? Should be able to knock out a few paysages . . . crumbling adobe walls, cactuses, dark-eyed señoritas—they've got some great stuff down there. Jesus, yeah, who the hell wants to go to California? You know I stretched a whole stack of fresh canvases last summer, and I've still got my old easel-paintbox from the Grande Chaumière—man, you couldn't have picked a better moment to walk in that door if God himself had sent you. And I got a hunch you and me are going to have us a ball down there . . . couple of gypsies, right? . . . no timetables, no intineraries, wander wherever the muse takes us, right?"

"A table, tout le monde . . . Mark and Debbie, go wash your hands, allez, vite!"

He stood basking gratefully in the domestic banality. And when Georgette enveloped him with her cordial smile, he did not think of resisting the invitation to supper.

"Let me try and make myself a little more presentable first."

"John's straight down the hall," Howell said, "to your left—hey, man, wait a second, what's all those little hairy things all over your mouth? Don't tell me you're growing whiskers on your lips too. Come here by the light—Christ, you got hundreds of them. Open your—Jesus, even on your damn tongue!"

"Oh those—I mean, they're nothing. A few cactus stickers, that's all. What happened was I got a little hungry up there on the mountain and tried eating some prickly pears."

"Cactus! For the love of God!" The friendly brows shifted up half-an-inch on Howell's forehead, and his short strong forefinger circled his temple like a carpenter's brace.

"Old buddy, you know, there's something I got to tell you. Sometimes I kinda wonder about you . . ."

At this, and for the first time in weeks, he laughed.

17

HE LAUGHED. Howell's words, Howell's face, wriggling in like a finger to the ribs, made him explode with laughter.

Instantly a woman screamed.

Not Howell's wife, not his *belle-mère*. Not there and then, in Albuquerque, Monday evening. Here, now, a woman screamed.

He pawed back up to the surface and saw her standing a few feet away, across the porch, scared stiff, her feather duster frozen in mid-motion, her gray *rebozo* pulled to her mouth. Monday's laugh had terrified the hotel maid.

"Oh! I you frightened you?"

She began to move again. The duster and shawl lowered, the swallow continued its descent in her bird-thin throat, her chest rose in breath. A Tarascan woman, sparrow-hued and tiny, less than five feet tall, her fine Asian hair drawn into two scant braids, her dress, patched and repatched, the dingy protective gray-brown of one of those tiny birds that are everywhere and unnoticed.

"*Perdón* . . . I you frightened you?" Again he used the wrong form of the Spanish verb.

"*Sí, Señor*," the automatic agreement of the humble poor. She began to dust again.

"I'm sorry. I didn't notice you. I was . . . thinking, that's all . . . about something funny." He smiled. "We *norte-americanos* . . . *usted sabe, somos un poquito* . . ." And made the same sign Howell had made, smiling.

She didn't burst out laughing. Or even smile. Her reaction was to turn away and move more rapidly through her work, dusting her way nervously around the porch. Her spread-toed feet in their *huaraches* were like pottery in leather carrying straps.

He watched her, forgetting Howell, forgetting himself, disturbed by an obscure guilt, as if these hours spent sitting here absorbed in himself had somehow been stolen out of her life. He felt a guilty need to communicate with her, throw out some binding strand to her, make her acknowledge the two of them were human beings together. But in the uneasy silence he could find nothing to say that would bridge the chasm. Her *huaraches* creaked on the terra-cotta tiles and her breathing was shallow and rapid and birdlike. The feather duster made no sound at all.

Then, like an old friend, the toilet reported in, gurgling and gargling from the floor below.

"The toilet," he said, "the toilet's not working?"

She stared around at him in a fresh flow of fear.

"*Perdón* . . . the toilet . . . it's broken."

"*Señor?*"

"What's wrong with it, do you know?"

She looked as if he were accusing her. God, what was he talking to her about the damn toilet for?

"I thought maybe I could fix it . . ."

239

"I will call *la Señora* . . ."

"No—no, don't. *Está bien.*" How old was she? He could no more say than with a sparrow.

He took his notebook from the round leather table, split it apart and pretended to read. February 7th, two months before his first breakdown, the "thrashing for answers." Another of his home-canned aphorisms, his pathetic attempts to stock the survival shelter.

The purpose of life: the struggle to love. Nothing is needed more, by the world or by you.

He glanced up and saw she was leaving.

"Oh . . . oh *Señora* . . ."

For the third time she was looking at him in the same way, with the same distrust, the same fear.

He stood up, removed a ten-peso note from his wallet and held it out to her. "*Por favor . . . tome . . . es para usted.*"

She looked at the gray wad of dirty paper and moved toward him, tense as a hungry sparrow toward a dangerously located crumb. As she took it, her hard dark little fingers, spare as birdfeet, scratched lightly against his own.

"*Muchas gracias, Señor. Que Dios se lo pague.*"

"Forgive me for frightening you."

And she was gone downstairs, the bill crushed against the fragile bones of her chest. Eighty cents, ten or fifteen hours of her labor. The gulf between them had not been bridged. If anything, the money had destroyed the possibility altogether.

He stepped outside and stared again into the purple cloud of the bougainvillaea vine. Above it, between two pieces of roof, he could see a segment of street. Three men sat talking casually on a curb. Two little girls swathed in communion gauze flitted past, a pair of cabbage moths. A load of split firewood came wobbling laboriously up the cobbles, a huge snail, the donkey ears poking out through the crusted shell like feelers.

Maybe this was enough now, maybe he should go down.

A church bell started up again, but only, after a grandiose overture, to tell the time. *Bong* and then *bong*. Two o'clock— was that all it was? Then another bell woke up, farther away somewhere near the lake. *Bong* and *bong* and *bong*. Three o'clock.

Yes, maybe he should go down now, go down and have some lunch. What would they make of it, these people there, of a gringo who comes hurtling down from the north only to sit alone on the roof of his hotel, dredging the channels of his private world in search of . . . in search of what? A key he'd lost somewhere? Were they isolated too, were all human beings, no matter where, under what circumstances, essentially alone? Or was it possible for private worlds to become communal worlds, private dreams one common dream? Did they feel this loneliness between the death behind and the death ahead, this imperative to find out who they were supposed to be? No—at least not the way we did. They already were, and it would take people like us more than one lifetime to be like them. To be. Like them. And yet, they envied us. We were rich, they saw, we were powerful, we were free, we spent maybe twenty more years in life than they did. What they couldn't see was the inner devastation, the wreckage—that took an educated vision. An X-ray camera, one of those that photograph warmth, would show them a truer picture. They'd see us bleeding internally, impoverished, wandering in the ruins, trying to tack makeshift shelters together out of hunks of debris. They'd pity us then, they'd send a corps of volunteers to our underdeveloped nation.

He felt his own throat constricting. All right then, wasn't this enough? It was two o'clock already, or maybe three. Was he or was he not going to leave this porch, go down there and have lunch?

He stared through the ectoplasmic beauty of the bougainvillaea vine into the gray-brown ugliness that supported it and fed it. He seemed to see again the thin throat of the frightened maid, the thin brown ankles of the Indian kneeling beside him in the Basilica, the fingers of the old man peeling the *tuna* on the way to Lagos de Moreno, the broken man on the broken truck near Francisco I. Madero. He heard the terrible little slap of the addict's face on the concrete floor of the police station in El Paso, heard Aguero shriek before electroshock, heard the cataclysm of the Navajo mother's cough. He heard Anne's static-filled Ohio accent over the phone, the multileveled unhappiness of Hoerchner's wife, the fatigue dragging at Hoerchner's voice. He seemed to feel the cactus needles in his flesh again.

He drew in breath and closed his eyes: "Children . . . your children . . . have mercy . . . don't abandon us to our own devices . . ."

18

He didn't sleep much Monday night. The first half of it he spent trying to bring a little order out of the chaos of home, working on one room after another, like a housewife. In the bathroom he gathered the seeds of Nembutal one by one, twenty-one of them, and flushed them down the toilet. An examination of the broken towel rack showed repair would take time, tools and plaster—he leaned it neatly in a corner. In the kitchen he scraped all the dishes, washed them and put them away in their cabinets, closing all the gaping doors. He swabbed all the dirty surfaces, swept the floor and even considered mopping it. As he was taking the smelly garbage pan from under the sink, he felt a surge of impulse and yielded to it: grabbing the radio from the table, he dropped it with a plop into the fermenting mash. In the main room he picked up, swept up, straightened up, and made the bed. Finally he went back into the kitchen to write Anne about what had happened to him today.

He spent an hour trying and failed, settling at last for a short cheery note.

Feel better. Leaving for Mexico tomorrow with Harry Howell—be gone two weeks. If you want to come home, you can any time. I think it'll be all right. Will write details from Mexico . . .

He packed his notebook and the Kierkegaard anthology in a small overnight bag along with a change of clothes, and went back into the main room to lie down. But seeing how neat the bed looked, he decided not to mess it up again with his body. So he sat down instead in the big chair, and there he spent the rest of the night waiting, thinking, and dozing.

Although he didn't cross over into actual sleep, he kept skirting its edges, blurring in the process the edges of time. Small confusions came and went. Had he passed his college exams yet? Did he have his lesson plan prepared for the morning's classes? Had yesterday occurred or been imagined? Had he really run to and from Hoerchner? Had that really happened on the mountain? Was Howell really coming by to pick him up? . . .

"HAWNNN-HAWNNN!"

At the bugle-blast he leaped up and pulled open the door. Howell's big station wagon sat purring quietly in the darkness, dimly aglow inside, like some craft from outer space. He made a hoarse sound of greeting as the front hatch opened, and out hopped its occupant.

"Bonjour, bonjour!" Howell said, punctuating it with a sock to the shoulder and putting down the tail gate for him to toss his bag inside. The car was already stowed with gear worthy of an expedition into the Sahara: jerry-cans of water and gasoline, mechanics' tools, entrenching shovels, nylon tent, Primus stove, medical kit, two ten-pound sacks of oranges, cardboard boxes of groceries, binoculars, a fancy camera and accessories. There was also the French easel-paintbox, a dozen stretched canvases, pastel and watercolor sets, and assorted sketchpads.

"That all you got?" Howell asked.

"Looks like you made up for it."

"Yes, sir. Be prepared, like a boy scout with a pack of rubbers. O.K., *en voiture, M'sieurs, 'dames,*" he shouted in a pretty good imitation of a Paris bus conductor. Howell was in high spirits, and he was grateful. For a while at least they were going to have to travel on Howell's energy alone.

The day was waking up in a bad mood, clogged with blue-black clouds, throwing tantrums of wind. Not until they reached Belen did enough sun seep through the wadded sky to let them turn off the headlights. Howell's mood was opposite. Driver talked away happily while in the seat beside him passenger lay back in silent depletion, listening and not listening as Howell aromatically repercolated the good old days and the great old times back in France, thanking him again for showing up at just the right moment and suggesting this trip, confessing he'd been "about to go nuts." For Howell this seemed to be, or this needed to be, one swift setting-back of time. And he too found himself conscious of time being rolled back, but in a very different way. Howell's thoughts were all inside, while his own—how strange!—were completely exterior. It was as if, after all those weeks of solitary confinement, all that incessant rubbing against the walls, his mind had finally worn a hole through to freedom. He felt "sprung," his liberated consciousness sweeping along outside, the flying landscape running through it as through a child's open fingers.

Howell was a fast, steady driver, and as they rushed southward they seemed to catch up with the advancing season. It slowed and slowed, and then, overtaken, it pulled to a halt, where, for an hour or so, it hesitated, until gradually it began to retreat, to reverse itself back into summer again. The half-nude trees began to replace their fallen leaves. The dry ochers relaxed into moist yellows, flecked again with green, until, more and more, wholly untouched trees basked complacently in the mild sun. The brittle cornfields grew humid again, and the alfalfa pushed high and bloodgreen, and flowered for yet another cutting. Below Elephant Butte the cotton harvest was in full swing, the slatted trailers wadded down with white and the roadsides snowy with fluff. At Las Cruces they caught sight of the first stumpy palmettos and a row of black Mediterranean cypress.

They were in El Paso before noon.

Howell held up his watch to prove it. "Pretty damn good time," he said, patting the dashboard affectionately like the neck of a horse. "What's it to Chihuahua—two fifty?"

Bob consulted the map on the seat between them. "Two thirty-four."

"Make it by dark easy."

He nodded.

They were both wrong.

The traffic trickled down the furrow linking the two cities and the two countries like irrigation water between crop rows. But this crop had been fertilized capriciously. Behind them, central El Paso shot up in clean and flawless gigantism, but in the direction of the border the buildings rapidly turned scrubby and grubby. The rich gleaming stores displaying fashions and jewels and sporting goods and electric gadgetry gave way to dingy caves of secondhand clothing and basic foodstuffs, as the metal and neon English signs gave way to hand-lettered Spanish.

Howell's fingers were drumming on the dashboard, and Bob sat in the comfort beside him as in a movie, taking in the cineramic travelogue that was being wide-screened past. At the border came a brief and snappy exchange of perfunctory words with a pair of curt and courteous blue uniforms, then up the camelback bridge over the dry riverbed and down the other side into the peeling green plaster of Mexican customs.

It looked like a rundown filling station selling some off-brand gas. But where were the attendants? Only one man appeared to be an official—a walnut-faced old man dressed in what might have been his original Pancho Villa khakis. It took several minutes of observation to deduce that some of those other men standing around in street clothing were also inspectors. Finally they established a connection with one of them, short and middle-aged, in a brown double-breasted suit-coat, a Miami sport shirt, and a pair of formal blue-serge pants. Either the man knew no English or didn't want to speak any. So that Bob, shaking his head clear like someone emerging from a theater, had to rouse himself sufficiently to act as interpreter.

"*Los documentos del carro,*" the man said in a fatigued voice.

"He wants to see the car papers."

"You bet." Howell shuffled through the cards in his wallet, picked one out and handed it over. The Mexican studied it a moment, looked up at him with an odd squint, and handed it back.

"*No sirve éste—es pá un camión.*"

"He says it's no good. It's for a truck."

"What!" Howell gave it a glance, and then, as if the supporting bones had given way behind it, his face caved in. "Oh . . . oh-oh . . ." He eviscerated the wallet onto the car hood, rifled his pockets, thrust an arm through the window to gouge through the glove compartment. "Oh, shit!"

"What?"

"What a jackass, what an idiot! This here's for the pickup. In the mad rush I forgot to check. You know where the damn title is? Home. Back there in Albuquerque. Holy Christ."

Then, as his voice died dismally away, his tongue suddenly gave a little click, as if switching into a new circuit. He reached out for the inspector who was turning away after having exhausted his curiosity in a moment of bored amusement. "Hey, amigo," Howell said to him, pronouncing each syllable with the slow clarity of a diction teacher, as if by enunciating English sufficiently he could turn it into Spanish. "Listen, this car belongs to me, *compris?* It is mine. I bought it. I did not steal it. Look at these initials on the door—H.H. Mine. See the name on this inspection sticker? Mine. You got a Bible laying around here someplace? I will give you a sworn statement. Look, see this, my Chamber of Commerce card . . ."

The inspector's face split in a yawn.

"Tell this character it's mine, Bob," Howell said.

"*Es la verdad,*" he said. "*Éste es el dueño del carro.*"

They waited for the inspector's mouth to close. "You boys go back and get the paper," the Mexican said, in good English.

"You mean you're going to make us drive six hundred extra miles for a lousy piece of paper? Look at me, buddy. Can't you tell an honest face when you see one?" Howell slipped a ten-dollar bill from his pocket. "Look, here's another piece of paper, a better one. Why make it hard on all of us, when you can just accept the word of an honest man and let me and my friend through. What do you think we're going to do in your country anyhow? Nothing but spend money, boost the economy. So what do you say, pal?"

The man contemplated the bill. "You know, I like very much to take your dollars, *compadre*. The government, he don't pay me that much in one day. But they get you anyway. Inside at the checkpoint. And those guys down there, they pretty mean. People they don't care. People not worth nothing. But cars—you know how much cost this station wagon in Mexico? Seventy-five thousand pesos."

"So, we're just—how you say 'up shit creek' in Spanish, Bob?"

"I don't know . . . *chingados.*"

"So, we're just *chingados?*"

The inspector, into another yawn, recurved the corners of it into a laugh. He laid his hand on Howell's shoulder. "Look, I tell you something. You go back to El Paso, get a *certificado* from the *policía* that you are the owner of this car, and I pass you. But this is not official *consejo.* It's private. I take two dollars." He accepted a bill from cach, folded them carefully and inserted them into his blue serge pants. There was something very appealing in this action, the dimensions of his corruption.

As the now stern and suspicious American guards went through their luggage and papers and removed for destruction several items of supermarket food, including the bags of oranges with *California* stamped on them, Howell looked on dismally, but didn't bother to protest.

"Off to a great start," he said, driving north into central El Paso. ". . . can you imagine, a lousy slip of paper? . . . hell, I almost feel like calling the whole deal off. How you feel about it?"

Feel about it? He realized then that he felt nothing about it. But he was feeling, and his feelings, though weak still, were better. "It's my fault, Harry, for rushing you. But we might as well relax. We'll get there."

"I know. It's just the goddamn waste of time."

He said nothing to Howell. But inside, something said something to him: "Either it's all a waste of time or none of it is. Either it all matters or none of it does."

They found the police headquarters itself imprisoned, inside a gigantic yellow cube that looked like one single block of quarried stone. The room they entered was large and low, seemingly windowless, lighted by banks of livid fluorescent tubes. He felt the crushing pressure immediately, as if the ceiling were on some hidden hydraulic mechanism that had already lowered it considerably, and would, at some pre-calculated moment, force it to the floor, flattening all contents into one large thin sheet.

The farther section of the room was behind glass walls, and in the cubicles beyond they could see, moving, smoking, sprawling on desks, talking to telephones and microphones, tilted back in steel chairs, sipping out of disposable cups, a dozen figures who, at first glance, seemed a special breed of men, brothers out of the same sire. Ballistically compact, ballistically clean-surfaced, some in, some out of uniform. A locker room behind some very grim kind of athletics. The burping monotones of intercom voices, the spastic clicking of teletypes, filled the large low space like electric crickets and frogs.

They were directed to the desk of the official charged with the protection of motor vehicles. His glance swept over them like a flame-thrower, searing them with a taste of his senti-ments towards molesters of cars. But he doused his look as Howell explained they were not rapists, but virtuous hus-bands, legally married to their automobiles, if temporarily without their marriage certificates. He became instantly friendly, called them "you fellers."

But the procedure he outlined was complicated. First you fellers phone the wife. Then she takes the title to a police officer who knows you fellers personally—there happened to be one such among the neighbors. The officer then shows the paper to the protector of vehicles in Albuquerque who tele-graphs the vital numbers here to his counterpart in El Paso. Upon receipt of which you fellers will be issued a police affidavit for the Mexican authorities.

As they emerged from the yellow building, Howell could only groan. "It'll take all day, for Christ sakes."

He realized that for the first time he felt more cheerful than Howell did, a peculiar sensation.

"How come you didn't offer him ten bucks on your honest face?"

"Yeah, that would have been a hot one." Howell shrugged and smiled. "Oh, what the hell, live and learn."

"Live and learn . . ."

Waiting outside the phone booth, he happened to glance at a clock. Five past two. His mind stirred, as if to remember where and in what condition it had been twenty-four hours ago, and then shuddered the thought away.

Howell came out. "O.K. Lucky I caught her—she was on her way to the beauty parlor. Well, what now . . . how about a beer?"

At seven, after tasteless beer, movie, and chop suey, they were back at the police station. "Nope, nothin' come in yet. Whyn't you fellers just park yourselves in the reception room and wait?"

They parked themselves in the parking area, a row of gray metal chairs lining the wall in the main section of the room. He stretched his legs and looked up. The ceiling seemed to have been lowered an inch since this afternoon.

"What a goddamn waste of time," Howell muttered once more. Again he didn't reply, nor did anything inside say anything to him either. He looked without curiosity around the room.

Over in the far corner, under a battery of long glowing tubes, was a large metal desk behind which an obese man was pecking lethargically away at a typewriter. A brown man, but beneath this light his complexion was a sallow gray. Sitting on the big desk were two other men, slimmer and more agile-looking, in body-hugging suntans, with revolver butts poking provocatively out of well-polished hip holsters. One was a black man, but in this light a pale ecru or beige, with a large silver ring of keys dangling from his belt. The other, a white man with a blotchy red face, was playing boredly with his thick billy club. All three men were smoking cigars. At intervals they pulled their mouths back to regard the wet ends with the concentration of suckling infants. From atop a file cabinet, a small transistor radio rattled away in muted frenzy. Periodically, each in turn stopped to look about vacantly or search his uniform for specks and threads; now and then their bodies all shook in brief laughter at a remark none of them seemed to have made. From the glass cubicles, the teletype-intercom chamber ensemble droned forth its interminable sonata. Everything was charged with potential, waiting for drama . . .

Enter a new sound. A scratching on metal, from the steel door in the wall behind the booking desk, solid and heavy as a bank vault's. The man with the keys slid down from his perch, sauntered casually to the door and unlocked it.

Enter a new figure. Stooped, capped and clad in prison denim, it came lugging a mop, a bucket, and an atmosphere of carbolic fumes. As the steel door slammed shut again, there was a swift glimpse of a long corridor, tiled in amber and leading back into depths. And then in the very corner, a small window came into notice, through which could be seen dozens of other small windows, dimly lighted and facing onto some kind of inner yard. All these windows had bars.

The new character was already at work, slopping white water onto the asphalt-tile floor and squeezing it back into his bucket. His skin was corpse-white. His head, his hands, his hair, everything that wasn't hidden by blue cloth, looked completely depigmented, the same dead white as the soapy liquid in the scrub-bucket, which might have been juice wrung from his own body. His face was a record of so much intimate intercourse with fists and nightsticks, sidewalks and gutters, that not a feature seemed to remain in its original shape or position. It looked one-directional, as if food, light, and air could still enter, but everything inside could no longer get out. He and Howell watched him approach as they would a large albino salamander, hatched and raised in a vat of mop-water. So that when he actually spoke, and to them, saying, "Mind liftin' ya feet a minute, gents?" they nearly leapt from their chairs.

Forgetting the trio at the booking desk, they watched the old prisoner slosh, mop, wring, saturate the air with his chemical fumes. From time to time he rested a moment by lifting his face to the low gray-white fluorescence, as if this were the only sun he had ever known. It was during one of these poses that his act was superseded by another.

Enter a new commotion. From the main doorway this time, followed five seconds later by its source—a small dancing body with a big blue shadow. Flying into the room it came, a foot off the floor, pedaling the air furiously, like some fantastic circus act with a no-wheeled cycle. As it rocketed across the room, it emitted a piercing whistle—"Aaaiiiiii . . ."—directing itself unerringly at the big metal desk, at the trio of waiting cigar-nursers, who looked up with the avidity of a litter of fox-whelps when papa brings home a squirming rabbit.

Because no, this rabbit was not self-propelled. Behind this performing body was that of a big blue cop at least twice its size, one meaty fist clamped on the scruff of the coat-collar, the other on the seat of the pants. So this was no gymnastic stunt, after all; merely a small man trying frantically to keep from falling on his face by means of this mad air-pedaling.

Frantically but futilely. As he arrived at the booking desk, the custodial hands released him suddenly, the one in his pants with a skillful little tug to make sure that what threatened to happen did in fact happen. Down went the rabbit, face first, with a soft dull slap as it met the cement floor.

The four big bodies looked down at the one small body. It did not move, just lay where it fell, a sack of palpitating clothing. The fat clerk leaned over the desk to get a better view.

The red-faced white man was the first to speak to it.

"Get up."

The head on the floor lifted itself an inch or two and fell back again, to the other side. The victim was a Mexican, dark, thin to emaciation, small-boned. Black-socketed eyes a blinking stare, lips drawn back from teeth, nostrils dark air-sucking holes.

The red white man slid his buttocks slowly and deliberately off the desk and stood spread-legged over the body, eyes slitted, as if taking aim.

"I said get up."

The only thing to rise was a whimper.

"Pick him up." Red jerked his jaw toward the cop, who was standing by, big and blue and puffing with exertion.

The cop bent forward. His left hand shot to the Mexican's seat again. Instantly the body jack-knifed up from the floor. For a second it seemed he would let it flop back down again, but the other hand, hooking the neck, snapped it upright and planted it on its feet in front of the desk.

The Mexican looked a foot shorter and a hundred pounds lighter than any of his captors. His fawn-colored sport coat had huge padded shoulders and wide lapels. He himself was little more than a dark wire hanger inside.

"Name?"

No response or reaction. The zoot suit stood wobbling before the big desk. If the cop released his grip, it would certainly crumple back to the floor.

"Search the bastard."

The pale black man, without rising from his perch, slapped quickly over the suit, rotating it as necessary, netting a wallet, a pack of cigarette paper, a small brown bottle and a dirty piece of rag. He piled the articles on the desk. The captive, evidently recognizing his belongings, started to lean in their direction, only to be snapped erect again by a sudden blue knee to his spine. His low whistling wail was stifled by a twist of the blue arm on his neck.

The red white man picked the wallet out of the pile and began to recite while the gray brown man, slipping a fresh form into his machine, began to type to the dictation.

"Still live at this address?" The question was directed to the prisoner. A low silibant blubbering came forth in response, as if his condition were improving a bit.

"What's he say?"

"Ah, he don't savvy nothin'," the blue cop volunteered.

"You ask him, Rod."

"¡Oye, jodido! ¿Dónde vives tu?" the gray faced man said, looking up from his machine.

The beige man bent down and picked up the prisoner's hat, which lay crushed on the floor, placed it carefully on the small dark head—much darker than his own—appraised it like a hatter, and then mashed it down with a swat of his hand.

"¡Dónde vives tu, te digo!" the fat clerk said again, his gray face purpling.

The Mexican mumbled something which evidently failed to meet the clerk's standards. Lunging like a bull walrus up across the desk, he slapped the dark little face hard, hard enough to send the hat sailing back to the floor. The victim's hand came up to catch his head, which had been tossed backward like a flower bud. The wide fawn-colored shoulders of the padded jacket began to shudder.

255

"What the son-of-a-bitch say, Rod?"

"Shit, I can't understand the sucker."

"We'll get it out of him later. Throw the bastard in the tank."

But nobody stirred to carry out the red white man's order, as if some ancient procedural canon had first to be fulfilled. There was a moment of stillness in which the three at the desk gazed on the trembling suit of clothes with the same deliberate concentration they had been directing at their cigars.

"Don't want to forget his hat," said the man with the palest complexion, the black man.

"Pick up your hat," ordered the red white man.

"*Tu sombrero, jodido,*" echoed the gray brown man.

The Mexican simpered and shuddered and held his face between both hands.

The turnkey placed his large hand on the man's small head and rotated the face down toward the floor where the hat lay inert and shapeless.

"Your hat," he whispered, almost politely.

As the Mexican began to bend shakily toward the hat, the red-faced man gave him a short swift shove on the buttocks with his foot, too swift to let him break his fall with his arms. His face and the linoleum-coated concrete met with a soft sickening thud. A dull scream rose like a curl of smoke from the clothes-heap, and it began to vibrate convulsively, like a body under electroshock.

The red man's starched khaki behind eased back down onto the desk. He slipped a small silver implement from his pocket —a nail clipper—and began to clean his already clean fingernails.

The turnkey sauntered lightly to the steel door, unlocked it, and held it wide like a footman. The big blue cop reached

256

down for the crumpled heap, and it rose like a phoenix and bolted directly for the door. The dimly lighted tile corridor beyond seemed now a vertical chute under a trapdoor. And unlike his entrance, the legs of the flying man were no longer pedaling at his exit, but dangling and swaying limply, as from an uninhabited suit of clothes on its way to the cleaners.

"His hat." The red white man scooped it up and sailed it casually down the shaft after the disappearing figures. The steel door slammed shut, and everything became what it had been. The pale prisoner, who had never ceased mopping, was still mopping, over by the main entry . . .

He sat staring—at his hands. Had it all been an hallucination? He turned to look at Howell, whose face confirmed that it had indeed actually taken place. He turned back to the booking desk. The clerk was sweeping the little residual heap of belongings into a brown manila envelope.

Suddenly he was on his feet, blind and quivering with outrage. He felt hands grab up at him desperately. "Christ man, where you going!"

"To the police. We're witnesses."

The hands pulled down on him with all their strength. "You *nuts?*"

Again; two little words. The strength went out of him, and he allowed himself to be pulled back into the chair. A moment later, a form passed through the entry, clutching several yellow envelopes.

"Hey, that's it! It's got to be it. Listen, do me a favor and just sit tight here a minute. Don't move, O.K.?"

"I'll wait for you outside."

But as he made for the door, he felt the red-faced white man's voice strike his back. "Hey!"

He stopped.

A low, dog-summoning whistle.

He neither moved forward nor turned back to look.

"Hey, Smitty! Come on over here and mop this mess up."

"Yessir, Boss, on the double."

They exchanged no conversation again until they had crossed the border into Mexico. But as they moved into the Spanish-twisted neon of Juarez, they gave almost simultaneous sighs of relief, and laughed, each knowing what the other was thinking.

"Yeah, but you think it's any different in Mexican jails? Cops are cops, man, the world over. I remember one night in Paris after the Beaux Arts ball, me and a buddy were walking down the Rue de Seine having a little fun, and the flics hauled us in. Weren't too gentle on us, either. But you should have seen the way they worked over two other bastards, couple of Algerians—hey, that looks like a pretty decent motel over there. What do you say?"

He said yes, and ten minutes later he was at work repairing his first Mexican toilet. Not that there was anything seriously the matter with it actually—just a question of straightening a bent plunger rod and adjusting its angle of fall.

19

S‍LEEP GAVE HIM BACK as easily as it had accepted him last night, without transitional thinking or dreaming, and he lay in the big double bed taking in the surrounding unfamiliarity with all his senses, like a child. The underlying odor, faint but there, a curious pungent muskiness between cedar wood and cigar smoke—he tried placing it, but couldn't except literally: he'd smelled it here in Juarez before, and only here. The heavy muslin sheets looked fairly clean but limp. More than possibly, the linen wasn't laundered and sanitized nightly, or even between guests. Over on the far side of the bed, Howell's wave was still rising and falling like a peaceful ocean, its rhythm unruffled when an impassioned argument blew up in a sudden squall from the other side of the partition wall. He lay and listened to the Spanish invective as to a squirrel raging, making no greater effort to decipher it. When, a moment later, it died out again, he got up quietly, dressed and stepped out into Mexico.

Across the courtyard the sun was also just getting up from one of the facing units. The same sun, which seemed to have followed them down here yesterday, to have chosen the same motel, and to be now having its first look at this very different world. The motel itself was aerodynamically streamlined, as if designed for flight, with many small fancy flourishes in paint and tile, even a crude Orozco-type fresco that crammed together conquistadores and Toltecs, revolutionaries, bull-fighters and Mexico City skyscrapers. But everything was conspicuously falling apart, fissuring, flaking, reverting to dust. The far end of the court hadn't even been finished—it was not under construction but abandoned, as if its builder had gotten bored with the project. The last unit had been converted into a chicken yard.

This state of disrepair he'd noticed so often in Mexico, was it all due to poverty? Or did it reflect a state of mind, a state of vision, that simply did not come to a focus at the same level American eyes did? Was it lack of ambition and organization, or was it a centering on other centers?

He strolled through the miniature formal garden around which the compound was built. The roses and dahlias were in full ultimate bloom, untouched yet by frost. They looked tended. But the fountain they bordered was bone-dry and littered with rubble. In the middle of it, a muscular "Mother Mexico" with square concrete breasts stood holding triumphantly aloft an unconnected section of half-inch galvanized pipe.

He stood by the chicken yard watching the chickens, looking at them as if he had never really seen chickens before. And they looked just right to him. Their comb, beak and feather construction, the way they jerked, scratched and strutted, their choice of life-interests, all seemed to be excellent answers to the questions of sentient existence, as valid as any others, as valid, certainly, as his own.

Suddenly they all rushed forward, clucking and gargling, to converge on one corner of the enclosure. In the adjoining motel unit, a door opened and a very old woman came out, a black shawl over her shoulders, she was cradling a dented tin pot of yellow corn.

"*Buenos días,*" he said.

"*Buenos días de Dios.*"

Behind him he heard the creak and slam of the station-wagon door. Howell was up. Turning, he caught a sudden and fantastic sight: El Paso's skyscrapers, glittering up like extensions of the hotel roof. Only a mile or two away. But in another country. A very other country.

Back in the room Howell had the instant coffee steaming on the camp stove. "Sorry, no juice," he smiled. "Some bastards stole the oranges. But plenty cereal." On the dresser-top eight different boxes of breakfast food were laid out to pick from, krispies, toasties and pops.

All morning long he sat gazing out at the vast empty aridity they were whistling through, its boney rock-green growths like intermediate forms between vegetable and mineral. Only his reason insisted that this was merely a continuation of the American desert of yesterday, that these great remote blue peaks belonged to the same chain of mountains as those around Albuquerque. Everything else assured him this was a completely new and different world.

Howell was happy again, eager again, reminiscing again, as if this were France, not Mexico they were entering. "It's different, I tell you, over there. Over there they appreciate artists, they respect them. And not just the big shots. Even me, I was '*Monsieur le peintre.*' And we used to call our professor '*Maître.*' In the states artists are bums, worse than bums . . . hey, look over there, the way those hills kind of fold in on each other, all siennas and Mars yellows and blues, really cubist."

"Why not stop and do a sketch or something?"

"Huh? I almost feel like it, but if we keep stopping, we'll never get there."

"Get where?"

"I don't know, wherever we're going. I'd rather get there first. Then we can relax and take our time—by the way, what time you got? Guess I forgot to wind my watch."

It was then he discovered his own wristwatch was gone. He remembered taking it off last night when he reached into the toilet tank. He must never have put it back on.

Below Chihuahua the desert gradually grew less arid, or else it had reconciled itself to its aridity and decided to make the most of it. The strange groveling growths grew bolder, began to reach outward and upward. The yucca multiplied its heads and stretched its necks. The cholla expanded. But it was the prickly pear he noticed most, the same species on whose stunted northern fruit he had gorged himself Monday night—the night before last night? really?—and the remaining few of whose stickers he still felt as a sort of subliminal itching pain in his mouth and between his fingers. (He'd got rid of most of them yesterday by semi-conscious nipping and plucking as he drowsed beside Howell.) Now with every passing hour the prickly pears pushed up higher and spread out wider. The flat green hands which were buried to the wrist on Sandia mountain slid their arms up from the earth, then their bodies; the lowly plants turned into bushes, and finally into sizable trees with strong trunks, thick limbs and heavy fat leaves. In some places they seemed to have been gathered and cultivated in orchards, in others men and animals sat resting in their shade.

Because, as the cactus grew higher, animate beings began to enter the landscape in ever greater numbers. Human figures, walking, squatting, reclining along the road, carrying all kinds of burdens, singly, in groups, lining the walls and filling the tiny plazas of the hamlets. And with men came animals:

burros, cows, horses, pigs, goats, dogs, chickens. It struck him as odd, this proliferation, disquieting somehow, and he realized how conditioned he had become to seeing a countryside populated by motor vehicles, so that the presence of so much life unpackaged in glass and steel, moving in its own flesh and under its own power, felt almost like an infestation. He caught himself wondering what they were all doing out there. Whatever it was, it was clearly nothing terribly urgent. Hardly any creature, man or beast, was too busy to stop and stare at their whizzing capsule of metal and glass.

The accumulation of all this slow anonymous life around them was having the same effect on Howell.

"What the hell they all up to out there?"

"I don't know. Just living, I guess."

"Call that living?"

Yes, now he was sure. That was exactly what you called it: living—though living in a sense he'd never thought of before, at least not in connection with the human race. But that was what they were doing, that and nothing else. Living the life that was given them . . .

Howell put off stopping as long as he could, but eventually the need for gas forced him to. He pulled into a tiny station set alone in what looked like the middle of nowhere. But even before the car had ceased to roll, it was crawling with people like a sugar lump with ants. A young man in grease-stained coveralls was turning the crank of the non-electric gas pump, another with legs of unequal length was limping toward the tank dragging the hose. A small boy had twisted off the cap. An old man who looked like Masaccio's Saint Peter was ineffectually smearing a paste of smashed bugs over the windshield. A tall man was holding up the hood while a short one climbed in after the dip stick. A short one was splashing a few drops of dirty water into the radiator from an old oil can. A child of eight or nine with ringworm over half its scalp was polishing the chrome trim with a piece of pants leg. To extricate themselves and get back into untouchable speed again meant inserting unfamiliar coins into half a dozen open palms like some very complicated vending machine.

They were both unnerved. In him, this incident, underscoring all those anonymous stares, had begun to release a guilty self-awareness. The year-old Ford wagon became an ostentatious limousine. The shirt on his back felt excessively clean and whole, the dollars in his pockets like stolen treasure. Even the unused space in the car seemed to have been robbed from somebody, its speed a fleeing from justice.

With Howell, he saw, the process was working differently. The shoots of guilt were clipped off below ground level, and his defenses became offenses.

"Jesus, don't they give you the creeps? The way they look at us, they hate us, they hate our guts. Man, I wouldn't want to have a breakdown in this place"—he meant throwing a piston rod or wheel bearing or something—"I can just see a mob of them closing in and stripping us to the bone in nothing flat like those South American beetles." And for thirty miles he reeled off a program of film clips of friends of his being gypped, robbed, insulted and conned by Mexicans. For an encore he threw in a handful of similar stories from his Paris days, including the time he'd had a sixty-five-dollar overcoat swiped in the Gare Saint-Lazare.

He himself said nothing. Not only was he too weak to contend with Howell, he was too grateful. Howell was saving his life.

They spent Wednesday night in a town called Jiménez. This time the toilet was a little more challenging: a corroded pivot pin on the shut-off mechanism, plus a leak in the copper float. He devised a replacement pin by clipping off a length of the heavy electric wire that was sticking out of a dismantled air-conditioning unit, cautiously, since it was live. The float he patched temporarily with a gob of Permatex gasket compound from Howell's tool box. Howell promised him the plumbing sub-contract on his next job.

The first awareness Thursday morning brought was that he was cured. For now at least, cured. The depression had completely lifted, and he felt more than neutral. He felt eager for the upcoming day. He went out to the market to buy bananas and tangerines and rolls for breakfast, and when he offered to relieve Howell with the driving, his offer was accepted. Howell too seemed to sense that something had happened to him, that now he could be trusted.

As he drove he tried for the first time to think about what happened to him. From the feel of it, his very metabolism had altered, as radically as the natural and social metabolism around him. What, he wondered, if he had happened to be born down here rather than up there, one of these people, would he still have—no, he felt certain of it, he wouldn't have. Or at least it was very improbable. Like the plague; people still caught it once in a while out of the blue, even back in the United States. But where they were dropping of plague right and left, the odds went up. He wished he could see comparative mental health statistics for Albuquerque and, well, a place like this—it looked about the same size.

They were cruising about, temporarily lost, in Torreón, Coahuila, through modern commercial streets that looked little different from American ones, and the unchanged *barrios* of the poor—wide, shallow canals of standing sunlight, the little family *tiendas* splashed with brilliant primary colors.

Howell too was showing the effects. Instead of worrying about the lost road, he was enthusing over the light, the textures, the reds, the oranges, the blues, the yellows, undisturbed now that they were "wasting time." "Now, that's the first Pepsi sign I ever felt like putting in a painting—reminds me a hell of a lot of the Côte d'Azur—and will you look at all those palm trees!"

The palms were out in force, and he realized that from here south to Argentina there was no winter worthy of the name.

It was glaring hot siesta weather. Having driven all morning, he sat drowsing in the seat beside Howell, and for the first time since he screamed himself out of the cement on Monday morning, he slipped back into dream . . .

It was glaring hot siesta weather, and he had come to consult Dr. Jorge. The doctor sat on a stump behind his packing-crate desk, while he himself lay in his manta pajamas slung in the hemp patient's *hamaca*, his sarape bunched into a pillow under his head, and his straw *sombrero* over his loins like a fig-leaf. Chickens were walking in and out of the consulting room, scratching on the dirt floor, while two or three bare-bottomed children were peeing on it to make mudpies. The doctor's wife was poking at a charcoal brazier in the kitchen corner, and a skinny yellow dog snored and twitched over near the doorway.

He himself, as usual, was discussing his problem. As he streamed consciousness, the psychiatrist streamed sweat. It flowed down his round brown cheeks and dripped from the eaves of his thatch moustache. But he was obviously listening keenly nonetheless, interjecting a critical "Sí sí—sigue, sigue . . ." as he swabbed his shining face with a large pink bandanna. He did not take notes, but periodically reached over to the sheaf of corn tortillas stacked neatly on his desk,

266

peeled off the top sheet, rolled it into a six-inch tube, swished it in a little saucer of blood-red chili, lifted the furry blackness beneath his nostrils, parted the pink wetness of his lips, and with the sharp whiteness of his teeth, bit off the end.

Then suddenly he raised his hand. *"Basta."* He leaned down, still chomping noisily, and proceeded to isolate the source of the trouble in certain unsavory desires which were not being gratified.

He felt the doctor's words streak to his heart like an arrow. He was right, Dr. Jorge was right. Yet he found himself sitting up, almost spilling from the hammock to protest.

"Sí, pero no consciously, Doctor, no consciously!"

"Claro que no consciously, hermano, only sub- and un-. Bueno—ahora tienes insight, no?"

He shook his head sadly. *"No. Ni insight ni outsight, Doctorcito."*

Dr. Jorge threw out his arms. *"Compadre, we can go no farther with talk. We must act. Our only recurso now is my little black box, mi cajita negra. Listo? Then kindly open your boca."*

Saying which Dr. Jorge donned a great welding helmet and a pair of asbestos gloves, and uncoiled a long corrugated rubber esophagus which he attached to Bob's mouth. He then began to whirl a pair of huge chromium dials. Instantly the juke-box colors swirled, the fireworks shot up, and the box struck up a hooting rendition of *Allá en el Rancho Grande*, while he himself lapped eagerly at the trickle of ice-cold beer that was being piped onto his tongue . . .

"Hey, Bob, take a look at that!"

He shook awake just in time to catch it. A crew of men and machines were working on the road. A tremendous yellow dump truck ahead was loaded high with green gravel, and atop this mound, fifteen feet in the air, a man stood urinating, describing a thin, brief, glittering parabolic arc to the ground. With his free hand, he waved down to them.

"Boy, that reminds me of France."

"That the way they do it in France, off of dump trucks?"

"No, I mean, they're not so . . ."

"I know what you mean."

"You know," Howell said a few minutes later, "Navajos are the same way. Had a couple of them working for me one time—had to lay them off, they'd bring the whole damn family along. When they had to go, they just went—anyplace. Even the women—they'd just lift all those skirts of theirs and squat."

"Is that so?" What would Dr. Hoerchner say to that? he wondered. Or for that matter, Dr. Jorge?

The road was in bad shape, cracked, cratered and chewed. And now it had begun to squirm up hills and around bluffs. They found themselves trapped behind a third-class bus, unable to pass. It had slowed them to its own laborious crawl. Ahead the view was filled with people, cartons, crated fowl, cardboard valises, burlap sacks, bamboo baskets, lashed and clinging to the roof and sides of the monster, cramming the interior to black opacity. A boy was straddling the spare tire, which was worn down to the fabric. A woman hunched high in the baggage rack, clasping a pair of large striped pumpkins to her breast like children. The bus itself, where it showed through, was a scabrous hunk of convulsing scrap-metal. Forced to climb, it sent forth howls of torment, while a thick wake of oily black smoke jetted from its underbelly as from a mortally wounded whale. And when the road suddenly tilted downhill, there was added a terrifying barrage of explosive flatus.

They stared, both of them.

"Will you look at the shimmy on that rear wheel!"

Howell no sooner spoke for the rear wheel than the rear wheel spoke for itself—one deafening and terminal concussion that drowned out all exhaust pipe artillery. The bus, heaving and pitching in a sort of death-ecstasy, shuddered to a thumping halt as a low choral moan of anguish rose from man and machinery.

For a few seconds nothing stirred. Then the boy leapt lithely off the spare tire. After another moment, the driver, dripping wet, came squeezing forth like a birth. He walked slowly to the flattened rear wheel and gazed at it enigmatically, all the lines of his face downflowing, as if to channel off the sweat. Then he began to auscultate the shredded rubber carcass with a few indifferent kicks. Finally, seeming to rise above the situation entirely, he reached around to scratch the small of his back.

"Let's give somebody a ride, Harry. How about that poor woman there, the one with the pumpkins?" She had not moved, but was still wedged in the baggage rack, now at a thirty-five-degree list, hugging her *calabazas* even closer, as if before a rising sea.

"I'd like to, I really would. But if we stopped for her, you know damn well what'd happen. The whole bunch of them would try to pile on. Anyhow there'll be another bus along pretty soon."

"Sure, the sister ship to this wreck."

Tapping his horn, Howell swiveled deftly around the bus and away. "Look, Bob, these people are different. They're used to waiting. Time doesn't mean the same thing it means back home."

"You mean time is *not* money down here?"

"That's it. Too much time and not enough dough. But maybe they get more out of life than we do, who knows?"

"Yeah, who knows . . ."

But one thing he did know. The next time he had the wheel he was going to stop and give somebody a lift without even asking Howell.

His chance came a few minutes after he took over from Howell at Francisco I. Madero, the last town north of Durango. Far ahead he made out the figure of a man standing beside a parked truck, raising his arm languidly and letting it fall again, as if he had lost hope of anybody's paying attention.

First he slowed down, and then he asked, "O.K. if I give him a ride?"

"Go ahead if you want to . . . but it looks to me like he needs more than just a ride."

The man came trotting across the road, looking anxious and frightened, but trying to smile. When he realized these were Northamericans he became speechless, just stood looking mutely in at them. He was in his forties, or maybe younger, and he was very dirty. His eyes were liquid and broken, like those of a workhorse. His hand, rising in a kind of salute, and his head, lowering in obeisance, conveyed an unmistakable message: "Behold your unworthy inferior. I have not the words to express my gratitude that you have noticed my miserable existence." But not a sound came from his mouth.

"What's the matter?" he asked the man in Spanish. "Having trouble?"

"Yes, sir, much trouble. We have been waiting here since yesterday morning. The truck doesn't want to go."

They all gazed across the road at the truck, a large black and blue panel delivery. A mass of contusions, it looked not merely beaten up and worn out, it looked posthumous, an exhumed hearse.

"Do you have perhaps a *bobina?*"

"*Bobina?*" He had never heard the word. "Well, let's go have a look at it." As he climbed out, he became aware that his voice had a new tone, a cheery, easygoing American egalitarianism. "How about it, Harry, want to come along?"

They crossed the highway. The air smelled sweet and mild. After the roar of driving, they began to hear the pulsating ring of insects, the soft rushes of breeze.

They stood staring at the black and blue hulk as at the carcass of some blubbery marine monster on a beach.

"Jesus, what a heap," he heard Howell whisper under his breath.

"Since yesterday morning we have been waiting here," the man said again

The "we" made them look around. There in the dusty hollow of the road shoulder sat a woman in a dirty black dress, painfully thin, her eyes an unhealthy dark, her hair stringy and matted, her front teeth brown and rotted, bent over a tiny black-haired infant and suckling it from a breast like an empty pouch. Two other small children were squatting beside her, staring at Howell and himself in gaping languor. From inside the truck, amid a heap of mattresses and bedding, a half-grown girl was staring at them with the same expression. Still another small body seemed to be lying in a dirty quilt. The view before him now could have served as a dictionary illustration for the word *poverty*. He nodded to the group on the ground and tried to force a friendly American smile to his lips. From them came nothing.

"*Bueno*, what exactly seems to be wrong with the truck?" he asked, glad that Howell couldn't understand the question.

"I think this, the *bobina*. At the garage in Durango they said the *bobina* was no good. A new one cost one hundred pesos. I had no money." The man's finger tapped the ignition coil. One quick glance revealed that the fanbelt was badly

271

frayed, oil was leaking from the head gasket, and a plug was missing from the carburetor. He pried off the ignition cap and asked the Mexican for a screwdriver.

"Señor, I have nothing. In Durango they stole my tools, they stole our money."

"Who stole—wait." He looked up at Howell who was standing there shaking his head slowly, as one does over a corpse. "*Dice que es la bobina.*"

"Huh? *Comment vous dîtes?*"

"Oh . . . sorry. He says it's the coil. You wouldn't happen to have a spare coil, would you?"

Instantly a mini-drama played itself out on Howell's face. He did have a coil, but he wasn't about to give it up. His features tussled with each other a moment, and then he said; "Yeah, I think maybe I got one in there, but I doubt like hell it'll work. It's for a Ford and God knows what this clunker is."

Asked what make the truck was, the Mexican replied it was a Fargo.

"A Fargo? What's that, the outfit that built Noah's ark? This idiot's got no business on the road in this piece of junk in the first place—I'll go see if I can find the damn coil."

"And bring the tool box while you're at it. He doesn't have any tools."

"You bet. But it'd be a heck of a lot simpler just to trade cars."

"Now, who stole your things?" he asked the Mexican, whose expression made him repeat the question in Spanish.

"Who knows, sir? Last night—no, the night before last night—we were sleeping behind the gasoline station. They stole our boxes, the one with the tools and the one with my brother's money."

"Did you tell the police?"

"The police are for the rich people."

"But isn't there some kind of welfare agency to help people in emergencies?"

"Yo no comprendo, Señor."

"So you have nothing?"

"Nada, nada . . ." The defeated eyes began to fill. "Since yesterday morning we have not eaten . . . the children . . . my wife has no milk . . ."

He looked at the Mexican, feeling the primitive alert signal go off inside him, the release of some self-protective hormone. Was this a trap? Was this some kind of elaborate performance designed to bilk dollars out of the naive and soft-hearted *turistas?* He peered at the others, looking for cracks in the façade of this tableau of misery. Four pairs of eyes were fixed back on him. No, five: the baby had given up on the breast and was staring at him as well.

"Wait here a minute. I'll be back," he said, in English, but not pausing to translate.

Howell was at the wagon.

"What's up now?"

"Those people, they're starving. Somebody stole their money. They don't have a cent, nothing. They haven't eaten for two days!"

"Hold it, just hold it. Calm down. Don't be a sucker for everything these guys tell you. They're sly buggers. Here they've hooked onto a couple of gringo do-gooders and . . . well, what've we got? There's the rest of the bananas back there, and the rolls from this morning—oh, what the hell!" He rummaged into his supermarket provisions and came up with a can of Spam, a box of Corn Toasties, and two cans of evaporated milk. "Wait . . . here's some Hershey bars for the kids."

They carried the food back across the road and distributed it UNESCO-style. From all but the baby came a barely audible "Gracias, Señor."

"*Banana bueno pour bébé,*" Howell said to the mother, standing over her like a public health nurse.

The woman took a bite of the banana and sat chewing it for a minute. Then she spat it slowly back into the baby's mouth as Howell's face recaptured some of the horror he'd seen it register in the El Paso police station.

"*Vamos a ver,*" he said to the man, turning back to the truck. He touched the screwdriver to the distributor. "First, let's see if there's a spark. Is the ignition on?"

"Yes, but the battery is dead from trying. I do it this way." The man had the crank inserted—the truck was that old—and was turning the engine.

"No spark. Think it's the coil, Harry?"

"I think it's everything. Of course, the coil can just blow like that, like a light bulb."

"Did the truck stop suddenly?" he asked the Mexican feeling like a doctor in the wrong specialty.

"It was going and then it didn't want to go."

"Try my coil on it," Howell said.

They tried it. Still no spark.

"Might be anything—generator, battery, short—anyhow that's not the right coil for it. Mine's twelve volts and God knows what this—hey, will you look at the gas pouring out of that carburetor."

With each turn of the crank a jet of gasoline spurted from the carburetor, like arterial bleeding.

"Tell you one thing—it's not the fuel pump."

"Stop," he said to the Mexican. "*Basta.* What happened to the screw that goes in this hole?"

The man shook his head hopelessly.

Howell had found a stick and was stuffing it in the hole. "It's just a drain plug. This'll hold it for a while."

He handed Howell back his coil and reconnected the old

274

one. "I am sorry," he said to the man, "we cannot fix it. You need a real mechanic . . . where were you going?"

'To Monterrey. There is work there. My brother went last year. He sent us the money to come, and in Durango they stole it."

"Where did you come from?"

"From Navojoa."

"Navojoa! You came all the way from Navojoa in—in *this?*"

"Yes, sir."

"But that's on the Pacific coast, isn't it? How far is it anyway from Navojoa to Monterrey?"

"Very far." His brown eyes were beginning to waver under the pulls of his anxiety. "It is impossible to make it go?"

"I don't say that. It may be something very small. But you must get a mechanic. We are not mechanics."

"You are not mechanics . . ." It came ten seconds later, like an echo, as if he thought los yanquis could accomplish everything they attempted.

"I'm sorry." Again he glanced back at the little group eating in the roadside dust, a wretched parody of the American family picnic. He heard the truck utter a small creaking sob as the man's body sank suddenly down onto the front bumper, and sat staring vacantly at the ground "*Vale más que morimos todos,*" he heard him breathe in one low sigh.

"Better that we all die"—and for him then it was almost as if the man had indeed died before his eyes; he seemed to see, rising from the bent body, a vapor of mild light, an effulgence of such infinite sadness and beauty that it almost drew him in, almost made him lose his grasp on time and place, his sense of "me here and that Mexican there." He stepped back quickly and averted his eyes, and his arms gave a little shudder to regain his balance.

On the bumper itself, he saw that something had been

written in blue paint, one of those mottoes in Gothic letter-
ing he had noticed on many Mexican commercial vehicles. It
had been almost completely effaced by scrapes and rust, but
still he could make it out, the last words of it at least: ". . . es
mi guía" The first part of the phrase was covered by the man's
body.

"So what's the deal?" came Howell's impatient voice. "You
rattle away with him in Spanish and never explain the situation to me."

"What's there to explain, Harry? You've got eyes. Any
suggestions?"

"How about that little town back there? There was a bunch
of guys working on cars in that garage where we just gassed up.
Why can't he go down there and bring out a mechanic? It's
only a mile or so—hell, we'll take him in the car."

"What about money?"

"O.K., let's give him some money, for God's sake. How
much you think?"

"He says they want a hundred pesos for a coil."

"A hundred? That's eight bucks! All right let's give him a
hundred. He might not even need a coil, or maybe they can
fix him up with a used one."

"I'll tell you what. Let's each give him a hundred. It won't
get him where he's going, but it'll help feed his kids for a
couple of days."

The Mexican was still sitting on the bumper, still looking
at the ground. He put his hand on the man's shoulder to get
his attention, told him the plan, and handed him two olive-
brown hundred-peso notes.

The Mexican stood up slowly, his eyes on the money, and
then lifted his face. His expression was the same as it was
when he first approached the car. Again he seemed to have
been struck dumb. The eyes looked more than ever like those
of a workhorse. Embarrassed, he averted his own and bent

quickly to pick up the tool box. A foot away he saw the hidden first word on the bumper, now disclosed. It was "*Dios.*"

They were at the garage before the man spoke again. He asked to borrow a pencil and paper. They watched him print out his name and address in Monterrey, carving it painstakingly, as if into stone: "José I. Montes de Oca G. *Al cuidado* Valentín R. Montes de Oca G."

"Got a name like a Conquistador," Howell said. "He ought to sell it."

"Please, *Señores*, write here your address in the United States. I will pay you back."

"No no no, forget it. Someday, when you're a rich *capitalista* in Monterrey, you may find my friend and me broken down along the highway somewhere." What was it that made him retreat once more into this role of American good egg?

The irony was lost on the Mexican. "Then God will repay you," he said, using the formula with which beggars receive alms.

"*Bueno* . . . well, *hasta la vista* . . . and good luck."

"Yeah, take it easy now . . ."

"*Que Dios les acompañe, Señores* . . ."

As he drove out of Francisco I. Madero for the second time, he felt himself silenced, left musing on the contrasts between their modes of farewell. "Good luck . . . take it easy now . . ." All this accumulation of power, all this prying loose and categorization of nature's secrets, all this sophisticated knowhow, and we knew nothing, we were back again with the most primitive and shallowest of understandings. We had no place to lay our lives but on the altar of the great god Luck.

Howell too seemed uncharacteristically quiet; he gave him a sidelong glance that found him staring out the window ahead, thoughtfully, as if musing along the same lines. For the first time he felt intimations of Howell's being something more than a useful but rather tiresome adjunct to his own purposes.

"Thanks a lot, Harry."

"What for?"

"You know what. You didn't have to. I appreciate it."

"Oh, what the hell, case like that. I mean, my God, who wouldn't?"

He turned quickly away and concentrated on the road, suddenly fearful lest he see that same mild effulgence start enveloping Howell as well.

As he drove, he found himself thinking, for the first time since they had left home, about his wife. Not about the present, but about their first stages together after they fell in love. Fell in, very apt. The golden pool bathed not merely the two of them, but seemed to wash over onto even the most ugly aspects of the world around them. And now he could no longer doubt that there existed a higher and greater level of this same thing. He knew for a fact now that it was possible for the human being to rise into love as well as fall into it.

Far as he was from such a state, just this brief distant intimation of it, the certainty it was real, was enough to make him feel a happiness beyond time. Actually it could only have been a minute later that Howell was reaching across his body to wave as they passed the old black truck. "So long, so long, kids . . ."

He stuck his arm out, too. In the rearview mirror he saw two small arms flutter in return, like David and Cassie behind the plane window.

"Hey, I meant to ask you, Bob—what was it that guy had painted on the bumper of that thing? 'God is my—what?' I got it all but that last word."

"Guide . . . guía."

"Guide, huh?" Howell shook his head. "Poor bastard, I guess maybe when you're in that sad a shape, God's the only guide you can afford."

* * *

278

When they reached Durango it was already dusk, but for some reason neither one of them felt like stopping, not at another tourist court. Without actually discussing it, they both understood they would like to spend the night in a little less insulated way, a little closer to real Mexican existence. And so they stopped at the first small village beyond Durango, Nombre de Dios by name, and after some asking around, located a small clean windowless room in a "guest house" for one-eighth of what they had paid the night before. They ate at a hole-in-the-wall restaurant off the tiny *mercado*, a place with a wood brazier, three clay *ollas* and two frying pans, and two raw wood tables. Beans, tortillas, *huevos a la ranchera*, spicy, greasy and satisfying. As for the toilet, the only problem was finding it in its little cubbyhole off the pigpen. It required no repairs nor would it, being merely a pit in the ground.

"One thing," Howell announced as they shifted gears into Friday morning. "No more good deeds, *compris?* We've already earned our merit badges for this trip. No stops for nobody till we get where we're going, O.K.?—Say, where are we going?"

"Don't ask me." They had neither discussed the subject nor even thought about it. "I didn't know you wanted to go someplace. I thought we were just going to zoom down two thousand miles, turn around and zoom back up."

"Where'd you get that idea? Listen, Georgette said stay two weeks and two weeks I'm gonna stay. My in-laws aren't leaving till the first. And besides, I really think I got the old urge to do a little painting. Funny, I don't know why, but I feel different, I mean, like the old days almost. You know, Mexico reminds me a heck of a lot of France."

"Oh? Lots of peasants in sarapes sitting around the cafes?"

"No, not that. I can't explain it. It's more a feeling."

"You mean neither one feels like Albuquerque."

"Albuquerque? Where's that? Never heard of the place."

"You're feeling pretty good today."

"Slept good last night. You know what those mattresses were stuffed with? Straw, just plain old straw. Georgette and me, we used to go on long bicycle trips, sometimes we'd sleep in barns, or little country auberges—oh, brother, that sweet smell of hay, sometimes we'd make it five times a night."

"Got to make it while the sun shines, they say."

"Sun's still shining, buddy," Howell said, pointing at the brilliant sky. "But no kidding, I feel like finding a nice spot and doing some painting. You know any place?"

"Not really. I've never been down this far."

"Hey, that reminds me." He leaned across and pulled a booklet from the glove compartment. "Here, I picked this thing up at one of those places back there. You find us somewhere to go."

He began to leaf through the newsprint pages. It was a magazine called *Mexico This Week*, and it contained road maps and brief descriptions of various tourist attractions.

"Yeah, I'm getting sick of just driving. If it's O.K. with you, what I'd like to do is find us a good town and settle down maybe five or six days and do a bunch of watercolors, anyway. I go for these crumbly walls and these big splashes of wild color and these old feathery trees. And the way the people dress—I don't know, I never felt like painting people with Monkey Ward clothes on. It's a lot more primitive, but still it feels like France down here."

"Any idea of what kind of place you'd like, Harry?" he asked, scanning through the pages.

"Oh, I don't care. Any old picturesque town, not too big, not too small, maybe on a lake or something, not too far south, though. You know, any old place, just as long as it's delightful."

"All right, I've found it." His eyes had just fallen on the phrase "Tarascan: Place of Delights."

"Ooo-là-là!" came Howell's falsetto.

He tried not to have heard. " 'Pátzcuaro, state of Michoacán. Pop.: 9,557; sit. on shores of picturesque Lago de Pátzcuaro. Founded 1540 by Fray Vasco de Quiroga, protector of Indians, who watched after their interests, taught them crafts, organized villages into guilds and made the first butterfly nets . . .' "

"Yeah, I think I heard of those things somewhere. But I thought that was Lake Titicaca . . . Lake Titicaca, if that isn't some name to give a lake! Titty—caca . . ."

In one of their discussions, he remembered, Frank Hoerch ner had remarked that middle class males, almost without exception, felt more at home in the anal than in the genital, most at ease as twelve-year-olds. Fighting back the sarcastic remarks to this effect that rose for his use now, he figuratively stuffed his ears and kept on reading, a little louder with each interruption.

" '. . . many attractions for the tourist, including the Basilica, La Colegiata, intended as Cathedral of Michoacán, but See moved to Morelia and church was never completed. La Colegiata contains the celebrated—' "

"Co-le-gi-a-ta, Ti-ti-ca-ca . . ." Howell was singing, to the tune of "Frère Jacques."

" 'La Colegiata contains the celebrated image of Nuestra Señora de la Salud, patroness of the sick and suffering. She is said to have been discovered miraculously by a fisherman, floating in an empty piroga in the middle of the lake. She has been observed to perspire on occasion—' "

"On occasion? What's so great about that? Look at me, I sweat every day. I'm sweating now. I just hope the lady uses an effective—"

281

" '. . . the image itself is fashioned of maize paste and orchid glue and has not deteriorated in four centuries. The faithful believe she is endowed with miraculous healing powers and can be seen any day in the Basilica walking on their knees—' "

"Oh, don't read me any more about sweating statues, man. What's it say about the delights of the place of delights? Anything about delightful señoritas?"

"There are 9,557 inhabitants. Conceivably one or two of them might be a delightful señorita."

"That settles it. Off we go to Whatz—cuaro. Whatzcuaro, Michigan. And no more stops for nobody, *compris?*"

But that afternoon they did stop for somebody: Howell. Three or four times. "Oh, it's nothing, a little touch of Lucy Bowels . . . just something we had last night at that greasy spoon."

And then, at the end of the day, as they glided through the warm mango light toward Lagos de Moreno, they stopped again, and for a nobody. It was Howell who did it, on his own. Once earlier he himself had been on the point of stopping —they were again tailing an overloaded third-class bus, and ahead saw a small puddle of waiting humanity, steaming in the hot sun. The bus didn't even slow down. He was tempted to pull over, but he read Howell's face and did not.

Yet now he felt the abrupt swerve of the car as it came to a halt at the crest of a hill, and it was for a single wayfarer, an old man. They had seen his bent figure from several hundred yards down the slope, in silhouette against the orange sky, seated on a large box and leaning forward on a stick. The man had not signaled but Howell had stopped.

They got out and stretched. Howell went off into the brush while he walked over to the old man, who looked up at him curiously but remained perched on his box, which turned out to be a homemade crate of thin branches bound with fibers of maguey.

"¿Adónde vas?" He found himself, without planning to, using the familiar "tu" form.

"¿Qué dices?" The old man craned his neck to get a better look at him.

"I said where are you going?" He raised his voice, unsure whether the old fellow was feeble-minded or just hard of hearing. His face had the color and texture of ancient leather, and was covered with a long stubble of shining white beard, rosy in this light. The hair beneath his stained and wilted hat was white, too.

"Where am I going? To Lagos, where else?" He tapped the crate beneath him with the end of his stick. "To sell my *tunas.*"

"Good, we are going to Lagos too."

"Good." He smiled and nodded and didn't budge.

"Don't you want to come with us?"

"Bueno, if you are going to Lagos, I will go to Lagos with you." He eased himself slowly down from the crate, and stood short and slight and stooped, like an old Indochinese peasant.

Meanwhile Howell had returned and was arranging things inside to receive the box. Together they heaved it up onto the lowered tail gate. It felt surprisingly heavy.

"You have sure caught a lot of *tuna.*" He had no idea what *tuna* might mean.

"Oh, yes, it took three days to catch this many. A lot of walking. Right now there aren't many, you know. It is not the season." He realized the old man was just gathering that, besides being *ricos*, they were foreigners as well. He was using the word *catch* out of courtesy.

He began to climb up on the tail gate.

"No, you ride up front with us."

"I will stay with the *tunas*."

"You will fall out."

"I won't fall out."

"Very uncomfortable back here."

"*Estoy muy bien*." There was no arguing with him.

They wedged him and the crate inside as well as they could and started off for Lagos. After a while he glanced back and saw the old man had resettled into the same quiet immobility in which they had found him, as if he could sit like that for a month without getting restless. His face was that of a Moses relieved of all historical responsibilities.

"Why don't you ask him what he's got in that crate? Weighs a ton."

"He already told me. *Tunas*."

"Come on . . ."

He turned around in the seat. Somehow he felt reluctant to ask baldly, "What is a *tuna*?"

"Would you like to sell us one of your *tunas*? Are they very expensive?"

"What are you saying?"

He repeated the question in a shout.

"Oh, forgive me, my *tunas*. Do you mean you like *tuna*?"

"Sure. I like *tuna* very much."

"I didn't think . . . I didn't think that foreigners like Mexican *tuna*." He grinned, seeming to find the idea very amusing, showing a full set of teeth, worn short but still strong and white. "Well, if you really like our *tunas*, I will give you some, without charging. You are taking me to Lagos without charging . . . aren't you?"

He looked, waiting for an answer to this.

"Of course without charging."

The old man carefully unlashed a corner of the crate, reached a hand inside, and pulled out two objects. "Two pretty ones," he said, holding them up. They were a bright magenta, about the shape of hen's eggs, but at least twice as large.

As he recognized them, he felt a tremor run the length of his body, as if some very long nerve had been plucked like a guitar-string.

"God, what are those things?" Howell asked, glancing quickly around. "Don't tell me you're going to *eat* them."

"Why not? Those are cactus fruit, off those big prickly-pear trees. I bet they're delicious."

"Well, please count me out . . . I don't know, my stomach's not feeling too sharp. I'm afraid I'm coming down with the damn G.I.'s. Used to get them once in a while in France, too. I'm not eating anything tonight—just maybe some bouillon, if they've got such a thing down here." He glanced into the mirror and grimaced. "Oh, now, look—he's peeling them for us. You better tell him—oh brother, those hands. Every tropical crud known to man under those fingernails."

The dark fingers were deftly rotating the fruit against a silver blade, while the brilliant purple peels curled off in spirals to the retreating road.

"Don't they have thorns?" he yelled back.

"Thorns? Sure they have thorns. Roses have thorns. But they don't bother me. My old hands are used to them." He held up a palm. It looked plated with tortoise shell.

Howell nudged him with his elbow. "I told you to tell him no-thanks on the cactus."

The old man was handing forward a glistening, blood-purple lump of flesh. He received it into his grasp and felt it there, slippery, wet and warm. Both the others were watching him with their different expressions, the old man gravely amused, Howell horrified, as if this were a fresh Aztec heart. Closing his eyes, he took a sucking bite. His mouth filled with the familiar succulence, ample now and sweet.

It took the remaining miles to Lagos to make clear to the old man why Howell was not eating his *tuna* too. It was wrapped conspicuously in Kleenex and stowed carefully in the glove compartment. "For later."

They descended into Lagos de Moreno just as it was soaking peacefully in a lukewarm violet bath. Howell pulled the station wagon up in front of the huge *mercado central* which formed one side of the main plaza, at right angles to the mountainous bulk of the church. The warm air rippled with the chattering of thousands of long-tailed black birds that were fidgeting and flapping among the green of the plaza's trees like some strange animated fruit. They unloaded the crate and carried it into the market after the old man, setting it down deep in the interior beside a great red mound of yams. There they said goodbye. The old man didn't thank them for their services. He commended them to God. They wished him good luck with his selling.

For a few moments they wandered about among the stalls of fruits and vegetables until they came to a section where old women were frying scraps of meat in grease and bubbling dark concoctions in clay pots over smelly kerosene flames.

He looked at Howell's face and asked, unable to resist, if he felt like having supper.

"Christ, let's get out of here before I throw up."

Along the way out, they passed a row of little booths, about the size and design of carnival concessions. But here the shelves in the background were neatly stacked with cans and jars and packaged grocery items. The relative order and sanitation slowed Howell, and he stopped to examine the wares.

Suddenly his face illuminated and he pointed to a high shelf as if he were seeing a vision. "Bob, look up there. Do you see what I see?"

He looked and saw cans and small packages. On the top

shelf too there was a little votive candle in a red glass, burning before a faded and fly-specked lithograph of the Virgin of Guadalupe, such as they had noticed all through Mexico. In the dim recesses of the market, too, they had just passed a shrine to her set up among the cabbages and bananas.

"Campbell's soup! . . . Campbell's chicken noodle soup, for God's sake. Can you imagine . . . here! Incredible. That's for me, old buddy. Nice pure food tonight, how about it, stainless steel vats, unmushed by human hands—and I'll be damned, Ritz crackers!"

"There's some Alka-Seltzer too, while you're at it."

"Alka-Seltzer I got."

As the woman was wrapping the soup and crackers, they noticed, standing mutely at the far end of the counter, leaning on his stick, their friend of the tunas. He obviously hadn't recognized them and instinctively quieted, they observed him. He said not a word to the woman, nor she to him. She merely reached routinely under the counter and brought forth a pair of small white paraffin candles which she handed to him, accepting in exchange an oxidized copper disk which the old men peeled from his palm like a patch of skin. Then he left the mercado.

They followed him outside as he made his slow way across the corner of the plaza to the craggy stone mountain of the church and disappeared through the arched entry as into a cave. Howell went back to the car, but he himself stopped to have a glance inside. A hollow reverberation of low voices, indistinct forms moving slowly among the stalagmitic pillars, masses of weak flickering points of light that did not penetrate into the shadowy heights above, a pervasive odor of cold dust, of smoking resins . . .

He did not enter but drew back, feeling he had violated privacy, the intimacy of somebody else's home.

Back at the car he found Howell very upset. "I'll bet that

was the last centavo the old guy had—and what's he spend it on? Candles! Candles to burn up in a church! It's criminal." He reached for the ignition key. "Oh my God, now what's going on out there?"

Outside was a very strange sight. The crowd, which as usual filled the plaza with its quiet activity, was collapsing and bowing down in a moving swath, like wheat before an invisible scythe. It took a moment to find the cause of this phenomenon. Which turned out to be a single man, large and portly, who was striding along, a civilian topcoat thrown over his long black gown in perfunctory deference to the law prohibiting robed clerics from appearing in public. On either side of him bodies were bending in veneration. The man's blubbery jowls were dimpled with annoyance, as if he were in a hurry and could well do without all this. Yet his pale hands kept rising to bless them right and left, as if sprinkling crumbs to pigeons.

It took several minutes for Howell to collect his revulsion and arrange it into utterance. "I tell you, I've seen it all now. If somebody was to tell me about this, I'd call him a liar. In this day and age . . ."

"It must have been the archbishop, or maybe a cardinal."

"Hell, I don't care if it was the damn Pope, I mean, I thought stuff like that went out back in the Dark Ages, for Christ sake. That's it exactly, that's what keeps these poor people so backward and ignorant, the damn church. Fat rich priests like that, fancy gold-plated churches—and these poor superstitious suckers groveling before the slobs, and spending their last pennies on candles! Talk about con outfits—the church makes the Mafia look like a bunch of pikers."

"What do you think he should have spent his money on, Campbell's soup?"

"Sure Campbell's soup, why not? Something that's got some nourishment to it, at least Something *real*."

"Real? What's real, Howell?"

"What's real? Like finding us a real hotel with a real toilet so I can take a real shit."

He had instinctively let the subject drop, but an hour later, in the Motel California, the town's fanciest motel, over canned soup and crackers, Howell picked it up again. "No kidding, Bob, wasn't that the most nauseating sight you ever saw?" It was more than diarrhea that was irritating him. Some major psychic nerve in him had obviously been inflamed, and he wanted somebody else to soothe it by joining righteous indignation to righteous indignation, by seconding his resolution to condemn the church as a monstrous parasite sucking the life out of humanity, a colossal fraud. But he himself felt as far away from Howell now as he had felt close to him yesterday after they had helped the family in the broken-down truck. And he knew that this wasn't simply due to Howell's attitude toward religion, which was, after all, commonplace. No, it was because these paired incidents were also having their disruptive effect on him. Or was it the taste, the re-taste, of the cactus fruit that made him feel so alone again, so isolated?

Whatever it was, he felt loath to talk to Howell about it. But Howell persisted. "You mean it doesn't even bother you, seeing a poor old guy like that who should have retired on Social Security twenty years ago, who has to sweat blood for every lousy centavo, go spend it on superstitious crap like that?"

"Yes, it does. It bothers me. I've been thinking about it for an hour."

"Yeah, I thought it would. Poor old geezer—and you know damn well they'd never get away with it if they didn't keep him so ignorant. Bet he can't even read. Education, that's what this country needs, a good airing out—get rid of all this musty old—"

"You really want to know what I think, Harry? I think you

and I are ten times more ignorant than that old man."

"What?" Once more Howell was giving him a look of incredulity, and his face seemed to draw itself back several feet to observe him better—"you don't even feel sorry for the old man?"

"I feel ten times sorrier for us."

Howell's features had arranged themselves into a queer strained expression and held it for a long quiet moment. It was something like that look he'd given him on discovering the cactus stickers Monday night in his Albuquerque living room, except that now it was deadly serious. Possibly some mental muscle, unexercised since café days, had given a twitch in him. But it had been idle too long now to start flexing again without warning, especially not on a queasy stomach just now undergoing a mild lavage of sterile chicken solution. He got up without a word and went into the bathroom.

Half an hour later, he opened the bathroom door, came out in his undershorts, and thrust forth his hand. "No hard feelings?"

"What? . . . No, of course not, Harry." He took the shower-damp hand.

"Want to come in here and take a look at this John?"

"What's wrong with it this time?"

"Nothing. Works perfect—superperfect. Watch."

Howell flushed the toilet. From a central drain a low geyser bubbled up to rinse the entire bathroom floor.

"Wait, that's not all. Stand back."

He turned the shower handle. A hard stream of water shot down not merely into the stall but doused the toilet, too.

"Now, that's what I call advanced sanitary engineering. Think I might steal the idea for my next job."

20

ALREADY, HE SAW, IT WAS LATE IN THE AFTERNOON. The porch was transfixed west to east with thick horizontal bolts of orange-yellow sunlight. They hung in the air in front of him, diaphanous prison bars.

The hotel's owner had just left the porch, but the perfumes of her cosmetics lingered coquettishly behind like an astral body. She had climbed all those stairs to ask if the American gentlemen would be having supper here at the hotel, because she was about to start cooking. An overblown rose of a woman, her powdered pallor and rouged blush a painted ideogram of widow's dread and widow's loneliness and widow's avarice, she gasped and puffed and held her breast as if about to swoon with the exertion. Clearly she was far from healthy, this *patrona* of the Hotel of Health.

"Yes, I think so, we'll have supper. But please, something very, very light and simple, nothing fried and nothing *picante*. My friend's stomach is very sensitive."

And with a prelusive sigh, she began to tell him how sensitive her own digestion was, detailing the symptoms—sharp cramps, churning, much gas—confiding her fears of cancer, obviously on the long shot that he might be a medical man, and finally putting the question to him outright.

"I'm afraid not," he said. "I know a little about plumbing perhaps, but not human plumbing."

"Oh, yes, the girl was telling me, you can fix our toilet."

"Possibly. What's the matter with it?"

She threw up her hands. "Who knows? About such things I understand nothing, but nothing! We use a pail of water. You pour it in . . . of course I have been meaning to have it fixed. But the prices they ask, they are insane. And besides, all my money goes to doctors. Not here in Pátzcuaro, of course. Here we have only *carniceros*. I take the bus to Morelia. There I have my *especialista*." At the mention of her specialist, her voice dropped to a silky pink whisper, behind which, though now there was nothing of interest, she had formerly kept veiled her womanly treasures.

"Have you tried your Nuestra Señora de la Salud?" he asked, to tease her a little. "You are a Catholic, aren't you?"

She ruffled like a grouse—no, like a politician queried on his patriotism. "Certainly I am a Catholic. We Mexicans are a very Catholic people." Like an old stenographer she scribbled a shorthand sign of the cross over her gallbladder, and her large, once-beautiful black eyes showed their whites in an abbreviated Murillo uproll. "But of course"—and again her voice reassumed an intimacy, but of a very different variety— "well, she is more for the simple people, you understand . . . *los inditos* . . ."

He suddenly felt her further presence would be tedious and useless to either of them. "Well, I'll have a look at the toilet for you. I'm becoming a sort of *especialista* in toilets."

She gave an admiring sigh. "Yes, you Americans are such clever people . . . my late husband always used to call you 'las llaves inglesas.' "

292

The monkey wrenches. He laughed, and she smiled back at him with a smile that was a faded photograph of the smile of Eros. "All right, I will fix you some nice poached eggs and plain boiled rice and *manzanilla* tea and toast of Pan Bimbo, *estilo Norteamericano*. That is what I often have myself . . . easy for the digestion."

"Fine, that sounds fine . . ."

And she was gone down the stairs again, the invalid who ran the Hotel of Health.

He pushed himself stiffly out of the leather chair and passed through the bars of sun, feeling almost as if it were he, not they, that was disembodied. He stood by the west windows looking out at the daylight which had boiled down to a thick and syrupy gold. The day was all but over now. And his story too, it was close to its end. The mass in La Colegiata, that was the only gap left open between past and present, that kept then from now. And strangely, having finally reached this thing that had set him remembering in the first place, he felt less desire, less need to speak about it, even to himself. Or rather he felt its unspeakability. This week, this week of re-genesis that had seemed, as if by fiat, to form him out of his chaos, had revealed the vital secret of human being. But to try to recapture it, surround it with words, to try to think it even —well, it was like taking a glass specimen jar, filling it with ordinary air, and pasting a label on it: *"This is what sustains all life."*

And who had this been for, anyway, all this recapitulation, this week-long *revelación*? For those strangers, his country-men? For Frank Hoerchner?

He tried one last time to summon up the psychiatrist, to picture him, but he could not. Frank was gone now, irretrievable. And had he ever been there in the first place?

Again he felt a little thrill of sadness, like fingertips skimming across the exquisite membranes of the heart. The pain of separation. Hell had been defined by that phrase, the pain of separation. And that was the pain of mental illness, inside sanatoria and outside sanatoria, of an individual's mental illness and a civilization's mental illness. An inability to reach, a sealing off, which seems forever, which seems ordained by sadist nature of things . . . but which, he had now been taught and could teach no one else—was a lie!

No, Frank had never been there.

But he felt like saying goodbye to him anyway, as people are constantly saying goodbye to people who have never been with them. "Goodbye, then, Frank, you exhausted Atlas, staggering beneath your world of suffering, you friend and father by the hour to the well-heeled tormented, you master of the psychic enema, wizard of the chemical brew and the artificial lightning, goodbye, goodbye. May evolution bless you."

No, he thought, no, not like that. "Goodbye, dear Frank, goodbye, brother sentience. May you also be reached."

And suddenly he seemed to see his face, his own adolescent face, looking out from its coop in the high-school yearbook, naive and bright-eyed as a young pullet. And the motto they had chosen to print beneath it: "Nothing is impossible to diligence and skill."

They were mistaken. Some things were impossible to diligence and skill. Yet, partly, they were right. Nothing was impossible.

Just then his eyes registered an elongated sightseeing limousine passing across a segment of street leading up from the lake. Several white arms were crooked out the windows. Probably that was Howell now, on his way back home.

21

THAT NIGHT, FRIDAY NIGHT, at the Motel California, he had slept as fitfully as Howell. But for him the inner occupant that kept him turning and thinking disconnectedly wasn't confined to the chambers and tubing of the digestive system, but roamed like a wraith through his nerve centers and brain cells with all the awful familiarity of his old Doppelgänger, anxiety. Yet the resemblance was less than the difference. This, whatever it was, posed no threat, aroused no fear. It was positive, not negative, a kind of yearning-outward, a beam searching through a haze. But to illuminate what exactly he did not know —did not know, that is, on Friday night.

So that when they finally reached Pátzcuaro late yesterday afternoon, neither one of them was feeling himself as he was accustomed to feel it. The chicken soup had not quieted Howell's tracts. They had, as he remarked, ignored it, shot it through untouched. He himself drove the entire way from Lagos, stopping to let Howell out every hour or so. The "sights" were scarcely seen. The beauty of the shore drive down from Quiroga, the lake beneath a woolly *rebozo* of mist, the only cloud in a brilliant sky, the flat-topped volcanic hills that bordered the lake, with the conic islands lying in the water like their missing peaks, lopped off by a titan's machete—such things were lost on them both. Howell sat slumped and silenced in the seat beside him, their roles of the first morning reversed, the militia of his consciousness obviously marshalled down in the rebellious provinces, the remainder no doubt praying that the bottle of Pepto-Bismol he had gratefully located in the unlikely town of Irapuato would be up to the job of coping with these Latin bacilli. When they passed the sign that read *TZINTZUNTZAN*, he did glance over wanly, but uttered not a word.

They were driving slowly up the lane of tall feathery trees leading into Pátzcuaro when something leaped up at them out of nowhere, hooked itself to the car window and hung there chattering like a monkey. "*¿Hotel? ¿Buscan hotel?*" A small boy.

Nodding yes, they stopped to let the child in. He directed them into a sumptuous courtyard, full of hibiscus, date palms, clipped lawns, dark men in white coats and light women in shorts, signs in English, and polished cars with American plates. An animated travel brochure.

"No. No, too fancy. We want something very simple. We're poor."

At the word poor the boy flashed a smile like a moving mirror catching the sun. "*Bueno, conozco uno, barato pero limpio,*" and led them through alleys to the Hotel de la Salud. There they had to swim their way through the incoming waves of the *patrona's apologia*, nodding into her explanations for the run-down condition of the place, nodding into her plans for a gala revamping for the holidays, nodding at the sudden death of her husband six years ago, nodding at how hard life was for a widowed lady alone, nodding, doggedly nodding their weary way into privacy. In their room at last, Howell sucked a few more swallows of the bloomer-pink cream from the bottle, climbed into bed, and was asleep before Bob could ask him about supper. He decided he too would rather sleep than eat.

When he woke up, Howell's bed was empty. Back on the toilet. For the first time he was beginning to feel serious concern, when the object of the concern appeared in the doorway, obviously not returning from the bathroom but from the outside world. "How's this for color?" he asked, setting down a new fiber shopping bag in pink, green, yellow, purple, orange and blue.

"Feeling better, eh?"

"Great. Think we got it licked. Hey, there's this grand tour thing starting in half an hour—the whole works, butterfly nets, the islands, lake villages, Janitzio, and that volcano—you know, it's famous, what do they call it?"—he consulted the leaflet in his pocket—"Paricutín, you must have read about that one— just popped up out of this guy's cornfield. Come on, get dressed . . . and you know what else? There's this little *boîte* that serves a *café au lait* as good as you can get on the Boul' Mich'. If you get the lead out, we can grab some breakfast before the bus . . ."

"Harry, if you don't mind, I think I'll just stick around here today."

"Huh? Don't tell me you got it now?"

"No, I'm all right. I don't know why, I just don't feel like doing anything, not today." It was true. He didn't know why, and he definitely did not want to sightsee, not today.

"Oh, hell, if you're not going . . ."

"No, please, you go. You could take your paints . . ."

"That's what I was figuring on—O.K., I guess maybe I will." He looped his Japanese camera around his neck, and put its accessories into his new shopping bag. He hefted the easel-paintbox from La Grande Chaumière, decided against it, and packed instead a sketch-pad and a set of pastels. "What about you? What are you going to do all day?"

"I don't know, just take it easy. If that thing's really good, maybe I'll go tomorrow. Enjoy yourself—and don't forget to show all the señoritas pictures of your wife and kids . . ."

"Maybe it's a good thing you're not going." And with a laugh and an "à bientôt," Howell bounced away down the terra-cotta stairs like a rubber ball.

As he stepped out into the narrow ravine of the street, the church bells, which had been drizzling on and off, came teeming down like a flashflood, drenching him with the sudden realization that this was Sunday morning—once again, Sunday morning. His thoughts, which might have drifted backward, were drowned in the din.

The next thing to catch his senses was a sweetish, yet salty smell: blood. It came just as the narrow street was about to debouch into the open plaza, from a butcher stall above which a stained red flag was drooping, as from some demoralized party headquarters. His eyes caught a passing glimpse of yellow-veined purple hunks in various sizes and shapes, impaled on hooks, draining into enamel trays and dancing with flies.

The plaza he was entering now reached him with a look and feel that was different from all the other plazas before it—it seemed older, organic and moldering, and shadowy as a forest. Stone arcades bordered it like caves, and great dark trees hung over it in a slowly undulating canopy of leaves. All the vegetation seemed to be growing more wantonly here, nurtured no doubt by the warm humidity from the lake: algae, lichens, moss, green in the gutters and black on the crumbling lime of the old colonial walls. As usual, the human species was quietly everywhere, the men in loose white pants and heavy sandals soled with used tire-tread. Almost everyone was carrying a burden of some kind. Many of the men wore wool ponchos that looked heavier and more somber than sarapes elsewhere, and the women, in full skirts, often enclosed an infant in the folds of the gray and black shawls that enveloped their heads and shoulders. Most of the people were scaled small, a third, it seemed, beneath his own milk-fed American dimensions, and their poverty did not seem carefree at all. It had the feeling of India.

He wandered into a small open cafe, but as he went to sit down and a swarm of raisins buzzed up from the plate of sweet rolls on the table, he turned and walked out again, realizing he still felt no real desire for food. And so he began to drift aimlessly in a sort of loose investigation of this place he was in. There were, it turned out, two distinct and separate plazas lying in the bottom of the basin in which the town was built. On all but the lake side, white and pastel buildings rose up the steep hillsides as in an amphitheater, divided by narrow cobbled alleyways. At the top of each of these ascending aisles, it seemed, there stood a church.

The two plazas were not alike. One was relatively open and orderly, with benches, grass plots and a round pool in which Don Vasco de Quiroga stood in his verdigris habit, a staff in his hand, giving forth a bronze benignity like that of Saint Francis himself. The other plaza, dirty and teeming, was the open market. There, under makeshift shelters of canvas and tin, men and women sat before little mounds of oranges and bananas, hawking them with curiously muffled cries of "Peso la pila . . . cincuenta el medio . . ." Others sold long stalks of sugar cane and small fat-bellied fish laid carefully out on plantain leaves. Strung side by side on long racks were rebozos of cotton and rayon, utilitarian grays almost all of them, but here and there a bright streak of orange or yellow or pink stood out like a snip of laughter, a spectrogram of the human lot. One corner of the square was given over to craft items, wood carvings, pottery, textiles, most of it obviously directed to the tourist trade.

He continued to meander, he didn't know how long, through the maze in the bottom of this bowl. The outer reality that sieved in through his senses joined and diluted in the stream of his inner reality, which had begun to flow again, if anything more strongly now than it had on Friday night in Lagos de Moreno. Maybe the lightness from fasting had something to do with it, this interior eddying, this anxiety that wasn't anxious, or afraid, or depressed, or hurried. But it did hold the physical world a little farther out from him than usual, since whatever came in from the outside was instantly dissolved in this flowing tincture of poignancy, puzzlement, and patience. He felt it collecting in quiet potential, filling an untapped reservoir.

Then, as he walked for the fourth or fifth time through the market plaza, he knew that it was about to be tapped. Something was going to happen to him—now, in the next few seconds. What? He hadn't the faintest idea. Perhaps he was about to drop, fall unconscious, die, here, now, on this spot. A sudden stroke, a heart attack? Perhaps one of the complex systems of this time-space craft he was in was about to fail. His mind made an electric survey of the trouble that would follow on this—for Howell, for Anne, for the authorities. This bothered him, not his dying. For a second. Then he relaxed. If death was what it was, then death was what it was. He felt peaceful in his anticipation. "The good is good, and the bad is also good," he found his thoughts thinking, and he understood these words, literally and perfectly, without having to submit them to his reason at all.

Then it happened. Immediately—it seemed immediately— new words entered, from outside, from behind him, a snatch of dialogue, in English.

"Come on, Bob, don't be a fool. You know you never pay them what they ask. Virginia told us to offer half."

"O.K. I'll do Ginny one better, I'll offer a third. Say there" —a hollow rapping of knuckles on wood—"I'll give you seven for this big devil here."

"No, sir, I cannot. To make that I work too long. Twenty pesos."

"What d'ya say, Hon? You really want that darn thing?"

"I just thought it might look cute over the bar—nah, I guess not. We got too much junk to lug around already. Why don't we just take that little green monster there; what was it, five?"

By the time he finally turned to look, the main actors in this little performance had vanished. There was only the young Mexican and his small display of demon masks carved from wood, snag-toothed witches, snarling devils, and grinning bug-eyed fiends with snakes coiled at their temples: objects once part of the Tarascan religious rites, now tourist items.

"You like to buy . . . ?"

"No—no, thanks."

In a way he was sorry he'd lost the others. He would have liked to thank them, too. Because their little skit had catalyzed the murk inside him into crystal clarity. He knew exactly what he wanted to do. He wanted to go to a church. He wanted to see Nuestra Señora de la Salud.

22

THE CHURCH ONCE INTENDED for the Cathedral of Michoacán was built on the flat summit of a steep hill above the plazas—partly built. The right bell tower had never gotten its cupola, the left had never gotten off the ground at all. As a structure it wasn't particularly impressive: barnlike, except for its catheral dimensions. Reddish stone and discolored white lime plastering. Atop the stump of the truncated bell tower, weeds two feet high were growing, and black moss or lichens stained the baroque cornices. In the clearing around it grew more of those tall slender trees. Along the walk leading to the entry gate was a double row of dark pines, and he moved slowly down it, focused now, and fully observant. Before the twin gate-pillars he stopped at a small wooden booth to look over the display of religious articles and souvenirs. Racks of pale translucent tapers hung by their wicks in long, even rows, and most of the medallions, booklets, pictures, statuettes, and postcards featured the famous image inside. For two cents he bought himself a little wallet-sized card with a cheap reproduction of the statue on one face and a prayer to her on the reverse.

At the gate to the churchyard were three beggars. The first had a scarf drawn across his face like a woman in purdah, apparently to hide some hideous disfigurement. Only his eyes, milky and gummy, looked out from a slit. The second was seated—no, had been placed—on the ground against the stone post, his gnarled legs and arms twisted under and about his trunk like some huge singed bug. The third was an idiot, tilt-eyed and drooling from thick palsied lips. All three of them were intoning prayers at a furious rate, as if plunging through space to destruction.

He pressed a bill into a hand of each, not bothering to check the denominations, and stood for a moment in the churchyard examining the façade. In four sandstone niches were four sandstone saints, the evangelists, executed with the crude power of sculptures done in institutions for the blind. Above the massive wooden door was a painted sign, offering tourists the information that a church was the house of God and one should not enter it in immodest dress.

As he stepped through the doorway, his senses underwent a sudden shift. His sight was momentarily blacked out, while his nostrils were charged with the odor of mildew and stone and centuries of aromatic smoke. As his eyes adjusted to the comparative darkness, he could make out, as if at the far end of a tunnel, the light-bathed apse and altar, and the tiny yellowish flames of burning wax coming on in the dusk. And finally he heard the droning reverberations of the priests. The mass was already underway.

He tiptoed down the left side-aisle and slipped into a pew halfway to the altar. For a moment he sat looking down at the bare worn wood of the kneeling plank, and then raised his head and looked up at the image of Nuestra Señora de la

303

Salud. She was large as life and elevated ten or fifteen feet above the altar on a white marble dais, in such a way that she seemed to be floating in a cataract of sunlight, in dramatic contrast to the dimness of the rest of the church. She was dressed in sumptuous robes of blue and white cloth embroidered with gold, and stood, like her better-known counterpart at Guadalupe, on a melon-slice of moon. Her plump white hands were clasped piously over her breast, and her hair was long and flowed in dark tresses over her shoulders. On her head was a heavy jeweled crown, and around her was a sunburst halo of gold rays. Her face had the pallor and shadow of the classic Iberian beauty, though she was no lovely señorita, but a rather buxom matron in her forties. She looked, in fact, a little like the *patrona* of the Hotel de la Salud.

He was not taken in by her. Nor was she by him.

Yet he couldn't help admiring the superb theatricality of this whole setup. What an environment of sublimated sensuality they'd created here, all designed to seduce the naive imagination into believing some kind of supernatural intercourse was taking place. There she floated, high and golden in this radiant mist of light, as four hundred years ago she had been found floating on the lake, with these tendrils of perfumed smoke curling amorously up about her, amid the hypnotic incantations of her adorers below, the silvery tinkling of bells, the hidden choir of disembodied voices, the aromas of myrrh and frankincense entering one's body with every breath. What an assault on the senses.

His eyes wandered over the ostentation of the great interior, the ornate pink fretwork, the lavish curls of gold, the glittering crystal chandeliers, the Corinthian pilasters, the banks of white gladiolus and the vases of purple orchids. It imparted a sense of fabulous luxury, even to him. What effect did all this have then on the unsophisticated poor coming in from their low-roofed squalor? And as he watched the mechanical actions of the ruby cassocks and the fine lace surplices, he began to have feelings of indignation close to those that had burst from Howell the other night. The faces of the celebrants as they went through their ritual dance, bowing, kneeling, turning, praying, kissing, holding up the golden chalice, looked impassive and cold, even bored. Two of them were young and fleshy, the third old, wizened and skull-tight. But all seemed the faces of actors, nothing more. And he felt he was witnessing just one more variation on the old, old play of religious deception, meant, in the final analysis, to keep the rich in their riches and the poor in their poverty, in no sense more spiritual than in any other version. The rites of Christianity were no better than the pagan rituals in which those Tarascan demon masks had figured—worse, for their hypocrisy, their grandiosity, and their ostentation . . .

He felt the board he was seated on quake beneath him as the bodies that shared it slipped down to their knees. He would have liked to kneel along with them, but he simply could not. So he sat with lowered head, in sudden remembrance of the church he had sat in exactly a week ago, the A-frame Motel of God in Albuquerque, with its orange velvet pews.

Was he losing his grip on reality? What was he doing in this place? Why had he come here when he knew in advance what he was going to find, what he wasn't going to find? Dr. Hoerchner's smile seemed to rise in stereoptic projection on the screens of his lowered eyelids . . . "Don't you think we might get farther if we cut down on all this mystical crap and stick closer to real things?"

At the first chance, he'd get up and walk out . . .

As he waited for that chance, he noticed in his hands the little card he had bought at the stall outside. He began to

305

focus on what was printed there, and to read it, purely for distraction and to kill time, as he would have read anything that happened to come beneath his eyes.

Oh María, Salud de los enfermos del alma . . . Oh Mary, Health of the sick in soul and body, who have a heart overflowing with pity and mercy for all: through You sinners are moved to penitence and obtain pardon for their sins; through You weak souls find the strength to struggle against their passions and triumph over them; through You lukewarm hearts flame up with divine love; through You the just receive the extraordinary grace to reach perfection. You console the afflicted and teach them to bear miseries of this vale of tears with resignation. You heal our spiritual pain, which is like a grievous wound that sickens our souls. You comfort the sick man on the bed of his pain and make his suffering easy and worthwhile. You watch lovingly over the dying man in the trance of his agony. You, when it suits You and when you wish it, can . . .

He flicked the card over. For a moment he scrutinized the elegantly gowned little woman who was in possession of all this incredible power. Then, slowly, he sealed his fingers over her.

Into his ears drifted the singsong chanting from the altar: *"El Señor está cerca"* . . . the Lord is close by. *"La muerte es una ganancia"* . . . death is a gain . . .

When they got up from their knees, he would leave . . .

He felt the wooden board beneath him move again, as somebody new slipped into the pew beside him and knelt, blocking his escape. Without shifting his eyes, he could see it was an Indian. Thin brown ankles emerged from dirty frayed trousers and entered rough leather sandals of almost the same color and texture as the feet they wrapped. The coarse woolen edge of a heavy brown poncho grazed against his arm. He felt it stir with each breath the man took, heard the air going in and out of his lungs, the swallow moving down his throat, almost his very pulse.

After a moment he began to feel this new presence as a sort of insistent pressure against his left side. He lifted his head and turned, in the other direction, to the right, toward the center aisle and the opposite bank of pews. For the first time his focus rested on the worshipers themselves.

There weren't many. Less than half the benches were occupied, and these almost exclusively by people who seemed the poorest and drabbest in the community. Most of them were holding burning tapers in their praying hands as they knelt, tiny droplets of flame that trembled perilously and threatened to go out, even here in the still air of the church, that would never survive the slightest stir outside. The faces behind them were dark and Asian. Their eyelids were lowered, and their lips were whispering soundlessly. They wavered too in the flickering yellow candlelight.

As he studied them one by one, he became slowly aware that they had begun to move as a group, these faces with their buds of light. Without rising to their feet these bodies were sitting into the wide center aisle, and a thin procession of them, tapers held fixedly before their eyes, were shuffling toward the altar on their knees. The church now echoed with the soft sounds of dragging cloth and scuffing leather and bare skin sliding across stone. An old woman and a small child of three or four, sharing a single taper between them, moved past as one, the woman's shriveled face turned up at the virgin, the child's smooth and wide-eyed and wandering as they inched together toward the light. A middle-aged husband and wife, life-worn and threadbare, formed another single pair, her stockings rolled down to her ankles, his trousers rolled up above his knees. The soles of their cheap shoes showed almost identical holes. Pregnant women waddling like seals, skinny old men with stained hats drooping in their praying hands like large dead leaves, the bottoms of their *huaraches* revealing the zigzag tread of discarded American tires. Two children alone, hand in hand, an adolescent boy holding his taper in his left hand, while his right arm, withered and useless, dangled at his side. A hunchback woman who had to sit back on her calves and pant every few feet. A slow, steady trickle of humanity that gathered into a pool beneath the altar and remained still, kneeling and waiting. A baby's cracked cry was snuffed softly by its mother's breast . . .

A sudden tremor, brief and swift, coursed through his body, as if the bench had shaken, as if the church, the town, the earth had shivered a seismic shudder. Something thin, hard and brittle cracked inside him, something sealed began to give way. The keg of self was springing leaks. The outside did not cease to flow into him, but now he felt a new and strange counterflow—himself outward. The realities of in-here and out-there, so sanely, so painfully separate an instant ago, had begun to intermingle. His chest heaved. It was as if his very heart had begun to breathe.

The wooden board he sat on seemed to have tilted sharply beneath him. He felt himself being spilled down from buttocks onto knees and he did not resist. As his knees touched wood and took over his weight, the life-flow heightened inside him —pure oxygen seemed to be pouring into the air. Into his ears came the whispering murmur of the man whose body and life knelt side by side with his own, repeating and repeating a single phrase:

"*Oh Señor, yo no soy digno, yo no soy digno* . . ."

The resonations of that voice, those words, reached him as notes of a perfect pitch, setting up reverberant echoes. In unison he found his lips murmuring the same Spanish syllables.

"*Oh Señor, yo no soy digno* . . . Oh Lord, I am not worthy, I am not worthy . . ."

A wine of sadness was pulsing through his bloodstream in exhilarating waves, bathing his mind, welling up in his eyes. How sad, how sad it was to live a human life, how beautiful and how sad . . .

His luxuriations were punctured by a choking sound beside him, and he turned and looked at his neighbor for the first time. The man's brown eyes were also filled with tears, and his shoulders were quivering in a silent paroxysm of grief. A young man, not out of his twenties, handsome and brown as potter's clay. Huddled against the other side of him sat an infant of two, ragged and dirty and immobile as a statue. There was no mother beyond. Tear after slow tear spilled from the father's open unblinking eyes which were fixed to their magnet, the floating image of the Virgin of Health. The brown cheeks beneath them glistened in the reflected light like the earth in a sun shower.

The tide of sadness and beauty rose higher in him and once again, in sudden terror of drowning, of being swept from his moorings, he turned his face away, as he had done before, from the man on the truck bumper, from the addict in the police station, from the Navajo in the drug store, from Griego, from Aguero, from Howell even, struggling one last time to keep his head, his balance, his distance, his control, by clutching tight to the physical solidities around him. Desperately he fastened his eyes to stone, studying the details of the architecture, the intricate baroque fluting and scrolls, the painstaking way the quarried blocks had been shaped and fitted to one another . . . trying to find the precise words to label all he saw.

But from the corners of his vision part of him slipped out and escaped to those ruby forms dancing their ritual dance beneath their corn-paste goddess, to that thin procession of fragile yellow flamebuds that made its slow and inexorable way out of the obscurity and toward the flooding daylight. And part of his hearing ignored his inner lecturing and sought out the creaking of wood, of bones, of leather beside him, the swallows of anguish, the supplicant murmur. Still he smelled the rancid wool of the poncho, felt its scratching touch on the skin of his arm. Still he was being drawn from his selfhood by the gravitation of that neighbor life. He drew back against the pull.

Suddenly he was tricked. The current reversed itself. Negative turned positive, the pull became a push. Thrown off balance, he turned his face again. Eyes caught him full in the eyes. Toppling inside, he leapt out, into nothing. Nothing caught him, full. Instantly, what had been threatening to happen happened. Everything—time-place, here-there, now-then, this-that, I-other, all the landmarks of human awareness—went up in an explosion of light. All emotion incinerated, the waves of sadness and beauty, tragedy and separation, pleasure and pain. Consciousness volatilized in the sun of being, the unthinkable splendor of human being . . .

23

"Bob . . . hey, Bob . . ."

Howell, downstairs, calling him. Something was wrong. He could tell by the voice.

"Harry . . . be right down," he shouted. He gave his body a convulsive shake, like a dog coming out of the water, took up his notebook and came down from the porch.

Howell was not in the room, but he'd been there. The Mexican shopping bag and the Japanese camera had been thrown on the bed. On the dresser was the tour leaflet and a packet of medicine in silver foil. He picked it up: *Entero-Viotormo CIBA.*

Howell appeared. "Oh, there you are. Listen, do me a big favor, will you? Go look at that goddamn toilet. I'm not up to fucking with it . . ."

"What's this stuff?" There was no need to have asked. Howell's face was enough.

"Some guy from L.A., he gave them to me . . ." He sat down heavily on the bed, pushed the bag and camera to the floor, and lay back with a moan . . . "Said it knocked his out in twenty-four hours . . ."

"You must have had quite a day."

"Oh, Jesus, don't ask . . . sometime maybe I'll tell you about it . . . right now all I want is sleep. But please, go see if you can get that son-of-a-bitch to flush . . . don't want to leave a mess . . ."

He went and had a look at the toilet. He lifted the tank lid and saw it was gutted inside, entirely devoid of mechanical viscera. Instead luxuriant algae were growing there, minerals were building tiny stalactites, it had been leaking so long, as if some underground stream had chosen this plumbing fixture for a spring. On the floor stood a chipped enamel pail full of water. He poured it quickly into the bowl. With a hearty, gulping chuckle, the toilet flushed . . .

Howell was laid out on the sheets, prostrate and pale, his eyes half-open in a kind of deathbed stupor. Bob stood for a moment looking down at him. He'd better go ask the patrona for the name of a doctor.

"Bob . . . ?" Nothing on Howell stirred but his lips.

"What?"

"Fix it?"

"It works."

"What was wrong with it this time?"

"Nothing. What can I get you? How about a little supper? The landlady's fixing some—

"God no! . . . You know this guy from L.A., he claims he had it worse than me, these pills worked miracles . . ."

"Hope they do. If not, I'm getting a doctor. Now you better get some rest. I'll go buy some soda pop, you don't want to get dehydrated." He turned and tiptoed toward the door.

"Hey, Bob, wait . . ."

"What?"

"Listen . . . let's say I'm feeling O.K. tomorrow morning

. . . you know, would you mind a hell of a lot if . . . well, what I mean is, I've had all the Mexico I need, I'm ready to head for home . . ."

"I'm ready too," he said.

It's been a long time now since Bob headed for home, and that week in October, those seconds in the Basilica, have receded into perspective. From this here and now they no longer just out as one single divide of miraculous intercession. Nor have his constants and variables altered very radically this side of that week. His life has remained his foolish human life, forever wandering to the brink of forgetting, forever being drawn back. The miracle of our regenesis is always.